WOLF BOUND

PACK BOUND SERIES BOOK 4

LEISL LEIGHTON

PERMIEN PRESS

Published by Leisl Leighton as Permien Press. For more information, email: leisl@leislleighton.com

First published 2018 by Escape Publishing Australia. Rewritten and republished 2022 by Permien Press.

Cover design – Samantha Marshall

Ebook ISBN: 978-1-922836-09-0

Print ISBN: 978-1-922836-10-6; Amz: 978-1-922836-11-3

❀ Formatted with Vellum

PRAISE FOR WOLF BOUND

Wow! I have found a new author to read! Leisl Leighton has created a world full of intrigue and captivating characters that draw you into the story and hold readers hostage until the very end. I was certainly spellbound throughout.

— EVA MILLIEN - STORMY VIXEN'S BOOK
REVIEWS

Leisl Leighton is an awesome story teller. This whole series so far has me wanting to keep finding out more about other characters and read her other books.

— JESSICA - GOODREADS REVIEWER

I was hooked!

— CYN - GOODREADS REVIEWER

Leisl has out done herself again ... Strong characters and a great story line that will keep you entertained ... I can't wait to read more of her work either too. I have come to love this series.

— KIM - GOODREADS REVIEWER

I found the premise very cool...I recommend to all shifter and witch fans because this is an intriguing story with tons going on and a new spin that you will love! I can't wait for the next book!

— CASSANDRA LOSKOT - CASSANDRA LOST IN
BOOKS BLOG/BOOK REVIEWS

WOLF BOUND

To my readers,
Your faith in this series has been amazing. So many of you have been
waiting for Adam and Shelley's story.
This one is for all of you.

PROLOGUE

Edinburgh, Scotland, 1502

Morghanna stared out at the crowd gathered to see the spectacle of a witch trial. Their greedy, avaricious faces taunted her. They were so eager to see her pronounced guilty.

These people she had helped through childbirth and sickness.

They wanted to see her burn.

She closed her eyes, sick of seeing the hate-filled faces around her, numb to the pain of her injuries. Even so, she couldn't escape their hatred and fear. It seeded the air with a foul stench. They clamoured and yelled, less than animals. She should hate them, but her hatred was held for one Were and the son he had never had the strength to control.

Her lip curled.

Iain MacCrae was to blame. If only he had done something about Lachlan when he began to show the seeds of his insanity; or if he'd allowed the Hunters to do their job as they should have done when Lachlan escaped, none of what had come to pass in the last ten years would have occurred.

She had lost so much because of his inaction, but never so much as in the last few weeks.

Alistair was dead trying to save her from Lachlan. And now Lachlan had done this! Turned her in to the Witch Finder after tricking her and Alistair to come on this supposed mission of mercy. He had known she would never be able to ignore a message from villagers who had once given her and her coven shelter.

She wasn't truly surprised by his actions. Nor was she surprised by Iain's continued lack of action where his son was concerned. But she was surprised by the others. When she had realised it was a trap, she'd called through the Packbond to ask for their help. She knew Iain would refuse to come, but his remaining lieutenants should have wanted to protect her, for she and Alistair were their last hope to keep their foundering pack together. But they refused. They blamed her for the fact they'd lost three quarters of their pack and nearly all of their coven to the exiled Dougal's new pack.

But she wasn't to blame. The Alpha they protected—an Alpha who, like the leech he was, drew on their strength and power to stay alive and keep his son from harm—was to blame.

If only she and Alistair had gone to join Dougal sooner, then this may not have happened. But like a fool, she'd stayed behind, Alistair along with her, the last of their coven to do so, their aim to convince those Were who stayed to leave the sinking ship that was Pack MacCrae and join them in Dougal's new pack.

She was only glad that Bridgette had come for the birthing of their son and had taken him to safety.

She was also thankful her sister, Morrigan, had not been there too. Although, why would she be? Her sister had begged her from the start not to listen to Bridgette Colliere. She'd begged her over and over not to share their powers with the Were. But Morghanna had believed as Bridgette did—she still did believe—that it was the only way they could survive.

And they'd been right. It had been the miracle they had prayed for. All the covens were safe now with their bonded packs.

It wasn't the fault of the Pact that things hadn't worked so smoothly for her coven. They couldn't have known they would be crushed under the weak leadership of an Alpha who wouldn't give over his position to Dougal and the others who were prepared to do what must be done:

Kill the insane Lachlan MacCrae.

But she'd taken care of that and her coven was now safe. However, was that enough? She'd been betrayed. Alistair was dead and soon she would be too. How could she make certain this would never happen to another one of her kind again? How could she make certain her son would be forever safe?

Her eyes burned with tears as she tried not to think of the son she was leaving behind. Tried to remember instead her mate's laughing face, his tender kisses, the way he'd held her face as if she were the most precious thing he'd ever beheld.

But all she could think of was that Lachlan's jealousy and Iain's weakness had killed Alistair.

Just as it was about to kill her too. Because of him, she would never see her child again. Never hold him to her breast. Never hear his first laugh, see his first stumbling attempt at walking, run to him when he was hurt, filling him with the certainty of her love. Iain and Lachlan had stolen all of that from Alistair and her.

For that, she could not forgive those who stood by and did nothing when they should have done what their Alpha was too weak to do. They were supposed to protect their coven as well as they protected themselves. Instead, their inaction had destroyed her and split her coven in a way she feared it would never recover from.

She *had* to do something to make certain this could never happen again.

Flames leapt to life around her as torches were put to the pyre at her feet.

And as it did, her need to pay back those responsible became a living flame inside her, building and building until everything she was focused with single-minded intensity on ending what remained of Pack MacCrae and ensuring this never happened to her kind again. She must protect her son and his progeny; only that mattered now.

The words of her curse leapt into her mind, and as they did, she spoke them out loud. Her words rang out above the angry cries of the mob and the crackling of the fire that licked at her with its hot, burning tongue.

Then the words were gone and she was empty, her power having been almost fully expended on making certain the Curse would carry through the ages.

It was then she truly felt the pain of the fire hungering for her flesh.

The flames weren't even touching her, but she swore her skin was blistering. She gritted her teeth, closed her eyes against the smoke. She wouldn't cry out. Wouldn't give those watching the satisfaction of her pain.

A prickling awareness shuddered through her and her eyes snapped open, going to the hill beyond the village.

A woman stood there, lit by the light of the moon above.

Morrigan.

No!

Oh, Goddess, no.

Her sister shouldn't be here. Not to witness this. Not to be touched by its evil.

She focused her magic so as to see Morrigan's features; she needed to read her to figure out what she had seen and heard. Despite the heat of the flames, cold slithered through her bones at her sister's expression—pure unbridled rage and hate. Oh Goddess, what had she done in speaking that curse aloud for her sister to hear?

Morrigan lifted her hands, drawing power.

Morghanna shook her head, whispered her denial, hoping the Goddess would carry her words to her sister's ears. *'No Morrigan. The Witch Finder will see you. Do not bring destruction upon yourself. Carry our line through the ages or all I have suffered will have been for nought.'*

Morrigan's hands stilled, the power falling away as devastation and grief pulled on her stunning features. Then her face screwed up and she shouted into the night, 'I told you this would happen. I warned you no good could come from aligning with those animals.'

'I know what you said. But I was right too. For many of our kind, the Pact has been a blessing.'

'How can you defend them?'

'Morrigan, listen. Not all of them are bad. Just this pack, and not even all of them.'

'Is that so? Then where are they now? These so-called good Were? They are supposed to protect you, so where are they?'

'I forced them away, to build a pack of their own where all of our coven can be safe.'

'And they let you?'

'They had no choice.'

'If you love some of them still, then why did you invoke that curse?'

'I had to. I had to ensure they protect Alistair's and my—' Her voice cut off as the flames licked closer and a cry of pain left her lips.

'Morghanna! I will kill them for doing this to you.'

Her sister's words helped her ride out the pain and say, *'No Morrigan. Do not go down that path. Believe me when I say, those responsible will pay. As will any others who seek to treat their covens as Iain McCrae and his ilk treated ours. The Curse will make certain this happens to no other witch or warlock again.'*

Morrigan shook her head, her rage and grief almost a physical thing. A dark shadow crept towards her down the hill.

No. It couldn't be. Panicked, she said, *'Please, Morrigan. Listen to me. You are inviting the Darkness to you. Can you not feel it all around you? It is what we have fought off with the Pact. Please, do not allow it entry into your heart. I beg of you not to—'*

The flames leapt higher, obscuring her vision, the smoke choking her, the flames catching her dress, touching her skin. She screamed, unable, despite her vow, to hold it in.

Through the pain, she cried out with her mind, desperate to make her sister hear. To make her stop from taking this most terrible of steps because of her hatred of the Were and her need to take revenge for something that only a few were responsible for. *'No Morrigan. Don't! Not for me. Never for me.'*

'Only for you,' she cried. 'They will pay for this. The Were will pay, but first every man, woman and child taking delight in this horror will feel each moment of terror and agony you endure.'

'No, Morrigan. It does not have to be like this.'

'You are wrong. They sealed their fate the moment they laid hands on you.'

'Then you give me no choice.' Morghanna looked up to the heavens and cried out, her voice carrying over the rabble, over the crackle of flames once more. 'Please, my Goddess. End this now. Take me as you always promised you would.'

There was no answer and as the flames took hold, Morghanna screamed again.

'Our Goddess has failed you,' Morrigan cried. 'I will not.' She raised her hands but Morghanna didn't see anything more. Light streamed from the heavens, surrounding her in a golden glow.

The pain fell away and she lifted her head to the heavens as the touch of her Goddess wrapped around her.

The light brightened, white and pure, as flames exploded around her. 'I knew my Goddess would never forsake me,' Morghanna cried out. Then in Morrigan's head, Morghanna said, *'It is not too late for you either my beloved sister to change your path. Fill yourself with the Goddess' light and love. Do not let the Darkness have you.'*

The light around Morghanna brightened, white and pure. Her bindings evaporated and she lifted her hands, crying out to the stars above, 'Save me.'

Flames exploded, whipping into a tornado that shot up into the sky. Screams sang out on the air as the mob fell away from the explosion of white-hot heat and flame. There was a brief flash of pain.

And then there was nothing.

She never saw the destruction her sister wrought in her name or the moment the Darkness wrapped itself around Morrigan's heart. It wasn't until much later when she was able to pull her consciousness together, that she looked down on the world and saw what had been started by her Curse.

She sobbed and railed and eventually cried out, 'Oh Goddess! How can I make amends for what I've done?'

'You can help me,' the Goddess Arianrhod said as she appeared beside her. 'Together, we can work to defeat the creature at the heart of this madness.'

'My Curse already took care of the MacCraes.'

'Not the MacCraes. The thing behind all the evil in this world. The thing I warned you we would have to face all those years ago when I helped save your mate the first time.'

'You did not save him this time.'

'No, I did not. But that was out of my hands.' A sigh. 'As you promised me your fidelity all those years ago, I now promise you I will do all I can to help lead you back to your soul mate in some future time.'

Hope thrilled through her. To be with Alistair again! 'You can do that?'

'I can try. But only after you do what must be done now.'

'And that is?'

'You will help me to destroy the Darkness.'

1

The smell was the first thing that hit Adam, a horrible burning of flesh and cotton. Then the punch as he was flung backwards. Time slowed, every bare millisecond separated as he flew through the air, giving him a chance to look down.

Fuck, there was a hole in his chest.

Time sped up as the pain tore through him. He hit the wall and there was a strange popping, wrenching sound that made him stagger. A thump behind him. He spun to see his body splayed on the ground, a stupid look of surprise on his face.

Marcus landed beside him. A black charred hole smoked in both their chests. Marcus' body was still in the super-empowered form that had allowed them to break down the door. Adam's was returning to normal. Well, as normal as it could be with a big black smoking hole in his chest.

Hang on. Why was he looking down at his body and not up at the ceiling?

The room span. There could be only one explanation.

He was dead.

Holy shit!

He was dead?

It had all happened so fast. One moment he'd been rushing into the room, feeling stronger than he'd ever felt before, the next—bam! Struck by warlock lightning. Dead.

It was the most curious sensation. Not at all like he'd thought it would feel. Quite freeing actually if you discounted the initial pain. Although there sure was a lot of wind in the afterlife—he couldn't feel it, but it was a loud whooshing in his ears. It made hearing anything else difficult.

Shelley had never mentioned it. Maybe she didn't hear it. Maybe you had to be dead to hear the noise of the afterlife.

He laughed, couldn't help it. It was so absurd.

Shelley's gaze snapped to him. His laughter died. She wasn't looking at his body lying on the floor with the smouldering hole in its chest. But at him. Ghost him. And the expression on her face made him want to howl.

Horror. Grief. Realisation.

He *was* dead. And there was no way they could ever be together. Not that there was ever really a chance that they would have been, but now that chance was completely gone. Whisked away between one breath and the next. It was like being punched in the chest with something worse than warlock lightning. He couldn't breathe. Couldn't breathe. He was dead! And every hope he'd ever had was gone.

Something brushed past him and he became aware of the pandemonium around him. What the fuck was he doing standing here worried about what he'd lost? There was a battle raging around him. Cain was about to throw a lightning bolt at Shelley.

No!

He threw himself in the way but he needn't have bothered. Power sizzled in the air as Shelley waved her hand and shouted out a word. Something buffeted him; the spirits around him wavered and crackled, like bad transmission on the TV. There was a faint amethyst outline hanging in the air around them all, like a bubble—holy crap, it was a shield! —protecting her, Cordy and the two bodies lying on the floor.

Cain loosed his lightning. It hit the shield, flared and skittered up to the ceiling, exploding there. 'Fuck, Shelley, that was amazing. I didn't know you could do that.'

She simply stared at him and then her gaze darted around him and he became aware of hundreds of spirits surrounding her too. He wasn't sure if they were being protective or staying in her protective cordon. He didn't have a chance to ask. Another bolt of lightning hit the shield. Sparks sprayed everywhere, delineating the edges of it; the strange amethyst tinge around the translucent edges fluttered. The bolt slid up and hit the ceiling. Rocks and plaster bounced off the shield and clattered onto the floor.

Shelley winced as if they'd hit her.

She was being hurt. Protective rage surged inside him. 'You bastard,' he shouted at Cain and leapt towards him—then fell right through him and onto the floor.

He rolled over, swearing, and rose, ready to try again. One of the spirits was whispering something in Shelley's ear. Another—he identified him as Harrison, Skye and River's grandfather, from photos he'd seen—shouted something, a general organising his troops. Half the spirits surged towards Cain.

Eloise's brother shrieked, his words lost in the strange wind that seemed to be a constant whistle in Adam's ears, then loosed another bolt and ran to the door.

'Don't let him get away!' Iain shouted, loud enough for Adam to hear. Shit. Iain was there. With Eloise cradled in his arms on the opposite side of the room. He'd forgotten about them. He turned to do as Iain bid, but Cain was already out the door, loosing another lightning bolt at Shelley as he went. More rocks and plaster rained down from the ceiling.

Cain was gone, but Adam didn't really care. He turned to check on Shelley.

Her look as it met his, it slayed him. Well, it would if he wasn't already dead. His lips quirked and he shrugged. 'I'm dead, aren't I?' he asked softly.

She didn't answer, but her eyes blinked faster.

'Am I supposed to go towards the light?' He glanced around, but he couldn't see any light except for what came from the lights in the ceiling.

'Don't go,' she said raggedly. His gaze snapped back to her as she whispered again, 'Don't go.'

He frowned. Strange that he could hear her so clearly when everything else was almost drowned out by the damned wind.

'Marcus. Marcus. Come back to me,' Cordy cried, her grief echoing through the wind. 'Don't you leave me alone. Not like this. Not like this.'

Her plea was useless. Marcus' spirit stood over Cordy, tortured grief written in every line of him. Adam swallowed hard then said, 'Shelley. Help her.'

Shelley jumped a little then started forward.

'Shelley.' Iain's voice, a sharp, desperate shout. 'Shelley. You can't help them. They're already gone. Eloise is still alive. We have to help her. Shelley!'

Cordy's wailing became even louder, the sobs so grief-filled they lashed him. He could see they were lashing Iain as well, the grief in his friend's eyes for him as well as the Alpha of Pack McClune and the mate he'd left behind. Yet, like a good lieutenant always would do, he put aside his grief and did what he could for the living. Adam understood. Just as he understood Iain would do anything to save his new mate.

Marcus was saying something to Shelley but Adam still couldn't make out his words through the howling wind—he could barely make out what the living were saying. Except Shelley. Her words were clear.

Shelley blinked and then very slowly turned to Cordy, her brow creased. She touched the grieving witch on the head and said, 'Sleep.' Cordy slumped over Marcus' body, the absence of sobbing a shocking silence. Shelley nodded slowly as Marcus said something else. 'I know. Are you sure?' She paused, then nodded. 'I'll tell her later.' Marcus looked pleadingly at her, then nodded and turned back to his mate.

'Who are you talking to?' Iain asked.

She swallowed hard. 'Marcus. He's standing right there. He couldn't bear Cordy's grief and asked me to make her sleep. She'll be no use to us anyway.' Her eyes slipped to where Adam stood and then away.

'We have to help Eloise,' Iain repeated.

'Yes.' Shelley blinked again and turned to look at him and the woman in his arms.

'Bron will be here soon.'

'We can't wait for Bron. We have to do something now.'

'You're holding her here.'

He grimaced. 'She's holding herself. She's using the bond and I'm holding her to it, but she's weakening. She's lost too much blood. The bond will tear if we don't do something. Please ... help. You're a nurse. Surely there's something you can do.'

She looked lost. Adam couldn't bare that look in her eyes. He had to do something. Had to bring her out of her grief and shock and bring her back to the here and now. He began to sing 'Suicide Blonde', doing his best Michael Hutchence impersonation. He knew she hated it. Knew it would make her angry. And anger would snap her out of her grief and make her move.

Her eyes flared wide and she snorted out on a laugh, 'Shut up you idiot!'

'Sure. As soon as you snap out of it and do what you're trained to do.' He pointed at Iain. At Eloise. 'She needs your help.'

She stared at him for a moment longer, her chin wobbling, then she moved, ripping the bloody sheet off the bed and racing to where Iain lay with Eloise clutched in his arms.

He smiled. *Good job Adam.* She was nurse Shelley again, action girl. One of the many sides of her he loved.

He watched her go to work, directing Iain to place Eloise on the bed, snapping out instructions. Despite Iain's injuries and obvious weakness, he complied, even to the point where he allowed Shelley to hook him up as a blood donor when they found no blood—Iain was a universal donor, thankfully.

As they worked, Adam became aware of a curious pull on him. Almost as if one of the pack pulled on the Packbond. Weird. He would have thought that bond was sliced clean the moment he died. Maybe it didn't fully go until the ceremony of light had been completed and his body taken in the flame of the power of his coven. He knew dead Were didn't stick around once the ceremony was done. Shelley had never seen any Were spirits—just human and witch and warlock. Perhaps he would be here, linked, until then. As Marcus was.

The pull became stronger, dragging him towards Iain and Eloise. He let it. He'd give everything he could to help Iain save his mate.

Jason, Skye, Bron and River charged into the room. Jason's gaze arrowed immediately to Adam's body, the gaping wound in his chest smouldering and black.

'Oh, my God!' Skye gasped.

'Adam!' Jason yelled. His brother's cry echoed through the wind; it was another tearing wound in his chest. Fuck! He'd never wanted to cause anyone that grief, let alone his big brother who had already been through too much. But what could he do? He was dead.

'Bron! Help.'

Alistair and June charged in behind them. They howled at the sight of their dead Alpha and went down on their knees next to Marcus and Cordy, keening at the ceiling.

Bron dropped down on her knees beside Adam's body, hands held over him, the anguish in her eyes only a fraction of what was in Jason's.

He held his breath, waiting for her to say the words that would make their grieving real.

Shelley's gaze flickered to him again. She took a deep breath and gripped Bron's shoulder. 'Don't. He's gone.'

Bron shook her head. 'No. He's still here. The bolt missed his heart. It's still beating. It's faint but still beating.'

'What?' Adam stared down at his body as Shelley slowly turned to look at him.

'That's impossible. I saw—'

He wasn't dead? Did that mean he was alive? He reached out to touch her, made contact.

She jumped, sucking in a breath.

'Holy shit. What was that?' He stared down at his hand. He'd felt her. Felt her! He looked up at her. She looked just as shocked as he felt. 'Shelley? Tell me you felt that.'

'Saw what?' Skye's voice intruded.

Shelley shook her head, at Skye or at him, he wasn't certain. 'I must have been mistaken,' she whispered and turned back to Bron. 'Can you heal him?'

'I'm trying. I'm trying.'

Skye and Jason began to question Shelley about what had happened. Adam waited for her to answer, for her to finish with them. Marcus began to speak to her again, gesturing at his pack-mates. She crossed to Alistair and June, spoke softly. They stopped keening and stood, fury and grief in their eyes. 'You have to stop them from doing something stupid, Shelley. You're the only one who can.' Shelley's gaze shot to him and then away, her lips working as if she was holding back some terrible emotion. He wanted to talk to her, wanted to ask her so many things, wanted to try to touch her again, but she got up and hurried back to help Iain with Eloise. Then she went back to Alistair and June.

More of the McClune pack arrived, and with words that Marcus spoke to her, Shelley managed to keep them focused, settling Cordy comfortably on a bed, covering and then carrying away Marcus' body. Some went in search of Cain.

'Catch the bastard and make him pay,' he whispered as they left.

There was a tug on him again and he stumbled a little towards Iain and Eloise. They needed his strength. He was happy to give it to them. He glanced over to where Bron worked on him, Jason's hand on her shoulder feeding his strength and Alpha power into her to use in healing his horrific wounds. He expected to be pulled back to his body any moment; Bron was the most powerful Healer they'd seen for centuries. She'd save him.

Minutes passed. Longer. But there was no tug back towards the shell that was once his. It was as if whatever had held him to his body had been completely severed.

But Bron would fix it. She had to fix it.

No point worrying right now. He was still needed even in this form.

He concentrated on Iain and Eloise, on the sensation that pulled at him. He needed to give them more.

'Don't do that.'

He turned. Shelley's eyes were wide, slightly panicked, as she stared at him. 'Don't do what?'

'Whatever you're doing. Stop it. You're fading.' Her voice was a mere whisper, but he heard it as clear as a bell.

'What do you mean?'

She looked around the room. Everyone was busy with what they were doing and took no notice of her. Not that Shelley talking to spirits was anything new—she tried to ignore them, but they weren't always ignorable. Except now. They weren't trying to talk to her now. They all hovered near his body or Iain and Eloise. Marcus and a few others stood over Cordy.

For the time being, Shelley had some peace from them all.

She turned back to him. 'I don't know.' She gestured with her hands, waving them up and down. 'You're less real looking. And flickering a little. I don't think it's good. What are you doing?'

'I felt Iain pulling on the Packbond so I channelled my strength into it to help him with Eloise.'

'Well stop it. I don't like the look of what it's doing to you.' She went to move past him.

He grabbed her arm. She hissed. He let go. 'Sorry. Did I hurt you?'

'No.' She stared at him, down at his hand, back up. 'It's just, you touched me. How did you touch me?'

'I don't know. All I know is I can. That I felt it. And so did you.'

She nodded. 'It's icy cold.'

'Oh. Sorry. I'll try and warm up a bit. I wonder if the fire pits of hell are close by?'

Her lips twitched. 'You're such an idiot.'

He couldn't help but smile at her epithet. 'Even in death.'

Her eyes clouded, gaze flickering to his body. 'You're not dead,' she whispered.

He leaned closer to grab her attention. 'Shelley. What's going on? If I'm not dead, then why can you see me? Why can I touch you? What am I?'

'I don't know.' Her gaze met his, a thousand troubled questions clouding the clear, almost violet, blue. 'I don't know.' Iain called her then. 'I have to go.'

'Don't tell them you can see me, Shelley. I don't want them more upset than they already are. I don't want them to give up hope of me. Not until we've figured out what's going on.'

She didn't look at him again, just pressed her lips together, nodded and walked away.

He turned back to the room, his thoughts whirring. There had to be some way he could find out what was going on. Why he was so separate from his body and yet wasn't dead. Was he a Shade like Cain had been? No. That couldn't be it. He'd touched Shelley and hadn't sucked her life energy from her as Cain had done when he touched others. There was something else going on here. Maybe one of the spirits could help him. According to Shelley, some of them were ancient and had knowledge of things that had been lost to the modern packs.

Perhaps there was one in the room with him now.

He caught a woman with long, tangled black hair, staring at him from across the room, her eyes a startling violet glow in the darkened corner in which she stood. She wore a gown that looked like it might be from the fifteenth or sixteenth century—although historical fashion wasn't his forte, so he could be completely off there.

But she was the only one showing him any interest. She floated over to him.

'You should touch her again. Do it as often as you can.'

'I can hear you.'

'Of course. We are the same. The others are not.'

'What are we?'

She waved her hand back towards Shelley. 'You must tie yourself to her more firmly through your bond.'

'Our bond?' He shook his head. 'There's nothing but the Packbond.'

She tipped her head, assessing. 'You truly believe that?'

'What else could there be?'

She opened her mouth as if to answer and then shook her head. 'You must come with me.'

'And why must I do that?'

'You want to know who you are, don't you? Why you're here? What your role is in all this?'

'What role? I'm here because I was stupid enough to get hit by warlock lightning.'

She tutted at him. 'You are important, Adam McVale. More important than anyone has ever given you credit for. But to learn all you need to learn, you must come with—' She jumped and looked behind her, then back at him, her face lined with worry. 'I must go. You need to come with me now. There is much you must learn.'

She reached for him. He edged away. The tug of the Packbond pulled insistently. He couldn't leave, no matter what the strange woman said. His pack needed him.

'They will always need you. But your role as Trickster is more important than you know and staying here won't teach you what you need to learn to save your pack.'

Her words skittered down his spine and he shivered, as if touched by magic or prescience. 'Who are you?'

She jumped again, looked behind her. She turned quickly back to him, eyes flared wide. 'You must come with me. Now.'

'I'm not going anywhere until you tell me who you are and what this is about.'

Frustration twisted her face. 'I can't. Not here.' She looked behind her again and when she turned back, her eyes were full of fear. 'You can stay, for now. Do what you must to help. But when I come back, I won't give you any choice. I only hope it won't be too late.'

'Too late for what?'

She glanced behind her, her fear palpable, and then, tossing her hood over her head, she turned and ran through the wall to his left, disappearing from view.

The roaring of wind around him crescendoed to ear-splitting proportions. He clutched his ears, trying to cut out the sound. It barely made any difference. By the Moon, it hurt. He bent over, trying to shield his head, his ears, from the ear-splitting noise. A dark shadow of movement emerged from the shadows in the corner, rushed across the room then disappeared through the wall where the spirit woman had run just moments before.

The deafening sound disappeared with the shadow.

'What the fuck?' All he could hear now was the whistling whoosh of wind that had been in his ears ever since he'd been kicked from his body.

He shuddered and looked around to see if anyone else had noticed the strange woman and the shadow that followed her.

A woman who looked strangely familiar—although he couldn't figure out why—was frowning at the wall. He strode over to her, waving to get her attention. 'Did you see that?'

She said something to him, but he couldn't hear her above the noise of wind all around him. He waved he couldn't understand. She shrugged then pointed over his shoulder.

He swung around. Shelley was staring at him. Their gazes met. She looked away and went back to tending Cordy.

For some reason, she didn't want to talk to him. Didn't even seem to want to see him.

But that was okay. She couldn't ignore him forever.

In the meantime, he had to figure out a way to hear one of the other spirits. That other spirit had seen her, he was sure of it. Someone here had to know who that woman was.

Perhaps he should have gone with her, but how could he, with the bond tugging at him like it was?

He sighed. The Packbond. At least he still had that. The violet-eyes woman had said he didn't know who he was or understand his true role of Trickster. What he did know was that he was still tied to his pack. Iain's need to keep Eloise alive pressed on him, pulling at him. He had to do whatever he could to help. It was what he'd always done. And despite what Shelley had said to him about not pushing his power through the Packbond, he had to help. It was the only thing he could do and he would keep on going until he could do it no more.

2

Morghanna ran. Her enemy was close. Its breath was cold death, whispering down her neck, promising finality in the way the death of her body never had. She'd never let it get so close before, but then, there had never been so much to lose.

Goddess-damn its persistence. She'd worked too long and too hard to let it close now. She could turn and fight, but then it might sense more than fear for herself, and she couldn't allow that.

She couldn't allow it to touch another one of her family. She was only lucky it hadn't seen what she'd done here tonight. She'd been so elated with her success that she'd almost missed the sound of it coming; the icy dark tingle that had chased along her skin, rippled up her spine. She'd been an idiot.

But then again, she'd been trying to grasp for what she'd worked centuries to bring about—a way to defeat their enemy once and for all. It had been difficult to turn from that.

She hadn't planned on Adam being so stubborn, refusing to follow the path she'd laid out before him. He was a Trickster through and through. She almost laughed at the irony. She needed him to be who he was; but being who he was had forced her to stay too long, too close to the very danger that hunted her, to try to make him take the step towards his destiny.

Thank the Goddess the enemy hadn't seen Adam. It had been too single-minded trying to chase her down. The only problem was, now she had to find some way of getting back to the Trickster. Had to find some way to get him to trust her. However, she couldn't do that with her enemy so close.

The moment it turned its attention towards Adam's soul, all could be lost. Without him, the triad of Skye, Bron and Shelley would not become the triumvirate. And if they didn't become the triumvirate, they wouldn't be able to pull on the true power that was theirs, feeding it into the Nexus so she could use the Goddess Stone. It all hinged on Adam doing his part. And it was up to her to ensure he was ready.

The whirl of sound around her became louder, a heavy thud in her veins, through her heart, pounding into her head. It pulled at her, making it harder to run, to move. She gritted her teeth and pushed.

It's swiping hand just missed catching her.

She couldn't let it touch her now. Not after all this time. It had reached out and snared her sister; had somehow caught Bridgette and almost turned her reincarnated soul to its black intent. It had destroyed so many good people.

And now, after so long working for her Goddess, they were so close to defeating it.

Something that would not eventuate if it captured her now.

Damnation. There was only one choice. She must return to the light of her Goddess. But if she did so, she would have to bargain something to be allowed to return. Her Goddess would let her come with her blessings if she could—but she did not make the rules.

What would she be made to forsake this time?

No matter. There was no time or choice. The pounding of the enemy was too close behind her. She could not escape its hateful maw if she did not do this. She would have to call on the light of her Goddess—the light that would allow her into the home of the Gods. The one place the enemy could never go. She'd have to bargain with the guardians to be allowed back, pay them something important to her so they wouldn't send her back this way, into the arms of the enemy, but forge her a new path.

She sighed. Why did travel through the realms have to come with such a cost? The guardians, eternal, infernal, had sent many to their deaths, smiles on their faces. Well, she would have to be smarter than them. But that was okay. Her Goddess hadn't chosen her because she lacked intelligence. She always gave her what she needed to scrape her way through.

It would help to keep her eye on the final goal: being reunited with Alistair once more as the Goddess had promised.

If he was here, he would tell her that if there was a way, she would be the one to find it. He had always believed in her, no matter what. She couldn't let him down now.

Her heart tightened in her chest, a little twist, anxiety and old grief moving their claws in her flesh, reminding her of all she'd lost.

But there was no time to let it take over her now. The enemy's noise was close behind her, deafening, its malevolence a cold burning pressure. She glanced back; it stared at her with more than hatred. There was longing and putrid jealousy and want and desire.

It ebbed towards her, threatening to swallow her whole.

Useless. Hopeless. Alone. All Alone. Always alone.

The horrifying whisper was in her ears. All around her. Pulling at her aching heart. She almost stopped. Almost gave herself over to it.

Her lurching movement made the heavy fist-sized locket she wore swing loose and bang into her chest. It flipped open and the coruscating colours of the Goddess Stone shone over her chest, light illuminating the portrait set into the lid of the container; a portrait of her beloved and her long-lost son.

The son who lived on in Pack McVale. Her son, whose features lived in the face of the one called River. Whose power called to her in the one called Skye.

Family. Her family.

Alone. Always alone.

No!

She cried out into the noise of the enemy all around. She shook her head against its invasive hold, putting her hands over her ears, humming inside her mind to shut out the noise that would thread its way through her. She wouldn't allow the little barbs of its hatred, its evil, putrid need, to let her falter now. She couldn't let it take her over. Because if it did, it would take over her family and then everything would truly be lost.

Love. Hope. Friendship. Family.

All gone.

No!

Her plan might not have come to fruition how she'd wanted it to —plans rarely did— but that didn't mean she couldn't find a way. She'd just have to be cleverer than her enemy.

Cleverer than the Guardians of the Hall who found it funny to stand in her way.

Turning the open locket, she aimed the light of the Goddess Stone at the greying dark in front of her and channelled her power into opening a doorway. A sliver of light widened quickly, large enough now for her to slip through. 'Thank you, my Goddess.' She tightened her grip on the locket as she stepped through the doorway, the warmth of the light chasing the cold chill of death from her limbs.

The door snapped closed behind her. The grasping hand that had reached out to grab her pulled back from the burst of power exhaled into the ether from the Goddess' light. Alone in the purpling dark it howled its misery into the silence.

CAIN STUMBLED on through the scrub and trees. Morrigan was waiting for him. The Darkness had told him. She had a car. Not far now. He just had to keep going.

His legs were wobbly. He'd been out of his body for too long and the bloody Were hadn't done enough to keep his muscles from getting weak. Thank the Old Ones the Darkness was still with him. A living presence in his chest and mind, it had been driving him forward since he'd come back to his body and all their plans had fallen apart.

Ruined. By Eloise.

He still couldn't believe it. His quiet little mouse of a twin had somehow managed to grasp a hold of the power that should never have been hers and use it against him and the Darkness.

She'd pushed him out!

His lip quivered, a throb in his heart. His sister had rejected him.

She had never rejected him before.

She'd always loved him. Looked up to him. Deferred to him. Had thought it only natural when Morrigan showed him preference over her. He'd always been the more powerful. The one with more talent. He'd always been everyone's favourite, the golden child. The one who never disappointed. Who could do no wrong. And Eloise had always been there for him, happy to live in his shadow, never aware that he fed from her power to buoy his own.

Truth be told, he'd been unaware of what he'd been doing for a very long time. It was simply a natural part of their relationship. Starting in the womb, continuing on afterwards.

It was Morrigan who'd made him aware of it. Had taught him how to refine his use of his twin's power, to gather more of it to himself, to twist it to his use so that it wasn't just a bolster to his own, considerable powers.

Eloise had never said a word in complaint. She'd never been jealous of his ability or shown any inclination to stop him taking from her what was meant to be his to use anyway. That's what Morrigan and the Darkness told him. She was his twin. She was supposed to share everything she was with him. What was hers was his.

Besides, she was lucky to be alive. She wouldn't have been without him. He was the stronger. He could have subsumed her in the womb, all of what she was becoming his—but he hadn't. He loved her as he thought she loved him. She'd given a part of her essence to him, and in return he'd protected her. Gladly. Even when he began to grow away from her in his work with and for Morrigan, he'd still done what he could to protect her from her own weakness.

They were one being.

But tonight, they'd become separate and she'd done the separating. She'd chosen a filthy Were over him. She'd brought him back as promised, returned soul to body, but then she'd denied him what was his by rights and chosen another path that was truly her own.

It was wrong. Infuriating. Inconceivable.

'The power of the Nexus should be mine!' His voice, harsh and angry, echoed in the branches of the trees overhead.

'Shh. They'll hear you.'

'Fuck them!' he snarled to the Darkness. 'I'll kill any who come after me just as I killed those two in the caves. I'll make them pay for taking my sister from me.' He began to turn around but the Darkness stopped him.

'You don't have the energy. You need to keep moving. You need to get to Morrigan. Once safe, we can plan your revenge.'

Yes. Yes. His revenge. He'd kill all of them. The filthy Were. He and Morrigan would do it together. And once they were gone, Eloise would be free to come back to him.

'We don't need her. I already have a plan. You simply need to get back to Morrigan.'

'But what about the Nexus' power?'

'You have what you need of her inside you already.'

'No. She took it. She took it all.'

'You are wrong. You took some of her power inside you during the ceremony. Look inside. You'll see I'm right.'

Cain stopped—not for long, the Were weren't far away. He closed his eyes and went inside himself, to that central place in his mind where he could not only tap into his power but see it.

The Darkness was there. It had grown larger. Which made sense, given he'd taken on the shard that had been inside Eloise. He stroked it as he went past. But he didn't stop. The Darkness wasn't near his power. He'd always kept it separate, no matter how much the Darkness had said they would be stronger if he allowed it access to his power centre. Cain loved the Darkness, had let it guide him all these years, but something stopped him from giving over to it completely.

He travelled deeper inside.

There.

A deep spark of red, glowing like lit coal, deep inside him. His power.

So beautiful.

And there, at its heart, was the flame of green that had always signified Eloise's power.

It was diminished. Less emerald and more of a faded grass colour. But still there. Still imbued with the power that was unique to his sister. A part of the power that made her the Nexus.

His to use.

He smiled and continued to run.

Everything wasn't ruined. In fact, it was going to be fine. He had his sister still in the deepest heart of him. She hadn't abandoned him completely. She never would. And somehow, he was going to use that bit of power to get everything he wanted.

He began to laugh as he ran back towards where Morrigan waited for him.

3

Shelley was in the dam again. Her head ached with the pounding of a million wails, a million needs, a million cries for help. She was sick of it. So sick of it. She just wanted to be left alone.

Then he was there. Wading through the water, reaching for her. When he touched her, it didn't pull from her in the way the touch of others did. He'd never needed anything from her except her smile, her laughter, her happiness.

She looked up at him, unable to hide the longing, the want, her own need, from his gaze.

He seemed to know, as he always knew, what was deep in her heart, what her emotions cried out for.

He took her face in his hands and then his lips were on hers and everything turned to flame.

She'd been cold in the water, but now his lips on hers drove fire through her veins, a fire she was helpless to fight anymore.

'Adam,' she gasped.

'Michelline.'

Her real name on his lips loosed something inside her. She dug her hands into his hair, pulled his lips tighter against hers. She opened to him, giving him her tongue, tasting him, the deep searing intensity of his scent filling her, heating her further. She loved the way he smelled; the fresh citrus and sunshine smell of him always made her want to smile, even as she fought its attraction. Now she breathed it in, soaking it up, tasting it on her tongue. His tongue.

His hands pulled her closer and he whispered her name against her lips once more.

The sound of it drove her wild. She ran her hands down his back, digging her fingers into his jeans, pulling him closer. She groaned as his erection pressed into her pelvic bone.

So close. But so far. Separated by wet clothes and too much time.

She'd wanted him the first time she'd seen him the year before, up at the snow. Wanted even though she had vowed never to trust anyone with her heart—not after her family and her ex-fiancé's betrayal. Hated that she'd wanted him, and so she'd been prickly and sarcastic. An absolute bitch. And yet he'd kept being nice to her, flirting and trying to make her laugh, annoying her and attracting her in equal measure every time he walked into the room with his stupid smile on his stupidly handsome face, his stupidly enticing scent wrapping around her, his stupidly deep voice full of open emotion reaching out to stroke the most intimate, secret places in her heart. Touching her soul.

'Stupid. Stupid,' she whispered against his mouth.

He pulled her tighter against him, deepening the kiss and she let him. Oh Goddess, she let him. She wanted to tear at his shirt, to rip off his jeans, to fill her hands with the hardness of his erection, make him groan and jerk and come so hard that she'd feel it as deeply as he did. And then she wanted to clamber up his body and impale herself on his amazing cock and ride him until she couldn't think, until she was nothing but the pulsing, aching need firing through her blood and let it build and build until it wiped away her frustration and emptiness, the horrifying sense of being alone in the constant crowd around her, until she screamed her repletion into the night sky as she came like she knew only Adam could make her come.

She jerked against him as just the thought brought her almost flying off the edge of the precipice she teetered on.

Water sloshed around them, pushing at them. She wanted to push back. Drag him out of the water so she could fulfil in reality the images filling her mind.

No. Not entirely filling her mind. There was something else there too. A noise had begun in her head, a low hum.

She wondered briefly if Adam was purring.

She'd made a Were purr.

Her lips curved against his as pure satisfaction shot through her.

He sucked her lip into his mouth in response. Oh Goddess, that was good.

The sound continued. Became louder. Began to push out the erotic images, replacing them with something else. Something dark and horrifying and desperate.

It wasn't coming from him. The noise was in her. Coming from her. No.

No!

She was dreaming. She knew she was dreaming, and yet, she couldn't bring herself out of it; couldn't stop what was coming any more than she could in reality.

Even so, she tried to stop it now. To shut off the sound. But she had no control over it.

Another sound joined the first. Wings beating, swooping down out of the night sky, grabbing her and hauling the essence of her away until she was nothing but the bleak desperation.

Death.

It was coming.

And she could do nothing to stop it.

She could only sound out its arrival and hope it didn't touch anyone she loved.

But it was too late—it already had.

The world swirled around her and she found herself standing in the room she'd had as a child in her family home. Someone was lying in the bed—herself as a ten-year-old. Sound asleep. But not peaceful. No, even then the burden of her gift brought shadows to her dreams.

'What is this?'

She turned with a start. Adam stood beside her. 'You shouldn't be here. You can't be here,' she said, wanting to push him away. Never wanting him to see what was coming. But once again she was helpless, unable to stop the inevitable from happening in this memory she'd forgotten.

Hands appeared over the edge of the open window, followed by a head, covered in cuts and blood that showed through the brutally short hair. Pale blue eyes glowed in the semi-dark, lit by the moon that gave her lunacy its name. The woman smiled as she spied the body in the bed and pulled herself over the window ledge, her lips a horrible mess of bites and scabs and scars where she'd chewed them.

'Who is that?' the Adam of her dream asked.

'My aunt.' The admission was a sword slash to the gut. Lilyanna had once been the most beautiful of her family, gentle and loving and kind. She'd helped Shelley when she was younger, protected her from the needs of the family. She'd taken the burden of their "gift" on her shoulders in full, until one day she'd begun to slash at herself with a knife and scream and scream until she'd been dragged away.

However, even when she was long gone, Shelley could hear those screams. She could hear them now as she watched this memory unfold in her dream, unable to stop them from joining in the song of the banshee that was building to a wail inside her.

Lilyanna began to scratch at her arms, digging her nails into the cuts and sores as she rocked back and forth, the grin never leaving her mouth as her gaze skittered around the room. 'I know. I know. I must warn her.' Her head snapped to the side. 'Of course I won't hurt her. I would never hurt Michelline.'

Shelley swallowed. She knew her aunt was talking to the spirits who had gathered around her bed, and she willed, with everything in her, for her sleeping ten-year-old self to not wake up, to not bear witness to what happened next. 'Don't wake up. Don't wake up.'

Lilyanna's gaze snapped to her suddenly, eyes widening. 'You cannot stop this, Michelline. It has already happened. You may as well try to push water uphill with a sieve.' She laughed, a wild shriek of sound. It was her laughter that finally woke Shelley's ten-year-old self. 'Oh good, Michelline, you are awake.'

Then Shelley was on the bed, in her childish body, looking up at the thing that looked like her beloved aunt if she'd come from hell. 'Aunty?' She edged away, knowing even then something horrible was about to happen.

'Yes, it's me, Michelline. They took me away. Wouldn't let me see you. But I got out. I had to come to you. I had to tell you what I saw. What I learned.'

'What? I don't understand.'

'No. You won't. Not for many years. In fact, you will forget this until the time is right.'

'I don't—'

'Shh.' Lilyanna put her bloody finger against Shelley's lips. 'There's no time to talk. The spirits tell me *they* will be here at any moment to take me away and I must tell you what I saw.' She paused, her wild gaze pinning Shelley to the spot. She could barely breathe, couldn't move, as her aunt's words wove around her, her tone soft, mesmerising.

'There is a winged creature inside you ready to take flight, little Michelline. When it opens its mouth, it will swallow you whole and the entire world will shudder with the death its scream will foretell. But do not fear the scream, because if you do, if you give in to the fear of what you could become, it will drive you insane.' She leaned in closer, her breath smelling of blood and rotting things. Shelley gagged, but couldn't move, could only watch in horror as this thing that had once been her aunt climbed onto the bed and laid her head against Shelley's small chest.

'Ah, your heart. It beats so strongly. I can hear the flutter of wings in it already. A promise. A whisper of what is to come.' She pulled away, replacing her head with her hand, the stickiness of her blood seeping through Shelley's cotton nightie. 'Your heart is the only thing that can save you from the madness. Trust it more than you trust anything else. It will lead you true.' She swayed back then and laughed, a mad shout of sound, and turned and pointed right to where Adam still stood. 'Don't let the madness kill your love. It is the only thing that can save you.' She turned back to Shelley, her eyes dark wells of insanity that caught at Shelley, sucked her in. 'Now, let the wail rise and shape the world to your will.'

Her aunt dissolved and Shelley stood in the dam again. With Adam.

Her mouth opened—she couldn't stop it—and as the wail released, her gaze found the Were she found so horribly, attractive and annoying.

His face was screwed up in pain. Blood poured from his nose and ears and mouth. His gaze met hers; in it was the shadow of Death.

No! No. She was killing him. She was killing her love with this insanity and she had no idea how to stop it.

Pain shot through her, worse than anything she'd ever felt before. The only sound coming out of her was Death's cry. Tears ran down her face, smelling of salt water and the copper of blood. Her heart was truly broken and could never be made whole again.

'Shelley. Shelley. Wake up!'

No. No. She shook her head. There was no waking up from this.

'Shelley. You're dreaming. A nightmare. Wake up.'

Something cold touched her shoulder. Her eyes snapped open and she jerked upright—and cracked her head on the shelf on the wall next to the desk.

'Fuck a duck! That hurts.' She rubbed at the bump on her head and scowled angrily at the offending shelf. 'The fuck who put that shelf there is a fucking moron.' A laugh behind her startled her into turning around.

Adam! It was his voice that had woken her. He was grinning at her in that way that both infuriated her and made her hot all over.

Craptastic. She could still see him.

But maybe that wasn't because ...

Her gaze flitted over to the bed where his body lay. Nope. Still there. She swiped at the tears on her cheeks. Goddamned dream.

'Off with their heads!' he said in a squeaky, English-accented voice. 'Death to all makers of shelving over desks!'

Her gaze was pulled back to the image of him despite her best efforts not to look his way. She wanted to laugh at his ridiculousness —trust him to quote a line from one of the most ridiculous and annoying of all literary characters. She hated *Alice in Wonderland*— and he knew it—particularly the bloody Queen of Hearts. There was no sense to her! She'd never understood people's infatuation with that stupid story or the stupid characters in that stupid book. She bristled to argue with him about his choice of quotes.

No. She couldn't engage. Not again.

He wasn't really there. Couldn't really be there. Because if he was really there, that meant he was dead—or as close to it as made no difference. She only saw dead people. It was what people like her did. She was a banshee and a Medium. Not that she fully understood what the banshee side was, but from what she'd gathered, it was more than just being the Medium she'd always thought she was. But even though it was different, it was still tied entirely to death and the afterlife. She could feel when death was coming. Her banshee wail proclaimed deaths—like Marcus'. Not Adam's. He wasn't dead. She wouldn't let her aunt's words be true. They couldn't be true.

She remembered that night now—how had she forgotten it? But her aunt was insane, and despite the fact that she'd predicted the banshee rising inside of Shelley, nothing else made sense. Especially the part about Adam and her heart and killing him. She hadn't killed him.

Her gaze went back to his body. He had a hole in his chest, but his heart was still beating. He was still breathing. She hadn't killed him. He wasn't dead. So there was no way she could see his spirit or ghost or whatever the hell people like her called them. *The Sixth Sense* wouldn't have been such a huge movie if Haley Joel Osmont had said, 'I see the images of still-living-but-not-attached-to-their-bodies-people.' No. 'I see dead people' was much more dramatic. And eerie. And correct. Mediums and banshees saw dead people.

They didn't see the spirits of those who were still alive.

So, ipso facto, she was either going completely insane, or Adam was dead.

She shouldn't be so surprised by the insanity. It ran in her family. It had hovered at the periphery of her mind for years. This was obviously just the first encroaching fingernails-down-the-blackboard announcement of it descending. The dream memory of her aunt was a reminder of what was in store for her. The only choice she had was to ignore it and press on and hope she could keep it at bay with sheer stubborn will.

Why her insanity had to take on the form of Adam was beyond her. It was cruel. Simply cruel. But then, why should she expect insanity to be kind? It had been a horrifying nightmare for her once beautiful and intelligent aunt. She closed her eyes against the image of Lilyanna as she'd last seen her, lips a mass of sores, scars on her arms and face, fresh wounds from where she'd scratched deeply at the insects only she could see crawling under her skin, hair shaved off so she couldn't pull it out, more scabs all over her skull. Horrifying.

Simply horrifying.

'Come on. That was funny. Or if not funny, annoying. I know you hate the Queen of Hearts.'

She jumped at the sound of Adam's voice and turned to see the hallucination of him move towards the desk. She shot up out of the chair—back creaking in protest—and walked to where his body lay.

The hallucination-Adam stopped in his tracks, frowning in consternation at her. 'That nightmare looked pretty nasty. You were crying and shaking. Want to tell me about it? I might be able to help.'

Her breath puffed out of her, fast, hard, painful in her Nullarbor-dry throat. She scrubbed at her face, forcing herself to slow her breathing before she hyperventilated. Of course, her subconscious would want to go over the nightmare. But she was in no mood to parse over the useless feelings the memories brought forward. There was nothing she could do now to change any of it, so why think about it? Especially that kiss and what happened after. Only a masochist or insane person getting off on their own misery would do that, and she certainly was no masochist. And she had no wish to let insanity dig its teeth in any further.

Busy. She just had to keep busy. That was all.

She picked up Adam's hand, her fingers finding the pulse point on his wrist. His heartbeat was strong, despite the hole in his chest. It was so strange, but it had to be a good sign, surely? She pulled the sheet away from his chest. The bandages covering the wound were turning black. The wound was still seeping. She'd have to change them again. The only problem was, hallucination-Adam stood right in front of the cupboards where all the supplies were kept. Which meant if she wanted to get to them, she'd have to walk through him. Walking around him wasn't an option—that would be accepting he was real.

She swallowed. She could do this. She hated walking through spirits—it was cold and shudder-inducing—but he wasn't really there, so she wouldn't feel anything. Right?

Her fingers curled on the edges of the sheet. She had felt something. He'd reached out and touched her the night it had happened. Grabbed her wrist. Touched her arm. And while it hadn't felt like when his actual fingers touched her, it had still been solid enough to let her know he was there.

But he wasn't. She was imagining him. Because his body was here. In front of her.

Lying unconscious on this bed.

Not dead.

Just walk through him, Shelley. Prove to yourself he's just some stupid figment of your imagination and get over it.

Right. Sounded like a good idea.

So, turn around and move. Now. Do it.

The door opened behind her and she almost sagged onto the bed in relief.

4

'Hey Shels.' Bron walked in, River close behind. 'How's Adam?'

She looked down at the body in front of her. 'His wound is seeping. I was just going to get some new bandages.'

'I'll get them for you,' River said, heading straight to the cupboards. He moved so quickly, the Adam hallucination wasn't able to completely get out of the way and River's hand went through him.

'Hey!' Adam said, rubbing at his side.

Shelley frowned. How had he felt that?

River didn't give any sign that he'd heard or felt anything. Which he wouldn't if the image of Adam was a spirit. Or a figment of her imagination.

She turned back to the body on the bed and busied herself stripping off the old bandages.

'That doesn't look any better,' Bron said from beside her. 'I was hoping the last Healing might have changed something.'

Shelley gave her friend a one-armed hug. 'You're doing your best. I think the problem here is a lack of understanding about warlock lightning and its impact on the Were body.'

'I know. You're right. It doesn't make it any less frustrating.' Bron gingerly touched the edges of the wound. 'I don't understand how I could heal the entire pack last year at Yule when my power fully kicked in and yet I can't heal this. It doesn't make sense.'

Shelley rubbed her back. 'It might if we knew more.'

'What are you thinking, Shelley?' River handed her the saline irrigator and new bandages.

She began cleaning the wound. 'I think maybe it's time I headed back to Melbourne and started researching the diaries more thoroughly for clues as to what's going on here.'

'You want to find out more about banshees?'

'No.' Her fingers clenched on the pad of bandages she was using to mop up the black gunk seeping out of the edges of the wound. The only research she wanted to do about her own powers was on finding more ways to shield herself from them. The things she'd learned so far about shielding had been incredibly useful—it had saved her and the others from Cain that night.

'But surely that's an important part of all this?'

'Understanding what I am isn't as important as finding out more about what could be causing Adam to stay like this, despite all the Healing energy you've poured into him. This can't be the first time this has happened. And given the Pack Witches liked to record everything, there has to be some mention of it somewhere. We just need to find it.'

'Patrick is already researching for us. He's using the notes you put together and is going through the other chests you suggested he go through. He's follow your instructions to a T.'

'I know. But you know Patrick can only get so far.' The diaries were spelled so that many passages looked like gobbledygook unless you had witch or warlock blood. They were full of hidden information that could only be pulled forth by those with the power of the covens running through their veins. 'It took us a while to get a handle on how to use them, and that was only with Cordy's help.' She looked over at Cordy, still in the magically induced coma. 'Besides, I was always the one who managed to get the diaries to spill their secrets the best.' She had no idea why. Possibly because she'd spent more time with them, more desperate to find out information about her powers so she could block them or learn to shield more effectively. She'd also found out a lot about Skye and Bron's powers to help them, her friends being uppermost in her mind a great deal of the time. 'Besides, you and Skye are needed here. I'm more a shag on a rock. It makes sense for me to go back.'

'What about the other McClune witches? They might be able to help.'

'They probably would if we asked them, but given what's going on, I don't really want to, do you?' She looked at Bron, whose eyes were clouded with worry and sadness.

Bron shook her head, whispered, 'No. I don't. They're barely handling keeping their coven and pack together without Cordy's abilities to steady them. What about Eloise? I know she's still recovering, but she's itching to get into the diaries and will follow your instructions too.'

'I know. I spoke to her before she and Iain left last week. But Eloise really needs to concentrate on finding out about what a Nexus is. We know it's important in the coming battle but not why. I need to get down there to help her with that. I need to teach her how to use the diaries.'

'She's under strict instructions not to start until she's better, so you have time.'

'Do I?' Shelley firmed her lips as she squirted saline into the wound. Black gunk ran out of the edges and down the side of his chest. Bron grabbed a bandage and helped mop up the foul stuff. 'I don't think I do. There's just so much to read through and as I've just said, the diaries can be tricky for a novice to use.'

'I could help.'

She looked up questioningly at River as he handed her a clean pad and took the one she was using, disposing of it in the toxic waste container he'd brought over.

'I have warlock blood in me from my father. If the books are blood-spelled to open for those with magical powers or magical blood in their veins, they might work for me.'

'Hmm.'

'He's probably one of the only Were who could read them properly,' Bron added.

'Adam could read them too.'

'Could he?' Bron said, frowning. 'That's strange. I wonder why that is?'

'Probably because I'm a magical being,' Adam said from behind her.

She had to stop her lips from twitching in amusement at his tone. 'Maybe there's more to the diaries than we know,' she suggested.

'Or maybe there's more to Adam than we know,' River said. 'He is different from the rest of us.'

'You're not wrong,' Shelley said, unable to stop herself from looking at the hallucination over her shoulder. He smiled at her. Heat flooded through her. She cleared her throat, focusing back on what she was doing.

'Perhaps we should look through the genealogies to find more like River,' Bron suggested, seemingly oblivious to the turmoil inside Shelley. 'He can't be the only Were from matches between Were and witch or warlock. I mean, Bridgette Colliere herself was mated to a Were. And we now know that River and Skye are both descended from Morghanna Cantrae, whose mate must have been at least a half Were.'

'It's an interesting thought,' Shelley said slowly, and then shook her head. 'But we really don't have the time and manpower to spend wading through all the genealogies right now, do we? And you really need River here to help you with the Healings.'

'We could have them brought up here,' River said. 'Then neither of us would have to go back to Melbourne at all and I could help you when I'm not busy helping Bronwyn.'

Shelley wanted to shout 'no'. She needed to leave. She was certain if she could get away from Adam's body it would help her to suppress the hallucinations of him. Being so close to his body, death riding so close to him, couldn't be making the situation easier for her, especially because of this new banshee thing inside her responding to death like it did.

It was no wonder she was slipping into the insanity that rode through her family like the horseman of Death wielding a scythe. She refused to let that scythe swipe at her yet.

Leaving here, not seeing Adam's body, was key to that. She was sure.

She swallowed hard. 'I don't want to take the chance that Morrigan might intercept them. The last thing we want is her getting her hands on them.'

'I guess you're right,' Bron sighed.

Shelley finished irrigating the wound with the saline and wiped the area around the wound clean. She began to ready the new bandages as Bron swabbed the edges of the wound with the antiseptic.

'When will you leave?'

'As soon as possible.' Shelley turned her face so Bron couldn't see anything she didn't want her to see there. Bron was too good at reading her worries and fears. She and Skye knew about her family and their weakness, knew she worried about it. It was imperative now that neither of them knew how urgent that worry had become ever since she'd melded with Skye's power to save her friend.

She cleared her throat and began to apply the new bandages. 'Before Morrigan and Cain come at us again. We need to be stronger, to find out more about your powers, Eloise's and Skye's, and what's happened to Adam. Especially what's happened to Adam. As River said, there is something different about him, but I think that difference is essential to the wellbeing of the pack.'

'I agree,' River said, shifting his shoulders as if reacting to an itch. 'There is something missing, something not quite right in the Packbond ever since this happened to Adam.'

'That could just be Jason's reaction to almost losing him,' Bron said.

'No. It's more. You know it's more.'

She nodded, her gaze meeting Shelley's. 'You're both right. I feel it too. I was just playing devil's advocate—which is usually your job.' She frowned.

Shelley pressed her lips together. 'The lack of his presence is detrimental to all of us. I need to find a way to bring him back to us.' Her fingers brushed over Adam's warm skin to smooth the tape in place, lingering longer than necessary.

'I didn't know you liked touching me so much, Kitten. I'm sure when I'm back to full fitness we can explore this need in you.'

She hissed and pulled her hand away.

'You okay, Shelley?' River was watching her curiously.

'Fine. I just thought I felt a sudden surge of power from the wound.'

'Really?' Bron put her hands over the wound. After a moment she drew them back. 'I can't feel anything. What did it feel like?'

'Static electricity maybe.' More like a big jolt of electricity she felt every time she touched him or heard his warm, rumbling voice. 'I must have imagined it. Or rubbed up against something that built a charge.'

'You can rub up against me again any time, Kitten. I'm happy to help you build a charge.'

She clenched her fingers, willing away the tingle, the sound of Adam's laughter-filled voice ringing in her ears as if he stood right behind her. He wasn't there. He wasn't. She couldn't hear him. She couldn't!

She backed away from the bed, away from the body and the image that now stood next to Bron and River. 'I need to get out of here. I think my brain is a little fried being around all these spirits. There's more here than ever before. The fucking sticky-beaks.'

'Oh, Shells,' Bron said, reaching out to take her hands. 'Is it really that bad?'

Shelley could only nod, her throat clogged with stupid tears. Why the fuck was she feeling like she was going to cry? This had to be part of the insanity—a complete inability to control her emotions. She hated it. Hated it. 'I read some new information about shields before I came up here. I need to read it again before I feel confident to implement it. If I can do this, it will help. I'm sure.'

'Then go. Get your shields where you need them to be.'

'Gareth is up giving Jason a report from Iain,' River said. 'He could drive you back down today if you want.'

'Good idea,' Adam said.

She pointedly didn't look at him. 'I can drive myself.'

'Like hell you will! I may not be able to be your Shadow at the moment, but that doesn't mean you can go unprotected. Morrigan and Cain are still out there.'

Fuck, fuck, fuck, she wanted to retort to his heavy-handed pronouncement. It was just like him to go all macho-Shadow bullshit on her about something like this. Her mind knew that. It was why it imagined those words coming out of his imaginary mouth.

'I don't think Jason will like that.' Bron paused and then looked to her left where Adam stood.

'What are you doing?' Shelley asked her.

'Seeing if there's something on my shoulder. You keep looking slightly past me.'

'I'm not. I'm just tired. My eyes are wandering.'

'All the more reason you shouldn't drive yourself,' Adam said

'Then I'll call Gareth. You're too tired to drive back to Melbourne.' River pulled out his phone. 'Besides, Bron is right. Jason won't allow you to go by yourself anyway. Not with Morrigan and Cain out there. Probably not even if they weren't.'

'See!' Adam said, pointing at River. 'I'm not the only one saying it. Listen to him if you won't listen to me.'

'God! I hate how overprotective you all are. I was driving myself around just fine before you Were came into my life.'

'But we didn't have an insane out-for-revenge witch hunting us then. Nor her equally insane student,' Bron said reasonably.

'All courtesy of the Were.'

Bron gasped. 'You don't really think that, do you?'

Shit! She was really slipping. She ran her hand through her hair, dislodging her ponytail. Raking her fingers hard against her skull, she pulled the band out. 'No. I know it's not their fault. Any more than it's Skye's fault I'm a banshee.'

'You were always a banshee, Shelley. No power can turn you into what you're not.'

'I know. It's just the influx of power allowed it to surge to the fore when it might have always stayed dormant.' Fuck. She was saying too much. She jerked her hair back into the ponytail, pulling it tight so it almost hurt. She needed that little bit of pain to keep her grounded right now. 'I'm sorry.' She glanced at River. 'You're both as much a victim of all this as I am.'

'You're not a victim, Kitten.'

'You're not a victim, Shells. And neither are we.' Bron was suddenly there in front of her, thankfully blocking out hallucination-Adam. He looked so distraught. So pained for her.

She couldn't bare it.

Shelley forced herself to look directly into Bron's eyes, not flinch away at the worry there. 'Wrong choice of words. I just meant that none of us could help what's happened. You and Skye have had just as many issues with these new powers as I have. Worse maybe. I need to stop being a baby about it.' She rubbed her eyes.

'You need to get more sleep.'

Shelley laughed. 'I think that is most definitely the pot calling the kettle black, my friend. If the bags under your eyes got any bigger, you'd be able to keep the kitchen sink in them as well as everything else.'

'Good one!' Hallucination-Adam laughed.

'It's difficult to sleep with so much going on,' Bron said.

'My point exactly. And with Morrigan and Cain out there plotting who knows what next, it's difficult to go to sleep.' She gritted her teeth together. 'If I could get my hands on them ...'

'You and everyone else,' Adam said.

She ignored the comment. 'If anyone is to blame, it's Morrigan and Cain. I need to keep focused on that. Working to make sure they don't get to do whatever it is they plan.'

'Damn right,' Adam said.

Hell, she wished she could block out his voice like she'd blocked out her ability to see him right now, but it wasn't that simple.

'Sounds like a good plan,' River said.

'So does going home.' Shelley firmed her face against the wistfulness that thought evoked. She didn't like feeling wistful. It made her think of all those "what ifs" she studiously avoided. There was no room for "what if" in her life. There never had been. 'I need to surround myself with something normal for a little while. Go back to work. They've been calling me, offering any shift I want if only I come back.'

'That's great.' Bron put her arm around Shelley to give her a little squeezy hug, the kind she'd only ever allowed Bron and Skye to give her. 'Go back to work and do the research you enjoy. If that's what you need, that's what you should do.'

Shelley nodded and headed towards the door. As she got there, she swung back, being very careful to look nowhere but at Bron and River, their arms around each other, comforting, supportive. A united front. A matching pair. She was happy for her friend. For both her friends. At least they had found the one person on this earth who would love them and look after them and see to their wants and needs. It was enough.

It had to be enough.

'What is it?' Bron asked.

'Just make sure you look after Adam's body while I'm gone, okay.'

'Of course.'

'And yourself. And call me if you need me back.' Her gaze darted to just behind them. Adam stood there, near his body, worry, pain and something else in his eyes. Something that hurt too much to try to figure out. She looked away. 'I'll come back if you need me.'

'We know.'

She turned and left.

She was in the lift on her way to the surface before she realised that hallucination-Adam hadn't followed her. Huh. She'd been right. It was being around his body, seeing him so quiet and still, that had made her mind conjure him up. It was part of the psychology of grief.

People often felt their loved ones nearby when visiting them in the hospital. She'd seen it time and time again. That's what this was. Not that Adam was a loved one. But she did feel something for him. She couldn't push away that fact, no matter how much it aggravated her.

The doors dinged and opened to show Gareth waiting for her.

'That sneaky bastard. River called you the moment I left the room, didn't he?'

He smiled broadly as she frowned at him. 'Yep. He told me to take you back to Melbourne and to ignore your scowls and any temper tantrums you might throw about overprotective Were.'

'Did he just?' Shelley's eyes narrowed as she stalked out of the lift.

Gareth's smile broadened as he fell into step beside her. 'Yes. And then Bron got on the line and told me to tell you that if you tried to ignore my offer of a lift back to Melbourne, that I was to call her and she would come up and use her Healer powers to make you unconscious so you wouldn't be able to drive yourself back.'

'Did she?' She shook her head. She should feel angry at her sneaky friend and her equally sneaky mate, but right now she just didn't have the energy. Leaving that room after being there for so long, leaving Adam's body, the hallucination of him, was harder than she realised it would be. It almost felt like she was tearing herself in two.

Was that insane?

No. Now she was being ridiculous. Tiredness. That's all it was.

The sooner she got back to Melbourne and filled her time with things other than tending to Adam's unconscious body, the better. 'Lead on, MacDuff.'

Gareth faltered, a cloud of sadness crossing his expression before he nodded and led the way out of the barn to the SUV parked just outside. For a moment, she wondered why he looked so sad, then she remembered.

Lead on MacDuff. That was Adam's saying. Tears pricked her eyes and she blinked them rapidly away.

She really needed to get away from here. The sooner the better.

5

The room was deathly quiet, the only sound the constant wind that seemed to whistle around him at all times. It had got worse since Shelley had left. Everything was worse without her around.

He wanted to talk to her. It didn't matter that she'd been studiously ignoring him pretty much since the night he'd ended up like this. He was used to Shelley ignoring him. She'd done that on and off ever since they'd met at the snow last year. It was kind of their thing. Besides, even when she ignored him, he knew she could hear him. Being heard. He never realised how important that was. What a difference it made. It made him feel something. Like he was still part of things.

Since she'd left, the depth of his loneliness had been almost crippling. It was a new and unwanted sensation. He'd often felt different in his life, like he was apart, but never lonely.

He wanted Shelley to come back.

Fuck, you're pathetic! He pushed away from the wall where he'd been staring glumly at the room. *And seriously selfish.* Shelley had needed to go back to Melbourne. Apart from having work there and the diaries to go over, she needed to get away from this room. More than anyone else, the memories of what had happened, the level of grief that hung over the room like a shroud, affected her. It was a withheld pain inside, like a knife slashing in his chest every moment she was here.

He'd done what he could to cheer her up, but every time he'd almost surprised a laugh out of her, she'd shut down further. He was glad she was gone. Sort of. When he wasn't being a selfish prick.

He had to look on the bright side.

What bright side? the depressive voice in his head mumbled.

The up side of him tried to rally. *Now she's gone, I can focus on what the fuck is going on with me.* He clapped his hands together. *Lead on MacDuff. Let's get shit done.*

He glanced at his body lying on the bed in the corner.

The wound in his chest was still blackened and horrifying to look at. His chest rose and fell without the help of the machines arrayed nearby. Thank the Moon. Seeing himself with that tube shoved down his throat had made him want to gag. Thankfully Bron had decided he didn't need it and had taken it out after a few days.

A light shone on the bed from above. His usually golden skin was so pale, it looked like he was glowing in the light—apart from the blackened ring in his chest that Bron hadn't been able to heal, no matter how much Healer energy she'd shot into him. Staring at the light glowing off him and the hole in his chest, he couldn't help but snort a laugh.

'Fuck, I'm holy.' He looked around, waiting for someone to groan and tell him how awful the pun was, and then he'd torture them by explaining why it was so brilliant. But Bron was the only other living person there—and she'd fallen asleep in her chair.

Aside from her, there were only the spirits who constantly hung around his and Cordy's bodies. They were next to useless insofar as an audience went. Despite being able to see them, he couldn't hear them, and unless they were seriously having him on, they couldn't hear him either. Although he hadn't really tried to talk to them when Shelley was here. That was about to change.

'Right. Here goes nothing.' He walked over to the closest group.

They turned to look at him as he drew near. One of them said something, but all he heard was the wind in his ears. 'What was that?' She said it again and he tried reading the ghost woman's lips. He only caught every other word and none of it made sense. 'Can you say that again? I seem to be in a wind tunnel. Is that the same for you?' She said something else—he really wasn't good at the lipreading thing, as it seemed she'd called him a nobbin tup thumper and followed it up by saying that erstwhile ferrets were all around and something else he really didn't catch at all. He tapped his ear and shook his head. She gestured with her hands. Some kind of sign language? If it was, he had no idea what. He knew a bit of Auslan but this had nothing in common with that. When he shook his head again, she rolled her eyes and turned to a ghost at her side and said something to him. They laughed.

Huh. At least that answered one of his questions—they could hear each other. So why couldn't he hear them or vice versa?

He tried talking to a few more spirits but with no success. Then he noticed one of them looking at him. She was standing beside where Bron was asleep—he'd noticed her around Bron a lot. He'd thought she'd looked familiar that first night and suddenly realised why. This had to be Adeline. Bron's dead grandmother. There was a definite familial resemblance, especially around the eyes.

He approached her. 'You're Adeline.' He pointed at Bron. 'Bron's gran.'

She nodded and said something back, some of which he caught. 'No, I can't hear you properly.' He gestured around his head. 'Some kind of wind.'

She nodded again, as if she understood. He sighed in relief. It was nice to be understood.

He turned and gestured back at his body. 'Do you know why I'm here, like this? Why I'm different from you?' He moved his hand between himself and her. It took some time, but he eventually managed to understand most of her answer—a combination of her talking slowly and making hand gestures.

Nothing she said was good.

She had no idea what he was, why he couldn't hear her, or why his wound wouldn't heal. He thought maybe she was going to ask some of the other spirits she knew but wasn't sure that's what all the hand waving in a circle had actually meant. He didn't get a chance to clarify though because she abruptly turned and disappeared.

She didn't come back for days.

And days.

And days.

He spent those days trying not to sink into the depression he'd been in when Shelley left. It was difficult. He couldn't talk to anyone. Couldn't make himself heard. Could barely make the other spirits listen to him—even though they seemed so very interested in his body and what Bron was doing to it to keep him alive. He just had to concentrate on the fact he'd managed to communicate with someone and they were trying to help him.

When Adeline finally came back, he almost wept with relief. That was until she told him she had no answers but that she'd keep asking around. It might just take time.

He had to be happy with that because, quite frankly, he didn't have any other choice. But it was aggravating not to be doing something more. Especially for someone who was known for his frenetic energy. And the whole thing was made worse by the fact his Pack-bond still seemed to be operating.

The pack's worry was like fingernails raking down his spine. He usually helped them through stressful situations by making others laugh or see the light side of things, but given they couldn't hear his amazingly funny quips, that was no use.

He tried not to think too much about the fact that he was as useful as tits on a bull now, but as days slipped into weeks, he couldn't help focusing entirely on that fact. Or the fact he needed Shelley to come back. It was like a pulse inside him, getting stronger every day. He needed to talk to her. Needed her to hear him. Needed someone else to focus on other than himself.

And wasn't that just the most pathetic and arseholish thing of all! The fact he wanted her to come back to a place that caused her so much pain just so he could feel better was a sure sign that something in him was horribly wrong.

Fuck. He had to find a way to get back into his body or he'd go stark raving nuts. But how? Bron had tried everything she knew. So where did that leave him?

Maybe it wasn't something that someone could do from the outside. Maybe it required the direct approach. That usually worked for him.

He should just go and try to force his way back into his body.

He stilled as the simplicity of the idea took hold. Why hadn't he thought of it before? Kicking himself mentally, he walked over to the bed and looked down at his body.

How best to do this? Probably if he hovered over the body and then sank straight down into it—except for the fact that he had no idea how to do the hovering part. So far, the most ghostlike thing he'd done was walk through a wall, but he'd done that with his feet touching the floor. Maybe if he just moved into the bed and into the middle of his body, that might do the trick.

He tried it. Nothing happened. Except for the fact that he felt really stupid standing in the middle of his body. He tried to crouch down, to fit himself to the body. Nothing. No sucking or popping sounds or sensations. He was still completely separate.

He walked out of his body and thought about it again. Maybe something smaller. Maybe if he held his own hand. People often said they experienced feelings of intense connection just through the joining of hands with others. They always did it in séances, right?

He reached out, touched his hand—and sank straight through it. Tried again. The same. Bugger.

Bron woke up then, rubbed her eyes and put her hand over his wound. A Healing golden glow lit under her hand tugging on his Packbond like it did whenever she'd used her powers like this when he'd been ... not this.

Maybe that was it. Maybe he should use the bond to his pack as a way back into his body. It was as good an idea as any of the others he'd had.

The warmth of the Healing was like a faint echoing buzz in his chest. He closed his eyes, tried to anchor to the strength of it, to her bond with the pack, to travel back through it to himself. Something happened, like sliding through a warm, golden shower of water—a waterfall—but then he hit a wall and was thrown back across the room.

Head reeling, he staggered to his feet. What the hell? That shouldn't have happened; it was as if his body had rejected him!

He returned to Bron's side and tried again.

Wham—he was smacked back, harder this time, so hard pain tingled in his chest. He looked across the room and saw Bron rubbing her fingers as if she too had been hurt.

'Are you okay, Bron?' He raced back to her side, touched her shoulder without thinking about it.

She jerked and stood up, knocking the chair back. 'What the?' She looked around, her gaze grazing over him.

'Did you feel me, Bron? Did you feel that?'

She looked blankly around then breathed out slowly. 'I think I need a break,' she said, righting the chair. 'I'll be back later. Don't go anywhere.' She kissed his body's cheek and left.

'Damn it!' What the fuck was going on? None of it made any sense. If he wasn't a ghost and he wasn't a Shade, then what the fuck was he? He needed Shelley here to talk it over with. She'd go straight for the books and find something. He knew she'd find something. But she wasn't here and the part of him that wasn't a selfish prick knew she couldn't come back. Not yet. He had to figure this out himself.

Okay. First things first. Why could he still feel his wolf and the Packbond if he was separated from his body like a Shade? The bond was weaker than it had been before he'd been hit by warlock lightning, but it was still there, a small tendril of connection to his body, his wolf, his pack—although apparently not enough to allow him to find a way back in, to reconnect. Maybe he needed to strengthen it before he could do anything else.

He stood beside his body and looked deep inside, to that place in his mind and heart and soul that held the bonds to wolf, to self, to pack. His head started to ache. There was a flickering sensation that shot up and down his body. He lifted his hand. It didn't seem as solid as it had before and was definitely flickering.

Was this what had happened when he'd focused his energy into helping Iain keep Eloise alive? Shelley had yelled at him for it. Told him whatever he was doing he was giving too much of himself. Making himself fade. But he couldn't stop. Not until he'd strengthened the thread connecting him in an essential way to life.

The flickering began to get faster. A burning pain shot through him. But he wouldn't stop. Wouldn't stop until … There.

In his body, the bond strengthened. It still wasn't what it had been —an earthly twine, laced with threads of silver and gold that glowed with health and the power of his wolf and pack—but it was better.

Thank the Moon because he didn't think he could give it any more right now. He leaned against the bed, head hanging down between his shoulders, breath a pant in his throat, every part of him aching. 'Shit, that was exhausting.'

As the pain faded, his mind cleared a little and he opened his eyes.

Adeline stood there yelling at him.

He couldn't hear her, but he could make out exactly what she was saying.

Stupid.

Stubborn.

Idiotic.

Male.

Was she channelling Shelley? Sure sounded like it.

He grinned at her and waved his hands in a gesture he hoped she would take as meaning he was sorry for worrying her and that he wouldn't do it again.

She calmed down but was still giving him the stink-eye. She mouthed something at him that he took to be, 'Why would you do such an idiotic thing?'

'I thought maybe it would help me to reconnect with my body.'

She frowned and shook her head. She didn't understand, and

right now he couldn't be fagged trying to explain. Eventually, when no further explanation was coming, she shook her finger at him and mouthed something about him not doing it again before she wandered off.

He smiled after her, but even that felt like too much effort. He slumped to the floor and sat there for what could have been an hour or a day, semi-dozing, aware of others moving in and out of the room. Bron came back in with River and did another Healing.

Nothing changed. The wound remained the same. She got up and staggered away, River at her side, urging her to lie down on the bed on the other side of the room to rest.

Adam watched them for a while and then pushed to his feet, feeling more himself again. Now he'd strengthened his bond with his body and his wolf, he had to try to reconnect again. That wasn't going against his promise to Adeline. It was a different thing entirely. In fact, it should give him energy.

He closed his eyes, found the silver-gold bond again, but this time, rather than thinking about strengthening it, he thought about blending with it, following it along its thread to his body and sinking in, enveloped by flesh and blood and sinew and bone. Whole.

The bond was strong, throbbing with the power of his unconscious wolf and body and the strength of the pack. He let the sensation filter through him, wrapping it around himself, sinking down, down.

He was thrown back, smacking against the far wall so hard that dust fell from the ceiling.

What the fuck?

He slammed his hand on the ground and pushed to his feet, anger a hot boil in his chest. This was bullshit! His body couldn't deny him access. How could it push him away like that? Maybe he had to try harder.

He rushed back to his body, reached into it where he could see the thread of the bond in his mind and grabbed it. It pulsed in his hand, glowing brighter for a moment. He smiled. Yes. He was going to be able to bring himself back to his body and his wolf.

The link twisted, pulling tight, hurting, the silver-gold threaded with black. No, that wasn't right. There was something wrong, something terribly wrong. It was burning—it shouldn't be burning. Then it tightened, cutting into his ghostly skin.

What the holy fuck? The link shouldn't hurt him. It was supposed to welcome him. Holy crap. It felt like it was going to cut his hand in half.

Wisps of something like silver-tinged smoke began to rise from the place where the bond was wrapped around his hand. But it wasn't blood even though it had the faintest tang of copper. Ghostly blood?

No. Worse. Ghostly essence.

Weakness wavered over him as the bond coiled tighter and more of the smoky substance rose from the point of contact and then was sucked into the thread of bond where it glowed for a moment and then disappeared. The bond throbbed, thickening, gleaming sickly.

Then he realised what he should have realised before. He shouldn't be able to touch the bond with any physical part of him. This wasn't the bond hurting him. It was something else entirely. Something with a dark tinge to it. Something sick that wasn't part of him at all. Something that came from the wound in his chest.

He'd been so angry before at his failure, he hadn't noticed that what he'd grabbed wasn't quite like what he saw in his mind. Rather than succouring him as the bond was supposed to do, it was draining him.

Shit. He began to pull at it, trying to loosen it, but the more he fought, the more it tightened.

His head began to spin as more essence leaked out of him. Was he actually, truly going to die? If this spirit self faded away, then his body would die. The one could not exist without the other—or so Eloise had said. He wasn't sure what he was, but that at least was something he did know. He could feel it.

This thing from the wound was going to kill him. He had to stop it, but how? He was getting weaker with every minute and he couldn't get free.

He couldn't go out this way. This wasn't how it was meant to go for him. With a whimper, rather than a bang. No. No.

There was a roar in his mind, a howl that shook through him, that was a part of him but was outside him as well.

His wolf. It had woken up.

It surged up from its dormant state, lunging forth to protect, savage and strong. The rainbow of change glowed over his body. There was a shriek and the cutting burning sensation in his hand ceased as the thing from his wound let go.

He staggered back, head spinning, eyes watering.

In front of him, his body began to change into the wolf. Then it snapped back to human. And back to wolf. Over and over. The change couldn't form properly. The wound in his chest was stopping the natural process. It was as if the warlock lightning had damaged something at a cellular level. Bits of him began to change, moving from wolf to human and back again, over and over. It was like what happened when one of their kind was hit by a powerful surge of electricity—it made their system go haywire and they couldn't control any part of the change. It was painful and horrifying—and could kill if not stopped.

His body began to vibrate violently on the bed, his face—human then wolf—contorted in a rictus of pain.

Fucking hell in a handbasket. This day was just going from bad to worse.

The thing that had tricked him into thinking it was the thread of bond flipped around, retreating back into the wound, which pulsed, thick black gunk seeping out and over his chest and onto the bed. The linen began to smoke.

The wolf was howling in a way that sounded like a scream as Adam's body heaved and surged, slamming against the bed, knocking against the wall, slamming him up against the bed edges. The cannula in his arm was ripped out. Blood sprayed across the white sheets and up the wall.

There was a shout behind him and someone ran through him—

Bron and River. River tried to hold him down, but needed more arms and legs, especially because the changes that were happening all over Adam's body were so unpredictable and violent.

The door smashed open and Jason ran in. 'What the fuck!'

'Jason—hold his body still. River—take care of his legs. Try and hold him as still as possible. I need to give him this.' Bron gestured to a large needle in her hand.

Jason leaned over him, trying to grab hold of limbs that were changing faster one heartbeat to the next. 'I can't grasp him. There's nowhere that's not flipping in and out of the change and I'm afraid I'll hurt him.'

'I don't think he's going to notice if you do.'

'I wouldn't bet on that,' Adam said. 'But let's just say, I give you permission.'

Of course, none of them heard him. Even if they could, they'd have difficulty hearing over the sound of his wolf's howls. He winced. It was in so much pain. He wished he could do something, but it wasn't taking any notice of him at all. Maybe he would take notice of the Alpha. 'Try to get through to my wolf, Jason.'

'Try to use the Alpha-link, Jason.'

'Bron—I love your beautiful mind,' Adam said.

Jason closed his eyes, face creased with concentration. Beads of sweat shone on his brow and ran down his temples. He shook his head. 'He isn't listening. Something has stressed him.'

'Well, try again, because if he doesn't stop this, he'll die. Adam's body can't take much more.'

Jason leaned over Adam's body and grabbed his face to keep it still and leaned his forehead against his. 'Wolf. Adam. Listen to me. Stop fighting. You're hurting yourself.' Nothing. The howling got worse. He held on tighter. 'Please. We love you. Don't leave us.' The violent heaving of his body seemed to lessen a little.

'You're getting through,' Adam said at the same time as Bron. 'Keep going.'

'I know this whole thing upsets you. I can feel your hurt, your anguish. I know you can't feel the human side of yourself and it's making you panic. But he's still there somewhere. Just unconscious because of the wound. We're trying to fix that, but we need your help.'

'Keep going. He's listening.'

'You have to stop trying to take over the body. It's not helping. It's harming Adam.'

The wolf stopped howling, and Adam could feel it settle, but for some reason his body kept changing.

Holy fucking dog's balls.

'The wolf is calm,' River said. 'Why hasn't he stopped changing?'

'There's magic fuelling the change,' she said on a gasp. 'I can feel it.'

'Where's it coming from?'

She narrowed her eyes in that way she did when she checked someone's aura. 'The warlock lightning. The power of it is still there and it's somehow funnelling magic into the change. But not like normal magic would because it's dark and sick and twisted. I have to stop it. Think. Think.' She knuckled her hands against her temple while Adam's body continued to change over and over on the bed. 'I know!' she cried, head snapping up, and then she raced over to a cabinet on the other side of the room, tearing open the draws and doors, pulling out boxes and searching madly through them.

There was a clang and smash of glass hitting the floor as she pushed things aside, not careful of what she was doing, as she mumbled, 'Where is it? Where the hell is it?' She glanced over at Cordy's still form. 'You told me you kept one here. It has to be here.'

Adam wanted to help, but the more his body changed violently, the more the room span. His knees trembled and there was a squeezing in his chest. He couldn't breathe. Which was kind of stupid, given he was a spirit-thing and so didn't really need to breathe. At least, he didn't think he did.

He sank to the floor, gasping, helpless.

Obviously wrong about the breathing thing.

'Come on. Come on,' Bron said, stepping through him. 'The cuff has to be here. Cordy is always so organised and ready for everything. It's here. I know it's here.'

'I saw that the other day.' River raced over to a set of drawers and pulled out the top one, grabbing something out of it. 'Bron, here!'

Her eyes lit on what he had in his hand. 'Thank the Moon!' she breathed, snatched it out of his hand, and snapped it onto Adam's body's wrist.

His body flexed, the rainbow glow of change chasing over him and then his body fell back onto the bed. Completely human.

'Thank you Bron,' Adam said on a deep breath in. 'I and my wolf thank you.' His wolf! His head snapped up, gaze going to his body. Something was wrong. Something was terribly wrong. He couldn't feel his wolf now at all. Couldn't sense his body. It was as if they'd been torn from him. He couldn't even find the bond inside him. It was gone. Shit. Shit.

'What did you do?' Jason asked, panting.

'The magic in the wound, the thing that's stopping me from healing Adam, was doing something to the bond. His wolf was fighting against it, but it somehow managed to poison the change with its dark magic. I thought if I could cut off the source of that magic, the change might stop. The magical suppression cuff was the most effective way to do that.'

'Will that help the wound heal now?'

'No. It's not destroying the dark magic, just holding it at bay. Besides, while that's on there, I can't heal him at all.' She chewed at her lip. 'I don't even know how long the cuff will hold it at bay. The magic is so insidious. So powerful.'

Her words were becoming lost in the panic howling inside him. He began to shake. He tried to take deep breaths, to calm himself, to pull on the reserve of strength that had always been inside him to overcome his fear. But it wasn't there, because that strength had always been tied into the bond with his wolf, and it was gone.

First Shelley and now his wolf.

He was alone. Truly alone.

Panic reared in his chest, an ugly, clawing beast. The wind howled and screamed around him. Louder than ever. Tearing at him. Calling to him.

What the hell?

It was calling to him. His name. He distinctly heard his name in the sound. The panic lessened at the realisation, enough to allow him to ask, 'Who are you?'

The wind howled louder, the call of his name nothing but an echo inside.

'Where are you?'

Nothing. And then, 'Adam! Come find me.'

He knew that voice. It was the voice of the ghost who had talked to him that first day. He spun, trying to find the source of that voice, but there was nothing. Just the noise of howling wind all around him and his brother standing over his body, River bringing back bandages and something else in a kidney dish, and Bron returning from the sink with a wet cloth in her hand.

'Where are you? Where have you gone?'

His voice echoed in the vast cavern of noise, but apart from the wind, it was the only sound that came back to him.

'Where are you? I need your help. I've got no idea what's happening to me. What's going on. I need some answers. Come back. You were right. I should have gone with you. I need your help.' He spun around, desperation a claw in his throat. 'Please. Don't leave me here by myself.'

The wind howled louder. His heartbeat became a loud thump-thump-thump in his ears, so loud he could barely even hear the wind anymore. The burn in his chest was unbearable. He realised he'd stopped breathing. He gasped. Gasped again. It didn't seem to help. He couldn't get any breath. No breath.

He scrabbled at his chest, his throat, gasping like a fish. The room about him began to spin.

His heart thumped hard. Slower. Slower. Stopped.

He looked over at his body, his brother, Bron, River, reached out to them. They didn't see him. Would never see him.

This was it. They'd always been told the Were couldn't live without their wolves. He'd been torn from his. So this was it.

He was dead.

The room spun and black rose up around him.

6

All around him was horrifying black nothingness. Was this what being dead was like? Aware and surrounded by nothing?

Ah shit! He'd gone to hell. This was hell. At least, it was hell to him. Some people might find peace in being surrounded by nothing, with no sound, no light, no colour— eternal rest.

It was his worst nightmare. He loved sound. Loved colour and light and the bustle of being around people. He craved their presence as much as he craved touch. And laughter. Smiles. How could he bear an eon of this? What had he done to deserve being sent here?

Light flooded over him, so bright it pierced his light-starved eyes, a shard of pain in his head. He slammed his lids shut, but it wasn't enough. The light flared red behind his closed lids. Moaning, he rolled into a ball, his arms wrapped around his head, trying to shield his eyes from the painful glare of light.

'Adam. Adam. You're okay. Open your eyes.'

'Too bright. Too bright,' he moaned.

'Sorry.' The light dimmed a little. 'Is that better? I haven't had to do this for a very long time.'

'Do what?'

'Talk to one like you in this place.'

'What place? Who are you?' This voice wasn't the voice he'd heard earlier. Richer. Softer. And yet somehow piercing him through with its bell-like quality.

'I will explain everything once you lower your hands and look at me.'

Slowly, he lowered his hands. Opened his eyes. Shadows danced on his retinas, making it impossible to see. He closed his eyes again, lifted his hands and gingerly massaged them. As he did so, he became aware that he was lying on something soft. And gritty. It was cold. He shivered. 'Where am I?'

'Can you not hear?'

Yes, he could; a deep, steady roar that rose and ended with a thump and rush.

Waves.

Scents began to follow the sound—briny scents mixed with the tartness of electricity and fresh earthiness of growing things.

A beach. With a storm brewing in the distance.

'Very good. Now open your eyes and see.'

Cautious, he dropped his hands away. The light wasn't too bad now. He opened one eye a fraction, opened it further. The foam of waves dumping on the hard-packed sand filled his vision. He opened his other eye. There was grass in the foreground—the kind of tough, thick grass found on sand dunes—and now he had both eyes open, he could see he was a good five metres from the waves landing on the beach.

He still couldn't see who was talking to him.

He rolled over. His muscles spasmed. 'Fuck.' He stopped moving, eyes squeezing closed as he tried to deal with the pain. Why did he hurt so badly?

'Because I pulled you from the aether and you weren't ready for it. Here, this might help.'

There was a slight tinkling sound. A strange sensation, like warm water, rushed through his skin, along his muscles. The hair on the back of his neck stood up. Magic.

'Thanks,' he managed to pant as the spasms faded. He relaxed and flopped onto his back, breathing deeply. The tingles of pain drained away. 'Why did you have to pull me from the aether?'

'It was the only way I could speak to you.'

'And who are you to pull me away from my body? My wolf? My pack?' He opened his eyes.

A woman stood over him, face in shadow.

'Oh, I didn't do that. That was someone else entirely. I just moved your spirit form from where it was, through the aether and to this place.'

'But why did you do that?'

She gestured impatiently. 'I already said. I needed to speak with you.'

Okay. This was going around in circles. Puffing out a breath, he prepared for pain and sat up. His muscles groaned a little, but nothing more than if he'd gone for a good run. He looked up at the woman. He still couldn't get a good look at her face, but he could make out her form. She was tall and curvy and dressed in what could only be described as battle armour, and her long golden hair—it was sparking bright in the dim sunlight—hung in a plait over her shoulder. 'Who are you?'

'I am the Goddess.'

He laughed, but the sound choked in his throat as he realised she wasn't joking. 'Which one?'

'I have many names and many aspects, but the name you best know me by is Arianrhod.'

'The Goddess who spoke to Eloise.'

'The very one.'

'Huh.' What was she doing speaking to him? He wasn't a witch or warlock. He had no magic. He also wasn't female. So why was the goddess of fertility and rebirth and the cosmic weaving of time and fate, coming to him now? If any Goddess should come to him, wouldn't it be Cerridwen, Goddess of the moon, magic and agriculture? Were worshipped the moon for everything it gave them, so why wasn't she here instead?

'Cerridwen is my sister. She has been punished enough for helping me in the past. I cannot call on her further.' There was pain in that statement. He was about to ask why when he realised something else.

'You're reading my mind?'

'Of course. I am a Goddess.'

Oh, yeah, of course. Why hadn't he thought of that?

'Because you're not a Goddess.'

The simple statement made him laugh. And once started, he couldn't seem to stop.

'You're hysterical,' she said after a few minutes, head tipped to the side like a curious cat.

Her comment made him laugh even harder until he was gasping for breath.

'Stop.'

'Would ... if ... I ... could,' he said between bouts of laughter. 'Stop ... me.'

'I cannot. I already used too much power to bring you here and to help you with the pain of the transition. Any more and the others will know what I've done.' She sighed as he tried to ask her about what she'd just said, but could only gasp for air, the laughter dying as the need to breathe became imperative.

'Are you able to talk yet?' He shook his head. 'Well, think to me. I will hear it.'

'Tip who off?'

'The other Gods who do not want me to interfere in the things that should be below me.'

'Why won't they let you interfere? You're a Goddess. Can't you do what you want?'

'There are rules that even I must follow.'

'Have you broken the rules by bringing me here?'

'Not quite. Bringing you here is skating along the edge of our laws.'

'Then why do it?'

'Because I cannot do nothing. It is our fault, what has happened, what will happen. I must do something to fight it.'

'The Darkness?' he said out loud, the hysteria gone now in the wake of his curiosity about what he was learning.

She nodded.

'Then why have you brought me here? How on earth can I help?'

'What makes you think you can help?'

He looked up at her. 'You brought me here. I assume that wasn't just for shits and giggles.'

She came down on her haunches in front of him and he could see her face properly for the first time. She was frowning at him, but that didn't belie her loveliness. Or the fact she looked distinctly familiar, with eyes that were the same brilliant violet blue as ... 'You look like Shelley.'

'She is a distant relation.'

'Huh.' He should have known she was related to a Goddess. Perhaps he should start calling her that rather than Kitten. He smiled. She'd hate that. Oh yeah, the next time he saw her, he was definitely calling her Goddess.

'Your mind is very strange.'

He barked out a laugh. 'You're not the first to say that to me.'

She frowned. 'You say that as if it's a bad thing when it is the very thing that will help us the most. In fact, it is your Trickster nature that will be ...' A pained expression crossed her face and her lips pulled tight. For a moment, she looked as if she was fighting something, her hands curling into fists, fingers red, knuckles white. Then with a gasp, she stood and spun away from him.

'Arianrhod?' Adam forced himself to stand, even though his muscles were still weak and trembling. He took a stumbling step towards her.

She swung back, hand outstretched. 'No. You mustn't touch me. If you do, you will become a permanent resident of this place.'

He looked around. 'What is this place?'

'A place of the Nexus' making.'

'Eloise? She made this?'

'Yes. When we spoke last year, this is what she created as a place that enabled her to speak with me.'

He stared out at the turbulent ocean, the storm, dark and threatening, on the horizon. 'Holy crap.' He turned to face the Goddess again. 'What the hell are you doing calling me here and not her? She's the one with the power. I'm nothing.'

Her frown was back. 'You cannot truly think that of yourself.'

Of course he did. What else was he to think?

'You are the Trickster. You are the one who is going to ...' Her mouth snapped shut again, jaw white, lips pulled back in a rictus of pain.

Adam reached for her. She was in pain. Distraught. Angry. Frustrated. Desperate. He wanted to do something to stop the roiling emotions inside her. To make her feel better. But she stepped back, hands raised, warding him off, and he remembered what she'd said. 'What can I do?'

She shook her head and turned away, shoulders stiff, clenched fists shaking at her sides. Long minutes passed before her shoulders and hands finally relaxed and she looked up at the sky and yelled, 'Damn you and your rules!'

Adam looked up at the dark, stormy sky. 'Damn who?'

She spun to face him again. 'One of those things I am forbidden to tell you.'

For some reason, her words really pissed him off. 'So, if you can't tell me anything, why the hell did you cause me so much pain? Why'd you make me think I was dead? Why the fuck did you bring me here?'

'Because you would have been dead if I had not!' Her shouted words flew over the waves. Above, lightning flashed across the sky and thunder rumbled from horizon to horizon, a rolling echo of her anger. He cringed under the onslaught, hands over his ears, as the sound grew louder. It flew overhead and then flapped away, dissipating in the distance.

He stayed crouched on the sand, hands covering his ears. Slowly, he looked up at her.

She stood there, hand over her mouth, eyes full of sadness and apologies. They stared at each other. The only sound that of the distant storm and the thump of his heart in his chest.

Finally, he dropped his hands from his ears and cocked his brow at her. 'That was some temper tantrum.'

She made a short, growling sound. 'Do you know how maddening you are?'

'Of course.' He shrugged a shoulder. 'It's my calling.'

A bubble of laughter burst out of her. 'I can see why Michelline finds you so irresistible.'

'For a Goddess, you sure can get things wrong.'

'I am the Goddess of fertility. I think perhaps I know what I'm talking about.'

'I am far from irresistible to Shelley.'

'That is your stubborn human brain talking. If you look into your Trickster heart, it will tell you the truth.'

He closed his eyes against the pain of her words. 'I don't have a Trickster heart anymore.'

'What are you talking about?'

He opened his eyes, met her gaze unflinchingly. 'How can you know so much and not know this?'

'Know what?'

'I am separated from my wolf. It's gone. I can't access it while the dark magic from the warlock lightning is still in my body.'

'Your wolf isn't what made you the Trickster, Adam.'

'Yes, it is. Without it, I'm nothing special.'

'You are as bad as Eloise was for not seeing what is right in front of you.'

'You don't know what you're talking about.' He spun away, staring out at the oncoming storm.

She was suddenly there in front of him, blocking his view of the bilious green-black clouds. 'I do know what I am talking about. I know only too well about the truths we all hide inside ourselves, holding them safe. Even if that means we keep them from ourselves.'

'Oh yeah? And what is your great truth?'

'That I am one side of the coin. This is your truth as well. You are not a Trickster because your wolf is a Trickster, but because both of you are. What you had with your wolf, you still have. It is what binds you to him—and your body—despite the Darkness' influence.'

Adam stared at her. 'No. You're wrong.'

'About many things, yes, but not this. You are right—you cannot return to your body or use the bond while the dark magic of the warlock lightning poisons your flesh. But none of that will stop you from doing what you were brought here to do.'

'And what is that?'

'As the Trickster, you ...' Her mouth locked again, eyes going large in her face. She trembled, looking like she was fighting it. Tears welled in her eyes and spilled down her cheeks, glistening crystal clear as diamonds as they fell from her chin, towards the sand. Her hands spasming at her sides. Blood dripped from the corner of her mouth.

'Don't. Don't tell me,' Adam said, holding out his hand. 'Not if it causes you pain.'

She closed her eyes, spun from him as she'd done before. Adam stood still, not saying a word, but in his mind saying over and over again, 'It's okay. Let it go. It's okay.'

Finally, her shoulders stopped shaking, her hands went limp and she hung her head. 'I'm sorry.'

'Don't be sorry. You're trying to help. You helped Eloise when she needed to believe in herself, and look at her now. And you brought me here because you wanted to help me. It's more than others ever do.'

She turned her head, gaze arrowing in on his. 'I always thought kindness a weakness, but in you it is a terrifying strength.'

He lifted his chin. 'I've always thought so.'

Her lips lifted into the breath of a smile. 'You are very wise. But then, that is the heart of the Trickster. It is what makes you so very important.'

'How?'

She opened her mouth and for a moment he thought she was

going to lock up again, but then she just shook her head. 'Somebody other than me must tell you that. I simply brought you here to see you safe for now. To tell you not to try to re-enter your body or join with your wolf yet. Not until it's time.'

'And when will that be?'

Her mouth worked for a moment.

He held his hand up. 'It's okay. I know. You can't tell me.' She shook her head. 'Then how will I know? Who can tell me?'

'You have already met her.'

He frowned. 'That ghost. The one who was there when I became this.' She nodded. 'Who is she?'

'I cannot tell you that, unfortunately.'

'Does she work for you?'

She shrugged and managed to say, 'In a manner of speaking.'

'Where is she now?'

'Hiding.'

'From the thing that was chasing her? Was it the Darkness?'

'A shadow of the Darkness caught in the aether. More than that, I cannot say.'

'Can I go to where she is?'

'No. For now, she is ...' She tipped her head, gazing off in the distance. 'Elsewhere. But she is trying to bargain a way back to you. I hope she is successful sooner rather than later. We are running out of time.'

'For what?'

Her gaze ran over him. 'You cannot stay like this forever. The force that is keeping you in this state will fade eventually and at that point, if you haven't done what you need to do to help your friends cure your body so you can return to it, then you will simply cease to exist.'

'Well ... crap.'

'Yes, well put.'

He pulled his thoughts away from the horror of her words and asked, 'You said she's bargaining. Can't you help her with that?'

'The rules forbid it.'

'The rules. Right.' He frowned. 'What happens if she takes too long getting back from wherever she is?' Arianrhod shrugged. 'Does that mean that I still have hope or that there is none?' She looked as if she was about to shrug again but he pointed a finger at her. 'Do not shrug at me again or tell me this is one of those things you can't tell me. Find a way around the rules. If I remember my mythology correctly, the Gods were always pretty bloody good at finding loopholes.'

'I am trying to find one here, believe me, but so far, I am unsuccessful.' She gestured at the stormy sky around them. 'There is a storm coming.'

'No shit Sherlock.'

She frowned at him. 'I am Arianrhod, not Sherlock.'

'It's just a saying that means ...' He shook his hands in front of him. 'Never mind. You were telling me there is a storm coming, which I can see.'

'No, you do not understand. This place is what your friend, Eloise, created, when she came to speak to me. It is a special place that she, as the Nexus, was able to pull out of the aether. It is a reflection of her power, but also shows the emotions of the universe at a deeper level.'

'You mean it's like one big mood ring?'

She blinked. 'I have heard of those.' She smiled, but the smile was bleak. 'Yes. It is like a big mood ring. And the mood is not happy.'

The hair rose on the back of his neck as lightning played in the roiling dark green clouds overhead. There was something evil hanging over this place like a threat. His Trickster senses were going haywire—she was right, he still had them despite not being able to feel the bond with his wolf. Edgy nerves danced under his skin. He tried to comprehend the needy desperation and unforgiving sense of loneliness mixed with raging anger lowering from above. 'Saying it's not happy is the world's greatest understatement.'

'Hmm, yes. Things that have been brewing for some time are about to come to pass.' Her gaze met his again. 'It is not a good time to be a human or Were on your earth. An ancient evil is about to take a step that will allow it to enter into your plane of existence and there is nothing that me and mine can do to stop it.'

'If you can't stop it, what chance do we have against it?'

'You have the Nexus. And you. Aligned with the power of the triumvirate, you have all you need.'

He snorted. 'Eloise and Shelley, Skye and Bron I can understand. They have incredible power. But me? You've got that wrong.'

'No.' She swiped her hand, her frustration making the air zing around them. 'You are one of the most important tools at our disposal in this war. It is prophesied that the Trickster ...' Her mouth snapped closed and she rolled her eyes but didn't fight it this time.

It didn't matter. She'd got out something he could use. 'There's a prophecy about me.' Crap. He didn't like the sound of that. It kind of felt like his life was being taken out of his hands. 'And this ghost woman is going to be able to tell me about that? To help me learn what it is I need to do to be of use against this evil? An evil that somehow we can fight even though you Gods and Goddesses can't?'

She nodded. 'Not only that,' she managed between clenched teeth.

'What else?'

'You must ... find out ... who she is. That will help when ... the time comes.'

'How do I do that if I can't communicate with anyone?'

She held up her hand. For a moment, he could only see her tension, then it released again and she let out a shaky breath. 'That's fucking annoying.'

He barked out a laugh.

She blinked at him, lips curling a little before continuing. 'Michelline is also key. The banshee-Medium is as important in this as you. You must work with her to find the truth of both of your roles. It is essential.'

'Uh, that's going to be a little difficult.'

'Why?'

'Well, for one thing, she hates her power. I can feel it every time she's forced to use it. It's like an open wound and we keep making her pick at it.' He shuddered.

'I'm afraid you're going to have to get over your empathy and she her hatred. She is key. What must be done cannot be done without her and her unique abilities.'

'Ah, that brings me to the other difficulty.' Her brows rose. 'Shelley's ignoring me. It's like she's refusing to believe she can see me. I know she can, but she hasn't openly responded to anything I do or say since the night I became this. And she's left the McClune's compound and gone back to Melbourne, so I couldn't even talk to her if I wanted to.'

'Of course you can. You can go wherever you like. You are not stuck in one place.'

He frowned. 'How do I do that?' He knew that other spirits seemed to come and go as they pleased, but he didn't know how they managed it. He'd walked through the wall into the corridor many a time but wasn't able to go further unless he was with someone. He couldn't make the lift work—his hand kept going through the operating panel.

'You think of where you want to go, or who you want to go to, and you just will yourself there. The aether will take care of the rest.'

'As simple as that?' She simply smiled. 'Okay then.' He clenched his hands, knuckles cracking. 'So, I can make myself go to Shelley at will. That doesn't solve the problem of her ignoring me.'

'Make her see you. Make her listen.'

'You don't know Shelley.'

'No. But you do. And you need her. Make her see that she needs you too. That she needs you more than anyone else.'

By the Moon, he wished that was true, but he might as well wish to not have been hit by warlock lightning. 'Do you want to tell her that?'

'I have done all I can. For now. When there is great need, I will come again, but until then, you are on your own.'

'Figures.' He looked around. 'So how do I get out of here?'

'Like this.' She waved her hand and everything went black again, then purple, then unbelievably bright. So bright he cried out and covered his head. For a moment, there was nothing but the pain of the light and the absence of all sound and then there was a pop in his ears and the brightness faded away as suddenly as it had come.

'He's stable for now.'

The voice came to him through the noise of wind that surrounded him. He opened his eyes slowly and looked around.

He was back in the room where his body was. Jason still stood beside the bed, Bron and River beside him. How much time had passed since he'd been taken by the Goddess? There was no clock, so he couldn't tell. He moved closer to see what Bron was doing. She was bandaging up his body's arm.

There was blood on the sheet from the wound. Black gunk drying on his chest and sides.

Holy hell! Hardly any time had passed at all. Maybe half a minute if that.

'I wish I could do more for him,' Bron said, her hands shaking as she finished with the cannula wound. She seemed smaller somehow, diminished, like her light had been dimmed.

'We'll find a way,' River said, his hand on her shoulder. Where his hands landed, there was a faint glow of gold. It grew brighter, growing thick around the point of contact and then, like a wave, rolled out and over and through Bron. Bron breathed in deeply and sat a little straighter, her usual glow steady and sure around her.

Adam drew in a quick breath. Holy shit! River was like some kind of power conduit for Bron. Probably the reason they were fated to be mates. He was a ready-made extra battery pack or something. He knew they worked together when she was doing a Healing—they all helped give her more energy for that—but this was something deeper, something more personal.

Love and strength and trust all bound into one.

A surge of something bitter chased up his throat. He was happy for them, that they had what they had together, but by the Moon, he wished he had something similar. Shelley's face was suddenly before him and he knew with a certainty he'd been fighting, that she was that for him.

She was his mate.

He wanted her. Wanted to be with her. Needed her more than he needed his next heartbeat. And according to Arianrhod, he was meant to be with her.

'Kitten,' he whispered. The room around him faded into swirling colours. Dizziness rose over him but before it could catch and toss him up, the colours stilled, became the blue of sky overhead, the greens and browns of the Australian bush.

There was a sound to his left. He turned. His mouth dried.

Shelley.

She was jogging out of the bushland of Westerfolds Park, along the walking track that passed by the bottom fence of the Templestowe Packhouse. Her face was red and beaded with sweat, her long, golden hair caught up in a double loop high on her head, bobbing up and down a little with her movement. She wore figure-hugging workout gear—all black. Tight calves and thighs led up to tight hips and butt. Holy mother of God, her butt looked good. He'd never really thought himself a butt man—more into breasts, really. Large breasts that spilled over his hands. But since meeting Shelley, his appreciation of the female form had changed. Don't get him wrong—she had a beautiful pair of breasts. Goldilocks breasts—not too small, not too large, but just right, set between a trim waist and wide shoulders. But by the Gods she had a glorious back. And butt. He wanted to run his hand over those firm globes. He bet her skin would be even silkier than the silkiness of the pants that encased them.

His cock stirred and he looked down at it in amazement. He could get a hard-on as a ghost-spirit-thing? Would miracles never cease? Although it would be a true miracle if he could use the damn thing. He had a sad feeling that it could get excited all it liked, but that it would lead a distinctly lonely existence until he could get out of whatever this place was. 'Down boy,' he whispered to it as Shelley got nearer. 'No use fantasising how hot Shelley looks in her workout gear. Wait until we can show her.'

A gasp.

Then total silence. Well, not exactly total silence—birds were calling between the trees and wind rustled through the branches close by—but the pounding of feet on gravel had stopped.

He looked up to see that Shelley stood stock still on the path, staring at him, face red and glowing with perspiration. Her violet-blue eyes were even more purple-violet than blue now; a change that had been happening slowly ever since the banshee had broken free.

They glowed in the twilight like sun-lit amethyst. Stunning. Simply stunning.

And they were focused entirely on his groin.

His cock hardened as her gaze stayed fixed on it.

'Crap, Kitten. Don't look at it like that unless you mean to do something about it.'

Her gaze snapped back to his, her nose scrunched as if she was in pain and then she looked at the sky and yelled, 'Oh, that's just perfect! Well, you know what you can do, universe? You can just go fuck yourself. I'm not playing the "Shelley is nuts" game. He's not there and I'm not going to talk to him like he is.' She lifted her middle finger to the sky for good measure, and then charged ahead.

She would have run right into him if he hadn't jumped out of her way.

He watched in stunned silence as she ran like the dogs of hell were at her ankles, up the path that led to the back gate of the Pack-house's garden.

Just as she reached for the gate, he yelled out, 'I'm not imaginary, you know. I'm really here. And I need your help.'

She paused. He thought she was going to turn and talk to him. But then she pushed the latch up with a jerk and shoved the gate so hard, it slammed against the fence, making the whole thing shudder. The gate swung back with the momentum and slammed shut behind her.

Adam shook his head. 'That went well.'

'Make her see. She is your only hope.'

The voice whispered to him out of the air. He didn't even bother to look around, knowing he'd see nothing but the breath of wind in the trees. He suddenly felt like Luke Skywalker watching Princess Leia's message with Obi Wan. It was an impossible task for them to go and rescue her and get the plans that were inside R2D2 to the rebels. Yet, they'd done it.

He wasn't quite sure if Luke and Obi Wan's task was harder than his. Infiltrating the Death Star seemed a cakewalk in comparison to making Shelley admit he was real and agree to learn how to use her powers. If stubborn had a Goddess, it was called Shelley.

'You have no choice.'

Sighing, he said, 'Yes, Master Jedi,' and trudged up the pathway towards the Packhouse.

7

Shelley leaned her elbows on her desk and pinched the bridge of her nose. There was a sharp pounding at the base of her skull that was slowly making its way towards her eyes and if she didn't take something for it soon, it would turn into a migraine.

She couldn't afford to have a migraine right now. There was too much to do. The only problem was, she'd already maxed out on medication. If she had any more, she could seriously compromise her liver and kidneys. If Bron were here, she'd make her take one of her disgusting herbal remedies. They worked, but urgh. She shuddered and tried to focus on the paper in front of her.

A figure rushed at her from the side, mouth open in a wail, hands reaching towards her. She jerked back. Damn it! She'd let the outer layer of her shields slip—she was too tired and her head hurt too much. Before she could do anything about it, the woman's wail reached her—'Help me! I'm alone. So alone.'

The wail hit her like a slap. As did recognition. This was the stroke victim she'd nursed earlier. The doctor said he thought she was going to make it. Shelley had known with a deep-down, pain-in-the-gut knowing, a low hum she now recognised as the banshee, that she wouldn't.

The woman's appearance here meant she hadn't been wrong. And now she'd come searching for Shelley, like a moth to Shelley's flame.

'No you fucking don't,' she said, pushing her chair back from the desk before the spirit's outstretched hands could touch her. She scooted across the floor on the wheeled chair, out of the grasping reach of the confused recently departed, and despite the sickening lurch of pain in her head, snapped the all-important outer shield in place and extended it beyond her.

The spirit of the old woman came up short a metre away, her wail coming to Shelley as if through water. Shelley shook her head at the spirit. 'I'm sorry. I can't help you. You died. You had a stroke.'

The spirit pawed at her shields—it was like nails on a blackboard.

She shuddered. 'Go back to your body. Your family is there, I'm sure. Go hear the nice things they're saying about you. Take comfort in their presence and try to comfort them. Sometimes they can feel you there. It helps.' The spirit held out beseeching hands. Shelley shook her head, the pain in her skull pushing her beyond the pity she would usually feel. 'I can't help you to communicate with them. I don't do that. It won't make it better for anyone.' Especially for herself. 'Go back to your body. Back to your family. Be with them or move into the beyond. Your choice. But there's nothing you can get from me that I'm willing or able to give.'

The old woman beseeched with hands and sad eyes for a few more, century-like seconds, then at last, turned and drifted off through the wall.

'Thank the Gods.' Shelley blew out a loud breath as she sank to her seat. They often didn't go so easily. Especially when she let her shields slip.

She moved the chair back over to the desk and noticed the mess of mug shards and coffee on the floor. 'Oh, fuckity fuck with a helping of shit on the side!' In her haste to get away from the spirit, she'd knocked her favourite coffee mug onto the floor. Just perfect!

'Bad night, Kitten?'

She flinched, stiffened.

'Anything I can do?'

Go away, she said inside her head. *Go away, go away, go away.*

'I can't help you if you won't talk to me.'

She really didn't need this now. In fact, she needed it like she needed a hole in the head. In fact, a hole in the head would be better. Where was a trepanning drill when you needed one?

'I could offer to kiss it better, but even though I've been told my kisses are magic, I'm not sure they'll be good enough to glue the mug back together.'

She almost laughed but didn't. Couldn't.

He moved back into her line of sight, lips quirked in a way he knew irritated her. And not for the reasons smirky, too-sexy-for-anyone's-good smiles usually did.

Oh, why did he have to smile like that? He was so goddamned annoying—in a sexy, hot, he-makes-me-want-to-slap-him-and-kiss-him-at-the-same-time kind of way. Even in her imagination he couldn't stop being annoyingly hot.

She'd been so hopeful after getting away from the McClune caves where his body was. She'd had weeks of not seeing any hallucinations at all. And then—bam. There he'd been. Watching her jog with that gleam in his eyes that made her feel all hot and itchy, his cock stretching the front of his jeans in a way that had made her want to reach out and stroke it.

She'd dug her fingernails so hard into her hand, she could still see the imprints.

She hoped it was just a passing insanity. A momentary slip. That he'd disappear again and not come back.

That hope had been useless. He'd been with her ever since, following her around, there every time she woke up, watching her, making smart comments about her murmuring his name in her sleep. She'd tried to ignore him. Ignored the fact that his presence meant this wasn't just about worry and grief brought on by his body's proximity. No. It went so much deeper. It meant she either felt something for him or it meant she was going insane.

Neither was a good alternative.

He had to go away. Her chest tightened, her breath stuttering. She rubbed at the pain, shaking her head against the thought that there was a reason her heart was aching. 'No!' She slammed her hand down on the desk, palm stinging at the impact. She winced, rubbed at the pain.

'Steady on, Kitten. What did the desk do to you?'

She closed her eyes. *I'm not going mad. I'm not. I won't be like the others in my family. I'm stronger than that. I will be stronger than that.*

At least nobody would say she hadn't gone down without a fight. It wasn't much, but it was all she had right now.

Sighing, she rubbed her eyes and turned her attention back to the paperwork in front of her. 'Okay. Just a few more forms and then home.' She only hoped no more accidents happened tonight. Or strokes, or heart attacks. Anything lethal. She couldn't take another death in the Emergency department. They were the worst of the newly departed to deal with. So much confusion and grief wailed at her as if she could do anything to change what had happened to them. And now it was made worse by the fact she could hear their deaths coming.

Being a banshee sucked as much as being a Medium.

At least she hadn't emitted another one of those horrible banshee wails since the night Cain had escaped—thank the Goddess for small mercies at least. That rush of sensation of oncoming death had been the most horrible thing she'd ever felt and to have to relive it over and over every night in her nightmares was ...

She shuddered.

Thankfully, outside of her nightmares it had been content to be a whimper, a hum inside her. She was pretty bloody certain that despite learning from the diaries how to build stronger shields, they would do nothing to help contain the wail if it wanted out. She shuddered again.

'Cold?' The voice sounded right behind her, so real and concerned and familiar, she almost answered before she could stop herself.

He's not real.

But he feels so real. Sounds so real.

Oh, crap.

She shoved the traitorous thought aside and told herself once more that he wasn't real. Hell. How many times would she have to say that to herself before it took hold? She only wished it would work. She'd simply have to work harder on the diaries and grimoires. There had to be some record somewhere of how to stave off the madness that inevitably came from walking the line between life and death. There also had to be information about warlock lightning and its effect on a Were. This couldn't be the first time a Were was ever hit by it. The Pack Witches had kept meticulous records of their lives and every spell they'd ever canted. She was obviously asking the wrong questions of the wrong diaries. There had to be a way to heal Adam and make him wake up again. If he was awake, she could no longer hallucinate about him being a spirit. Besides, if she didn't find a way to heal Adam, he might truly die and then he would haunt her for the rest of her life—he was that sadistically annoying.

The thought was enough to make her want to study until her eyeballs dried up and fell out of her head. Even with this goddamned awful headache brewing behind her eyes. She rubbed her temple. 'Finish the paperwork, go home, have some of Bron's disgusting headache cures and then get on with the research.'

'You forgot to add have something to eat to your list.'

She tensed at the sound of the voice right beside her chair.

'And when are you fitting sleep in there, I'd like to know? You look worse than me, and I'm half dead.'

She ignored him.

'Do you have any idea how lonely it is when the only person I can converse with properly won't speak to or even look at me?'

'Lonely,' she said before she could stop herself. 'You can't be lonely. You're not real.'

'Not real? I'm standing in front of you having this conversation, aren't I?'

'Yes. In my imagination. You're a hallucination.' She spun in the chair to face him, giving up to the insanity, and tapped her head.

'I don't think so.' He frowned and pinched himself. 'No. I feel very much real to me. Here in the flesh. Or spirit, would probably be more correct.'

Her lips twitched and she burst out laughing and then winced and clutched her head.

'Shelley? What's wrong?'

'Bad headache.'

'Then why are you here? You should go home, have something to eat and get some sleep.'

She opened her mouth to argue. 'Okay,' popped out instead.

'Okay, then let's get you out of here.'

Too tired and in too much pain to argue any further, she went to the staff room, collected her bag and coat, waved goodbye to the nurses on duty and then hopped in the elevator to the staff car park. The doors closed. She leaned back against the wall and closed her eyes.

'Why didn't you say your headache was that bad?'

Her eyes popped open and she stared at him. 'Because you're in my head so you should know anyway.'

An expression crossed his face, a shadow of sadness, pain. 'You really think I'm a figment of your imagination?'

'What else can you be? You're not dead. I only see dead people. Ipso facto—I'm imagining you. You're a product of the crazy that has felled every single one of my family who had "the talent". And now that crazy is finally getting me. Typical that you're the centre of it.'

He seemed lost for words for a moment, but then cocked his head as he looked at her consideringly. 'You're not going crazy.'

'Oh, really? Then why am I currently talking to you?'

'Because I'm here. Actually here. Just like the spirits you talk to, but obviously different.'

'Oh, you're different all right.'

His lips cocked in that smile that drove her nuts. 'How nice of you to notice. Is it my innate sexiness that makes me different or just my handsome smile that makes me stand out from the rest?'

She snorted. The lift doors opened. A couple of staff stood outside. They gave her a strange look.

'Sorry, just thought of something funny,' she said. 'Have a good shift.' She sidled past them and headed towards her car. She pulled out her keys and pressed the electronic opener. Her car blipped back.

'You taking me for a drive, Kitten? Got to say, that's always been a fantasy of mine. You, me, a car's back seat. A big bright old moon above sneaking a peek.'

She rolled her eyes. 'Why are you still like this? Why can't I make you behave even in my imagination?'

'Because I'm not a figment of your imagination.'

'Prove it.'

'Okay.' He reached out and grabbed her hand, stopping her from opening her door and pulling her to face him. 'How's this?'

She gasped at his cold touch, yanked her hand away and stumbled back into her car. 'You ... I ...' Her mind stilled as her gaze met his, caught for a moment in a wisp of memory that she'd tried to forget. 'You've done that before. The night it happened.'

'Yep.'

'I thought I imagined that. I was distraught. I wanted to believe that you were physically there. But I can only see spirits and spirits can't touch me.'

'I can.' He lifted one hand and pushed her braid back over her shoulder. She shivered but couldn't move back—she was already pressed up against the car. He stepped closer. His hand lifted, finger gliding down her cheek—an ice-cold glide that heated her all the way to her core.

'You can feel that, can't you? If I'm a figment of your imagination, then explain how.'

'I ... I ...' She couldn't. But if she could truly see him, that meant he was dead. But ... 'You're not dead. You're not dead. Your body is still alive.'

'You're right. I'm not dead. And I'm not like the spirits that plague you. My ability to touch you and the fact I still have a living body is proof enough of that.'

'Then why can I see you?' She gasped again as his fingers brushed down her neck, then back up. Shivered.

'Cold?'

'Your touch is cold, but also—' She stopped, not wanting to admit what it was truly doing to her. 'It's weird.'

'Good weird or bad weird?' He brushed his finger along her chin then up to her cheek again.

'I ... it's just not ... normal.' She wanted to lean into his touch, to hold his hand against her face. But she couldn't. She didn't need like that. Wouldn't. She edged sideways, away from his touch.

'But it feels real.'

'Yes.'

'It's the same for me.' He tangled his fingers in the ends of her hair, tugged. 'Soft. Silky. Not the same as when I felt alive, muted somehow, but it's real.'

'Why? How. How can you do that? How can I feel you?'

'I don't know.' His voice was a low whisper and she almost imagined she could feel the brush of his breath across her skin.

She stared up at him. If he wasn't dead and wasn't a figment of her imagination ... 'You're a Shade.'

His expression clouded and his hand dropped from her hair, but the action seemed to catch his attention and he lifted his hand again, stared at it. 'I had thought maybe that was it, but then ...' He touched her shoulder, slid his hand up to cup the bare skin on her neck. There was the cold sensation, a sensual glide, making her shiver in anticipation. 'Does that hurt you? Drain you?'

'No.' Realisation dawned. He could touch her. And it didn't hurt. Didn't drain her of witch power or life force. If he was a Shade, that's what would happen. But if he wasn't a Shade and he wasn't a spirit ... 'What are you?'

'I was hoping you would help me find out.'

She blinked away the sudden rush of moisture that blurred her vision. What the hell was wrong with her? She didn't cry. Didn't feel anything so deep as the kind of sadness or longing or grief that would make her cry. She'd had to harden herself against those feelings years before because of her "gift", otherwise they would have destroyed her. 'I've been trying to help you. I've been trying to find out about warlock lightning and the wounds it creates. And Tricksters; just in case it has something to do with your role in the pack.'

'I know. I've been watching you, remember. But there's so much more going on here than simply that.' He told her what had happened the night he tried to re-bond with his body. 'And then the most remarkable thing happened. I found myself talking to—'

'Shit, Adam. You almost died.' She blew out a breath, her aunt's words playing in her mind again. She'd left him, his body, and hadn't looked back because she was afraid. And her leaving, taking away the only person he could communicate with, had caused him to act in such a rash way, almost killing him. Was this what her aunt meant?

'Shelley?'

She blinked, shook her head. 'Thank the Goddess Bron realised there was black magic in the wound. You could have died, Adam.' She wanted to grab him, shake him. 'You could have died.'

'It's okay, Kitten. I didn't die. I'm fine. You can see I'm fine.'

She nodded. He wasn't really fine, still being in spirit form, but she knew what he meant. 'Okay. Okay,' she said on a shuddering breath. 'You were saying something about a remarkable thing happening.'

'I was trying to, before you got off topic.'

She hardly thought him almost dying was off topic, but she forced herself not to respond. 'Tell me now.'

'So, I ended up in this place that Eloise created and it was the Goddess Arianrhod who had brought me there.' He continued, telling her in detail what had happened. And as he did, she couldn't help but gape at him.

'Shelley? Did you hear what I said?'

'You saw the Goddess, Arianrhod?' she asked as if waking from a dream. 'And she said I was related? To her?'

'I know. It's a kicker, right. But somehow, it makes sense. Your powers are different from the other witches that I've met.'

'God-touched,' she whispered. 'It makes horrible sense.' His brow rose, questioningly. 'In the past, it was said that anyone who could see the future in any way, was God-touched. As was anyone who saw death. And being God-touched brought madness with it.' She laughed, an edge of hysteria to the sound.

'What is it?'

'My aunt Lilyanna said we were touched by the Goddess. I had no idea she meant it literally.' She shook her head, squeezed her hand tight around the car keys and met his gaze. 'I wonder what the link is?'

'Perhaps it says something in your family grimoire.'

She rubbed her head. 'No. I've read it back to front.'

'You've read it? How? I thought it was with your family.'

Her mouth quirked. 'I stole it a while back. I figured I needed it more than they did. I wanted to see if there was anyone with my talent in the past who hadn't gone insane. But there wasn't.' She wrapped her arms around her body. 'I guess I know why now.'

'It might not happen to you. You're different from the rest of them.'

'It doesn't matter.'

'Of course it matters.' He gripped her shoulders. 'Everything about you matters.'

She shrugged off his touch. 'Not at the moment, it doesn't. What matters is figuring out how to help you and why this has happened. What matters is finding out who this woman is that you need to talk to. My problems will just have to wait.' Pain lurched through her head with a sickening thump and she winced.

'It's getting worse, isn't it?'

She nodded carefully.

'Then let's get in your car and get you home.'

He backed up so she could turn and open the door. By the time she'd lowered herself inside, he was already sitting in the front passenger seat.

She stared, then shook herself and started the car. 'So, you can slip through walls like a spirit or Shade, but you're not one. And I can see, hear and talk to you clearly despite all the work I've put into my shields that helps me fend off other spirits. All of which means you're some other kind of thing that we've never heard of before.'

'That's right. I'm a not-Shade-spirit-thingy.' He tipped his head to the side. 'Hey, I like that. A not-Shade-spirit-thingy. It's got a ring to it.'

She snorted, put the car into reverse and backed out. 'I'm not calling you a "not-Shade-spirit-thingy".'

'Spoilsport!' He stuck his tongue out at her.

She turned her head so he couldn't see that her lips were twitching and began to drive carefully through the labyrinthine carpark. 'You know,' she said when she had herself under control. 'Going to the other side is supposed to make you more serene. Less of an idiot.'

'You'd think that, wouldn't you? I'd say it sounds good in theory but doesn't really work in reality.'

'For you.'

'For any of the spirits you deal with. I wouldn't say being dead has made Adeline or Harrison more malleable. They seemed pretty full on when they took you over last year.'

'Hmm.' She didn't like thinking of those times. It still hurt her head and made her feel sick when she did.

'Besides, I'm not a usual spirit. I'm a not-Shade-spirit-thingy.'

'Idiot,' she said as she pulled out into the traffic.

'You love me for it.'

His words shot through her; a short, sharp jab. A burn. She glanced over at him, but he was staring out the window, oblivious to how his thrown-away words might affect her.

So oblivious. Always oblivious. Except for that one moment in the dam the night of the blood moon before she had succumbed to the banshee wail. The night Adam had almost died and Marcus had. The night Cain got away.

Cain. She gasped. 'Do you think maybe Cain meant to do this to you? That it's part of their plan to weaken us?'

'I think maybe he's just an insane bastard who gets off on killing. Besides, going by what Arianrhod managed to tell me, being what I am now is essential to her plans to fight the Darkness. I don't think Cain would do anything that might help our cause.'

'No. You're right. I just wished we knew more. Maybe Eloise has come across something in her studies about the Nexus.'

'We'll have to ask her.'

She fell silent, chewing her lip as she thought about everything he'd told her.

'Hey, what are you thinking?' He reached out, touched her shoulder.

The ice cold of his touch was muted by her clothing, but still, the aching reality of it made her want to lean into it. But no good could ever come of giving into that need. Instead, she swallowed and said, 'I'm sorry I ignored you before now. It's just ... I didn't want to believe you were real because I thought that meant you were dead. Or were about to be. And I couldn't stand the thought of that. Not you. Not after all the other losses. It was too much.'

'I get it. All that matters now is that you are seeing me and you're going to help me.'

'Of course I am.'

She pulled into the street that led to the Packhouse. 'How do you want me to tell the others?'

He winced. 'Could we not tell them yet?'

'Why not?' She pulled into the driveway and parked, turned to look at him.

His shoulders were tensed, his mouth thinning as if he planned not to answer her question. But then he let out a loud breath, eyes glowing in the now dark car. She had no idea what he was thinking but knew whatever it was, those thoughts were deep and personal and very much about protecting the others in the pack.

'I'd just like to know more before we tell them.'

'You don't want to get their hopes up.'

'Something like that.' He tipped his head. 'So, how about it? We keep this just between us for now?'

She stared at him for long minutes before nodding. 'Until we learn something more.' She shook her head. 'I can't believe you spoke to a Goddess.' She frowned and stared out the window. 'You know, I read something the other day that indicated that the Gods couldn't speak to anyone unless they had a certain level of power. I know a Trickster is different from others in the pack, but maybe it's more of a difference than we ever thought. Maybe the source of your empathy comes from some magical power.'

'Oh, I'm different,' he snorted, 'but I don't think I'm special enough to have power.'

'Stop running yourself down like that.' She smacked him on the hand. He looked up at her in surprise. 'The fact you can read the diaries is proof you do have some form of magic inside you most Were don't. Besides that, I'll have you know that the Trickster was valued very highly in centuries past. Packs that had Tricksters in each generation always did better than those without.' She touched his shoulder, met his gaze when he looked at her. 'You aren't only for "shits and giggles". You're needed in a much deeper way. It's not only me saying it. The others can all feel it. You heard River and Bron say as much. And Arianrhod said something similar to you. You've been chosen because you are special. We just have to figure out why.'

'Okay.' He looked down at her hand where it still touched his shoulder.

She snatched it back. 'Anyway,' she coughed, clearing her throat. 'It's getting cold in here. We better go inside.' She hopped out of the car and walked up the path. Adam was at her side before she'd taken a few steps. 'You should ask Adeline if she knows anything about this woman you're supposed to go with. She was there that night. If she saw her, she might know who she was. Adeline knows a lot of spirits.'

'I already tried to ask her, but we didn't get very far.'

'Why not?'

'Communication is tricky. I can't really talk with the other spirits.'

She stopped at the front door and dug through her bag to get her house keys. 'What do you mean? I thought you said you spoke to that woman?'

'I did. But aside from the people who were still alive, she was the only one I could hear. The other spirit voices are brushed away in the wind that's here all the time. It even makes it hard to hear those who are alive if they aren't speaking loudly enough.'

'What wind?'

He stared at her as if she'd said something strange. 'You have to know about the wind.'

'No. Nobody has ever mentioned it before.'

'Huh.'

'Maybe that's another clue.' Although it seemed like a strange one.

'Maybe.'

'You can hear me okay though?'

'Yes. You're the only one I can hear with any clarity aside from the woman and Arianrhod.' He sighed. 'So, I hate to ask this, given how I know you feel about using your powers, but until I figure my way around the sound of the wind or that woman comes back, you're going to have to help me communicate with the others. They might have answers.'

'Yes.' She swallowed hard against the nausea rising inside and dropped the keys on the ground. 'Damn it.' She reached down to pick them up, fumbling them in the door.

Adam's hand over hers steadied her shaking. 'We don't have to start straight away.'

'Okay.' It was weak to be so relieved that he was giving her a reprieve—she should insist she could help straight away. But she couldn't. She hated engaging with the spirits. They always took so much out of her. It was exhausting. Even with the new multiple-layered shields she'd learned to raise—which she was supposed to be able to lower a few layers at a time so she could communicate but still keep herself protected from them with the inner layers—it was still difficult to be around them. And they were around pretty much all the time now. Always wanting something from her, always bludgeoning her with their need. It was one of the reasons for the increasingly bad headaches. Even with the shields, their need drained her. Since Oestra, it had gotten worse. She'd thought her head was going to split open earlier with the spirit in the hospital. Except ...

She frowned. Touched her temple. The pain had gone. As had all the spirits which constantly followed her around. In fact, they mostly weren't around when Adam was. Strange. Although, she wasn't going to look an Adam-shaped gift horse in the mouth. Besides, it didn't matter why the headache was gone, only that it had.

She pulled her hand from Adam's, feeling a little steadier now, and opened the door. Once inside, she dumped her bag on the hall-stand and continued down the hallway that led to the library.

'Where do you think you're going?'

'Library.' She kept walking.

Adam shook his head. 'Nuh-uh. Food and bed.'

'But my headache's gone.'

'You still don't look well. You've been driving yourself too hard.'

'Says who?'

'Says not-dead me.' He crossed his arms as he appeared in front of her, blocking the doorway to the library. 'Do I really have to get all alpha male on you?'

'As if you could,' she scoffed.

'I'll hide the diaries. You won't be able to find them.'

'You can't touch them.'

'Wanna bet? If I can touch you, I'm thinking I can touch anything I want.'

She glowered at him as she considered pushing past him. But then she'd have to touch him. And she couldn't do that. Not when the urge to do so was too great.

She ached every time he touched her, longing, loss and relief intertwined with a bone-deep need that she'd never been able to divorce herself from when it came to him. She couldn't touch him again or allow him to touch her. Not tonight.

He simply stood there as if he knew how much she wanted to, arms crossed, a shit-eating grin on his face. She clenched her fists at her side. Goddess, she wanted to smack that grin from his face. Or kiss it away.

No! No kissing. Definitely no kissing. He wasn't corporeal. Not that there would be any kissing when he was corporeal. Which he would be if she could only get to the diaries and start researching.

As if he could read her mind, his grin widened and he shook his head. 'Uh-uh-uh. No trying to guilt me into letting you have your way by "but Adam, I'm doing this for you" wheedling. Food. Sleep. In that order.' He unfolded his arms long enough to point in the direction of the kitchen. 'Be a good kitty.'

'Kitty!'

His smile widened. 'I thought I might start calling you Goddess, given your relations and all, but I think I still prefer Kitten.'

Her fists shook at her sides and she growled—actually growled!—at him.

He simply laughed. 'You purr nice, Kitten.'

'Argh! You're a misbegotten, sadistic arsehole, you know that?'

'Sticks and stones, Kitten.' He mock frowned. 'Actually, I'm not sure that holds true anymore. I don't think sticks and stones could break my bones as I don't appear to have any.'

'Your body does. Perhaps I should go there now and show you just how much sticks and stones can hurt.'

He bowed, grin firmly in place. 'You're welcome to. After you've had something to eat and a good sleep.'

'Argh! You're so annoying.' She threw her hands up and headed for the kitchen. Actually, now the headache was gone, she was kind of hungry. So it suited her to go and make herself a sandwich. Yes it did. She'd make herself a sandwich with all Annoying Adam's favourite ingredients and then she'd enjoy it so much while eating it in front of him, she'd give Meg Ryan in *When Harry Met Sally* a run for her money.

The thought made her smile.

'What are you smiling at, Kitten.'

'Just the thought of a bit of revenge.'

8

'**H**ow's Adam?'

Bron looked up as Jason came into the room. 'The same.' She rubbed her temple. 'I don't know what else to do for him.'

'You saved him.' River's hand on her shoulder calmed her.

She shrugged it off. She didn't want to be calmed. 'It's not good enough.' She stood up, pushed away from the bed, swayed a little.

'Careful.' River's hands caught her—he always caught her. 'You've been giving too much of yourself to the Healing.'

'It's not enough. And now I can't heal him because of the cuff that's keeping that thing—' her finger pointed shakily at the black seeping wound in his chest '—at bay. I don't know what else to do.' Her vision wavered, tears spilling over before she could blink them away.

'Hey, hey.' Jason came to stand in front of her, stroking her hair, brushing away the tears as River stood at her back, holding her steady, even when his heart was aching for her. She felt that aching now and she was sorry for it. It made her cry more.

Jason gripped her shoulders. 'You're asking too much of yourself.

94

More than anyone would ever ask of you.' He glanced at Adam. His voice dropped. 'More than Adam ever would.'

'Jason's right,' River murmured. 'If Adam saw you now, he'd be the first one to kick your arse. Then he'd kick mine for letting you do it to yourself. And I'd deserve it. I've not been a very good mate.'

'That's not true. You're the best of mates.' She stroked his face. He leaned into her touch.

'You're both overextended,' Jason said. 'You've not truly left this room since Oestra, and that's not good.' His gaze landed on River. 'It's not good for your wolf.' He turned to Bron. 'And it's not good for your powers. You need not only rest, but time spent out in nature, recharging. You can't do that properly in here. Cordy wouldn't thank you for it and neither would Adam.'

'Pot, kettle, black.' Bron gave him a look. 'You've been here as much as I have. But you're right.' She straightened, took a deep breath and waved her hand. 'We all need to take a break. I as your Healer command it.'

'But ...' Jason began.

She smirked at him. 'Uh-uh-uh. You know in instances of pack health that my word outweighs yours.'

'That's my mate,' River said, lips twisting into a smile. 'Put the Alpha in his place.'

Jason glared at him, but then softened it with a smile. 'Okay. You're right. I'll call June. She and Alistair and Ingrid can organise a roster to come sit with Adam and Cordy for the next twenty-four hours while we get some R and R.'

Bron lifted her finger and waggled it at him. 'No sneaking back.'

'Same to you,' Jason said.

'I'll make sure she doesn't come back until tomorrow.'

'And I'll call Skye and make sure she keeps you away until then as well.' Bron crossed her arms, a satisfied smirk on her face.

Jason brightened. 'Skye should be back from Melbourne by now. I wonder what the doctor said about her tummy bug.'

Bron snorted. 'I think you're dreaming if you think she went to the doctor.'

Jason sighed. 'You're right. Can you check her out later if she didn't?'

'Sure, but you'll owe me a big drink after. We all know she's the worst patient on the face of the planet.'

'She might be a little more malleable now she's had some time checking on her business and is bringing Tom back up here,' River suggested.

Bron snorted. 'Have you met your sister?'

River chuckled and Jason said, 'I'll bring two bottles from my own personal collection.'

'Nice,' Bron said.

Jason made the call. Ten minutes later, June and Alistair arrived, ready and more than willing to take up duty looking over their beloved coven leader and the man who was felled fighting alongside their Alpha.

ADAM WATCHED JASON, Bron and River leave. A few of the other spirits went with them, including Adeline, who seemed to spend a lot of her time hanging around Bron. Marcus, of course, stayed. He'd been there every time Adam came back to check if the mysterious lady had reappeared.

Adam could understand that Marcus didn't want to leave Cordy's side, even if it wasn't their way to hang around after death. He rather thought he'd do the same. He even understood why Marcus' attention was solely centred on Cordy and he had ignored every attempt Adam had made to communicate. Not that Marcus would be useful to him anyway. There was no chance he knew anything about the ancient witch Arianrhod said had the answers he wanted.

No, he really needed one of the older spirits.

He turned back to the room. There were fewer spirits here than the last time he visited. Maybe they'd been attracted by the excitement, the death, and now that was gone and things were quiet, they had gone to find amusement elsewhere. Maybe they'd gone to find

Shelley—although there hadn't been many spirits around her lately either, which was why he'd come up here at her suggestion because she still hadn't found anything in the diaries that could help them heal him or about who this ancient witch might be.

He wished he could ask one of the spirits here if she'd been back or not, but if wishes were fishes and all that. Shelley would have to come up here sooner rather than later if they were to find any useful information. He'd been trying to save her from that, but it looked like there was no other alternative.

Pain. In. The. Arse.

He'd had such high hopes today. The spirits had been a little agitated when he'd arrived. He'd thought maybe there was a special reason. But no. They were just chattier than usual. With each other. Not with him.

A big grade-A bummer of a wasted trip. Especially as he didn't like to be away from Shelley. It had already been too long. He needed to get back to her now.

Just the thought of her made the world around him change and then he was standing in a bathroom.

The bathroom in Shelley's house. A sound behind him made him turn.

The air left his lungs in a whoosh.

She was at the basin, nothing but a towel wrapped around her as she dried her hair with another towel. His mouth went dry and he could do nothing but stare at her.

Forget being related to a Goddess. She *was* a Goddess.

Her skin was the most amazing golden shade, smooth and silken and calling to be stroked. His fingers itched just at the thought. Water drops glistened on her shoulders. He wanted to lick those up like nectar, little laps before sweeping his tongue up to her ear, rimming that perfect shell then making his way back down her neck to where he could see her pulse thrumming under her skin. His teeth ached with the need to bite down on that spot, to claim her, just as he'd wanted to claim her the first time he'd seen her in that bar up at Mt Buller the year before.

She picked up a hair dryer and started blow drying her hair, the thick, golden-honey strands blowing away from her face, just like in those ridiculous shampoo commercials she always laughed at.

The whir of the hair dryer and the constant wind around him wasn't enough to cover the sound of her voice. It came through as clear as a bell. She was humming a tune. It was slightly off key, but he recognised it. 'Suicide Blonde'.

His lips curled. That was until he noticed her reflection in the mirror. She was crying.

Holy hell! Was she crying over him? Usually his Kitten had teeth —she rarely showed anything but those teeth to him—but right now there was a soft vulnerability that made him ache; an eternal sadness darkening the startling violet-blue of her eyes. Hand stretched out to touch, to comfort, he took a jerky step forward.

Her gaze collided with his in the mirror. 'Adam!' she shrieked, dropping the hair dryer. 'What the hell are you doing here?' The noise of the hair dryer as it whirred around the basin echoed around the bathroom, almost obscuring her words. With a curse, she turned it off, swiped the tears from her face and turned to him, eyes narrowed, crossed arms securing the towel firmly in place—damn! He so hoped it might slip down a little more.

'Adam!'

He blinked and looked up from staring at her crossed arms. 'What?'

'How long have you been standing there?' She blushed as she saw the answer on his face. But the embarrassment only lasted for a moment. 'You can't just pop into someone's bathroom. How many times do I have to go over this with you morons? There is such a thing as privacy and I need you to respect mine.'

'Sorry, I didn't mean to. I just thought of you for a second and then I was ...' He stopped, backtracking over what she'd just said. 'You morons? Plural? So not just me?'

'Yes. Not just you.'

A hot curl of anger burned in his lungs. 'Spirits have watched you while you're in the bathroom?' He looked around, couldn't see any.

Which was just as well, because he'd have to find some way of smacking their faces for seeing what he hadn't seen yet and invading her privacy in such a way.

She threw her hand out. 'Well they're not here now, because they've learned not to come near me when I'm in the bathroom, or on the toilet or getting dressed.'

'They've dropped in when you're on the toilet?'

'Yes. They have. Worse than that though, they've popped in when I've been with a man. It's a passion killer when you open your eyes and see someone staring at you from across the room.'

'Spirits have seen you having sex?' His fingers clenched, itching to hit something. 'Bloody peeping Toms.' There was nothing to hit, so he kicked at the bath mat on the floor.

It flew up and sailed through the air.

Shelley's mouth dropped open. 'I didn't believe you when you said you might be able to touch something other than me.'

He blinked at the mat. 'Neither did I.'

'Try to touch something else.' He raised his hand towards her. 'Not me, you idiot. Lift the hairdryer out of the basin.'

She moved out of the way, careful not to touch him as usual. Ignoring that little curl of hurt, he reached for the hair dryer. His hand went through it. He tried again. Again. Again. 'Bloody fucking shit.' He swiped at it. His hand connected with the handle, sending it flying out of the basin, skittering over the bench to crash onto the floor. A large piece of the plastic nose broke off and scooted across the tiles.

He looked up at her sheepishly, the anger dissolving. 'Ah, sorry about that.'

'You were angry then.'

'Yes. Well, more frustrated than angry, but a little angry too.'

'And you were angry when you flipped the bath mat up.'

'Of course I was. The idea that ghosts have invaded your privacy like that ...'

She lifted her hand up. 'So, it seems you can touch and move things when you're angry.'

'I guess.'

'You're angry when you touch me?'

'No!' He took a step towards her, horrified she might think that. 'No. That's something else entirely. I don't know why I can feel you and you can feel me. I've tried to touch others at times, but apart from the odd occasion, it hasn't worked. Not like with you.'

'What do you mean?'

'A few of the others have responded to me like they heard me or sensed me and occasionally, felt my touch; like they would a brush of a feather. Not enough to hold their attention though.'

'Who have you tried touching?'

'Bron. Iain and Eloise. Jason.'

'I thought you didn't want him to know you were like this.'

'I don't. I tried before I realised I was a not-Shade-spirit-thingy. Although, given we're not having any luck with finding out information, we might have to tell them soon.'

'Why? What's changed?'

He shrugged, but her gaze narrowed on him, head tipped to the side like she could see into the heart of him. 'It's horrific being invisible to everyone and not be able to talk with any of them.'

'I see you. I talk to you.'

'Yes, and that fact has kept me sane.' She blanched at the word and he wished he could pull it back. 'I'm sorry.'

She shook her head. 'It's okay. I know what you mean. It's not nice to feel like you're alone in this world.'

'No.'

They stared at each other for an age, or what could have been seconds, until Shelley finally broke the moment by taking a step back. 'I need to get dressed.'

'You look fine to me.'

She rolled her eyes, took a step towards him, stopped. 'Well?'

'Well what?'

She gestured towards the door. He was blocking it. She could squeeze past, but the bathroom wasn't big enough for her to do it without brushing right up against him.

Given her apparent aversion to touching him, he stepped back and gestured. 'After you.'

He followed her into her bedroom. She went over to a large, dark wood chest of drawers and pulled out some underwear from the top drawer, then a soft wool top from the one below it and a pair of jeans from the bottom drawer. The clothes bundled against her chest, she moved back towards the bathroom. 'Stay here. I'll be back out in a minute.'

The ensuite door closed behind her and he was alone. In her room. Shelley's room. He'd often imagined being in here. Of course, in those dreams she was here with him, getting undressed, not getting dressed behind the closed door of the ensuite. And the circumstances were completely different. In his imagination, she begged him to touch her rather than avoid it at all costs. And of course, in his imagination, he hadn't been a not-Shade-spirit-thingy. 'Whoever said dreams come true was a great big fucking liar.'

'What was that?' Shelley asked as she came back into the room.

'Nothing. Just talking to myself. I seem to be doing that a lot now given you're the only one who can hear me.'

'And that other spirit woman.'

'Yes. Speaking of which.' He told her about his visit to the McClune caves and what he'd discovered there. As he spoke, her eyes widened and she sank to the bed.

When he finished, she sat in silence for a little while, then looked up at him. 'So, I really am going to have to go up there to speak to them.'

'Adeline should possibly be your first port of call and she won't hurt you like the others.'

She snorted. 'That's if she doesn't try to take me over again.'

'I don't think she'd do that.' She arched her brow at him. 'Well, I hope she wouldn't do that.'

'Hmm.' She caught her bottom lip in between her teeth and looked pensively into space for a long moment. 'If I go up there, you're right, I will have to tell Jason and the others about you.'

Adam swallowed slowly. 'Yes.' He wasn't looking forward to it. But he hoped, if they did it the right way, then his brother would be relieved rather than feel more grief. At least, that's what he hoped.

Shelley pulled her boots on.

'What are you doing? You don't have to go now.'

She looked up at him. 'I'm not. I want to read more of the diaries. I want to face Jason with some reasons why this might be happening, and if that's not possible, I want to be able to ask Adeline about a few things and need to double check my understanding before I do.' She stood. 'One way or the other, Adam, we'll have some answers soon. I promise.'

She was so sincere, the tigress he loved sinking back behind a world of sadness and worry. 'I don't want you to hold yourself responsible if you can't find a solution for me.'

'I won't,' she said, heading to the door.

She was lying. He could smell it on her. She would blame herself. Was already doing so. She'd been crying over him after all.

He wouldn't forget that. Couldn't.

Even though he'd been blocked from the bond with his wolf, the echo of it was in his soul—and it was howling at the pain all this was going to bring to her.

He had to find some way of making her okay with all of this. It was essential to more than his equanimity—it was essential to her well-being. And apparently for some reason, his wolf's.

9

'Will you stop pacing. I can't concentrate when you pace like that.'

Cain stopped and swivelled to face Morrigan. She hadn't even looked at him. She still sat in the same position she'd been in for the last few hours, hands on either side of the basin, staring at the clear surface within. 'Can you see anything?'

'Not yet.'

'But you've been looking for hours.'

Her eyelash began to flicker, like she had a tic. 'Sometimes it takes hours. Magic isn't always easy. Sometimes, we have to work for it.'

'But you usually scry with no problems. At least, you haven't had problems in the past.'

'No, I haven't. But then, I haven't been up against four powerful witches who are on guard against me.'

He didn't like her tone. 'You can hardly blame *me* for that.'

The tic got stronger. 'No? And who else should I blame?'

'Yourself.'

Her lashes stopped flickering, and then slowly, so slowly, she lifted her head to look at him.

In the past, that look would have sent him scrambling away in terror after apologising profusely for disturbing and upsetting her. But now he straightened and met her gaze. She might be older and know more spells, but she wasn't more powerful than him. Not anymore. Not now the Darkness whispered in his ear, directly to him, not just to her.

'*Don't let her talk to you like that.*'

He lifted his chin. 'You made me become a Shade. Made me force Eloise to bring me back with her blood.'

'I didn't make you do anything. You agreed with me.'

'*Did you? You tried to argue against her. Don't let her only tell her side of the story.*'

'I was afraid of you, so I would hardly call doing as you bid "agreement". We were hardly on equal ground then, were we?'

'And we're on equal ground now, are we?'

'Yes. Neither of us got what we wanted that night.'

Her brow cocked, fingers twitching next to the bowl. The water began to bubble. 'Really? The fact that you got an extra charge of power when your twin came into her own—that wasn't something that you wanted? You would never have that if not for me. I would think you would be grateful.'

'*She didn't give that to you. You got that for yourself.*'

He let a smile twist the side of his mouth. 'I am grateful, but it wasn't what you promised. Not even close. My sister was supposed to be with us now. Her full powers were supposed to be twined with mine, making me even more powerful.'

'Making *us* more powerful.'

He forced his lips into a pleasant smile. 'Yes. Us. But it didn't work, did it?'

Her lips twitched and the water in the bowl began to boil. 'Nothing worked as it should that night. How was I to know that your sister actually had a spine? That she'd fight you? She never gave any indication she would do that. There was no way I could have known she'd choose that moment to show what she'd never shown before.' She tilted her head to the side, eyes completely black now. 'She is *your* twin. *You* should have known. *You* should have guessed what might happen and told me.' Her fingers twitched and the bowl began to rotate, faster and faster, lifting off the table, the water bubbling over the side.

His pleasant smile turned into a sneer. 'That would be more impressive if I couldn't do this.' He flicked his finger.

The bowl exploded. Water flew into the air, shards of pottery flying everywhere, but before it could hit her, it turned into steam and the pottery itself turned into nothing but a blast of dirty sand that flew around her.

'Spectacular. You're both so powerful. More powerful when you let your anger rise. Even more powerful if you come together. Especially today at the height of Beltane.'

By the way Morghanna's eyes flickered, it was apparent that she now heard the Darkness too.

'What do you want us to do, Master?' Cain asked before she could take the lead.

'It is the night of the bright fires. Light the spark that's in you both. Use the power of this day to create something special between you. Allow it to augment what you still have from your twin. I promise that something will grow from the spark you ignite tonight that will help to give you both what you long for. You have always hungered for her. Reach out and take what has always been yours, my child, my brother, my father.'

He was surprised by the turn of the Darkness' thoughts, but he could feel the truth of what it had said rising, deep inside him.

And suddenly, he saw Morganna as he'd never seen her before.

Her hair lifted in the fae wind that whipped around her. Beautiful. She was beautiful. Sensual. Luminous with power.

She stopped, something coming over her face as her gaze raked over him too. A glow lit her eyes and she licked her lips. Then she moved towards him, hips swaying.

Fuck, she was hot. His gaze ran over her, wanting, needing; a need that was reflected in her expression, in her eyes as they returned to their usual colour, glittering with desire.

'Perhaps you did know your twin would do what she did.' She moved, oh so slowly, seductively, towards him. 'Perhaps you planned it that way, to allow her to get away, to allow her to fully tap into her powers to bring yours fully to the fore.' She stood before him now, lifted her hand and ran her finger along his chest. 'It's what I would have done.'

He could hardly think, but the Darkness whispered in his ears and he let them come out of his mouth, pushing her, provocative. 'Maybe I would have done that—if I'd known she had it in her. I didn't. She surprised us both.'

She bit her lip, her gaze flickering to his lips and back up to meet his gaze again. 'But still, you won something out of that night. What did I get, aside from disappointment and a rather nasty headache that took a week to subside?'

He hooked his arm behind her and pulled her flush against him. 'You got an equal partner, rather than an underling.'

She licked her lips, gaze roving down to his lips again. 'Did I?'

'Yes.'

'Then prove it.'

'I will.' The Darkness didn't have to say anything to let him know what he had to do. He felt it now, that driving need to take, to have, to spill himself inside her, creating something new. Something whole out of the disparate parts they'd become.

He pulled her closer and kissed her.

Her smile blossomed under his lips, her fingers clenched on his shoulders, then dragged up his neck to wind in his hair. She pulled the strands causing a little tantalising hit of pain that made his balls tighten, his cock flex. He wanted to give her a little taste of that back. Wanted to taste her. 'Open your mouth.'

'No.'

He bit her lip. She groaned. Opened to him. He thrust his tongue inside her mouth.

Her tongue met his, duelling, tasting, sucking, teeth nipping. Her hands left his hair, fingernails raking over his bare arms. They were sharp, tearing through his shirt, the little stings of pain driving the heated rage of desire inside him higher.

'*Yes. Yes. Take her. Make her yours. Bind her to you with your seed.*'

Yes. That's what he had to do. She seemed to want that too, one of her hands dropping to undo his jeans, shove inside and clench around his cock.

'Yes.'

He held her tighter, closer, rubbed his engorged cock in her hand as she pressed her breasts against his chest, nipples hard nubs through the silk of her shirt. He pulled his mouth from hers, hissing as she caught his lip between her teeth before letting go. He tasted blood.

She smiled, licking his blood from her mouth.

He ripped her shirt open, shoved her back against the table, and tore her bra away. 'Mine.' He took her nipple in his mouth, biting down like she'd bit him, tasted blood, lapped it up with his tongue.

She groaned.

He tore at the button on her jeans, shoved his hand down, spearing his fingers through damp curls and then deep inside her as he took her other breast in his mouth and bit down. She screamed, a scream of impassioned delight, jerking against him, riding his hand.

'Yes.'

The sound of her cry drove him higher, drove him on. He wanted to mark her more than he had. Wanted her to know that she was his, just like he was hers.

'Put your seed inside her.'

Yes.

Her nails scored down his back—his shirt was gone. He wasn't sure when. Didn't care. Except for the fact that there was still too much material between them. He muttered a spell and their clothing dissolved.

She looked down her body at him, a wicked smile on her face. 'Clever boy.'

'I'm a man, not a boy.'

The smile grew larger as her gaze dropped to his engorged cock. 'Mmm. That remains to be seen.' She ran a finger down his chest, towards the cock that ached for more than the touch of her hand.

'Shall I prove it to you, then?'

'If you can.'

He pushed her legs wide, pulled her forward on the table and thrust inside her. She arched off the table, head thrown back, breasts high, nipples extended, mouth open on a silent gasp. She was wet. So wet. Wet for him, her body pulsing around him, begging for more. He thrust again.

'Yes,' she gasped. 'More.'

He thrust again, again, harder and harder. She rose up, legs gripped tight around him, hands in his hair, pulling, her lips at his neck, licking, sucking, nipping. Fuck! He was going to come if she didn't stop doing that and he didn't want to do that yet.

'Use your magic to maintain control. Twine it with hers.'

His magic was already rising through his skin so it was nothing to bring it forth and make it do what the Darkness bid.

Morrigan gasped as his power stroked over hers. 'Oh, don't stop. Don't stop.'

He shoved her back on the table, hard. She laughed up at him, breasts bouncing with the movement. He shoved into her, harder, harder, took her breast in his mouth, lathing the pebbled nipple, nipping it between his teeth, sucking. He speared his fingers into her wet curls again while pounding into her and began to rub his thumb against the nub of her clitoris.

'I love a man who can multitask,' she gasped.

The gasp turned into a scream as he worked her harder, faster, taking her higher, higher. Their power sizzled and crackled around them, making the joining stronger, deeper, special in a way he'd never experienced before and he was pretty certain she'd never experienced either going by the way she looked at him.

Her back arched, her skin slick. As was his. She panted, gasped, whimpered, as he worked her body with everything he had in him. She was his. She was his. And he was making a connection between them that would never fade. That would grow and develop inside her body, and when it came forth, it would be his to mould in any way he saw fit, in a way his twin could never have been his to mould, and it would never leave him. Not like the others had. Not like he knew

Morrigan eventually would despite what he was about to build between them, for them.

He was giving her a gift, and she would give one back to him. One the Darkness promised.

He would never be alone again.

'Yes, yes.'

'More. More.'

'Mine. Mine.'

The words—the Darkness', Morrigan's, his—wove around him, around them, binding them to each other, sinking into their skin. They rose above the table, hanging in the air, their power twining and spinning around them, a physical extension of their passion, their connection.

Then Morrigan clenched, her body arching high against him, almost pushing him off her.

But he held on, driving into her one last time, seated as deep as he could get. His cry met hers. Lifted, rising to the ceiling, making the world tremble.

Her body clenched around him as he came, milking him of his precious seed. And it kept coming and coming, rising with their cry, a magical incantation, sealing the promise of their binding, of what was to come, into their skin, their very souls. A binding that would never let them go until they'd seen it to its very end.

'At last!'

The Darkness' cry joined theirs and drove him into oblivion.

10

'Cain!' Eloise came out of her seat, the sound of smashing crockery and clang of cutlery a distant noise.

'Eloise? Eloise? What's wrong?' Hands ran up to her shoulders, cupped her face. Lips touched hers. A touch she knew. Wanted. Warmth chased the chill away and she leaned into the kiss, returning it.

There was a groan and then the lips pulled from hers. 'Eloise? Talk to me, Little Bird.' She blinked, her vision clearing to focus on the handsome male before her. 'Iain.' The smile bloomed, automatically, on her face.

His lips—those full lips she adored, the lips she wanted back on hers—didn't form into an answering smile but remained in a serious line. As serious as the frown between his brow.

She reached up, rubbed at that frown with her thumb. 'Why are you frowning?'

'Oh, I don't know. Maybe because you leapt from your chair, dropped your plate on the floor and cried out, "Cain".'

'I did?'

'Yes. And then you wouldn't answer me when I asked what was wrong.'

'So you kissed me.'

'It always worked in the past to bring you back when Bridgette took you over.'

'Bridgette isn't here.' He looked questioningly at her. 'Well, she is, but no more than usual. You know.'

He did know. He felt Malcolm inside him—the past presence that had been Bridgette Colliere's soulmate, tying his soul and Bridgette's together from that time for eternity. Those souls had been reborn inside Iain and Eloise and had helped them to come together.

Although, those past presences weren't the only thing that had drawn them to each other. Even without Malcolm and Bridgette inside them, Eloise and Iain would have chosen each other. Choice was always the most important thing in a mating. And while the past presences still made themselves felt on occasion, today wasn't one of those times.

Iain drew in a breath, careful, measured. 'Okay. Then what happened?'

'I don't know.' Eloise frowned. She was light-headed. And there was something there in the back of her mind. Something that made her nervous, nauseated. 'I think I need to sit down.'

He led her over to the couch and sat beside her, not letting go of her hands. 'Better?'

She swallowed. 'Yep.'

'Liar.'

She smiled at him. 'Maybe. A little.' She rubbed at his frown again. 'I don't like you worrying.'

'I know. But worrying is warranted when you scream your brother's name and fade out for a moment.'

'Right.' She'd screamed her brother's name. Why? Images swirled in her mind, but she couldn't grab a hold of them, just knew they made her feel edgy, sick. 'I felt something.'

Iain stroked her trembling hand. 'I thought you'd broken the link with him.'

She shook her head slowly. 'I thought I did too. But maybe that was just a surface link, created by Morrigan and the Darkness, and when I rejected them, I broke the link they were using to control me and my powers. But he is my twin. We've probably got a deeper bond that can't be truly broken.' Her frown deepened. 'I've been having flashes of him ever since that night; a sense that he was there still.'

'Why didn't you say something?'

She shrugged. 'At first I thought maybe it was like phantom-limb syndrome. But then when I realised it might be more, there seemed to be nothing worth worrying over. I never saw anything that could help and he never spoke to me; never even tried. His attention hasn't even been turned my way—at least, that's what it felt like. The connection was one sided, me seeing him, not the other way around. Maybe it was my power letting me do it, or just the twin bond that was still important to me, but not important to him.' Her voice hitched, the pain of that acknowledgement a deep cut in her heart.

Her mate just continued to stroke her hair, her cheek, down her arm, giving her time to pull herself together. She loved that he knew her so well. She tried to concentrate on the images swirling in her mind. 'I can't really see him. It's like a damaged film, the images flickering and distorted. I can't make sense of them.'

'But you must have seen something. Enough to make you shout his name and drop what you were doing.'

'Yes.' She rubbed her chest. There was pain there, like she hadn't taken a breath in too long. And she still felt nauseated. 'He was with Morrigan. He was angry. I could see that much. And then it changed and ...' She swallowed hard against the bile in her throat.

'What did you see?'

'I think ...' Her face screwed up. 'I think they were having sex.'

'Ew.' He rubbed her arms. 'I'm sorry you had to see that.'

'It was only a flash. I might have got it completely wrong. Sex was never part of their relationship before. It was more mother and son.'

'They could have been doing some ritual.'

She shook her head. 'I don't think so. But whatever it was, it didn't feel good.'

'When is it ever good where he's concerned?' He hugged her to him. 'I can understand why you dropped your plate and cried out.

Seeing your brother have sex with Morrigan.' He shuddered. 'I'm surprised you didn't lose your breakfast.'

He was trying to make her smile, but the more she thought about what she'd seen, what she felt, the less she felt like laughing. She pulled away. 'No.'

'Eloise? What is it?'

'I don't know.' She rubbed her chest harder. She really felt like she couldn't breathe. 'This is different from what I've felt before. He was always still himself, tinged with the Darkness. But now ...' She gasped, her hands clutching at him as she realised what she'd felt, what she'd seen, the reason for the horrible ache in her chest. 'He's given himself over to it. All of himself.' Tears began to pour down her face. 'He's gone. He's gone. My brother is gone.'

The sobs tore out of her as Iain pulled her into his arms, hands running over her hair, down her back, in long soothing strokes. 'I'm so sorry, Eloise. I'm so sorry.'

He let her cry herself out, his hand constantly stroking, the warmth of him spilling into her slowly, not ridding her of the cold ache of grief, but making it feel a little less chilling.

She thought she'd come to terms with what Cain had chosen, what he'd done, the fact that he was now her enemy. But obviously, in some part of her mind, she'd held onto hope; had denied that she'd felt this final change begin the night she fully mated with Iain.

Now that hope was gone. Cain was gone. Completely subsumed by the Darkness.

Her mate pulled back a little, enough to wipe the tears from her cheeks, kiss her forehead. 'Your loss will lessen with time.'

'I know. This ... it's not grief. Not really. It's the shock of what he's done. It's worse than when he made himself a Shade at Morrigan's behest. He was dangerous before—now he's worse. So much worse. He's evil now. Truly evil.' She pushed to her feet. 'We have to go tell the others. We have to prepare.'

'We're always prepared, ever since Morrigan came after us.'

'No, this is different. He is so much worse than Morrigan. She is fuelled by revenge. That can be overcome. But what Cain is now … it won't stop. Ever. Until it gets what it wants.'

'We've defeated the Darkness before. Bron expelled it from River. You pushed it out of yourself and broke its connection with you on Oestra. We can fight it again.'

She gripped his arms, fingernails digging in. 'No. You don't understand. What I felt in Cain, it's so much more powerful than anything we've gone up against before. Those were just small parts. Bits of the thing that Bridgette repeatedly expelled from the Were all those centuries ago. This is like … this is like it's becoming again what it once was. And it's not content with just taking over Cain completely, taking him from me forever.' Her gaze clashed with Iain's. 'It wants us all. And tonight, it's done something that will help it reach its goal.'

His throat moved convulsively as he took in what she said. 'Then we need to find out what that is.'

'How?'

'I don't know.'

'Should we look in the diaries?'

He rubbed his thumb against his chin. 'No. Shelley and others are taking care of that. I think we need to look at this from a different angle. I think we've overlooked a major piece of the puzzle.'

'What?'

'You.' He cupped her face, the warmth of his hand and his gaze chasing away the chill his words brought on. 'You are the Nexus. We've been looking into what that might mean, but we haven't looked at why.'

'Why?'

'Why you. Where did that power come from? Are you the only one in your family with this power, or were there others? And why did Morrigan and the Darkness target you and your family and steal you from them?'

'But how will we find any of that out?'

'We need to find out what happened to your family, who they were, where they came from. We might find the answers we need.'

'Or we might find nothing. Morrigan most likely murdered all my family when she took me and Cain.'

'We don't know that,' he said, cupping her chin. 'But I think it's important we find out for certain.'

She'd always wanted to know who her people were, where she came from, learn about her shifter heritage from those with blood ties to her. But now the thought that she would actually get the answers seemed one of the most frightening things she'd ever faced. 'I'm scared.'

'I know.' He kissed her, a soft kiss, full of love, support and encouragement.

It reminded her who she was now, not who she'd been. She was the only one who could tame the restless heart of a Lone Wolf, the only one who could add a fourth dimension to the powers of the triumvirate that was the McVale Coven—whatever that meant. They still didn't know. What she did know was her being here had strengthened the bonds in the pack in ways they were still discovering. She made them stronger.

She was the Nexus. And she must face her past to face her future. 'Let's do it.'

'That's my girl.' Iain kissed her again.

'Possessive Were,' she gasped when he finally pulled back from the toe-curling kiss.

'Damn right.' His smile made her insides flip in delight. 'You are mine. Just like I am yours.'

'Damn right,' she said, swinging her leg over his to face him, chest to chest, holding his face between her touch-needy hands, giving him back his possessive kiss.

A cough came from behind her. She didn't stop kissing her mate —she wasn't finished, and whoever it was could just damn well wait.

'Sorry for interrupting, bro, but you called?'

She gave Iain one more kiss and pulled away. 'You called Patrick?' she asked her mate.

'Yes.'

'I didn't hear it.' She heard a lot of his internal communications with the other soldiers in the pack now she was mated to him—it had become a constant flutter in the back of her mind, one she mostly was able to ignore unless they were swapping insults with each other.

Then it was kind of fun to listen in.

'I didn't want to interrupt your revelation, so I sent to him on the Alpha link.'

Ahh, that explained it. She couldn't hear that link unless they wanted her to. She knew it was the same for Skye and Bron—they'd chatted about the difficulties of being mated to a strong Were Alpha and his lieutenants many times over the past few weeks since she'd mated with Iain. Especially when they video messaged with her to chat about the mating ceremony they planned for her and Iain. She'd never had a sister, or even a close female friend, so it had been eye opening, but something she'd come to rely on.

She shifted off Iain's lap, holding onto his hand as she faced his brother. 'How are you, Patrick?'

'Not as good as you two, apparently, but pretty okay.'

She didn't blush as she would have a few months ago but gave him a cheeky grin. 'So I hear from the pack females.'

His brow rose. 'Is that so?'

'Okay, okay, enough preening,' Iain said, gesturing for his brother to take a seat. 'I asked you here because we need your mad computer skills.'

'He's got mad computer skills too?'

'Don't make his head bigger than it needs to be, Little Bird,' Iain said, squeezing her hand. 'But yes, given Patrick is our Lore Keeper and Librarian, he's pretty good with a search engine. I thought he could help us look into your past. And it seems more pertinent now than ever before.'

'What's happened?' Patrick asked, looking between them.

Iain filled him in on what Eloise had felt, her suspicions about Cain. 'I told Jason via the Alpha link. He wants us to go up there and discuss what we mean to do next.'

'What are we going to do next?'

Iain stared at his brother. 'Well, that kind of depends on what you've found out so far.'

'You've already started looking?' Eloise's stomach swirled and then sank through the couch as she turned to Iain. 'I thought you'd asked him here to help us look.'

He stroked the back of her hand with his thumb. 'I haven't asked him yet.' He angled a brow at his brother. 'Although, knowing my bro, I knew he couldn't possibly help himself trying to find some information that might help a member of the family.'

Patrick chuckled. 'You know me well. I started looking as soon as you mated.'

Eloise swallowed hard and leaned forward, intent on Patrick, trying to tamp down the hope building in her chest. She couldn't read anything on his face. 'Have you found something?'

He blew out a quick breath, elbows on knees, hands clasped together. 'Okay. Based on what you knew of time-lines and where you were when you ended up with Morrigan and her coven,' he began, 'I started to search for any information about missing children or suspicious deaths in that time and area. There were a few deaths that matched the criteria.'

'How?'

'The deaths weren't explained.'

'That could be said for many deaths.'

'Yes, except these had something about them that was familiar to me.' He paused for a moment, his gaze capturing his brother's, sending some message that Eloise couldn't figure out, but that Iain nodded to. Patrick focused on her again. 'These people were found dead, each one with a black hole in their chest.'

'Warlock lightning. Like with Adam and Marcus?'

'Yes.'

'You said there were a few? Were they a group, like a pack?' What if Morrigan had slaughtered her entire pack of shifters to get to her and Cain?

'I don't think so. I extended the search when I noticed a pattern. They were spread across the country, hundreds of miles apart. All unsolved murders. Each of them with a black hole in their chests.'

'Perhaps Morrigan was busy with finding more than Eloise and her brother.'

'Maybe. But I don't think so,' Patrick said, steepling his hands under his chin. 'There was a pattern to them. A stream of deaths that started in the January of one year and ended in the January of the next.'

'My birthday is in January.'

'Yes.' Patrick swallowed, his mouth tense. 'And they all happened along the major river systems in the different states.'

Iain let out a breath. 'She was tracking down shifter packs.'

'That's what I think.'

'How do you know that?' she asked, every muscle aching, trembling.

'Shifters tend to live by rivers and streams. Or the ocean. They like the water. They usually buy up farm land somewhere near running water.'

'Oh.' She hadn't known that. Iain's hands stilled hers on her lap— she'd been picking at the edges of her nails again as she'd been listening to Patrick.

'Why did she stop?'

Patrick looked at her, his deep brown eyes more serious than she'd ever seen them.

'She found what she wanted.'

'Me and Cain.'

'I think so.'

'All that death because of us?'

Iain cupped her chin, gaze meeting hers. 'No. Not because of you. Because of Morrigan. Don't take those deaths on your shoulders. The responsibility for them is not yours to bear, do you hear me?'

'You're right.' Anger flared through her at the thought of what Morrigan had done to find her. 'She has to pay for everything she's done.'

'Bloody oath she does.'

Both men spoke together, their voices a vow that tapped her anger, gave it a direction to flow in.

'How did she know about us? How did she know I was the Nexus?'

'That I don't know.'

'Is there something we can do to find out?'

'Shelley might be able to,' Patrick suggested.

'The diaries?' Iain asked.

'No. The spirits. There's all those ancient witches and warlocks that follow her around. They might know something of why Morrigan went searching for you. If there was a portent of some kind, they were bound to feel it on the astral plane.'

Eloise stood. 'Then let's go find Shelley.'

They headed to the door, but Eloise stopped as Iain opened the door and looked back at the tall Were behind her. 'Did any of my shifter pack survive Morrigan?'

'From what I found out, one woman survived the attacks.'

'I want to see her.'

Patrick's eyes filled with sadness. 'That might prove difficult.'

'Why? Did she die?'

'No. But from what I discovered, she's in a hospice. She's been in a coma ever since that night. With a wound in her chest just like Adam's.'

'That was twenty-four years ago!' she said, the horror in her tone making her voice rasp.

'Yes.'

'Have you told Jason and Bron?'

Patrick's gaze flickered to Iain's. 'No. I only got the message just before you called me.'

Eloise felt suddenly sick. If Adam was trapped like that in his body, his wolf howling and in pain, year after year ... 'The Darkness has to pay.'

'Yes, it does,' Iain and Patrick snarled together.

'Let's go find Shelley. Hopefully she can start us in the right direction.'

She led the men out the door and by the time she'd got to the car, Iain had ascertained that Shelley was at the Packhouse going over the diaries. It would take only a few minutes to drive there.

For Eloise, it was a few minutes too long.

11

'This can't be right. It just can't be.'

Shelley turned to another diary, one that was equally ancient, and thought the same question she'd asked about the Trickster when she'd opened the other ones. The pages flickered, the breeze of their movement fluttering her fringe, and then the pages stopped. The words swirled as hidden entries came to the fore. When they settled on the page, she bent over and read what the ancient witch had said.

Sept 1st: Uain Trickster has become weaker as his Yolanda improved. I noted a change in her aura, a wildness that had never appeared before. What my mother had been afraid of is likely true: Uain will pass beyond the veil and Yolanda will live. He is giving her his life energy. I have tried to stop him, yet he will not listen.

Sept 5th: I tried to bind him yesterday, however his empathy pathways are strong and have already found another path around my spells. I managed to slow the fading, but I could not stop it. From my reckoning, he has but a few days left. I do not know what else to do.

Sept 8th: Uain Trickster passed into the light of the Goddess yesterday. I have bound Yolanda to myself and the pack even tighter to stop her from following her mate into the veil. If only she and Uain had borne children, this task would be easier.

Sept 9th: I have written to Katelyn asking for parlay with the other Covens in the area. If what I have seen here has occurred elsewhere, it may be that we have created a problem in binding Coven and Pack that was never intended, for one thing is certain, Tricksters never gave of themselves in this way before the Pact. If I am correct—and I hope to the Goddess I am wrong—we have to find some way of stopping the Tricksters from using their empathy in this way. They are needed in the Pack. They cannot be allowed to falter and fail.

Shelley finished the section and rubbed her brow. 'But why would he do that? Why are you showing me this?'

The pages fluttered and flickered open to another entry. One on mating. Her heart lurched. Then anger burned in her chest. 'You don't know anything!' she shouted at the diaries. 'This wouldn't happen. Not now.'

The pages flickered again, flipping between the entry about Uain and Yolanda and the one on mating. Her aunt's words reverberated in her mind.

She slammed the diary shut and glowered at it. 'Why the fuck are you showing me this? I want to know how to heal him, not how to mate him.'

'Mate who?'

She jumped at the voice behind her. 'Bloody hell, Adam. Warn a girl before you appear behind her.'

He laughed. 'It's more fun this way.'

'Of course you'd think that.' She swung around in her chair and glared at him. 'Where have you been?'

'Why? Did you miss me?'

'Of course not,' she lied and swung back around to face the table before he could see the lie in her eyes, her face.

He chuckled, a soft sound that slid up her spine. 'I went back to look for the woman again as you suggested. So far no luck.'

'I wonder why she hasn't been back.'

'Well, that is the question, isn't it?'

'Hmm.'

He propped himself on the table beside her, his leg too close to her arm, his presence like static electricity chasing across her skin. She shifted, hiding the action by reaching to pull another diary across the table. It was a truly ancient one that smelled of dust and the sharpness of the herbs used, alongside magic, to preserve the parchment. She pulled cotton gloves on so as not to get the oils from her hands on the pages, and then opened it.

Adam slid off the table, turned and leaned over her, his stomach brushing against her shoulder, his hand coming down beside hers. 'What do you have there?'

She managed not to flinch at his accidental touch, gritted her teeth, wishing he'd move away. It wasn't fair that even in this form he could make her feel like this.

He leaned closer. 'This one looks really old.'

'It is.' She flipped a page, trying to think of a question, unable to think of anything but him.

'Whose diary is it? What does it say?'

'I don't know. You're in my light.'

'I'm see-through. How can I be in your light?'

'You're hardly see-through.'

'I don't cast a shadow.'

'Then you're standing too close.'

'Am I?'

She tried not to move, to concentrate on the words on the page before her, but they blurred and it was no use, she had to look up. He was smiling, damn him, as if he knew exactly how he affected her. 'Yes,' she whispered. 'You are.'

He moved closer, like he intended to kiss her. Her gaze flickered to his mouth, to his eyes, then back to his mouth. His smiling, sexy mouth. She licked her lips. Shit! Had she just made a little moaning sound? Had she moved closer to him? Or had he moved closer to her?

If he didn't kiss her soon, she was going to turn into a puddle. Her hand moved without her willing volition, reaching up to touch the cold not-quite-thereness of his skin. The sensation was like a slap.

She jerked away, turning to stare out the window. What the hell was she doing? She couldn't encourage him. Shouldn't. No matter how much she longed for it. Even if he was back in his body, it was more impossible than ever before. If what she had just read was true —and she was terribly afraid it was—allowing anything to happen with Adam would end up killing them both.

Words whispered in her head, her aunt's crazed whisper, and she knew it was true. She'd been shown in too many ways to ignore it.

Her love equalled death for him.

'Earth to Shelley?' A hand waved in front of her eyes and she blinked. 'Are you there Shelley?'

She swatted at his hand and growled. 'Of course I'm here. It's you who isn't here.'

'Well, that's just ghostist.'

'What?'

'I said that's ghostist.'

'What the hell is that?'

He smiled as he stared down at her, arms crossed over his chest. She almost sighed with relief that he'd taken a step back and was no longer touching her. 'It's racism against ghosts because we're disembodied.'

'That's ridiculous. You're ridiculous.' She turned back to the diary in front of her and thought a question at it. Words swirled on the page.

'I love it when it does that for you.'

She smiled lightly. 'I do too. It's like the TARDIS.'

'Yep. Bigger on the inside and changing itself to the needs of the individual Doctor. Or in this case, witch.'

She grinned up at him. 'It's nice that you get my Doctor Who references.'

'I didn't before I became this. But given you're addicted and I've been hanging around you the most, I've learned an appreciation.'

'Glad I could give you a proper education.'

'So, what question did you ask it?'

She returned her attention to the diary. 'I wanted to know how warlock lightning was first created.'

'Ooh. What does it say?' He leaned over her again, close, so close, and began to read with her.

The hairs on the back of her neck stood up. His breath—how did he have breath when he didn't have a body?—brushed over her arm, bringing tingles and heat chasing over her. The words swam in front of her eyes, the ancient scrawl harder than usual to read.

Fuckitydoo-da! Concentrate, Shelley. It's really not that hard. She rubbed her eyes and forced herself to ignore his presence and to concentrate on the words in front of her.

'Did you know that when you're lost in concentration, your brow furrows in the most endearing crease right here.' He touched a spot between his eyes.

She jerked back. 'Everyone's brows furrow there.'

'Not like yours does.' He cocked his head. 'It's different on you. It's also pretty endearing that you mouth the words you're reading.'

'You're supposed to be reading the text yourself, not me. And besides, I do not mouth what I'm reading!' She used to do that, right from when she was young, through school and university, but she'd worked really hard to stop when she was going out with Charlie, her arsehole ex-fiancé, because he'd found it annoying and distracting and childlike.

His lips tipped up in that infuriating shit-eating grin again. 'You do. So cute. And fun to watch. I'm trying to see how well I can read lips. I think I'm getting it most of the time—although that last section I'm pretty sure was wrong. I don't think Bridgette Colliere would have written about spanking her play with no dildos where man can do one as he anchored her soup porcupine.' She suppressed a laugh as he looked down at the words on the page and read out loud the sentence she'd just been reading. 'Astral travelling is best done in a Spartan place with no distractions so Malcolm may anchor my soul properly.' He looked up at her. 'Nope. Not even close.'

His lips were twitching and she couldn't help it. She burst out laughing.

'What?' he asked, lifting his hands, all innocence.

'You are the most ridiculous man I have ever met.'

'I made you laugh. That has to be at least one up for me, especially given that I'm not even truly here.'

Her laughter died, the reminder of his situation a slap in the face. 'Yes. It is.' She wished he wouldn't be so jolly about it. Wished he didn't make her laugh and feel like this whole thing was normal. If normal was Melbourne, then this was somewhere in far north Siberia. He was supposed to be here, in body, not just in spirit, so she could lean over and slap him when he annoyed her too much; jab him in his ribs when he was being overprotectingly stupid; reach up, pull his head down and kiss him if she goddamned wanted to kiss him. Even though she knew she shouldn't, couldn't. It could lead to nothing. Would just be a torment to both of them.

Tears pricked her eyes. 'Shit!' She threw her pen down and surged up from the table, tripping over her chair in her urgency to get away.

But she didn't hit the ground because he caught her.

As it always was, his touch was icy and was accompanied by the strange burn that ran through her limbs, making her hot and shivery. So familiar—too familiar—its power muted and yet filling her with such need.

She gasped, gaze jerking to his.

He had his arms wrapped around her, bent over, almost as if they were performing a wild dip in a sexy dance. Slowly, ever so slowly, he straightened, taking her with him. Her body slid against his, aligning breast to chest, hips to hip as they returned to an upright position. She was tall, but he was taller—the first man to make her feel dainty, protected, womanly, and not like some overgrown Amazon. She hated it and cherished it all at once.

He turned her inside out. How did he do that? She had no idea, but around him she was never certain about her feelings. And for someone who was always so certain about things, it was unnerving. She didn't like it.

So why did she keep seeking him out, going back for more? Even now when she was certain there was no point, she wanted him.

She must be some kind of masochist. Huh. Her aunt Lilyanna, before she went insane, used to say you learned something new about yourself every day. She'd thought that was rubbish. She'd seen a documentary when she was younger—*Seven Up!* it was called—where a filmmaker had interviewed children about their futures, based on the Jesuit motto of 'Give me a child until he is seven and I will show you the man'. She related to that series and had seen nothing in her life to indicate the premise wasn't true. Her gift had frightened her when she was seven and she'd vowed to not let it rule her life. That ideal had set her on her path. There was nothing new to learn. She was who she was going to be.

At least, she had been until she'd met Adam and Jason and their pack and they'd turned her life, and the lives of her friends, upside down. Bron and Skye were happy with the turmoil. But she couldn't be. The only certainty in this new life was that what Lilyanna had said was being proved right. She *was* learning something new about herself every day and it frightened the life out of her. Especially now those other words whispered by her aunt on the night she'd taken her life had new, meaningful significance.

'You okay?' Adam asked as he settled her back on her feet, not letting her go.

'Yes.' She licked her lips. His gaze slid to watch the movement. Her mouth dried. Her lungs burned. Breathe. She had to breathe. She opened her lips to take in a breath, her tongue darting out again to wet them.

He groaned, his fingers flexing on her back. 'Damn,' he whispered and lowered his head to hers.

'Shelley? Shelley! Are you in here?'

She leapt out of Adam's arms just as Eloise, Iain and Patrick came into the room. She stumbled over her still overturned chair and would have landed on the floor if Patrick hadn't caught her this time.

His touch didn't burn like Adam's. Her breath didn't catch in her throat as he held her close. Her heart didn't bang in her chest as his hands steadied her. Their eyes met but her mouth didn't dry, her words of thanks making it out clear and steady. Not for one moment did she long with everything in her for him to kiss her.

Damn, damn, damn, damn, damn!

'Are you okay?' Patrick asked as he let her go.

She forced a smile before turning to right the chair she'd knocked over. 'Yep. I'm fine. Just a clumsy clot today.'

'Did we startle you?'

'No. Not at all.' She brushed her hands down the front of her soft woollen jumper and plastered an even bigger smile on her face when what she really wanted to do was slink off into a dark corner and lick her wounds. Or tell them to piss off so she could kiss Adam.

She ran her hand through her hair, noticed her ponytail was askew, pulled out the band with a yank—the pain a kind of sharp relief—and pulled her hair back tight into the ponytail again, fluffing her fringe.

'What were you doing?'

'Reading the diaries.'

'From over there?' Eloise pointed to where she'd been standing when they entered the room a few paces from the table. Adam stood on the other side of the table, a troubled frown on his face as he stared at her. She shook her head at him, desperate for him to understand that she didn't want him to say a thing. If he spoke, she would lose her shit. And right now, she so desperately needed to keep a hold of her shit. It was the only thing she had any control over—however tentatively.

Thankfully, he seemed to understand. At least, he kept his mouth shut.

She turned her back on him so she didn't have to see the question in his eyes. It hurt to think what that question might mean.

She swallowed hard. 'Did you come to see me?'

'Yes.' Eloise gave her a considering look, but thankfully didn't press her. 'Actually, we came to ask you a favour.'

'Step into my parlour,' she said, trying to keep it light. None of them laughed. Or smiled. They just kept frowning at her. No wonder really. She *was* acting weird. She had to stop it. Blowing out a breath, she said, 'Sorry. I've been so lost in the diaries, I'm afraid I'm not quite myself. Take a seat and tell me what you need.'

'Perhaps you need a sleep first.'

'And some food.'

She rolled her eyes at Iain and Patrick. 'Why are the men in this pack always so certain sleep and food will fix everything?'

Eloise smiled at her. 'Because it does for them. And it makes them happy.' She patted Iain's arm. 'They're simple creatures.'

Iain snorted. 'Simple my arse.'

'No. Your arse isn't simple, I agree with that. It's delectable.'

Patrick laughed as Iain grabbed Eloise and kissed her breathless.

Shelley looked away and right into Adam's eyes. 'Sorry,' he mouthed.

She closed her eyes. She couldn't take his apologies right now. She didn't want them. She wanted ... Well, she wasn't quite certain what she wanted anymore. Tears prickled behind her eyes again. Damn. She pressed her fingers against her closed lids and breathed steadily until the sensation passed. When she opened her eyes, Eloise, Iain and Patrick were all staring at her. 'My eyes are sore. Damned hay fever. Anyway, where were we?'

12

They all took a seat around the table and Iain told her about his ideas surrounding Eloise and finding out about her past to understand what role she played and how it affected all of them.

'That makes sense. But I don't see how I can help with that. I'm already poring through the diaries trying to find out information about Skye, Bron and my powers and how we fit and work in the pack. I'm also looking for information on warlock lightning and how to heal it as well as discovering if there's anything about the Trickster that might help us in healing Adam. Oh, and I'm also trying to find out information on different kinds of spirit entities.'

'Why are you doing that?' Patrick asked.

'What?'

'Why are you trying to find information about different forms of spirits? I'd imagine there's only one.'

Fuckity-shit, she'd almost given away the truth about Adam. Although she supposed she'd have to tell everyone soon.

'What about Shades?' Eloise said. 'They're a kind of spirit entity and you didn't really know about them until Cain became one and I told you what I know, which isn't much. It would make sense for Shelley to try to find out more information on them too.'

Shelley pounced on Eloise's words like a drowning man on a life buoy. 'Yes. And then I thought, if there are Shades and we don't know about them, what else is out there that we don't know about?'

Eloise nodded. 'Makes sense to me.'

Shelley nodded. 'So, I'm not sure I can look for anything else while looking for all that, but if you've got something to keep my eye out for, I'll try.'

'No. We don't want you to look up anything else.' Iain gestured at the mess of diaries spread out over the table. 'You've got your hands full with that. Too full, perhaps.'

'I can manage.' She crossed her arms, straightening in her chair. 'So why do you need me then?' A prickle ran over her back—she was afraid to find out what they were going to ask of her.

'Well ...' Patrick paused, gaze darting to Iain.

'We need you to speak with Adeline and the other elder spirits.' Before she had a chance to respond, he held up his hand and rushed on. 'Eloise thinks that Cain has been completely taken over by the Darkness. Not like before when it was just influencing him. It's gone into him. Become him.' He looked over at Eloise.

She nodded. 'There is no more Cain.'

'It's like when Morrigan took over Skye's grandmother's body,' Patrick added. 'But worse.'

Shelley nodded. 'It makes sense.'

'It does?' Patrick said.

'Yes. Of course. The Darkness wouldn't be content with only being partly in control of people, of influencing them in bits and pieces. It wants to be in the world. More than it ever was before.'

'What are you talking about?' Eloise's eyes were large, and despite her questions, Shelley knew the shifter-witch had an inkling of what she'd realised weeks ago.

'The Darkness somehow got into the Were people centuries ago. It influenced them, changed them, kept their two sides separated in the cruellest way and turned them into savage beasts every full moon to do its bidding. It might have been content to continue down that path, but then Bridgette Colliere forced it out of the Were, made them whole again, and after those first few rocky years, managed to keep them too filled with power from the light for the Darkness to be able to slip back in.

'It was lost, alone, searching for a way back into the world. It found Morrigan—we know that much. But while it could use her to create havoc and sow the seeds of violence and division, it didn't have control over her like it did over the Were. It's not so ... personal. I always wondered why Morrigan has come after us like she has, and then it dawned on me it's because the Darkness wants back in.'

'No. Morrigan wants revenge,' Patrick said. 'That's why she's come after us.'

'Yeah, that's her reason, but it's not the Darkness'. It wants her to corrupt the Were, to break the flow of power between the covens and the Were so it can be a part of them again, to rule them like it once did. I mean, it's not like this is new to you. It's been trying to get back in ever since it was ousted.'

They were staring at her like they had no idea what she was talking about. She gestured at the diaries. 'It's mentioned here about its attempts in the first dozen or so years of the Pact. They thwarted it back then just like we've thwarted its plan three times now.'

'Three times?' Eloise asked.

'Yeah. First when Skye and Bron and I joined and brought her power forth to fight it in that cave. Skye and River lived, and in doing so, cut off the Darkness' path back into the Were. Then it focused again on River, having managed to get a foothold inside him when he was younger but couldn't utilise that because River and Skye's grandparents blocked his wolf. Thankfully, with your help, Eloise, Bron was able to help River fight it off and expel the bit of Darkness that had infected him once more. And then when he was mated to Bron, it meant that River was no longer its conduit into the Were.'

Iain and Patrick stared at her. How had they not thought of all this before?

'Most people don't see things as deeply as you do, Kitten.' She jumped at Adam's voice close behind her. It took everything in her not to respond verbally—although she really wanted to. How was it he could read her so well? She needed to find out so she could stop doing whatever it was—it was aggravating.

'Go on,' Eloise urged. 'What about me and Cain? How do we figure into its plan?'

She shrugged. 'This is only supposition, but I think it probably sought to use your power to make itself whole. But when you fought Cain at Oestra and expelled that bit of Darkness that had melded with Bridgette's soul centuries ago, mating with Iain and the pack to give yourself the strength you needed to do what Bridgette couldn't, things changed. You chose to bind yourself to the power of the light, expelling anything of the dark. It had no way of using you to make itself whole or even to get back inside the Were.'

'Why do you think that?'

'Well, from what we've discovered, your power ties into those elements of nature centred around creation and rebirth, so it makes sense it wanted to use you to make itself whole again—to be reborn into itself. Centuries ago, when it went into the Were, it split into countless pieces as it tried to influence as many beings as it could, but once expelled, it never fully managed to meld back together again into a whole, stronger entity.'

'How do you know? Do the diaries say that?' Patrick asked, pulling one towards him.

'No. Not as such. It's just ... if it had managed to make itself whole, I think it would have managed to do a lot more damage than it has, don't you? I don't think it would need to use Morrigan or Cain or any of us to do whatever it plans.'

'Good point,' Iain said.

'Of course it's a good point,' Adam said, crossing his arms over his chest.

Shelley ignored him, frowning down at the diary in front of her. 'I'm just spinning suppositions here, but I don't think it can put itself back together; at least, not without significant help.' She looked up at

Eloise. 'That's why it needs you. It's the only way it can get back to what it once was.'

'You're right,' Eloise said wonderingly. 'Oh my Goddess, you're right.'

'What about Adam's wound? We know it's black magic, but what if it's also a conduit for the Darkness?'

Something about Patrick's question rang a bell in Shelley's mind. Standing abruptly, she hurried around the table and opened an old chest pushed against one wall. Reverently, she reached inside and pulled out one of the grimoires stored there and returned to the table.

The binding crackled. She straightened her gloves and picked up the tweezers. The pages—animal skins scraped so thin she could almost see the shadow of her hand through them if she held it up to the light, turned with a soft shushing sound without her even touching them, falling open to the page she remembered. The crackle of magic prickled her skin. She scanned the page. 'I gave this a cursory look last year when I first started researching the diaries.'

'What is it? It looks older than the diaries,' Iain said.

'That's because it is. It's the Colliere Grimoire, one Bridgette had added to. It's mostly made up of spells and information particular to her coven but not necessarily the pack, which is why I've not looked at it deeply. I thought the diaries would hold more information to help us learn about our powers and how they relate to the pack. Much of what's in here relates to a time before the pact was made.'

'I can't read any of that,' Patrick said as he leaned beside her. 'It's more jumbled than some of the entries in the diaries.'

She looked up at him. 'Yes. It's more heavily spelled than the diaries so that only those with witch- or warlock-like power can read it.' She glanced over at Adam, horribly aware that his ability to read from the diaries and grimoires was even more proof of what she'd discovered about the Trickster genes.

'If you didn't really look at it, how do you know it can help us now?' Eloise asked.

'It was Patrick's question about being a conduit.' She tapped the page lightly. 'This didn't make sense when I first read it, but Adam wasn't hurt then.' She looked up at them. 'I believe this is the story of the first instance of warlock lightning.'

'What does it say?' Patrick asked.

'It's a suspension spell at its heart.'

'Then why does it kill?'

'It's not supposed to. This entry is written by Catellyn McCaeth, one of Bridgette's ancestors. According to her, the power was originally used as a Healing spell, to cauterise wounds and hold them in that moment, giving the Healer time to gather their power in situations where the patient would otherwise have bled out.'

'How was it turned into warlock lightning?'

She didn't look up at Eloise, her gaze skimming over the passages. 'It was to do with Catellyn's betrothed. He was a leader in their coven, but then he began to change. His power built inside him and none of the remedies or spells she used seemed to help him. He couldn't release the magic. He was going mad with it and she was terrified he was going to explode. He was preparing to leave so that he wouldn't injure anyone when their village was attacked.'

Her gaze skimmed over the words as her brain registered the information and tried to summarise it. 'Picts swept down from the north to raid the coven's winter stores. There was a fierce battle. Many were injured. The coven Healers were worn out with using their power; and all this while in their midst there was one of them bristling with power that was killing him. It was then Catellyn wondered if her betrothed used the excess energy to heal those lying on the battlefield, it might help to save him.' She took a breath, firming her mind to ignore Catellyn's obvious grief as she spilled out the agony of watching her betrothed be taken from her by the power that was at the core of who they were. But still her voice broke as she continued. 'It didn't.' She cleared her throat again, blinking back the tears. It was so hard not to feel the agony that had been cried into the page with the ink that created the words.

A cold touch on her shoulder firmed her resolve, fingers gripping, giving her a squeeze. Adam. She glanced at him briefly. He nodded, encouraging her to go on, his lips not in their customary aggravating grin as he whispered, 'You can do it. Go on.' She shook her head slightly, but he simply nodded, lips forming the words, 'You can'.

'Are you okay, Shelley?'

'Do you want me to read it?' Eloise asked.

She shook her head, took a deep breath, and returned to the text in front of her.

'He went out into the field, engaged the Healing power of the lightning, but something dark had touched him in his increasing madness and he wasn't able to contain control.' She hissed. She'd read these words before, but they'd had no true meaning then. 'The power was too strong, concentrating his magic into bolts of lightning. He killed everyone on the battlefield in one blast of power, Picts and coven alike. Everyone except Catellyn.'

'Did he survive?'

Her gaze skimmed ahead. She closed her eyes, then said the words that were printed on her eyelids. 'No. He cried out in agony at what he'd done, and then turned the power on himself. The force of the explosion knocked Catellyn back far enough that she escaped serious injury.'

She didn't want to read the rest. Not out loud. It would make the tragedy that followed somehow less meaningful. Words like these were meant to be read in private, to oneself. Maybe even never written down. Except that's not the way the ancient witches did things. If there could be a lesson learned, a new spell derived, an understanding of something hidden, then it was recorded. They never shied away from the lessons learned through hardship, grief and pain. Even their last words they wrote down, bidding those that followed to continue their journey.

Catellyn had done exactly that. Shelley knew if she turned a few pages on, a different hand would pick up the story. Catellyn, unable to bear her grief, had taken her life after her daughter was born. It was her sister's hand that wrote those words and continued Catellyn's work in the grimoire. It was a history of all that had gone before as much as a repository of spellcraft and witch lore.

Shelley cast her gaze over the grimoires on the tables, the diaries kept by the Pack Witches. They were all so much more than they appeared. If only she had the ability to see the truth of what lay within in an instant. But that truth often remained hidden until another one unfurled its petals to release its secret in its own time. Just like this story of the end of Catellyn's life. Shelley had seen its sadness before, but now, with the knowledge of what she was truly reading about—the birth of the destructive power of witch and warlock lightning and what created it—it touched her in a way it never had before.

'What did the blast look like? Was it black like the warlock lightning we've seen?'

Shelley blinked back the persistent burn of tears and scanned the page. 'No. That's why I didn't make the connection. Although, Catellyn does make mention that the colour was different, like there was a shadow on it.'

'The Darkness had got inside him,' Iain said.

'Perhaps. But I don't think it had. I just think it's an indication that it had become darker magic. Black magic isn't simply called that because of the evil often associated with it, but because the magic itself is not the brilliant colours seen in the light magic we use.'

'If it was black magic, that would make it the perfect vehicle for the Darkness to use to get inside someone,' Eloise said, her expression grim.

Iain nodded. 'Yes. It seems to thrive on taking something good and turning it to evil use. Like what it did with the Were centuries ago. What it did to River. And Eloise's foot.'

Shelley rubbed at her brow. 'In this instance, you're probably right. Cain was taken over by the Darkness, so it makes sense that it has become part of his power. And it's why Adam's wound isn't responding to Bron's Healing.'

'Could it turn him? Adam?' Eloise asked, voice threaded with worry.

'Oh shit. Could it?' Adam asked.

'I don't know.' She looked around, trying desperately to think, to ignore the pained expression on Adam's face. 'It never really took over the Were—just separated the human and wolf halves so they were in constant struggle with themselves. And it never had a proper hold of River either, only manifesting as the Beast when River lost control during the full moon. And it never really took over you, either, Eloise. In fact, it was kept so suppressed, the only way it could manifest was in the physical twisting of your ligaments. I don't think it can truly thrive in something that is, at its essence, good.'

'So you acknowledge that I'm good. That's an improvement.'

She couldn't suppress the snort of laughter at Adam's words, but she turned it into a cough and said out the side of her mouth, 'Good, not shit-hot.'

Adam's chortle of laughter warmed something needy inside her, and the sadness she'd experienced while relating Catellyn's words faded so it was no longer oppressive. Then she noticed the tears glistening in Eloise's eyes. Laughter died. 'Oh God. What did I say?'

Iain shook his head gently as he took Eloise's hands in his, stroking his thumb over the backs of her hands. 'It's Cain. What you said means that Cain was never good. Because, if he was …'

'Then the Darkness wouldn't have been able to take a hold of him like it has.' Oh crap. She hadn't thought of that. 'I'm sorry. I could be wrong. I probably am—'

'No. You're not.' Eloise rubbed her face with the back of her hand, wiping away the tears. 'Cain was always good to me, but there was always something wrong inside him. I knew it, right from when we were young. He didn't love me like I loved him. It was more … ownership to him.' She swallowed painfully. 'He was broken. Something is missing in him, isn't it?' She looked up at Iain, who nodded, sadly.

'He's a sociopath.'

Her brow furrowed at Patrick's words. 'Yes. But now he's something so much worse.' Eloise's eyes seemed to glow gold as she met Shelley's gaze. 'He's beyond saving.'

'You okay, Little Bird?' Iain slid off his chair and knelt next to hers, his arm hooking around her waist to pull her close.

She nuzzled into him. 'I'm okay.' She cupped his face and kissed his cheek. 'Really.'

'You sure?'

'I'm sure.' She kissed his lips, soft, gentle.

Shelley had to look away.

'You okay, Kitten?'

She shook her head but didn't say anything. Couldn't say anything. How could she when what she wanted to say would come out as a scream to the universe for its cruelty. She could barely stand her own pain and yet she was constantly barraged by other people's —the pain of the dead, the pain of the living. And it had become so much worse since she'd erupted with the banshee scream at Oestra. But the pain that was worst of all was the one bound up in the man standing at her side. A man nobody but her could see. A man, who, if she didn't figure out the secrets of the past hidden in these diaries and grimoires, might never come back to her. What would she do if he was no longer there, making her burn with a terrifying mix of anger and passion? Even though she couldn't—and never would—do anything about it, she didn't think she could stand him not being there.

How had her life come to this? It was meant to be controlled, easy, serene. Since meeting the Were the previous August, her well-ordered life had exploded in her face. She wished she could hate them for it, but it was no more their fault than it was hers.

It was Morrigan's. And the Darkness'.

She stood abruptly, her chair scraping loudly against the wooden floor. The others looked up, startled. But she didn't care. She simply turned to Adam. 'We can't let them win.'

'What do you want to do?'

'I have to talk to the spirits.'

He grinned. 'You up for that?'

'I've never felt more up for it.'

'Then let's get going.'

She started walking towards the door.

'Where are you going?' Iain asked.

'To the McClune Packlands. I need to talk to Adeline and a few others and they're not leaving Bron at the moment.'

Iain and Eloise stood, Patrick following.

'Who were you just speaking with?' Iain asked as he brushed past her to open the front door.

She looked questioningly at Adam. He nodded. 'Tell them.'

'I was talking to Adam.'

She shouldn't have said that. She really shouldn't have.

'You can see Adam?' Eloise's voice broke the deathly silence.

Beside her, Adam blew out his breath. 'Fuck, I'm glad someone spoke. That silence was beginning to kill me for real.'

Shelley choked on a laugh and glared at him. 'Yes. I can hear him. Annoying as usual.' He grinned at her.

'Has he died?' Iain asked, voice tight with grief.

'No!' She gripped his arm. 'No. His body is still alive.'

'Then how can you see him?'

'I don't know. I just can. I could see him right after it happened, the same time as I saw Marcus' spirit rise from his body.'

'Did I rise from my body?'

She blinked at Adam's question. 'No. You didn't. You were just suddenly there.'

'Weird.'

'You're talking to him now?' Patrick asked.

'Yes.'

'What's he saying?'

'Nothing particularly enlightening.'

'Sounds like Adam.'

'Hey!' Adam reached across her and punched Patrick—his hand went right through the younger Were, who didn't even move or indicate in any way that he'd felt Adam at all.

'Damn it!' Adam snarled. 'I was pissed. That should have worked.'

Shelley would have snorted, but his shoulder had brushed her breast as he'd reached past her. It was like touching an electric fence.

'What's wrong?' Eloise asked, her gaze pinned on Shelley's face.

'Nothing. We should probably get going.'

'Good idea.' Iain led them out to his four-wheel drive.

Eloise hopped in the front next to Iain, so Shelley had to sit in the back with Patrick. As she got in, Adam entered behind her, forcing her to shift into the middle seat, squeezing up against Patrick in an effort not to touch the annoying male spirit—or whatever he was. She still had no clue.

'I know you like me,' Patrick said, wiggling his brows at her. 'But do you have to sit so close?'

'Adam's sitting there.'

'Oh, right,' Patrick said, gaze running over what was an empty seat to him but to her was filled with an oversized smirking male Were.

As soon as they were on their way, Eloise swung around, her green-gold gaze disturbingly knowing. 'That didn't look like nothing before. You jumped. And your face went red. Did Adam do something?'

Shelley couldn't escape that assessing look. 'He just punched Patrick for what he said.'

'He did?' Patrick looked down at himself. 'Is he still doing it?'

'No, I'm not still doing it, you git,' Adam grumbled. 'What's the point of hitting someone if they can't even feel it?'

'Perhaps you shouldn't hit in the first place.'

Adam's eyes widened as he turned to look at her. 'Says she who hits first and talks later.'

She crossed her arms over her chest, surreptitiously rubbing the place Adam had touched—her skin still tingled. 'I'm not that bad.'

'Not that bad what?' Iain asked. 'You know, it's very annoying when you can't hear the entire conversation.'

'It's equally annoying when you *can* hear it.'

Patrick snorted. 'Especially when it's Adam you're hearing.'

'Excuse me,' Adam said as he reached behind Shelley—she ducked forward to avoid the risk of him touching her again—and smacked Patrick in the head. Patrick's head shoved forward.

'Hey!' He turned to look at Shelley who crouched forward on her seat. 'What the hell was that?'

'You felt him?'

'You felt me?'

'That was Adam?'

She sat up slowly. 'What did it feel like?'

'I don't know.' He touched the back of his head. 'It was like my head got shoved by a cold wind. Kind of. It wasn't really like a person touching me. More like ...' He stopped, mouth working.

'You'd been punched by a pillow?'

'I'm hardly a pillow.'

'Yeah, kind of,' Patrick said over Adam's complaint. 'But even less specific than that. You know?'

'Yeah. I do know.'

'You can feel him, can't you?' Eloise again. 'That's why you had that funny look on your face before when you said he punched Patrick. He touched you doing it.'

'Yes.'

Eloise frowned and bit her lip. 'It didn't hurt you though. And it didn't hurt Patrick.'

'No.'

'Speak for yourself, ' Patrick said, still touching the back of his head.

'You're not hurt,' Eloise said. 'Not like if a Shade had touched you.'

Shelley suddenly understood that look on Eloise's face—the deep concern in her eyes. 'Oh, Christ. No, Eloise. He's not a Shade. We've already established that. He's touched me quite a few times, and aside from feeling kind of ... ghostly, for want of a better description, it hasn't hurt me.'

'You don't feel a drain on your power or your energy?'

Quite the opposite, actually, but she wasn't going to say that. 'No.'

'And it's not uncomfortable in any way?'

Well, it was, but once again, she wasn't going to admit that either. 'Apart from it feeling cold, no. Why? Have you heard of anything like this happening before?'

Eloise twisted around further to face Shelley, her fingers flexing against the leather.

'No. Not like this. In every way, it sounds like his soul was cut from his body by the warlock lightning. That would usually create a Shade. But if he's not draining or hurting you, then he's not a Shade. I have no idea what he is. This is what you meant when you said you were looking for information about different types of spirits, right?'

'Yes. But I've found nothing useful.'

'But this couldn't be the first time something like this has happened. I mean, warlock lightning has been around for centuries. Surely someone's seen something like this before?' She sounded so hopeful, and after what they'd told her of their suspicions about what had happened to her family, Shelley understood.

'It might have happened before, but unless someone like me was around to see them, nobody would know. He can't even talk to the other spirits—there's some kind of noise like wind or static that gets worse when they try to talk to each other.'

'Like they're on a different wave length?'

Shelley stared at Patrick. 'Yes. That's exactly it. They're on different planes of existence.'

'Then why can he and the spirits talk to you and you to them?'

'I must have the ability to switch planes or channels or something. Maybe that's why he can touch me too. It's like he's out of phase and yet part of me shares the same phase molecules.' She laughed and shook her head. 'Sorry, too much science fiction.'

'No. I think you could be on to something,' Patrick said.

'It's a wonder nobody's ever thought of this before.'

144

'They might have,' Patrick said. 'But, like all written information that has to be preserved, things get lost, misinterpreted when translated so the meaning changes. War and social upheaval, even natural disaster, can destroy records. As a lore keeper, it's frustrating.'

'Adam and I were just talking about that before you came in.' She looked down at her hands, unclenched them and lay them flat on her knees. 'I'm going to talk to the spirits up at the McClunes Packlands. There's quite a few ancient witches who've been hanging around Bron and Cordy up there.'

'And Adeline,' Adam added.

'Yes. Adeline. I'll have to talk to her. She might know something about Adam's mysterious lady that she's not been able to communicate with him. At least we're hoping. She always seems to have her fingers in many pies.'

'Mysterious lady?' Patrick asked. 'This sounds intriguing.'

She explained about the woman who had come to Adam just after he'd first become what he was now and then his subsequent talk with the Goddess.

'You saw the place I created?' Eloise turned to stare at where Adam sat.

'He did,' Shelley said.

'I thought it was a place in my mind, not somewhere physical.'

'Nope. You created it. The Goddess said it's something that a Nexus can do—create actual places in the aether or something like that.'

Shelley repeated what he'd said.

'Wow. I had no idea. What was it like?'

'Stormy.'

Shelley kept translating.

'Huh.' Eloise sucked in her lip. 'The storm was coming when I was there. But I didn't create that. How is it still there?'

'The Goddess said your power could show the possibilities of the future. The storm is in our future—I gather it's the fight that's coming with Morrigan and Cain and the Darkness—but while it's there in the place you created, it's not taken over yet. It's kind of just hovering.'

'But what if—' Eloise began to ask, but Shelley threw up her hands.

'Look, can we not do this now? I know it seems really interesting and is possibly important info we all need to know down the track, but it's kind of annoying having to repeat everything Adam says so you can hear it.'

'You could let him take over your body,' Patrick suggested. 'That would make the conversation faster.'

'No!' Shelley and Adam said together.

She turned to stare at Adam. 'Why did you say no? Surely, you'd want to speak to others more easily? Isn't that what all spirits want?'

He grimaced. 'I'm not precisely a spirit, am I?' When she stared at him, he reached out and touched her hand. 'I don't think I could just slide into you. As you said, we're in phase with each other in some way. With the others, I could probably do it, but with you, I'm almost corporeal.'

'If you could, would you?'

'No. I'd never force you to do anything you didn't want to do. Besides, it hurts you when a spirit takes over your body and I'd never do anything to hurt you.'

'You know that?'

'Of course. How could I miss it? What I don't know is why you haven't told any of the others what it does to you.'

Shelley looked down at her hands, unable to meet his eyes. She hated talking about her feelings to anyone. Even with Skye and Bron she found it difficult—although they had a way of getting them out of her anyway. But it just felt so ... weakening to admit to her deepest fears, her deepest wants, those things that hurt her the most.

But Adam was persistent. He nudged her shoulder with his. The touch tingled outwards in ever-expanding ripples. But still, she didn't answer, just folded her arms and pinned her lips together more tightly. The others might not hear him, but they could bloody well hear what she was saying and she wasn't going to answer his question in front of them.

Probably wouldn't even if they weren't there.

He leaned closer. His cool breath brushed across her ear, making her shiver. Her fingers dug into her sides as she fought the unwanted sensations that shot through her body like electric prickles. She leaned a little further away but couldn't go too far. Patrick was sitting on her other side, his big shoulders taking up more than his fair share of the back seat.

Adam leaned closer. 'It's because it would hurt them to know, isn't it?' Her head whipped up, gaze clashing with his. He smiled knowingly. 'Thought so. You're such a martyr sometimes.'

She snorted. 'You're one to talk.'

He gave her a 'who me?' look, which made her laugh despite the fact that she was pissed off that he could figure her out so easily. His face lit at the sound and he sat back in his seat as if to say, 'my job here is done'.

She became aware that the others were all staring at her. She quickly scanned back through her memory, hoping they hadn't heard something she desperately didn't want them to hear. Could they have figured out what she and Adam had been talking about?

Eloise reached out and patted her knee. 'Don't worry. We wouldn't ask you to do that again.' Her gaze darted to Patrick.

'Sorry, I shouldn't have suggested it.'

'It's okay.'

'You're being a martyr again. You need to stop it.'

'I'll stop it when you stop it.'

Adam glared at her, fingers clenching in his lap, itching to do what his Were nature— and his Trickster side—was urging him to do: touch her. She was certain he could feel her need by the tension in his body let alone the way he looked at her. But she'd made it clear she didn't want him to touch her, so he didn't. Annoying man. She really wanted his touch right now.

She didn't care how contrary that was.

His fingers clenched and unclenched in his lap as his jaw tightened, worry shadowing his eyes.

She couldn't stand it. She reached over and put her hand over his. 'It's okay.' He stilled. Relaxed. 'Don't worry about me.'

He made a clucking sound. 'Can't do that. It's my job.'

'No, it's not.'

'Once your Shadow, always your Shadow.' His lips widened into his cheekiest grin. 'You can never get rid of me, you know. Even in partial death.'

His gallows humour would usually have had her chuckling. But instead of laughing, she just clenched her fingers around his. 'I don't want to get rid of you.'

Patrick was watching her, as was Eloise, their gazes heavy. But she didn't care. For the rest of the journey, she sat there silently, her hand wrapped around Adam's ghostly one, garnering a strange sense of strength and peace from his almost-not-there touch.

Adam held onto her. Something inside him surged forward at her touch, the neediness in it speaking to a need in him that he'd held back for so long. This was more than the sexual attraction he'd always felt for her. It was something deeper.

If he didn't know better, he'd call it the mating bond. But that couldn't be right, because he was no longer bonded to his wolf, and there was no mating bond without his wolf heart.

Whatever it was, Adam didn't want to let it go. Didn't want to let Shelley go.

The problem was, at some stage he was going to have to, because as he held her, he felt the secret need she kept hidden inside, the part of her she was too afraid to speak out loud.

She wanted out.

Somehow, after all this was over, he was going to have to make sure she got what she wanted, even if it killed something precious and newly awakened inside him.

'WHAT ARE YOU ALL DOING HERE?' Bron asked as they walked into the kitchen of the McClune Packhouse. 'I didn't know you were coming up.' She grabbed Shelley and then Eloise in a big hug.

'Nobody does. We didn't tell anyone we were coming,' Iain said.

'It just kind of happened,' Patrick agreed.

River walked in the door behind Bron, a towel in his hand, hair wet. 'Hey, what's going on here? Did someone organise a party without telling me?'

Shelley looked around. 'We're here to see Adeline and some of the other spirits.'

'You *want* to speak to them?'

'Yes. Adam needs me to communicate with them for him. He's been unable to talk with them so far, so I've come up with him to act as an interpreter.'

'What do you mean Adam needs you to communicate with them? He's unconscious. He can't communicate with anyone.'

'Shelley can see Adam,' Eloise volunteered.

'She says he's here now,' Iain said.

Patrick rubbed his head. 'He slapped me upside the back of the head.'

'Wait a minute.' Bron held up her hands. 'But ... he's not dead.'

'Here we go again,' Adam said, rolling his eyes, making Shelley feel like chuckling. 'Tell them I'm a not-shade-spirit-thingy.'

'I'm not calling you that.'

'What? What did he say? What's going on?'

Shelley sighed. 'I'm not explaining anything until Jason and Skye are here.'

River closed his eyes for a moment and when he opened them said, 'They're on their way.'

Jason and Skye rushed in a few minutes later, hands clasped. 'Shelley!' Skye said, racing to her friend and enveloping her in a hug. 'And Eloise!' Another hug for their new coven member. 'It's so lovely to see you in the flesh.'

'What's all this about?' Jason asked after doing the male-nod thing with Iain and Patrick.

'It's for Shelley to tell you,' Iain said, pointing at her.

She took a deep breath. Now the moment was here, she wasn't sure what to say, so she just blurted out, 'Adam is here. I've been able to see him since Oestra. But he's not dead,' she said quickly as Jason's face blanched. 'Something else has happened.'

Jason's gaze chased around the room. 'A?' He took a step forward. 'You're here?'

'I am.'

Shelley translated, indicating as well where Adam was standing.

'Why didn't you tell me? Why is this the first I'm hearing about it?'

'Don't yell at Shelley,' Adam snarled, standing in front of her. 'It was my decision. Tell him it was my decision.'

Shelley did no such thing. 'I believed that if I could see him, he was dead, so I didn't want to admit he was real. I thought he was a bad hallucination.'

'I'd call me a good hallucination.'

She screwed her nose up at him. 'But then he was too annoying to be a hallucination, so I realised he was real.'

'Why didn't you tell me?'

'Because I didn't know what he was or why I could see him. Neither of us wanted to say anything given we had no answers. We didn't want to worry you further until we knew more. I've been researching in the diaries, trying to look for specific references.'

'Have you found anything?'

'No.' She looked down. 'Not specifically about what he is. All we know is that he's not anything like the spirits I see and he's not a Shade. I don't know why I can see him, but there is something different about him. Something special.' Shelley's throat felt thick, and she coughed, trying to cover it.

'He is special. I've always known it.'

'Of course you have,' Adam said. 'It practically shines off me.'

Shelley rolled her eyes again. 'That's just what you need, a bigger head.'

'What did he say?' Jason asked. She told him. He barked out a laugh, as did the others. 'That sounds like Adam.'

'My job here is done.' Adam folded his arms and leaned against the table behind him.

Shelley stared around her. It was like something had lifted and been replaced with ... light? Laughter? Hope? All the things that Adam had always brought to the pack. Even in his altered state, he still did as he'd always done. Her gaze fell to Adam. He had faded a little. 'Stop it, Adam. Stop doing that.'

'Stop what?' He looked surprised at her vehemence.

'What's he doing?'

'He's giving you part of himself, just like he did the night of Oestra when he helped Iain to keep Eloise with us.'

'That was Adam?' Iain asked.

Shelley waved her hand at him, as if wiping away his question. 'It's not the only time he's done it either.'

'I'm fine, Kitten.'

'No. You're not. Look at you.'

He looked down, his brow furrowing. 'So, I'm a little paler than before.'

'A little? You're fading. You're giving your life essence to everyone else in this room to make them feel better.'

'It's what he's always done,' Skye said.

'We've known something like that was happening for a while now,' Bron added.

'But that doesn't make it right.' She shook her head, mouth working, trying to find the words to convince him—convince all of them—that he couldn't do it anymore. 'He will give you all he has if you ask for it. But he'll unravel. He'll use up everything he is and become nothing. You can't ask him to do anything like that again. You can't.'

Bron's eyes had grown wide, her face pale. 'I wouldn't let him do that, Shelley.'

'I know,' Shelley said, fingers twining, shoulders tensed. 'But it doesn't matter if you'd "let him" or not. Don't you understand Adam at all?'

'It's okay, Kitten.' Adam began to massage her shoulders.

She wanted to lean back, let him soothe her, let his hands run over her shoulders, down her arms, touching more than her tense muscles, but she couldn't. Wouldn't. She jerked away and spun to face him. 'It's not okay, Adam, you idiot!' She flung her hand out, pointing at the others. 'You don't understand. None of you do.'

'Then tell us,' Iain said.

'What have you found out?' Bron asked.

She was breathing heavily, skin tingling, words from the diaries coalescing in her mind, certain phrases jumping out at her, brighter now, more pertinent as she realised how true they were. Adam made himself look the laughing fool, never taking anything seriously, when all he ever did was take everything seriously. When all he'd ever done was give and give and give. Laughter and happiness wasn't simply a passing fad for him, an expression of the moment; it was something woven into the very fabric of his nature, who he was, what he must do, who he must be.

'Shelley. Kitten.' A hand grabbed hers—Adam. Held tight when she tried to pull away. 'It's okay. You don't have to protect me.'

Her gaze snapped to his. 'Of course I do. You need protecting more than anyone else.'

'No. I don't.'

'Yes, you do. Because you give too much. You give everything until there's nothing left anymore. I can't let that happen. I can't let them do it to you.'

'Nobody here would hurt me.'

'That's only because they don't know what giving too much means. What they take when they let you do that.'

His hands slid up her arms, captured her face, held her still, looking into his eyes. 'You're not seeing it right, Kitten.'

'I'm seeing it the way it is. You give too much, Adam. You always do. In fact, you're doing it now.' She tore away from him, horrified to see that he'd paled further as he touched her, as he soothed her. 'Look at you. You're definitely not a Shade. You don't take life. You give it.'

'Kitten.' He reached for her, but she skittered back. 'I'm fine. I feel fine. You're overreacting.'

'And I have a right to overreact!' she shouted. 'I see dead people. I talk to them. Hear them. I predict and scream out oncoming death.

Everything about me is about death. About the absence of life. About taking. Taking. Taking.'

Her breath came in hard, sharp gasps. Her skin buzzed and purple lightning sparked from her fingers. She looked down at it, horrified at the reality of her power, how it had changed since she'd become the banshee.

Purple lightning. Not the brilliant blue of Skye's or the warm golden orange of Bron's or the sparking life-fuelled green of Eloise's. Hers was darker. Amethyst with a dark heart of deeper purple at the centre—almost black. Black like warlock's lightning.

Fuck.

'Get back,' she said, stepping away from all of them. 'Get back.'

'Shelley. What's wrong!'

'I'm dangerous. Can't you see? It's me. I'm death. I'm death! Get them out of here,' she screamed at the Were in the room, gesturing with sparking fingers, purple lightning leaping from her fingertips to burst against the walls, the floors.

'Her power's built up,' Bron cried.

'Jason, help her,' Skye shouted. She tried to step forward, Eloise at her side, but Shelley screamed at them to keep back as her power snapped at them, carving a line of purple light between them and her.

'Shelley. No. Let us help you.'

'Stay back! Stay back! Someone's going to die if you don't. That's who I am.'

'It's not.'

She thought it was them who protested, but suddenly realised it couldn't be. Iain, River, Jason and Patrick had stepped in front of Skye, Bron and Eloise, all of them on the other side of the purple wall of light she'd created.

She swung around to see Adam standing right behind her, a smile of wonder on his face.

'You're not death,' he said. 'You are life.'

And before she could stop him, he grabbed her face and kissed her.

14

Adam pressed his lips against hers. Shelley stiffened, jerked. He held tighter to her face, knowing deep inside him that this was what he had to do.

There was a buzz of power over his hands, centring on his lips where they met Shelley's. Purplish light glowed around them and something whipped at his hair. There was no sound though. The howling that he'd become used to had disappeared, and all he could hear was the beat of his heart and the fast-paced beat of Shelley's—too fast.

'Adam? I can see him.'

Vaguely he heard Jason's voice behind him, but he didn't pull away from Shelley. Couldn't.

'Holy fuck. I can see him too.' Iain.

'Like a shadow.' River.

'He's getting brighter though.' Eloise, wonder in her voice.

'He's channelling her power.' Skye.

'By kissing her?' Patrick.

'Sometimes, that's what it takes to share the power.' Bron.

He had no idea what they were looking at, and quite frankly, he didn't care. Shelley's lips were warm under his. Bliss. He nibbled at her plump lower lip, sucking it into his mouth and forgot all about their audience.

Warm breath cascaded over his skin as she sighed and softened against him. Her mouth opened slightly, her tongue darting out to taste his lips. He opened and let her inside, let her control the kiss.

Shots of electricity prickled over his hands, moving up his arms, over his shoulders, encompassing his entire body. Her power—warmth and life and sexual caress all rolled into one—wrapped around him and pulled them closer, chest to breast, hip to hip, and held them there. He wanted to be this close to her just as much as it seemed her power needed him to be there.

It was right. It was good. Better than good. Perfect.

Her mouth widened, tongue sliding along his. He groaned. An answering sound came from her, buzzing through her chest into him, making him smile.

Her lips moved, slanting at an angle as her hands gripped his shoulders. Then she slid one into his hair, the other chasing across his back, fingers clenching, desperate.

He understood her need. He slid his hands to her waist, pulled her even closer, and deepened the kiss.

The air sizzled with her power. The purple brightened; light-shot amethyst with a golden edge spilled around him, into him. 'That's right,' he whispered against her mouth. 'Syphon the excess into me.'

Shelley pulled away a little, her gaze meeting his, the once bright blue now a brilliant violet. 'Adam, no. I'll hurt you.'

His hands gentled their hold, letting her know it was her choice to stay as he shook his head. It didn't matter if his wolf wasn't in his body. He knew with sudden certainty that was not the way this worked. It wasn't his wolf that took the power and used it, it was their spirit. The heart of them. It just used it to enact something essential to them, something magical that needed a little help when they couldn't borrow the power of the moon. 'The Trickster in me says you won't. It knows we need this. Both of us. Do you trust me?'

Fear flickered through her eyes.

He was asking a lot. Wasn't sure she was ready yet to take that step into trusting the pack. Trusting him. She really hadn't trusted any of them yet. She was here because of Skye and Bron and their trust. It wasn't that she didn't like the pack. She did. Even admired them. But trust? For Shelley, that was the biggest ask. He knew that deep in his soul. It was one of the reasons he'd always been so full of jokes and harmless flirting. He'd always sensed how much she needed things to stay light. To be able to brush away casual affection. To not let it anywhere near her heart. She'd been hurt deeply in the past, and not just by her bastard of an ex-fiancé. The pain ran further back than that. It was a fissure he wasn't sure would ever mend.

But right now, he didn't need to mend that fissure. He just needed her to trust in his Trickster instincts. After all the research she'd done, the things she'd said to him about his worth to the pack, he hoped she would meet him halfway with this at least.

Finally, the need to breathe a scream in his chest, she nodded.

His released breath fluttered her hair, the ends alive with the purple brightness of her power. 'Give it to me.'

She laughed—a brief snort—and then pulled him close again, lips meeting his in a long, searching, searing kiss.

The power surged around him. Into him. The kiss heated him, the power adding to the surge of desire cascading through him, firing him. He tried to hold on to it, tried to stay in control, to keep from taking over, but it built and built and built as Shelley slid her tongue into his mouth, twining it with his, sucked his lip, bit his chin, her hands tracing fire across his back, along his arms and shoulders, into his hair, down to his butt.

He pulled her tight against him with a groan and gave in to the desire roaring inside him to take, to hold, to have.

He half expected her to fight him, but she didn't. She leaned into him, giving him more, sharing control of the kiss and the fire and the power. The perfect beauty of what she gave surged through him, and with a roar he lifted his head to the ceiling and howled, the sound a note of triumph and satisfaction rolled into one.

He looked down at Shelley. She met his gaze, her eyes now velvety-violet-blue, her hair no longer purple-tinged flame. Her lips were kiss-stung and her breath came in short, sharp pants. 'Thank you.'

'Believe me, it was my pleasure.'

She didn't let go of him as he half expected. Her arms stayed slung around his shoulders, fingers playing lightly along his collar-bone and into the hair on his nape. 'I didn't realise the power had built up inside me like that.'

'It makes sense. A lot has gone on since you found out you were a banshee as well as a Medium.'

'Maybe.'

'Not maybe. Definitely.' He swept his hand across her brow, brushing away the strands of hair stuck to her face. 'Your power ... it's extraordinary.' She frowned. *No. No, no, no.* He didn't want to make her frown. He wanted her to smile. Needed her to smile. So, with a twist of his lips, he said, 'And if this is the way you need to release it, count me in as your release valve.' Her lips twitched. *Yes!* He had her. Now for the follow up. 'I thought that kiss at the dam was something. But this ...' He blew a breath. 'It quite literally lit me up.'

She laughed outright this time. 'You are the most ridiculous male I know.'

'You love that about me.'

The laughter left her face, the brightness in her eyes snapping off like the gas had been turned off on a flame. She edged back, her gaze darting everywhere, not landing once on him. He let her go, a hollow ache in his chest where warmth had just been. Her warmth.

Fuck, he was an idiot.

She cleared her throat, hands twining in front of her once again. He wanted to grab them, to stop the painful, lost movement of them, but after what he'd said, he couldn't touch her right away.

'Adam?'

Jason's voice sounded choked, wondering. He turned. His brother was looking right at him. In fact, all of them were looking right at him. 'You can see me?' He suddenly remembered hearing their discussion when he was kissing Shelley. 'You can see me.' Jason nodded, as did the others.

He looked down. His form was edged in sizzling amethyst. Eyes widening, he lifted his hands. 'Shelley's power.'

'Yes.' Bron said. 'It went into you, like it would to any of the Were.'

'He didn't change into his wolf,' Jason said.

'No. Because he's ...' she waved her hand, 'whatever he is. He didn't need her power to change into a wolf, he needed it to become corporeal.'

'He's not corporeal,' Eloise said slowly. 'But using Shelley's analogy, he used her power to bring him into phase with us.'

'He sucked energy from her,' Iain said, worry in his tone. 'Then he is a Shade?'

Eloise shook her head slowly, taking a step towards Adam. Iain grabbed her arm to pull her back, but she shook her head. 'No. He's not a Shade. We already determined that in the car. He's something else. Something born of spirit and man and Were. Something unique.' She turned to the others, eyes bright with wonder, with understanding. 'Shelley's power can light him up. I think, maybe, all of our power could. He's a conduit for it. More truly now than ever before.' She walked forward a couple more steps, Iain right behind her. When she lifted her hand to touch Adam, Iain hissed, fists clenching. Eloise smiled at her mate. 'It's okay. I'll be fine.'

'How do you know?'

Her smile was almost beatific as she met his gaze. 'I don't know, but something inside is telling me what I said is true. It feels right, like I need to do it. Do you trust me?'

His tension dissolved. 'Always.'

She reached out to Adam.

He let her touch him, trusting her instinct. Her fingers slid down his arm to his hand. He gasped at the sensation that surged through him. It didn't have the same heated sexual feel of Shelley's power. More innocent somehow and yet vastly more ancient. It sank into his skin, leaving a glow of green sparkles along with the purple of Shelley's where she'd touched him.

'Beautiful,' Bron said, moving to touch him too. Her touch, on his other arm, left an orange glow behind. It was warmer than

Eloise's power, but not as warm as Shelley's and made him feel lighter. Skye joined them, Jason right behind her. She touched his shoulder, leaving blue sparkles in the wake of her fingers. Bron touched where Eloise had touched, the colour of her power not overlaying hers, but mixing in, so that his skin looked like it was covered in tiny sparkling lights of orange, green and purple. The three of them laughed and then began placing their hands over where the others had touched.

Adam's lips twitched. 'Girls, I know I'm irresistible, but you don't want to make your mates jealous, do you?'

Jason, River and Iain snorted.

'How long will he stay like that?' Patrick asked in a hushed voice.

'I don't know,' Eloise said, her voice equally hushed, like they were standing in the Sistine Chapel discussing the Michelangelo paintings on the ceiling.

'Where I touched him seems to be fading already,' Bron whispered.

'Thank the Moon for that. I look like a bloody Christmas tree,' Adam commented, his arms out wide while he looked down at himself.

'If it was purple,' Patrick snorted.

'Whoever heard of a purple Christmas tree?' Iain said, laughing.

'All right you two. You can cut out the double act,' Adam said. Then he stared. 'You can hear me too?'

They all nodded and Jason said, tears in his eyes, 'Goddess, Adam. You're a sight for sore eyes.' He went to reach for his brother. His hands slid right through him.

Adam shuddered.

Jason turned to the witches. 'How come you can touch him?'

Eloise shook her head and looked at Bron.

'Maybe it has something to do with our power? Maybe he's only in phase with witches. I don't know. I've never heard of anything like this before. Shelley?'

Shelley didn't answer. They all turned to face her. She hadn't moved but her eyes were wide, face pale, gaze fixed on Adam.

'Shelley?' Bron closed the distance between them and touched her friend.

Shelley jumped. 'What?'

'What do you think of all this?'

She shook her head, sucking in a breath. 'I don't know. I haven't read anything in the diaries that could explain this at all. But then again, I haven't been looking for anything like this, so I am unlikely to have found anything about glowing still-alive spirit beings.'

'You mean that they're still hiding information from you?' Jason asked.

Shelley's attention snapped to him, fists clenched. 'Not hiding. Just not responding in the way I want.'

'Maybe you're not asking the right questions.'

She glared at Patrick and then closed her eyes, shoulders drooping. 'Perhaps. But if I'm not, I don't know what the right questions are.'

'Maybe you're just not picking up the right diary.' She looked questioningly at Skye. Skye waved her hand. 'When I've had a specific question in mind, when I wave my hand over them as Cordy told us, some of them flutter, indicating there is some information in them that could be useful, but often one simply jumps open, or flies into my hand, and I know that's the one I need to look at. Does that happen for you?'

Shelley sighed. 'Yes and no. I have so many questions, they're all fluttering and jumping. It's like watching a box of puppies trying to get my attention.'

'That's annoying,' Bron said.

Shelley gave her a look.

'Speaking of annoying,' Eloise said. 'I don't know if this happened for you, but sometimes I'll go back to a diary I've read before and the information I first read is no longer there.'

'Yes!' all three witches said.

'What's that about?' Skye asked.

'It's like ...' Bron added, '... like they also sense what you need to learn and if they feel you already have read or learned something, they give you something else. It's fascinating and aggravating all at once.'

'That means you can't really use them as a true reference material,' Patrick said, the idea obviously horrifying to his Pack Librarian sensibilities. 'How can you truly learn something if it won't show you the information again?'

Skye shrugged. 'But we are learning. The diaries have helped us all with understanding and controlling our powers.'

Everyone except Shelley nodded. Adam knew exactly why—she hadn't been looking for anything about her own power except how to mute it with better shields. He really had to do something about that.

Jason's voice cut into Adam's thoughts as he asked Shelley, 'Can you look into them about why Adam is able to suck in your power and be seen by all of us? I'd like to know if this is something that can be repeated or if it's a one-off.'

'Did you miss my handsome face?'

Jason smiled wryly. 'Perhaps. Although I didn't miss your lack of humility.'

Adam laughed, but then sobered when Shelley frowned again. 'What is it?' Her mouth twisted and she looked down and away. Adam was certain he saw tears. 'Kitten?'

She turned back to face them, misery and anger in her eyes. 'I just remembered I have read something that might help explain this.' She told them what she'd found about Tricksters, how they'd been affected by the Pact and the magic of the covens in ways that changed their empathy, making it magical in form, and far stronger than it was ever meant to be. 'I thought it meant emotions and some degree of physical health, but it possibly also allows him to syphon magic in a way we've not seen before and use it for something other than the change.'

'Fascinating,' Jason said. 'Then if he can—'

Shelley made a chopping motion with her hand. 'It might be fascinating, but it's pointless delving into it now.'

They all stared at her, obviously shocked by her outburst. She couldn't make herself care about that now. Adam stepped closer to her, but Shelley edged away. She couldn't let him touch her. She didn't want to be held, or comforted or made to laugh until her worry faded. It wasn't going to fade. 'This,' she said, waving her hand around, indicating Adam and her before any of them could rally enough to speak, 'still doesn't help us know more about what truly matters.'

'And what is that?' Adam asked.

'Finding a cure for you. Working out what Morrigan and Cain are going to do next. Protecting ourselves from whatever is to come.' She raked her hand through her hair and blinked rapidly, hating that she was so close to crying. 'I just feel like we're running out of time. The knowledge is building inside me, like the banshee is humming and it's getting louder and louder every day. I feel we're on a countdown and yet I can't see what the end time is. All I know is it's coming and I'm afraid I'm inadequate to the task of finding the solutions.'

'Kitten,' Adam said, reaching for her again.

She jerked away, glaring at him. 'Don't touch me.'

'Come on Shelley,' Bron said, taking a wary step towards her. 'You know that's not true. You've helped me and Skye so much in understanding our powers. You're found so much information and shared it. We've all learned from you.'

'But not now. I can't seem to find anything now. Except for information that's not relevant to any of this.' Except for her relationship with Adam. Not that they had a relationship or ever could. The diaries had made it perfectly clear that was well and truly off the table.

'We'll help. We'll all help more,' Skye repeated. 'And if we're not doing enough, you just need to ask us.'

'Skye's right. We never meant to put all of this on your shoulders,' Jason said. 'I'm sorry if that's the way it's felt. I'm sorry none of us has noticed what a strain this is putting on you.'

She shrugged. 'It's partly my own fault. I can't seem to ask for help.'

'I think maybe that's been a problem for all of us in the past,' Bron said. 'But now we're part of the pack. Part of a coven. It's not just us anymore. We've got everyone else to lean on too.'

And everyone else's expectations riding on her shoulders. Shelley sighed, unable to say it, refusing to look at Adam for fear he could read that very thought from her head. He didn't need to give more than he'd already given.

'So, let's take a breath and start again,' Jason said. 'Patrick, how about you do up a roster of those available and able to truly help Shelley and we'll make sure it's followed.'

'Put me down too,' Adam said.

'That's right,' Bron said. 'Shelley said you can read the diaries.'

'It's proof that he really does have some magical element in him,' Jason said.

Shelley tried to keep the terror of that fact from her face as she nodded. 'Yes. It's proof. I realised it after I read about the magic of his Trickster nature. It's why I was so upset about him draining himself before. It's not like when you give Skye or Bron some of your power, Jason. Or even what a mate does for a mate. It's more than that. It's even different from a witch using too much power and draining themselves, because from what I've read, the ancient witches realised a Trickster's power is tied into his life essence. There's a limit to what a Trickster can give because of it.'

'And you said you hadn't learned anything important,' Jason said, staring, horrified, at Adam. 'A—you need to be more careful.'

Adam crossed his arms. 'Don't get your knickers in a twist, Jas. I'm fine. I think Shelley's overreacting.'

'I'm not.'

Skye moved between them. 'I think we're all a little overwrought right now. How about we all have something to eat and then get a good night's sleep and come back to this tomorrow?'

'My sis, the peacemaker—will wonders never cease!' River said, smirking.

She clapped him on the back of the head. 'Ow! Bron, save me.'

Bron laughed. 'Nope. You asked for that one my love.' She leaned up and kissed his scarred cheek. 'Skye's right. Let's all eat and then sleep and start this tomorrow.'

'I need to go speak to the spirits in the hospital room.'

'Tomorrow will be soon enough to do that. You're exhausted. We all are.'

Shelley didn't argue—she was happy to put it off for a little longer and happy to fill her time with doing something other than worry about what they did and didn't know. For the first time in a long time, she shared cooking duties in the kitchen with her friends. It was the best she'd felt in ages.

15

It didn't take long to track down Adeline the next day or to discover she knew little more than Adam had gleaned when he'd managed his rough communication with her.

'I'm sorry I can't be of more help, Shelley.'

'That's okay. I guess I'll have to ask some of the others.'

'You don't have to do that if you don't want to,' Bron said, squeezing her hand.

The worry on her friend's face made her feel so guilty. She'd done the wrong thing by her friends by sticking her head in the sand about her powers for so long. She'd burdened them with her fears and that wasn't fair, especially when they had their own issues with learning about their powers. 'I want to do this. It's about time I put on my big girl-knickers and took my powers in hand rather than letting them happen to me.' She pushed her lips into a smile. 'Besides, it'll give me a chance to truly test my new shielding and see if it works as promised.'

'Sounds good,' Bron said. 'Do you want to do it up here?'

'No.' There weren't many spirits here and some of those that had arrived left when it became obvious she only wanted to speak to

Adeline. 'Let's go down to the hospital room. There'll be more down there, and who knows, Adam's mysterious ghost-woman might have turned up and then I can talk directly to her.'

'Okay. Whatever you think is best. You're the expert in this.'

Hardly, but she was going to try to be. At least until they'd managed to defeat Morrigan and Cain.

They headed downstairs, out to the four-wheel drives, and drove to the barn that hid the entrance to the mines. The others were already there—they'd left her to talk to Adeline with only Bron and River as an audience. Even Adam had left her when she'd asked him to go. He was a distraction she hadn't wanted when lowering her outer shield enough to talk to Adeline.

'Is Adam still with them?' she asked River when they were in the lift to the lower mines.

He closed his eyes for a moment and then nodded, a slow smile on his lips. 'Yes. He's busy being the life of the party while everyone can still see and hear him.'

Shelley's gaze whipped to his. 'He's doing it again, isn't he?'

River shook his head at her. 'No. He's not doing that.' She frowned at him. 'I'm telling the truth. Jason says he's still glowing as strongly as last night and making jokes about being useful at raves. Jason wouldn't let him do more than that. None of us would. Not after what you told us.'

'Good.' She still couldn't help but be worried. They were talking about Adam after all.

He closed his eyes again.

'What's wrong, baby?' Bron stroked his arm.

'Jason's asking if Adeline knew anything about what Cain and Morrigan might have been doing. I'm telling him she didn't know anything, other than something's going on in the spirit realm that's got everyone in a bit of an uproar.'

'Yes, it makes Eloise's vision of Cain even more worrying, doesn't it?'

'You're not wrong,' Shelley mumbled. 'Have Eloise, Iain and Patrick left yet?'

'Yes. But Iain wants to know if you can find out from the spirits if they know anything about Eloise's shifter family. It would be helpful to know before they speak directly to the nurse who looked after this woman we think is Eloise's relative.'

Shelley nodded. Patrick had told them over dinner the night before what he'd discovered about Eloise's shifter family. That morning he'd rung the hospital where the remaining relative was supposed to be but had discovered she'd been discharged by a distant family member some time ago. They didn't know anything other than she'd not woken in all the years she'd been with them and the family member was going to organise private care somewhere. They thought the nurse who had cared for her might know more. It was the only lead they had and Eloise was keen to follow it. Jason had agreed to them going, given if they found the woman or any of Eloise's family, they might have some answers that would help them figure out what was coming at them next.

'Anything else?'

'Would any of the spirits go spy on Cain and Morrigan for us?'

Shelley frowned. 'I don't know. I've never asked one to do that before. I don't know if they can. Or would.'

'Worth asking, though.'

'Okay.'

The lift bumped to a halt and the door opened.

She became aware of Adam's presence before she saw him standing outside the hospital room at the end of the hall.

She followed the others down the hallway towards him, feeling like a marionette, controlled by something outside herself.

'Can I have a word with Shelley alone for a moment?' Adam asked when they reached him.

Shelley looked at Bron, willing her to say no, but instead her friend nodded. 'We'll be inside,' she said and then disappeared with River through the door.

The click as it closed made her jump. She was alone with Adam. His presence was a stroke down her back, making her skin prickle with awareness. She had to stop herself from visibly shivering, but the tight coil low in her stomach—there since their last kiss—kicked up a notch. It was like a livewire had traced along her spine, sparking out through every nerve and synapse, making her more aware of everything around her, particularly the Were standing in front of her.

The night before, the dream she had every night of them kissing in the dam had changed. Rather than ending in the banshee scream, their kissing had continued. They'd fallen onto the embankment, naked, her arms and legs wound around him, skin gliding against skin, while he pounded his thick length into her until she screamed a different scream into the night sky. And then as she looked up at him, his kiss fresh on her lips, his body still warm and pulsing in hers, her power flared. She tried to hold it in, but it was too much. It blasted out of her and he took it in. Took more and more, even when she screamed at him to stop. He simply smiled and said, 'For you,' before her amethyst fire burned through him, turning him to ash.

She'd awoken screaming and he'd been there, wanting to know what was wrong, not believing her when she'd said it was the banshee pushing inside her mind and it had frightened her. She'd yelled at him to leave her alone, and he had, even though the request obviously hurt him. He'd done it for her, because she'd asked, because it would make her feel better.

And it had. With him not there, she'd been able to pretend the nightmare had been nothing but her fears, not a premonition. But now, looking at him, she wasn't so sure. She shoved her hands under her armpits.

'Are you okay, Kitten?' he asked. 'Adeline behaved herself?'

'I'm fine.'

'You don't look fine. She didn't try anything, did she?'

'She couldn't. Not with my new shields. I only have to lower the outer layer or two to converse with the spirits, so the inner ones are still there to protect me from them pushing too far or trying to take me over.'

'But it still takes something from you. I can see it in you. I felt it.'

Oh, Goddess! He could feel her like she could feel him? This was insane. Kissing him had just made it worse for both of them. She had to stop it from progressing further. The trouble was, she no longer knew how to do that.

He inched closer to her. She put her hand out, fist against his stomach, stopping him. Her fingers tingled. 'Don't.'

'Don't what?'

'Don't suggest what you're going to suggest.'

'What am I going to suggest?' He shifted against her, and almost as if it was beyond her will to control it, her fingers splayed out on his shirt, the coldness of touching him nothing to the heated fire building inside her at the feel of him, of the hard muscles of his abdomen, outlined by her power, making him feel more real than before.

She swallowed, willed herself to pull her hand away. Failed. Failed to even lift her gaze from the sight of her fingers flexing against his shirt, against him. 'You're going to suggest I let you help me. Let you give me some of your power, your strength, to help me control my shields. The answer is no.'

'Why?'

'It's dangerous for you to do that. I thought I made it clear last night.'

'Nope. Not good enough. I don't believe that claptrap about Tricksters having magical powers tied to our life force.'

Her gaze jerked to his, held. 'It's in the diaries.'

'Maybe, but it wasn't talking about me. It was talking about Were centuries ago who were still getting over the influence of the Darkness and being a part of the Pact with the covens. None of that has any relevance to who I am now. I can't be that weak.'

'It's not weakness.'

'Yes, it is. You think I'm too weak to be able to help you.'

'I don't. It's … it's … You were fading. I've seen it with my own eyes. Twice now. Proof that what the diaries say is true.'

'It's not proof.'

She was so frustrated with his pigheadedness that she almost stamped her foot on the floor. 'How can you argue that?'

'Because if I was so weak, if I could fade away to nothingness for doing something so small as to make others feel better, then why would the Goddess have singled me out as being useful to her? Why would she tell me that I am different? That I'm what they've been waiting for—integral to their plans?' He put his hand over hers. 'I might have believed I was but the pack's fool last year, but I've learned a lot about myself in the time since I met you. Do I have doubts? Of course I do. But then I think about you, about how strong you are, how intelligent, how you've told me over and over that I am essential to the pack. And do you know what has come of your belief in me?'

'What?' she asked, voice shaky.

'I believe in me. So, if you don't think I am strong and useful, that you've just been stroking my ego, just tell me.'

'No. That's not what this is.'

His fingers clenched against hers. 'Then why? Why are you so against letting me help you when you know that I can?'

'I …'

'It's because you're afraid. Of us. Of this.'

Afraid? Of course she was afraid. Sharing power with him the night before had been one of the most intimate moments of her life. It was as if she'd been inside him, and he'd been inside her, sharing their essence, their emotions, their hearts. How could she do that again? She was already having trouble keeping her distance. And she had to keep her distance, because it wasn't only the diaries telling her it was dangerous—that *she* was dangerous to him—but it was the banshee invading her dreams, showing her what would happen if she didn't stop this thing between them, not to mention her aunt's prophecy always clamouring in her mind.

She wasn't afraid of sharing her power with him, she was afraid of sharing other things and what that would ultimately take from him.

She was afraid of him giving and her taking it all.

Her fingers flexed on him again, under his hand. Her gaze snapped down to it. His hand spread over the top of hers, bigger than hers, making her feel oh-so-feminine against his masculine strength.

Heat rose through her as she realised how close her palm was to the jut of his penis outlined in his jeans.

Her fingers moved lower.

He made a little noise in his throat, breath playing in her hair. 'Michelline. You're killing me.'

She gasped, gaze meeting his, fire to fire.

He groaned again. 'By the Moon, I wish I could have taken you away and let that kiss last night lead us to where we both wanted it to go. I wish I could let you continue doing what you are doing right now, but very unfortunately, now is not the time.' His lips jerked into a self-deprecating smile. 'That seems to be our thing, doesn't it? Our timing sucks.'

'I don't want that.'

His fingers curled over hers, stopping the movement she wasn't even aware of. She'd been stroking back and forward with her fingers, scrunching his ghostly-soft t-shirt material up and stretching it back, making it play over the hard ridges of muscle in his stomach.

'Don't lie to yourself, Kitten. You can lie to me, but don't lie to yourself.'

She jerked her hand away, breath hard and fast in her chest, heat rising to touch her cheeks, and stumbled a few steps away. 'You're a … a… not-shade-spirit-thingy. Nothing could happen anyway.'

'Hah! I told you that was a good description of what I am.'

'Adam!'

He didn't seem in the least repentant. Instead, he edged a little closer, his hands sliding up to her shoulders. 'And in so far as nothing being able to happen anyway, are you sure about that? I can touch you. Kiss you. And right now, my cock is as hard as a pylon of concrete.'

His words rocked through her, making the tight coil even tighter. If he continued, she'd come standing right there in front of him, and everyone else just out of sight patiently waiting for them behind the door would hear it. 'You can't say things like that, Adam. Not to me.'

The look in his eyes turned burning and smoky. 'Only to you.'

It was clear that was the truth as far as he saw it, but ... 'I'm not worth it. I'm broken.'

He brushed a stray lock of hair back from her face. 'You don't see yourself clearly.' He cupped her face. 'Shelley, you are one of the strongest people I know. Your loyalty to those you love, the way you give yourself over and over again to them, to your job, to the pack, even when you don't think you have it in you to give more, you somehow find a way. You think I give too much of myself, but I have nothing on you.'

'I'm not loyal. I want to leave. Do you know that?' She pulled out of his hold. 'It's my greatest wish at the moment. To turn my back and leave all of this magic and power and fighting evil to those who are far more able to deal with it and find myself some semblance of a normal life. I want that more than I've ever wanted anything and I'm willing to give up my work, my friends, my family, your pack, to get it. I'm not loyal or loving. I'm closed off and snappish. At heart, I'm a selfish bitch.'

He grabbed her hand, holding her, gentle but firm so that she couldn't pull away again.

'Sometimes you are a bitch. But sometimes I'm a bastard. We're never only one thing. You've told me that over and over these last few months as we've been learning about my Trickster heritage.'

'It's not the same,' she said, her breath a hitch in her throat. She wanted to look away from his searing, knowing gaze but couldn't even though she felt stripped by it. Naked. As if he could see everything, past her skin to the person she was deep inside. The person she kept hidden from everyone, even herself. That lonely little girl who years ago curled up into a ball and cried because of the present she was forced to endure and the bleak future of insanity ahead. Her family revered her but were afraid of her and wanted to use her. She couldn't keep a friend. Strangers shied away from her as if they felt the terror of her like a prickly warning on their skin. She'd had nobody to love and trust, nobody who loved and trusted her.

Until Skye and Bron came into her life.

They'd changed things until she'd begun to think she could have a life if she shut everything she was down and shoved it into the deepest, darkest pit inside herself and never let it out.

Adam could see inside that pit. He'd always been able to. That's what made her so prickly with him. Not because she was attracted to him—although that in itself would be enough. But because he could see everything she never wanted to bring to light again and it made her afraid. So she pushed at him, shoving him away with her attitude and bitchiness. She'd said such horrible things to him. Had really never been nice. And yet he came back, time and time again. 'Why? Why do you care?' she choked out.

'Because, all that time you were fighting with me, you were also fighting for me. Trying to prove that I was more than the useless, shallow man I thought I was. That my existence is deep and meaningful. Now it's my turn to fight for you. I want to help you in the same way you helped me. You think you're closed off and selfish, but you are the opposite. You light up a room when you walk into it. You give and give and give. Your intelligence is a sparking flame. You're like some Amazonian angel striding amongst us mere mortals.'

She snorted. 'Sounds like you've been wearing your beer goggles too long.'

He chuckled. 'No beer goggles. Just reality. Everyone can see it but you, and it destroys me to know that. But do you know what really destroys me?'

She shook her head. 'I don't think I want to know.'

He cupped her face in his big, cool hands. 'What really destroys me every time I think about it is that, despite the pain your power has caused you, you took on more to save your friend. You took on more to help our pack. You let Harrison and then Adeline take you over, even though it took something from you to do so, just because others wanted it. Because it would help them. You did this despite the impact on you physically or mentally. And you have stayed to help us over and over and you're going to do it again, no matter how much it scares you to do it or how you long to go and lead a normal life, one free of magic. You might pretend that you're okay about going in there and talking to the spirits, but I can see underneath the bravado even if the others can't. I know it terrifies you. And yet you're still going to do it. If that's not strength, I don't know what is.'

She swallowed hard, wanting to deny his words, but no words would come. Her throat was Sahara dry.

'You say you're going to go after all this, but I don't think you will. I don't think you could. You don't have running away in you.'

'You don't know me.'

'You've got that wrong. It's you who doesn't know you.'

'Adam.' She ground her fist against her chest, against the burning in her heart.

His thumbs brushed over her cheeks as he captured her gaze, the cold of his touch shooting electric warmth through her body. Then, before she had time to take a breath and tell him to let her go, he brushed his lips against hers in an achingly sweet kiss.

She pressed up and into him, wanting more—she could give herself this one last time—but he kept it light and after a long, too-sweet moment that made tears sting and burn her eyes, he pulled away.

His breath brushed over her face, cool and clean like a spring breeze in the forest. 'By the Moon, Michelline. You undo me.' He leaned his forehead against hers. 'You completely undo me.'

She was rather undone herself, her legs shaking, her breath a shallow pant. 'Adam.'

He brushed his lips against hers again, a little harder this time, but before she could open to the kiss, give herself up to it, he let go and stepped back. And even though her legs shook, she stood firm and didn't reach for him again.

'See. So strong,' he said, smiling his knowing smile at her.

'I'm still not letting you give me any of your power.'

'Stubborn,' said with an even wider smile and moved away so she could open the door.

'Everything okay?' Bron asked, bounding over to give Shelley a hug as she entered the room.

Shelley allowed the hug before gently disengaging. 'Everything's fine. I just want to get this done.' It wasn't a lie. Adam was right about that. To protect her friends and their loved ones, Shelley would face death itself and shout 'fuck off you bastard' in its face. With that in mind, she dropped her outer shield and said, 'Who'd like to answer some questions?'

16

Spirits rushed at Shelley. Their cries, which would have normally been ear splitting, were a dull roar, like the ocean heard at a distance. Before they could get too close, they were stopped short, her shields doing what they were designed to do—allow her to talk to them without giving them power over her.

'Impressive,' Adam said from beside her.

He was right. She was more in control than she'd been in a long time. She shot him a cocky look.

He simply cocked a brow at her and waved her to continue.

Shelley turned back to the spirits, the confused expressions on their faces almost funny. 'I need information.' They continued to stare at her but didn't say anything. 'Okay. Right. I want to know if anyone here knows anything about the spirit woman who appeared to Adam on the night he was struck with warlock lighting?' Still nobody came forward. In fact, a few of them drifted away. 'If anyone's got some information to share, we'd be very grateful.'

More of them drifted away, some through the walls, others to stand behind a group of three women who were dressed in Jane Austen-era clothing. They were staring at her, gazes narrowed. 'What about you?' she asked, moving closer to them. 'Do you know anything that might be helpful?'

They stared at her balefully. The blonde on the left looked as if she was about to say something, but the grey-haired one in the middle wrapped her long, thin fingers around blondie's arm and pulled her back. 'We mayn't talk with one who does not come to us free and clear of that which rebuffs us.'

Shelley frowned. And then it dawned on her what the woman was talking about. They wanted her to lower her shields entirely. 'I can't do as you ask. I need my shields to protect me.'

'You insult us all with your ignorance and fear. If you truly understood your power, you would know you do not need protection from us. It is we who need protection from you.'

'I've never hurt any spirit, but I've been hurt by them.'

'Only because you deny what you are. It is your hatred and fear that hurts you, not us.'

'That's not true.' She waved her hand at the other spirits. 'Didn't you see what they just tried to do? If I didn't have my shields up to protect myself, they would have overwhelmed me. I would have become insane long ago if I didn't learn to shield myself from them all. They won't leave me alone. Ever.'

'Because you refuse to do what is yours to do.'

'And what is that?'

'Help us. If you helped us, we might be able to help you,' Blondie said.

'You're holding back help because you're miffed at me for protecting myself?'

'No,' the brunette said. 'You are the conduit. It is your duty to help as it is ours to help in return, and yet your refusal to do as your position decrees has caused harm, to you as much as us.'

'We want to help. We have always wanted to help,' they intoned together.

'That's not true. Any spirit who's ever come to me has just wanted to take. Wanted me to do things for them.'

Grey-hair nodded. 'It is true some spirits are like that, but the fault is partly yours. You surrounded yourself with the sick and dying in your work. It is only natural that in their confused state, the recently departed would flock to you, seeking guidance. And yet, you rebuff them.'

'I let them in when I was younger, but they hurt me. They often took me over and forced me to speak for them. It was beyond my control. It was forcing me down the path to insanity.'

Blondie shook her head sadly. 'You could have learned so much from us if you'd only kept yourself open, especially once you were free from the influence of your family. They were wrong in what they taught you, what they allowed to occur.'

'We would give you all that we are, all that we were,' the brunette said. 'And yet, since coming to live with the pack, you continue to rebuff us. All of us.' She gestured with her hand at the spirits standing around.

'I want to learn now. I'm willing to learn now.'

'Not with your shields still in place. We cannot share with you what we must if you have them raised.'

'Why? Why can't you simply tell me?'

'There is more to share than words.'

'You know something that can help me?'

'We do. However, we can only share with you what you need if you lower your shields. All of them.'

Shelley stared at them. What they asked ... could she do it? What if they were wrong? Or tricking her? But they looked so sincere. So hurt. And they were from covens attached to the pack, otherwise they wouldn't be here. There would be no reason for them to want to harm her. Besides, their belligerent expressions said they wouldn't bend to her will. She had to bend to theirs.

She didn't think she could do it.

'What are they saying?' Adam asked. The hopeful look on his face, his trust in her ... she couldn't let him down.

Shit. She was going to do this. Was going to drop her shields. It was the only way to find information that might help get him back.

Closing her eyes before she could think twice about it, she went into the part of her mind where her shields were and stripped them away in one wrenching burst of power.

'Oof.' She swayed on her feet at the impact of the shield breaking apart in her mind. There was a whooshing sound, followed by silence. She took a breath in. Perhaps the spirits weren't going to rush her. Perhaps they were going to help her this time. Perhaps their needs wouldn't pull at her and push at her, battering at her emotions, threatening to tear her sanity apart. She began to open her eyes.

They surged towards her. All of them. The noise of their entreaties made her slam her hands to her ears and curl in on herself. More and more of them appeared, rushing towards her.

'Shelley!'

Adam, Bron, Jason, River, all called her name as they reached for her, held her steady as she weathered the barrage.

'Why did you drop your shields? Skye cried.

'They won't talk to me otherwise.'

The three ancient witches were calling to the spirits, asking them to stop harassing Shelley. Some paid attention, others still came at her; their needs pushed at her. Her head began to pound, her breath coming in gasps.

She opened her eyes, gaze finding the ancient witches. 'This is why I have shields.'

'This is what your shields have wrought. You have made them desperate.'

The noise, the pressure of all of them was too much. Too much. She couldn't stand it. Felt herself slipping. She tried to grab for her shields but was too overwhelmed. They wouldn't respond. All she could do was clutch her ears to try to block out the noise of them. But it was no use. She could hear them anyway. Feel them.

'Enough!' Adam roared, standing in front of her, the purple of her power pulsing around him like a beacon. In the corner of the room, his body jerked on its bed. 'You will not hurt her anymore.' His eyes blazed, filled with the amethyst fire of her power.

'Adam!' she cried.

But he didn't seem to hear her. 'Piss off. Piss off all of you.' The purple power pulsed out, moving in waves that pushed the spirits back. On the bed in the corner, Adam's body jerked again.

'Adam, stop!' Shelley said, reaching for him. His physical body shook as if he was having some kind of fit. 'You're hurting yourself.'

'I'm helping you.' He closed his eyes. The purple power vibrated, then shoved outwards in rippling waves. It grabbed all the spirits up, tossed them about, sweeping them all before it, taking them away, out of the room.

All except the ones she needed to speak to. It moved around them, like a current around a rock.

Where there were a hundred spirits, there was now only three; and Adam.

He collapsed to his knees, shaking, but still, he smiled up at her. 'I did it.' Then he fell onto his back.

'Adam!' She went down on her knees, cradling his head in her lap. He was colder than before and not as solid. 'Hell, Adam. What did you do?' She blinked back tears. Angry. She was so angry with him. 'I told you not to endanger yourself.'

'I'm okay, Kitten.'

Her fingers trembled as she stroked his hair back from his face. 'No, you're not. You collapsed. You don't feel the same as before.'

He shook off her help and pushed himself up to sit beside her. 'I'm fine. See. I just got a little dizzy.' He stroked his thumb across the back of her hand then reached out to cup her face, tipping her chin up so their gazes met. 'See. I'm fine. I promise. You were wrong.'

'I'm not wrong, you fucking idiot. Can't you see?' The words came out husky and without a shred of the anger she was sure she should feel.

His smile widened and his thumb stroked across her cheek, making her want to lean into him. 'I see perfectly well. It's you who has the problem.'

'What's going on?' Jason asked. He stood by the bed, Bron with him, her hand over Adam's now still body. 'What's happened to Adam?' Jason's gaze roved the room.

Shelley frowned. 'Adam used the power he'd taken from me to make all the spirits go away.'

'I assume from you swearing he's still here?'

'You can't see him?' She looked at Adam again. Her power was still there, but only in the centre of his chest as a flicker around his heart. The sparkling purple that had tinged his skin, allowing the non-Mediums to see him, was gone. 'Adam, what did you do?'

'What I had to.'

'But only I can see and hear you now.'

He smiled at her, and the smile wasn't sad at all. 'That's all I need right now, Kitten.' He gestured to the witches. 'I don't know how much time I bought you, so you better hurry up. I don't think I can do that again.'

The witches! She'd completely forgotten about them. She turned to face them, scrambling to her feet, her anger with Adam now aimed at them. 'I told you! I said that would happen. It always happens.'

They'd moved closer together, their attitudes completely changed from the haughty, slightly pissed-off attitudes of before. There was now a wariness about them, their gaze flickering from her to Adam as he stood beside her.

She took a deep, shuddering, chest-hurting breath, then lifted her chin. She should probably find out why they stayed when all the other spirits had been pushed away by Adam, but instead she said, 'What he did just then is nothing compared to what I'll do if you don't answer my question and help us. Help the packs.'

'Ask us what you wish to know,' Grey-hair said.

'You know what I want. Adeline's asked around. So has Adam.'

'We need *you* to ask us.'

Shelley rolled her eyes. 'Fine. Do you know the witch who spoke to Adam the night of Oestra and do you know how to find her?'

'That is two questions,' Brunette grumbled.

Shelley glared at her.

Blondie nodded. 'She is one of those who tied us to the packs. One of those who saved us all from our excess powers.'

Shelley's gaze went from Adam to Bron then River and Jason before returning to Blondie. 'You can't mean Bridgette Colliere.'

'No. Her spirit resides in the one just recently joined to your coven.'

'Eloise.'

'Yes. The Nexus,' they said together.

'It is not her of whom we speak,' Grey said. 'It is her friend. The sister to the one you fight.'

Shelley's gaze met Adam's. 'They're saying your mystery woman is Morghanna Cantrae.'

Adam shook his head. 'But she cursed us. Her sister is seeking revenge on us because of her death. Why would she help us?'

'Good question.' Shelley turned back to the three witch-spirits. 'Why would she help us?'

'Ask her yourself.'

'I would if I could, but she's not here.'

Blondie smiled. 'Now your shields are down, she will be able to focus in on your power and come to us again.'

'Why? How?'

'Your shields block more than us from conversing with you.'

'She has arrived.' The three witches gestured behind them.

She turned.

A doorway of light opened in the wall between the beds where Adam and Cordy lay. Standing in that doorway of light was a slight, shadowy figure. She paused before taking a few steps forward, allowing them to see more than a shadowy figure.

She was tiny, her heart-shaped face sweet and youthful looking, but at the same time giving an impression of an old, old soul. Her dark hair moved in a fae wind as if alive, tendrils flying back from her face. Her eyes were so blue, they were almost purple—just like Shelley's—and they darted around as if she was looking for something. No, not simply looking. Guarding.

'You must come.' Her gaze went to Adam as she crooked her finger at him.

'You're Morghanna Cantrae?'

She darted her head to look to the side, then back at him. 'Yes.'

'Well, isn't that just a kick in the gonads?'

Morghanna blinked at him. 'I beg your pardon?'

'I was prepared to go with you because the Goddess said I must, but now I'm not going anywhere until you answer a few questions, lady.' He folded his arms.

'We do not have time for this.'

'Make time. You betrayed my kind. You instigated the Curse that almost wiped out my pack. Why on earth should I trust you?'

'Adam!' Shelley said.

'What? She can't expect me just to follow her without any questions.'

'Yes, she can. The Goddess told you to do exactly that.'

'What's happening? What's going on?' Jason asked.

'Morghanna Cantrae is here.'

'*The* Morghanna Cantrae?' Skye looked shocked. 'Bridgette's friend?'

'Morrigan's sister?' Bron choked out.

'Yes.'

'Is she the one Adam saw?'

'Yes,' Shelley said.

'Fuck.' Jason rubbed his chin, his fingers rasping on his bristles. 'What does she want?'

'She wants Adam to go with her.' Shelley frowned as Morghanna peered around again, as if worried she was being followed.

'And I'm not going,' Adam said at the same time Jason asked, 'Why? Why does she want him to go with her? Where's she been? Can we trust her?'

Adam pointed at his brother, face triumphant. 'My question exactly.'

Shelley glared at him to shut up. His interruptions added to the crawling feeling that had started climbing up and down her spine ever since Morghanna stepped through the door acting all twitchy. 'I don't know. She only just arrived.'

'Is Adam going to go?'

'Not right now he's not. He's being belligerent.'

'I've a perfect right to be.'

'Ask her why she wants him to go.'

'She can hear you.'

'Well, what's her answer?'

She put her hand up. 'Just give me a moment to sort this out, okay?' She turned to Adam, who was still glaring at the woman and the other spirit witches in front of him. 'The Goddess did tell you to trust Morghanna. If she wants you to go with her, you need to go.'

'Listen to your friend,' Morghanna pleaded. 'We need to leave. Now.' Her gaze darted around again.

'I'm not leaving here. Not with someone who cursed my kind.'

'I did not mean to curse all Were. I had no idea my curse would have those ramifications when I canted it. I had been beaten and starved and tortured, had seen my husband killed before me and knew I would never set eyes on my baby son again. I was being tied to a stake to be burned alive. I wanted revenge on the Were who had brought me to this point, an Alpha weak enough to use his pack and allow his son to become an unspeakable monster. I wanted them to pay. Him and those who remained unthinkingly loyal to him despite the fact he still used them and wouldn't stop.'

'The Alpha might have been to blame, but how could any other member of his pack have deserved what you did to them?' Adam asked.

'They should have protected me with their lives, especially after all I'd sacrificed for them. But they didn't. I wasn't as important to them as their Alpha and their dying pack. And I wasn't the only one to suffer because of their blind obedience. So yes, they did deserve it. But I promise you, I never intended for my curse to manifest the way it did. I was horrified when I saw what my moment of grief and pain and loss had wrought. Especially on the McVales. Your pack is more special to me than you could know.'

'We know. We carry your blood,' Adam scoffed.

She took a sobbing breath as she nodded. 'I am eternally grateful to the McVales because you took my child in, kept him safe. You helped him to grow into the adult he was always meant to be and to father a dynasty of strong witches and warlocks that has made me so proud to watch.'

'Your curse almost brought that dynasty to an end.'

'You cannot know how sorry I am for it. My curse was meant to safeguard my kind. To ensure my child would always be safe within the pack structure. I never wanted what happened to me to happen to another witch or warlock.'

'Our pack has held sacred to the Pact; we have kept our coven safe and happy and secure to the best of our abilities, and yet your curse still enacted through no fault of our own. It was because of the actions of your sister that our coven dwindled and then Skye and River were taken from us. Morrigan killed their parents. Not us. And yet we still suffered.'

Morghanna took a pleading step forward. 'You cannot know how sorry I am for it. They had you to help them through though. Your Trickster powers buoyed them until I was able to help Jason find Skye.'

'What?'

Shelley felt as shocked as Adam sounded. 'You helped them? But ... they found each other because it was destined to be so. They're mates.'

'Yes. But it was I who made Skye's father bond them when they were children. I whispered to him in his dreams, knowing what my sister planned.'

'Why didn't you warn him? Why didn't you stop Morrigan?'

'I could not stop her. I may be an agent of the Goddess, working to defeat her enemy, but I do not have her power. Besides, Morrigan shut herself off to me centuries ago when she allowed the Darkness to wrap around her so completely. I did what I could. I warned Skye's father through his visions so that he would ensure Jason and Skye would one day find each other and bring coven and pack back together when it was most crucial.'

Shelley couldn't believe what she was hearing. 'That ... but you ... How?'

'The Goddess helped me guide them back to each other.' She turned to Adam. 'Now she wants me to guide you as only I can. Please, let me do it. Come with me.' She held her hand out again.

Adam swallowed hard as he stared at the ancient witch's hand. Then he glanced at Shelley, his gaze piercing through her to grab at her heart. 'How long will we be gone?'

'That is uncertain. Time runs differently where we are bound.'

'Then I'm not leaving. I'm not leaving my pack. I'm not leaving Shelley. Not for some unknown time. Not when there is so much danger.' He pressed his knuckles into his chest where an ache had lived and grown for months. 'Not when they need me so much.'

'Adam! You have to go.'

'I'm not leaving you.'

'You can't sacrifice yourself for me. I won't allow it.'

'I can, and I will.'

'Adam. This is madness.' Morghanna stepped a little further out of the light from the doorway she'd come through, one hand stretched behind her keeping touch with the light, as if anchoring herself to it. 'You will be of no true use to Shelley or any of the others until you have learned what I am bound to teach you.'

He rounded on her. 'You don't know what happened, what I did for her.'

'You mean the beacon? The way you pushed all the other spirits away that were clamouring at her?' She waved her hand in a tight gesture that seemed confident but betrayed her nervousness; her fingers were trembling. 'I was able to follow those emanations to you.' She flinched, eyes widening as she peered around again. 'Emanations that are still embedded here and will draw other, far more frightening things to you if you do not leave with me right now.'

Her fear reached out to Shelley, making her skin twitch and goose flesh rise on her arms and neck. 'The thing that's chasing you?'

Morghanna's gaze met hers and an understanding passed between them.

'It's the Darkness,' Shelley said. 'It's chasing you.'

'Yes. It has always chased me because of what I know. Because of what I can teach. Because of my link to both witches and Were through my bloodline all the way to River and Skye. It would use me to take power that does not belong to it.'

'As it's used Morrigan.'

'Yes, but far worse, for my power is akin to yours and would give the Darkness the dominion over death it has always craved. I have spent centuries trying to help your pack but being hindered on this plane because I have to constantly run, constantly hide from it.' She turned back to Adam. 'I came out of hiding for you. Because of what you are and what you can do. I have waited a very long time for you, Trickster.' Her gaze met Shelley's again. 'As I have waited a long time for you.'

'Me? Why me?'

'You have blood from the Gods running through your veins. The banshee is of them. It is unique and powerful and when combined with your other gift, has power to rival a God.'

Shelley's breathing came hard and fast—she'd known, she'd known ever since Adam had told her what the Goddess had told him, and yet hearing confirmation wasn't a simple thing. She didn't want it. Didn't want it.

'You are also part of the triumvirate.'

'The triumvirate?' Adam asked. 'The Goddess mentioned that too, but I still don't truly know what it means.'

'I do not have time to explain now, other than to say it is something we have been waiting a very long time to come into existence. And now that it has, I must teach you, Adam, what you must know to bring it all together. Your tie to the pack, to the witches, to the banshee through your Trickster power, makes you key.' Her gaze flickered back to Shelley. 'And you must stop fearing what you are and embrace it. You must learn to see what a wonderful gift it truly is.'

'It's no gift. I see death.'

Morghanna looked at her sadly. 'I understand. I felt the same for so long. But I need you to see past your fear and understand that your gift is far more than simply seeing death. You are connected to the past and all that it offers for the future, and through the banshee, you see the future and what should or should not be avoided. If you learn how to master it, your power will be a gift beyond compare, one others will envy you for.'

'It will make me go insane. Like others in my family.'

'Only if you refuse to embrace what it is to be Medium and banshee. The key to your fears is knowledge—which is much more than most other people have. You are so close to—'

A shriek echoed through the room. The lights flickered in the wake of the shriek. When they steadied, they were dimmer than before.

'It is nearly here.' Morghanna reached out towards Adam. 'I have spent more time here than intended. You must come, now, before it catches up with me.'

Adam stubbornly shook his head. 'No. I said I'm not leaving.'

'Adam, you must,' Shelley said. Cold was creeping into the room, a sense of doom about to crash down on them, overwhelming her. In reaction, her banshee was waking, a low hum rising from her stomach, making her teeth chatter. Evil was coming, and if it entered this room, if it got Morghanna, or worse, Adam, then everything she knew and loved would be destroyed. If this banshee wail came into full effect, she might never recover the after-effects.

Even though she needed him—even though she desperately didn't want to lose him again—she had to make Adam go. It was the only way to stop the coming death.

The only way to save him from the Darkness. To save him from her.

'Sorry, Adam.' She reached up, pressed her lips to his in an agonising kiss and then grasping her powers in a way she'd only just realised she could do thanks to him, she slammed them into him, pushing him back across the room to Morghanna and the doorway.

'Kitten, no. You need me here.' He fought, shouting at her over the sound of the wind in her ears, each word a slash to her heart. But she couldn't listen. She had to make him go. It was the only way. The dark thing that chased Morghanna was drawing near, the feel of it a scrape along her skin, hard fingernails down her spine, a cloying presence that made her want to cringe, to gag. She had to get Adam through the door before it came otherwise everything, all of this, would be for nothing.

She didn't need to see the fear and desperation in Morghanna's eyes to know that was true. She shoved her powers at him, harder, forcing him towards the doorway of light.

His body began to buck and slam hard against the bed as he fought her, screaming, 'I won't leave you. I won't. You need me. You need me.'

'Bron!' Jason cried.

Bron raced over to his body, grabbed an injection and pushed it into the port on the drip. His body jerked harder. She looked up, eyes wide. 'That should have worked.' She looked at the monitor—his heart rate was climbing too fast, the heart monitor a screech. 'If he keeps this up, he'll crash.'

Adam's body slammed onto the bed over and over, so hard it made Shelley's teeth rattle and her bones ache. 'Adam, stop fighting. Please. Stop fighting me.' Tears streamed down her face. The evil coming closer was pressing heavier on her, making it hard to think, hard to breathe.

'Do it. Do it now!' Morghanna shrieked.

Shelley nodded, then grasping hold of all the power she could, looked Adam in the eye, whispered, 'Forgive me,' and shoved everything at him.

The power hit him, picked him up and carried him the remaining few feet towards the door of light. He cried out, the sound tearing at her heart.

Morghanna grabbed his hand as he flew past her and just before she was pulled through with Adam, shouted, 'Thank you. We will return to help you all.'

The door of light slammed closed.

Adam was gone.

17

A scream lit the air with its fury. The lights flickered and then went off as a loud whooshing sound filled the room. A swirl of foul-smelling air whipped around Shelley, shoving at her, pulling at her hair.

'Weak. You are weak and you are mine!' The voice screamed in her mind as claws raked down her spine.

She cried out at the pain, at the terror of the voice in her mind, and crashed to her knees.

'Shelley!' Bron screamed.

'What's going on?' Jason.

'It's the Darkness,' River said, his voice strong despite the thread of terror there. 'It's here.'

'You can't have them!' A brilliant blue light flared in the black.

There was a high-pitched screech as the blue light flared out, becoming more brilliant, pushing out to light more of the room.

'I command you to leave this place.'

A final screech and then an explosion of air that knocked everyone in the room backwards and sent furniture and medical equipment and papers flying.

The blue light flared again and pushed into all corners of the room. Shelley covered her eyes, blinded.

The light faded.

Silence.

'Jason. Are you all right?'

Shelley lifted her head to see Skye racing towards Jason as he picked himself up off the floor next to Adam's bed.

'Adam?' She raced to his side, picked his hand up. His skin was ice cold, body deathly still. 'Bron? Bron!'

Bron scrambled to her feet, then closing her eyes, ran her hands over him as Shelley stood breathless, waiting. 'He's okay. He's okay.'

Relief flooded through her. Adam's body was okay. Her knees buckled and it was only the fact she could lean against the side of the bed that she didn't fall to the floor.

'He got away. Thank the Goddess he got away,' she breathed. She wished she knew definitely he was safe but had to believe Morghanna would keep him so.

Hell. Would he ever forgive her for what she'd just done? He'd have to know why. Morghanna would tell him. Surely she would. He would have died if she hadn't done it. The banshee scream had been building inside her, telling her that he would die if she didn't make him go away. Something about what he was, what Morghanna was, made them more vulnerable to the Darkness than any other spirit, or human for that matter. She didn't know how she knew that. She just did.

'By the Moon, Skye.' Jason's words were full of awe and relief as he held Skye's face in his hands and kissed her. 'Are you okay?' She was trembling so hard, Shelley could see it.

She looked around her, eyes a bit dazed, teeth chattering as she spoke. 'I'm fine, I think. I haven't used that much power since the night I bonded with Bron and Shelley and mated with you to defeat Morrigan.' She leaned against him. 'It took a bit out of me.'

He held her close. 'Take what you need from me.'

She looked up at him, touched his face.

The tenderness of the gesture made Shelley's eyes sting, her gaze blurring. She blinked rapidly, but it didn't help. The room stayed blurred. Her breath was a shallow rasp in her throat. The voices around her ebbed and flowed in the rising sound of wind that roared in her ears. Her back stung. She reached around to touch it, but the movement hurt and she bit back a wince.

'I'm just so glad it worked,' Skye continued, her voice drifting in the distance. 'I felt the Darkness before, but never as strong as that. After what it did to River last year ... I was just so filled with fury when I felt it going for Shelley and for River again. Something inside me flared to life that it would once again dare to touch those I love. I wasn't sure what I was doing. I just did it.'

'You were brilliant.'

'Yes, you were,' Bron said, reaching over to take her hand. 'Thank you.'

'Yes, thanks sis.' River snatched her from Jason and into a great big hug, making her laugh.

Laughing, voice muffled against his shoulder, she said, 'I'm sure you would have managed without me.'

'I'm not so sure about that,' Bron said as River released her. Jason took her hand again and pulled her against him.

Skye shook her head. 'Of course you could have. You've fought the Darkness before. You and Shelley together could have done it.' She turned to look at Shelley, her eyes going wide. 'Shelley!'

Shelley tried to say something, but the room swung around her and despite her grip on the side of the bed, she crashed onto the floor.

'Shit!'

Bron raced over to her side.

'What's wrong with her?' Skye said, coming down beside Bron.

'I don't know. River, Jason, can you pick Shelley up and get her onto that bed over there.'

They did as she asked. Shelley moaned as they lifted her, eyes fluttering open. 'It hurts.' She tried to indicate her back.

'Roll her over,' Bron said as they lowered her to the bed.

Hands grabbed her gently and rolled her, but the movement made the pain rip through her like lightning. She screamed.

'Fuck. What's wrong?' Jason said.

'Oh, Goddess.'

In a distant part of her mind, untouched by the pain, she thought, *Crap. It couldn't be good if Bron sounded like that.*

'Skye, get me the morphine. Over there in that drawer. Yes. And River, I need the saline and bandages in that drawer there. Jason, keep holding her still.'

'What is it?'

'Her back is torn open, like she's been clawed by something burning.'

Shelley heard whimpering and realised it was her. She tried to stop, but the noise didn't seem to be within her control.

'It's hard to keep her still. She's shaking too much.'

'She's in shock. She used too much power getting Adam and Morghanna through the door and safe from the Darkness.'

'Oh goodness,' Skye said, fingers trembling over her mouth. 'Her shields. She'd dropped them. She had nothing to protect herself from it.'

Bron nodded grimly. 'I'll do a Healing, but we need to clean out this wound first.'

There was more scurrying, the sound of metal sliding open and closing, shuffling steps, packages being torn open. 'Here.'

'No. With magic. And then we'll have to erect some shields around her until she can do it herself. Skye, do you think you can help me?'

'Just tell me what you want me to do.'

The voices were now so far away, Shelley could barely hear them. Then a feeling of rushing cold and warmth flowed through her and she floated away.

It would have been blissful except that a wolf's piercing howl of distress punctured her bubble of happy and dug claws deep in her heart.

'HE WON'T STOP HOWLING. I can't seem to get through to him,' Jason said to Bron as she and River came back into the room after leaving to pick the herbs and plants she needed. Bron rushed over to where he sat next to Adam's bed, holding his brother's hand. Skye sat at his side, haunting worry shadowing her eyes.

'We've tried everything,' Skye said. 'I've tried to reach Adam's wolf through my Packbond. He quietens a little at my touch combined with Jason's but then he kind of pushes past us through the bond, like he's searching for something and when he can't find it, he starts up again worse than before.' She looked up at Bron, eyes beseeching. 'I feel so helpless. I don't know what to do.' She glanced over at Cordy.

Bron reached out and pulled her into a hug. 'I know. I wish Cordy was awake too. She'd know what to do.' She took in a deep breath and blew it out, fringe ruffling. 'I could try to waken her.'

They looked over at her, a heavy silence of pain and grief stilling them. 'No,' Skye said, her voice husky. 'It would be cruel to wake her before she's ready.'

'I don't know if she'll ever be ready,' Bron said.

They both nodded, looking over at their mates, and Bron knew that if either of them lost their mates, they wouldn't want to be awake to face the pain either.

'I'm not sure Cordy would be able to do any good anyway,' River said. 'The wolf started howling just after Adam went wherever he went with Morghanna. I think Adam coming back is the cure.'

'No,' Jason said, brow furrowing. 'I know I was a bit distracted with everything going on, but I'm pretty sure he began when Bron and Skye used their magic to put Shelley under and erect a shield around her.'

'You know, I think you're right,' River said. 'That's when I truly noticed him howling too. I just thought that maybe in the commotion I'd missed something.'

'You're saying he's distressed about Shelley?' Skye looked over at their friend lying still on the bed on the other side of the room. 'Is that because he's her Shadow?'

'Maybe.' Jason rubbed his hand over his chin, scraping the bristles. 'Although, I wouldn't expect this amount of distress. He'd more likely be angry with himself for not protecting her. I'd expect strong waves of determination not to let it happen again, but not this ... pain.' He rubbed his knuckles against his chest. 'It's extreme. Almost as if ...' His eyes widened.

'Almost as if what?' River asked.

Jason turned slowly, eyes wide, shocked.

River slowly shook his head. 'No. There's been no sign in the Packbond. Surely we would have felt it if that had happened? You would have felt it at the very least. You're not only Alpha, but his brother.'

Jason walked slowly over to Shelley. 'I know. But maybe ...'

'Are you talking about a mating?' Bron asked.

'Holy cow!' Skye said, joining Jason, brushing a stray hair off Shelley's face. A laugh choked out of her. 'Shelley will hate that.'

Bron laughed too. 'That's an understatement. She's been fighting her attraction to him ever since they met.'

'I thought she hated him,' River said.

Bron touched his face. 'That's what she wanted everyone to think. It was easier for her that way. A defence mechanism against being hurt again.' She stroked Shelley's hair. 'She was hurt so terribly by her family. They should have protected her, loved her, supported her. Instead, they used her, caused her pain and kept the truth from her of what happened to those in their family who used their talent. When she found out and refused to do their bidding, they outwardly ostracised her. That was when she met her fiancé. What she didn't know about him was that he was secretly working with her family to bring her back to them.'

'Her fiancé was working with her family? Is that why they broke up?' River asked.

'Mostly,' Skye replied. 'Despite her best efforts to keep the spirits at bay after she left her family, sometimes they got through. One came to her and told her something horrible was happening with her fiancé. She dropped everything at work and rushed home, only to find her fiancé in bed with her cousin.'

'Why? If he was working with her family, why would he have done that?'

'Because she wouldn't use her powers and he needed them to raise his profile in the coven, so he went to someone who would,' Skye said flatly.

Jason's eyes filled with disgust. 'Her cousin. She was a Medium as well.'

'Her family's coven believed those with the power to talk to the dead gave strength to the rest of the coven through using their power. The men believed it gave them virility to be able to create life with someone who dealt in death.'

'Did Shelley know why he was with her?'

Bron shook her head. 'He came from overseas so she had no idea he was from the European branch of the coven. He went straight for her, wooed her and made her feel loved and special. She had no idea he was using her or working with her family.'

'Fucking arseholes.'

Jason nodded his agreement at River's words. 'I want to tear them apart. How could they do that to her? It's no wonder she's kept herself so separate from us.'

Skye nodded. 'When she saved me by linking with my power and linking herself with the pack, it hurt her in ways I will always be sorry for. She hates that she's linked by blood to her family, but this is even stronger than that and she's struggled with it a lot. She doesn't trust the bonds of family. The only reason she trusts the bonds of friendship with Bron and me is because she met us before her family had truly destroyed her trust in love of any kind. But trusting Bron and me is as far as she's able to stretch her love and trust, especially since her bastard ex did what he did. I don't think she'll ever come to terms with the bonds of pack, of being tied to us all by something she can't bring herself to trust not to hurt her.' She blinked hard, her voice thick with tears. 'If I could find some way to release her from it, I would. I hate that helping me hurt her so badly.'

'Come here.' Jason wrapped his arms around Skye, stroking her hair. 'I wish I'd known she was struggling as much as this.'

'And I wanted to tell you. But Shelley doesn't even like the fact we know all we do. Besides, she knew Bron and I needed her and that you needed her. She said it was nice to be needed and she'd be happy with that. We asked Cordy if there was some way to release her, but she didn't know of any. She said Shelley could live away from the pack if she wished, like my grandmother had, but that she'd always be linked.'

'If she'd wanted to go, we wouldn't have stopped her. We would have helped her,' Jason said, looking at River, who nodded.

Skye leaned back and stroked her hand down his face. 'I know. But despite thinking that she's a runner, running is not in Shelley's nature. Especially when those she loves have need of her.' Her gaze slid back to Shelley. 'Maybe it's that loyalty that's allowed a mating bond to come into existence between her and Adam. Although, I would have thought it impossible.'

'I could be wrong. It could be something else,' Jason said. 'I mean, even now, I can't feel anything definitive.'

'But why else would his wolf be so distressed over her being hurt and unconscious?' River asked.

Jason shook his head slowly. 'I don't know. I've never come across anything like this.'

Bron huffed out a little laugh and pointed at Shelley. 'The irony is the only person who might know can't tell us.'

'She probably wouldn't tell us if she did know,' Skye said.

Bron nodded. 'Yeah. She most likely wouldn't even acknowledge it to herself if she did feel it.'

'And if she won't acknowledge it,' Skye said, a deep line creasing her brow, 'the mating can't truly come into being, can it?'

'No.' Jason's gaze went to Adam's still form. 'They'll both suffer and there's nothing we can do about it.'

'But surely, when she wakes, that will help. His wolf will stop howling?'

'I don't know.' He rubbed his brow. 'I just don't know. Skye, are you okay?'

'Just a little nauseous,' she said, then made a dash for the sink.

'I'm not cleaning that up,' a husky voice said from behind them. They all jumped and turned to see Shelley trying to push herself to a sitting position in the bed. 'Crap, that hurts!'

'Shelley!' Bron leapt towards her. 'Careful. Your wounds are only just mending. I haven't had a chance to do a second Healing. Roll over and I'll start now.'

Shelley gripped her friend's hand. 'Don't tire yourself further. I know what you must have done already. My back was bad and I—' Her eyes flared wide. 'My shields!'

'It's okay. Skye and I've put something in place until you've had a chance to rebuild yours.'

'You did what?' She nodded towards Skye who was standing heaving into the sink on the other side of the room, Jason holding her hair and stroking her back. 'I don't think you should do that again if it that's the result.'

Skye lifted her head. 'Don't worry about me. I'll be fine.' She wiped her mouth with the towel Jason handed her and sipped at the glass of water he passed her. 'But is the shield okay? The spirits aren't bothering you, are they?'

Shelley looked around. 'Actually, no. There's none here to bother me. Aside from Adeline that is.' She gestured to the woman standing in the corner. 'And the Macbeth trio over there.' The three witches looked insulted, and turning as one in a swish of gowns, they disappeared through the wall. Shelley would have chuckled at their dramatic departure, but the howl in her head that had woken her pulled at her, driving out all other thoughts. She gritted her teeth and swung her feet over the edge of the bed, frowning as she saw bare legs and a hospital gown. 'You undressed me? How long have I been out?'

'Slightly more than twenty-four hours. But you need more rest, and another Healing.' Bron tried to stop her from standing, but Shelley pushed forward and stood, wincing again as her muscles pulled tightly, like she'd exercised too hard.

'You did a good enough job. It's not me you need to be worried about. It's Adam. And his wolf.'

Skye gasped. 'You heard us?'

Shelley tipped up her chin. She didn't want to answer. It was too painful to consider whether what they had said about Adam and her was true. But she couldn't ignore the fact that his wolf was in pain and that, if they were right, she might be the only one who could soothe him. 'I guess there's only one way of finding out the truth.'

She began to walk stiffly over to Adam's body. Jason and River were suddenly at her side, helping her. She was aware of a draft on her back—bloody hospital gowns!—but she couldn't think about her modesty right now. The wolf's howling was awful. It had been a constant gnawing at the back of her mind, a tug of pain in her chest. She'd tried to ignore it, to sink back into the blissful, pain-free slumber where she could dream of being with Adam without any of the complications of real life, but the howl wasn't something she could ignore.

River pulled a chair for her to sit in when she reached the side of Adam's bed, but she didn't take it. Instead, she leaned against the hospital bed and put her hand on Adam's chest near the horrible black wound so near his heart. 'Shh,' she whispered. 'It's okay. I'm here. I'm fine. I'm fine.'

The howling stopped at her touch, but then it started up again, less painful, more a sad mournfulness, as if begging for forgiveness.

It pulled at her heart more than the other howling had. She began to stroke Adam's hair back from his forehead, fingers gliding through the dark silk. 'You couldn't have done anything to stop the Darkness. It wasn't your fault. You did all you could to keep your body safe, to help me make Adam go where he's most needed. I felt your strength. You helped me.'

A whimper and another mournful howl greeted her words. She cupped his face, fingers brushing his too long hair from his face.

'Stop beating yourself up. I don't blame you. Nobody blames you. You'll make me angry if you keep this up. You don't want me being angry with you, do you?'

There was a whimper in answer. An image fluttered in her mind, of Adam's black wolf rubbing up against her, bumping its head into her hand so that she'd stroke him from snout to neck, thumbs rubbing over his ears. She smiled at the image. 'I want to see you too. But you can't change. Not yet. It's not safe for your human body. But I promise, I'm going to work on some way to bring the human Adam spirit back so that you can come out to play. I promise I'll cuddle you then.'

Another image played through her mind of her lying down on the bed beside Adam's body, hands stroking his hair back from his brow, stroking around the black mark on his chest.

The image caused her lungs to constrict, her heart aching with every beat. Longing threaded through her veins, her limbs, making her want to do nothing but lie down next to Adam, stretching her body against the long, muscled length of him, the scent of him surrounding her like an enticing spring breeze.

She'd dreamed of being stretched against him, skin to skin, as his lips and hands roamed over her body making her gasp and cry out as her hands did the same to him. In those dreams, he hadn't just been lying there, as still as death. He'd made her feel special, treasured; his every touch a benediction, a worship.

So despite the ache begging her to do as the wolf wished, she couldn't lie down next to him right now with those images so piercingly tattooed on her mind's eye. Especially now that his human spirit was no longer there. With him gone, it was more difficult to believe that she could find a way to bring him back to his body. To bring life and light and laughter to limbs that lay so motionless, to features that were unnaturally still.

She shook her head, easing away. 'I can't,' she whispered. 'Not now. I've got to go. Do research to make you both better. But I promise, when you are back together and can change, I'll stroke your head as much as you want.' The wolf whimpered. 'Please. I just can't do it now. I'm sorry.' She trembled, waiting for a response, knowing that if the wolf began howling again, she would do as it asked, but that it would tear her heart apart to do it.

The image was withdrawn and the wolf inside her head snuffled against her, nudging at her in her mind before doing something that made her feel like her hand had been licked.

She jerked back. 'What was that?'

'What was what?'

'I felt him nudge me and then lick my hand.'

'He's in your mind?' Jason asked, the look he gave her significantly hopeful.

'Maybe. I don't know.' She withdrew from the bed. 'I'm probably imagining it.'

'I don't think you were,' Jason said. 'Listen.'

She listened. 'I can't hear anything.'

'Exactly. Adam's wolf is silent.'

'You did it,' Skye said softly. 'You know what this means.'

'It doesn't mean anything.' Guilt was a heavy weight in her chest as she denied the bond. She couldn't do it. Didn't want it. Had never asked to be bonded in that way with anyone. Especially him. She'd already let things go too far. Pain was already a livewire in her chest after forcing Adam to go with Morghanna. She couldn't let it get any worse. She had to shut it off. Turn away. It might hurt a little now, but it would hurt a whole hell of a lot more later if she allowed herself to hope for more than she knew she could have. Her gaze took in her friends; the hopeful expressions on their faces was more than she could bear.

'He's settled now.' She cleared her clogged throat, fingers winding together in front of her. 'I've got to go. I need to build my shields back up. Then I need to get back to Melbourne. Get stuck back into the diaries. Maybe I can get the Macbeth trio to help me understand my power better, given that they, Morghanna and Arianrhod seem to think it's so important. Of course, that's if they'll deign to talk to me again.'

'But they'll make you drop your shields.'

'I'm sure I can come to an understanding with them. I'm of no use to them if the spirits batter at me so much I fall unconscious or go insane.' She grimaced. 'It's necessary if I'm to find something to help Adam. To help all of us against the Darkness, Cain and Morrigan.' She backed away from the bed, away from her friends and their mates, with their hope and their expectations. 'I'll go find Gareth and see if he'll come back with me. If there's any change to Adam, give me a call. And if I find anything, I'll let you know.' She tried to smile, but her mouth was stiff and twitchy, so she stopped. She grabbed the door handle and pulled. 'I have to go.'

The door slammed closed behind her and she ran stiffly down the hall and into the lift, turning to punch the up button over and over until the doors shut and the lift jerked, taking her back to the surface, away from the others and Adam and his wolf and what had just happened down there. She shook her head, went to shove her hands into her pockets and realised she was only wearing the hospital gown.

'Fuck.' She'd have to get some clothes. Then she'd get out of here. The lift jerked again and she almost fell out the doors as they opened.

Gareth stood there, expression serious, a bundle of clothes in his arms. She didn't even bother thanking him or saying anything sarcastic about Were and their freaky communications, but just grabbed the clothes, went into one of the stalls, slammed the door shut and got dressed. There were no shoes, but she didn't care. She had to get away from here. Away from the need simmering in the air, from the knowing that had begun deep inside her when she talked with Adam's wolf in her mind.

When she had dressed, she ran outside to find Gareth waiting for her in one of the sedans. 'Go. Just go,' she said, slamming the door, hugging her arms to her. She was cold. She wasn't sure if she'd ever feel truly warm again. Not that it mattered. All that mattered was getting back to Melbourne. Back to the diaries, where she could lose herself in research and not have to think about the burning ache pulsing in her heart.

18

'**A**re you feeling okay, my love?'

Morrigan glanced behind her. Cain stood in the doorway of the bathroom, arms crossed, possessive interest in his gaze.

Since that night weeks ago, when he'd changed and become her lover, he'd become stronger—and not just in power. He was no longer the student with her the master.

She didn't like it. Especially at the moment when she was so weak and he was glowing with power and good health. 'I'm fine,' she snarled. 'Go away.' That was all she managed before the nausea rose up, forcing her to turn back to the toilet. The heaves were violent and empty, nothing but caustic bile coming up and filling her mouth with bitterness. She was vaguely aware of Cain leaning over her, holding her hair back, a cold cloth on her neck. It was unusually caring and sweet, something a true lover would do.

She didn't trust a moment of it.

Finally, the heaving stopped and she drooped onto the floor next to the toilet, hair sticking to her face and neck, stomach and back aching.

'Let's get you cleaned up, my love.'

She couldn't fight him as he lifted her up and helped her to the basin. She was so weak she had no choice but to lean against him and put up with his ministrations as he washed her face and held a capful of mouthwash to her lips.

'Spit.' When she had, he gave her a glass of water. 'Now drink this.'

She grabbed at it, thirst tearing at her throat, and gulped it down. The glass was pulled out of her hand. She glared at him.

'Slowly, my love, or you'll vomit this up too.'

'Stop treating me like a baby,' she said, voice hoarse and weak.

'I'm not treating you like a baby. I'm treating you like my lover. Like the mother of my baby.'

His words punched into her. She stumbled back against the basin. 'I'm not pregnant. It's just a stomach bug.'

His smile was gentle and patient as he stroked her arm. 'This is no bug. You know that's true. That first night together gifted us more than the best orgasms of our lives.' He brushed his knuckles over her still flat stomach. 'Our combined powers and the Darkness have gifted us a baby. A son to stand at our sides and help us to rule the world.'

He turned his hand over, fingers splayed over her stomach possessively, the look on his face so joyous it was frightening.

She flinched, but he didn't remove his hand. 'I'm not pregnant,' she grated out between clenched teeth. 'It's impossible. The process of taking over a body renders it barren. Not even the Darkness can change that, otherwise it would have done so long ago. Black magic cannot create life. If you knew as much as you think you do, you'd know that.'

His gaze met hers, eyes shining. 'Ah, but that was before Bronwyn did that remarkable Healing at Yule and we were all caught up in the power of it. Things that had been damaged by magical means were fixed that night. Your womb was one of those things.'

She gasped, her fingers clenching over her abdomen. It couldn't be. It couldn't be true.

She couldn't have a life growing inside her. Could she?

As if in answer to her question, something fluttered against the skin of her belly. From the inside.

'See.' Cain moved closer, his fingers pressing more firmly against her stomach.

'You felt that?'

He nodded. 'He knows we're here. His parents. Loving and accepting him. Don't you, little one.'

The flutter came again. 'It could be wind.'

His gaze burned into her, a distinct look of displeasure in his eyes. 'You know it's not. Stop denying what you know to be true.'

'But ... but ... it's too early.' She looked down, both their fingers splayed over the suddenly slightly rounded mound of her stomach. 'To feel anything, I mean. To know for certain.'

Cain dropped his hand and grabbed her chin, fingers pinching into her skin, forcing her to look up at him. 'He is the child of our power and the Darkness. This is not some normal pregnancy. He will grow faster, stronger, than any other child. He has to. He was created on Beltane, the day of light and so must be born on the opposite Quarter day, when the moon is at full potency.'

'Samhain?'

'Yes. The prophecy was about this, not about you taking over Skye's grandmother's body and trying to kill her and River last Samhain as a rebirth. That's why you've failed. You had it wrong. We all had it wrong. This is the true beginning. The true rebirth of the Darkness into the world. He can only come through on the day when the veil between the worlds is thin. On the eve of Samhain, he will be able to enter our world truly whole through the birth of our baby.'

Morrigan shook her head, unable to believe him even though what he said made some kind of horrifying sense. 'How do you know this?'

'The Darkness told me.'

Anger flared inside her. 'The Darkness wouldn't tell you and not tell me. I am its conduit. You are a mere servant.'

'I haven't been a servant for a long time, as you would know if you truly watched and listened. I was never meant to be a servant to you or the Darkness or anyone else. The prophecy wasn't simply about Eloise, it was about me too. It was why you brought us both with you when you killed our family. I have my place, and this is it. The part of the Nexus' power that's within me allowed this to come to pass. As the father to the baby that will become the vessel for the Darkness to enter this world, I will help shape the future.'

She stared at him, nausea rising again, but not because of pregnancy hormones. 'No human could survive the intrusion of the Darkness. Not fully. Certainly not a baby. It couldn't even fully take over the Were for fear of destroying the vessels it wished to use. It had to break itself into small pieces to go inside them. It has never been able to be whole for as far back as it can remember. So, what you say can't be true. It can't be.'

As if to prove her wrong, the thing in her stomach lurched again. She clawed at her shirt, lifting it up to look. There, pushing out from her skin, the imprint of a tiny hand. 'Oh by the dark Gods.'

'You see,' he said, crowing. 'Our child is strong. It will grow fast in your womb and be ready to come into this world as the Darkness has promised.' He grasped her hand, held it tight in his, a manic light in his eyes. 'And you will stand by my side, mother of a dark God, and together we will rule this land for him.'

She stared at him, speechless for the first time in her very long life, her free hand pressed protectively over the new life in her womb.

'Let's seal this ultimate blessing of our partnership with a kiss.'

She wanted to rear away from him, but there was something in his face, his gaze, that shrieked of power and evil and a darkness that had nothing to do with their mutual master. That look made her shudder deep inside, a little tendril of fear uncurling and gripping her dead husk of a heart, making her wary of him in a way she'd never been wary before. Something essential was missing at his core. Why had she never seen it before?

'Or perhaps you did see it and never cared because you had become the same through your need for revenge. The baby has changed something inside you. You are no longer the same as him.'

She jerked in his arms as the voice sounded in her head, a voice she'd not heard for centuries and one she'd longed to hear ever since she'd seen her disappear in a blaze of heavenly fire. 'Morghanna?'

Cain stilled just before his lips touched hers. 'What did you say?'

'Nothing.'

He tipped his head to the side and observed her for a long moment as she tried not to cringe from him. 'You are thinking of your sister. Why?'

'I always think of my sister. It is revenge for her that has driven me all these years.'

'But why mention her now?'

Her mind scrambled but could come up with nothing but the truth. 'I thought I heard her voice in my head.'

'Did you now? And what did she say?'

'What she always says. She wants her revenge.'

His lips curled into a cruel smile. 'Yes. Although revenge for your sister isn't the central goal. It never was.'

'What are you talking about? It's all I've ever wanted. All I've ever fought for. I want the Were gone, dead, scattered to dust, all evidence of their existence wiped from this world. The Darkness promised to help me do it.'

The smile fixed to his lips made him look like a painted picture of an angel. 'That was never the Darkness' goal. He wanted back into the Were. It was the closest he had ever been to having a body of his own. He was simply using you and your need for revenge as a way to get back what your sister and her friends had stolen from him.'

'No. That's not true.'

'You know it is.' His smile widened as he caressed her cheek. 'Silly Morrigan. So caught up in your own hatred that you failed to see you were being used just as you used others.'

'It's not true! The Darkness loves me. He would never betray me like that.' She'd begun to tremble again, but this time not from nausea. Despite her words, she knew he was right. The Darkness had used her and it was using her, and her baby, one final time.

'Oh, it wasn't a betrayal,' he answered, cutting into her thoughts. 'You wanted the Pact destroyed and he was happy to support you in that goal, because it meant he would get what he wanted—the ability to take over the Were once more and act through them in their animal form. He didn't want them destroyed. They were the only creatures on this earth he could enter without destroying their bodies after a while.'

'He entered me. And you. He hasn't destroyed either of us.'

'It's not the same. He can't control us. We are not his creatures in the same way the Were were. And even the way he took over them wasn't truly fulfilling. He longed to be whole again, to find a way around the punishment wrought on him by the Gods for his hubris in loving one of them. They tore him apart, made him so much less than he was, and so he thought he must remain. Which was why he wanted to get back into the Were. Why he wanted you to destroy the Pact.' Cain's eyes glittered as he grasped her arms, fingers digging into her flesh. 'But we have changed that for him once and for all. We have done what no other has managed to do in the history of the Darkness' existence. We've given him hope to be what he once was.'

His hand shifted to cover the small mound of her stomach. 'This child, the child you and I have made, makes the Were's importance to him insignificant. The Darkness will be the child and the child will be him. Isn't it magnificent?'

'But what of the Were? What of my revenge?'

'Oh, you will get that, don't you worry. The Were and their covens will bow down to our son or be destroyed.'

They would never bow down, which meant they would be destroyed. For some strange reason, it didn't give her the satisfaction she thought it should. Even so, she asked, 'You promise?'

He simply smiled and then bent and took her mouth in a kiss that was hunger and violence and passion and madness entwined.

And as she kissed him back, tearing the clothes from his back and letting him take her against the wall, instead of the exuberance of finally getting everything she'd ever hoped for singing in her head, she heard nothing but her sister's sobbing.

It hurt her more than it should have.

19

'Shelley!'

Adam's voice rang all around him as he screamed her name, reaching out to her, trying to stop the pressure that pushed him back through the door, away from the woman he loved. He could see her face disappearing as the light grew brighter around him, the pain and sorrow in her eyes as she forced him from her. He wanted to stop her, to stay with her, to chase that pain and sorrow away, to make her laugh, to have the only tears she ever shed be ones of joy, not sorrow.

But she was too strong and he couldn't fight the power of her as she pushed him away from her. The light flared and for a moment he was blinded and falling.

Then he stopped and the light faded.

He stood in a darkened place, alone. Still reaching for Shelley. 'Fuck.' His outstretched hand dropped to his side. 'Why, Shelley? Why did you push me away?' His shout echoed back to him, hidden barbs of truth underlying the echoes as they folded over him, fading away.

She didn't want him. She'd never wanted him. She had no use for him in her life. He'd always known that. But by the Moon, he'd never wanted to admit it because the truth was, he wanted her. He needed her. He loved her. And he couldn't stop. Shit, he'd fucking tried to stop. He'd tried so hard. Especially as she wasn't his mate. But it was hopeless. He loved her and she never would love him. She didn't even want him by her side as her Shadow. He really had to stop torturing himself and give up on her as she'd given up on him.

'She has never given up on you, Adam.'

He didn't bother to turn around to face the woman who stood behind him. 'She pushed me away.'

'She did it for you. You would have died if you'd stayed there. She knew that.'

'How could she know that?'

'Are you forgetting she is the banshee? She could feel the truth of it rising inside her. It's why she helped me and used her power to push you into this place. It was for your own good.'

'My good? What use is that if I can't be there to help her? I might as well be dead.'

A soft hand touched his arm, but he still refused to turn around. 'You have given her everything she needs to become who she must be. She would never have got this far without you. But she must go the rest of the distance by herself. You cannot help her with her personal journey. Just as she can't help you with yours.'

He stared down at his hands. 'She saw past my bullshit and saw me as I truly am. She's helped me learn so much about my Trickster side and what that means. She's helped me feel like I truly belong, that I have value within the pack. That I'm not simply a joke.'

'Yes. She did. But as she now must travel her path alone, so must you. By making you come here, Shelley is helping you to fulfil your destiny, Adam. Do not be too harsh on her.'

He hissed out a breath. 'I don't blame *her*. I would never blame her. I blame myself. For not being enough.'

'She would not want you to do that, would she, Adam? Just as you would never want her to blame herself for not being enough.'

'She is more than enough.' He spun to face her. 'Don't ever say she isn't enough.'

Morghanna Cantrae smiled up at him, hands splayed out in a gesture of acquiescence. 'I would never do such a thing. Shelley is all she is meant to be and now that you are not there to baby her, she might just grow into her potential.'

'Baby her! I've never babied her.'

'What I meant was that you have both been acting as shields for each other against the world and your place in it. Now it is time for you both to follow your own paths; to create your own shields by truly becoming who and what you are meant to be. Only then can you return to each other and truly be worthy of the love you hide from each other and the world.'

'She doesn't love me.'

She smiled at him. 'That is a lie you tell yourself because it makes things easier. Because it stops you from truly opening up and allowing the mating bond to become.'

'She isn't my mate.'

Morghanna shook her head. 'Of course she is. There is nobody else who could ever be mated to you. You know this at your core. Your wolf certainly knows this. Without you there to get in the way, it has already begun to link itself to her.'

'It's done what? How?'

She began to walk away from him, forcing him to follow. 'How or what does not matter. All that matters is what is and what is to become.'

'You're as bad as Arianrhod talking in riddles.'

She flashed him a grin. 'Thank you.'

'It wasn't a compliment.'

She chuckled. 'It is if I take it as one.' She looked up at him, having to crane her head back to look up into his eyes. She was a tiny, dainty thing, all cascading dark hair and violet eyes, but despite her dainty appearance, she wasn't fragile. Power radiated off her in waves that pushed and pulled at him at once.

'What makes you think you know so much about me and how I feel?'

'I have been waiting for you since long before your birth. The moment you sprang to life inside your mother's womb, I began watching you. And I am not the only one. Those of us who have fought the Darkness and the powers behind it for eons have been watching you, encouraging your Trickster side, trying to make you see the worth of who you truly are.'

'You did a rotten job of it.'

'Did we?'

'Yes. Before Shelley and Skye and Bron came into our lives, I thought I was pretty much useless to the pack. The only ones who believed in me were my family and even then, they often lost patience with me. I was too much of a joker. Never took anything seriously. So nobody ever took me seriously.'

'But Shelley, Skye and Bron did come into your life. Who do you think was behind ensuring their path to you and your pack?' The smug expression on her face faded, replaced with a desperate kind of anger and regret. 'I only wish I could have done more to stop the Darkness taking so much from you all. I wish I could have torn it from my sister and cast it into the void where it truly belongs.' She shook her head, violet eyes wells of sadness. 'I could not. I do not have that kind of power. I am not supposed to choose those who are to live and those who die. Who death comes to is not my ability to control—I was only ever a harbinger of it.'

'What?' It took a moment for her words to sink in. 'You're a banshee?'

'No. Nothing so powerful. I am a Medium and a seer of death. That is all.'

'Then if you can't control death, how did you tie death into your Curse?'

She looked down, and he could have sworn she looked ashamed. 'In my anger, I let the Darkness into my words. I wanted those who had hurt me and mine to feel my pain and the Darkness answered my call.'

'You used dark magic? But I thought you were the Goddess' creature.'

'I am.' She looked back up at him, brows creased. 'Your mistake, Adam, has always been that you think your actions make you who you are, but that is not true.' She reached out and touched his chest, fingers splaying over his heart. 'Our actions are only part of the story. It is what is in here,' her fingers pressed in a little, 'that truly guides what you are. I made a mistake, but that one mistake is not the sum of my being. Just as your ability to make people laugh and feel happy isn't the sum of yours. You have so much more to offer than that.' She pulled her hand away. 'Which is why you are here. And if you've finished sulking because Shelley did what she had to and sent you here with me, then we can get on with teaching what you must know to help your mate, your brother, your pack and your coven destroy the Darkness and its minions once and for all.'

'One of those minions is your sister. You would kill your own sister?'

She stopped abruptly, sighed. 'I do not wish to kill my sister.' She glanced up at him. 'But I would save my family. River and Skye are my descendants. They are my blood. I would not see them or their progeny destroyed because my sister thinks she needs to gain revenge for my death. I gained my own revenge, much to my never-ending shame. I tried to make her see that allowing such evil into her heart was not the way to deal with her grief, but she would not listen. She still does not listen.'

'What do you mean she still doesn't listen? Are you in communication with her?'

'Of course I try to communicate with her. She is my sister and I do not wish to give up on her, despite all she has done.' She pressed her lips together. 'But I am also prepared to sacrifice her if that is what must be.' She waved her hand in an impatient, chopping motion. 'We are wasting time. We must go.'

'Go? I only just got here.'

'This is only a transition place known as the God's Hall.' She held her hand out. 'Take my hand. I am about to drop the shield from around us. You might find it disorienting to see the truth of where we are.'

He swallowed loudly and took her hand. A dark curtain fell from around him to show they stood on nothing, surrounded by a field of stars. 'Holy shit,' he whispered, beginning to wobble as the stars moved across the endless sky around him. It was dizzyingly immense, its vastness too much for him to take in. He'd heard of astronauts suffering from a strange kind of vertigo when taking their first steps into space with nothing between them and infinity except their space suit and the tether tying them to their ship; no up, no down, no right or left, no gravity, nothing to shape their world or give them a sense of who they were and where they stood in the scheme of things. He'd never been able to imagine the sensation. Until now.

'I'm going to fall.'

'You will not fall.' Morghanna's hand tightened on his, acting as an anchor. He tore his gaze from the endless night sky around him and looked down at the hand that was the only thing stopping him from flying off into infinity and being lost forever.

'How are we standing here?' Was he standing? Or was he hanging?

'Let go of your preconceptions of your corporeal body. You have learned to walk through walls or sink down through the floor or fly through a ceiling. You have learned to close your eyes and think of someone and find yourself at their side in an instant. Time and place and space have no true meaning to a spirit such as yourself.'

'And you? What about you?'

She smiled, the violet in her eyes twinkling, the starlight mirrored in their depths. 'Have you not guessed it already? I am like you. I was taken from the earth before I ever truly died. I was hit by Goddess lightning before the flames could take me, but the effect was the same as what happened to you when you were hit with warlock lightning. My spirit was separated from my body in a way that was similar to a Shade, but without the true severing that is done by the dark deed needed to create a Shade.'

He looked around, but the sensation of falling and floating off, of being pulled and pushed at the same time, washed over him again, so he looked back at their joined hands.

'So, if you're like me, where's your body?'

'My body is lying somewhere safe, healed as yours is not.'

'Then why didn't you go back to your body and show your sister that you were alive and well and stop all this from happening in the first place?'

She sighed. 'Time moves very differently here from earth. What seemed only a moment to me was years to my sister. By the time my body was healed and I realised I had a choice to return to my body if I wished it, it was too late. Morrigan was already too far down the path that has led her here and would not have turned from it even if I had shown up in front of her. The Darkness would have made her believe I was a trick, especially as my body is now full of Goddess light. It does not exactly look normal anymore. And I realised I had to stay like this because only in this form could I truly help.'

'But you can go back to your body if you wish.'

'Not any longer. Once I could, but I made a bargain and my body is no longer mine to have.'

'What bargain? With whom?'

Her gaze was intense as she stared at him, a small smile on her lips. 'The one I made to get back to you. The Gods do not give free passes to travel between one plane and the next. They required a major sacrifice for what I requested and so I gave it.'

'You gave your life to come and get me? But why?'

'My life was over long ago. My husband and son are long gone. There was nothing to return to. Besides, all that matters is the task the Goddess set before me.'

'But what happens once you are finished with this? Do you just continue to go on as you are?'

'No. Once I am done here, I will have to make my way to the Well of Souls to be reincarnated into another life.'

'And what about your body?'

'It will die.'

Adam's breath stuttered in his chest. 'Is that what will happen to me?'

She paused, face creasing with withheld grief. 'Your situation is very different from mine. The bargain I made allows you to move from one plane to the next freely. However, it does not guarantee you will be able to get back to your body at the end of this. That will entirely depend on if we are ultimately successful or not.' She touched his arm. 'And much of our success is dependent on you learning what you need to learn about your powers.'

He stared at her, words lost to him—a thoroughly unusual sensation. But finally, he managed to gather his thoughts and ask, 'So, if I do what you ask, you'll allow me to go back to my pack. To Shelley.'

'It is not quite as simple as that—'

'Of course not.'

She narrowed her eyes at him. 'But yes, of course. You will go back. It is essential.'

'Essential?'

'Yes. You must be with Shelley. You must deepen your bond with her. You must show her your love. It is of the utmost importance.'

'My loving Shelley is important to the success of your great scheme?'

'Of course. Love is one of the most powerful things in the universe.' She gestured around them. 'It is what created and held together all of this. It will be our saviour. It is ultimately what I have sacrificed everything for.' Her voice choked up and she took in a deep, shaking breath. 'We need to go. We have stayed too long and my bargain only gives us passage through here at certain times.'

'Can the Darkness follow us here?'

'Not here. It was banished from this place eons ago. But there are consequences for not following the rules of what has been bargained. We must go to the Goddess' safe haven.'

'Safe haven?'

'Yes. It is where those of us who work with her stay when in need of hiding or rebuilding our strength for the fight ahead.' She looked back over her shoulder, beckoning him to follow. 'It is but a short journey, however, you must keep your wits about you and whatever you do, do not let go of me.'

He gripped her hand tighter. He had no intention of letting go.

'Make certain not to look back.'

He nodded. Then she stepped forward into the haze in front of them, tugging him to follow. Without a backwards glance, he followed her as she moved from the whorl of stars and into the violet mist beyond.

20

'**I**'m glad you came up here for the last few days. You needed to take a break from all that research,' Skye said, pouring some more tea into her cup. 'You look exhausted.'

'Pot calling kettle, baby,' Shelley snorted. 'Those who live in glass houses shouldn't throw stones and all that.'

'You're using mixed metaphors?'

'Ha! I'm just living outside the square.'

'Yeah, right. That's my line. Besides, if a best friend can't tell you that you look like shit, then I don't know who can.'

Shelley's brows rose. 'Wow, I must look bad. You're swearing.'

'At least I didn't say the F word.'

'I would have fallen off my seat if you had.'

Skye laughed, but then the laughter died. 'Seriously, Shelley, now we've got a moment alone, you can tell me, how are you?'

Shelley stared down at her tea, swirling the dregs in the mug. 'I'm fine.'

'Really?'

Shelley looked up at her friend. She knew Skye and Bron had been worried about her since she'd pushed Adam into the void or the veil or wherever it was he'd gone with Morghanna. They'd texted and called her every day to check on her. It was one of the reasons she'd come back to the McClune Packlands—to show them that she was fine. All recovered. Not even a scar left from her ordeal.

She should have known that they weren't simply worried about her physical wellbeing. Of course they had questions about Adam and that kiss and why and how she'd pushed him away. But she didn't want to talk about any of that. Didn't know the answer to any of those questions. Didn't even know the answers to the questions she actually searched for. However, she knew it was useless to keep on pretending there was nothing wrong with her at all—Skye could teach classes in stubborn—so she sidestepped with, 'Well ... I'd be better if I could find something that was helpful.'

Skye tapped her fingers against her mug, eyes narrowed.

Crap. Her friend wasn't going to let her get away with such an obvious sidestep.

Skye sighed, put her mug down with a click and said, 'The diaries still not giving out the goods?'

Shelley almost sagged in relief at the reprieve but knew Skye would jump all over that sign of emotional weakness, so she held her back ramrod straight and waved her hand. 'Oh, they're giving out lots of things, just nothing that will truly help us find a way to unspell the black magic keeping the wound alive in Adam's chest. I thought maybe if I came up here and had another look at it, I'd see something I hadn't seen before that might help.' Not entirely a lie. She had to give herself points for that.

'And have you?'

'Have I what?'

'Seen something in Adam's wound you didn't see before?'

Shelley rubbed her hand over her face to cover the impact of that question. Hell, her friend was a fiend when it came to pushing her to give up the goods. But although Skye was past mistress of avoidance techniques, Shelley was the reigning queen and she wasn't about to let go of her crown. 'Yes, actually.' She almost laughed at the surprise on Skye's face as she let those words hang in the air. Then she leaned forward, as if she was going to reveal something secret and personal, and whispered, 'It's not simply black magic. There's a piece of the Darkness in him.'

'Oh.' Skye looked extremely disappointed.

'You don't seem surprised.'

'Bron thought as much when she put the cuffs on him.' She tipped her head to the side, her eyes blanking for a moment.

'Skye?'

'Sorry,' she said, gaze snapping back to Shelley. 'I just had a thought. Would the spell Bridgette used to expel the Darkness from the Were all those centuries ago work?'

'I thought it might, except ...'

'Except what?'

'If it were that simple, then Bron should have been able to oust it with her Healing magic like she did when the Darkness was inside River.' Shelley rubbed her forehead again. 'I asked Bron about it, and she said I was right. What she'd done already should have rid him of the Darkness if it was in him like it had been in the Were and in River. But it's not. It's like it's wielded to his cells and I can't find a spell that would make it just let go.' She rapped her knuckles against her temple. 'It's so frustrating.'

'We'll find a solution. We have to.'

'Yes. We have to.' Shelley stared stubbornly at Skye, but her friend stared just as stubbornly back. Shelley shook her head, willing her friend not to go there.

Skye smiled apologetically and said, 'Shelley, it's been three weeks since Adam went with Morghanna. I know you miss him. I know you regret pushing him away like that. You need to talk about it. It's eating you up inside. Everyone can see it.'

'They can?' she said, horrified at the thought.

'Well, maybe not everyone. But those of us who care about you can feel it through the Packbond.'

Shelley bit her lip against the rising tears. 'It's fine.'

'Shelley.'

The love and friendship in Skye's eyes broke her.

Blinking rapidly, she stared down at her hands. 'It's just I've heard nothing. Found nothing. And time's slipping away. I can feel it. Something horrible rising inside me.'

'What kind of horrible?'

Images. Of death and destruction and hopelessness with the banshee hovering above all. But she couldn't speak of those images that came to her in her nightmares and flashed in her mind with increasing intensity. To speak the words would be to make them real. Yet she couldn't say nothing. Fingers tightening around her tea mug, she stared down at the cooling brown liquid.

Adam. She had to concentrate on Adam. So she met her friend's gaze and said softly, 'Like if I don't find something soon, he's going to slip away and I'll ... we'll lose him.'

'You can't think like that, Shelley. We're going to do everything we can and we're going to get Adam back.'

'You don't feel it then?'

'Feel what?'

'That we're running out of time?'

Skye swallowed hard. 'I do. But I try not to think about it, because if I do, it will overwhelm me. You can't let it overwhelm you either.'

Shelley blinked hard. 'I know. It's just ...' She sniffed. 'I just miss the stupid bastard.' She scrubbed her hand over her face and laughed a little. 'He manages to piss me off at least six times a day. I feel more alive, more aware of myself when Adam is around than I have ever felt in my life.' She clapped her hand over her mouth. Oh shit. Had she just said that out loud?

'You can't cram those words back into your mouth now they're spoken. And pretending you didn't say it doesn't make it less true.' Skye smiled softly. 'You love him.'

Shelley sucked in a breath, the words a punch to her chest. No. She didn't love him. She couldn't. 'This isn't about love.'

Skye shook her head. 'Of course it is. He's the exact right man for you. You knew that the moment you met him—which is why you've always been so snappy with him.'

Shelley looked around, as if she were going to find some convincing argument to prove her friend wrong, but it was useless.

They'd seen the proof of it—her feelings for him and his for her when she'd settled his wolf all those weeks ago. 'I don't want to love him.'

'I didn't want to love Jason either, if you remember. But when I stopped fighting it, everything changed for the better and I've never regretted it.'

'It's not the same.'

'It could be.'

'No. It can't. Adam and I can't be together.'

'You've begun to bond with him.'

Shelley shook her head, mouth a thin line. 'It can't go further.'

'Why not? Why not let yourself be happy?'

Shelley's eyes widened. 'You don't think I want to be happy? You don't think I want love?'

'I think you're afraid of it because of what's happened in the past, but you've no need to be. It's more freeing than anything I've ever experienced. My love for Jason strengthens me in ways I never imagined.'

'And I'm so thrilled that's true for you and Bron and Eloise. But it's not true for me. I can't have what you have. Certainly not with Adam.'

'Why not? He's perfect for you.'

Shelley stared at her, blinking rapidly, chin wobbling, her breath coming in short, sharp gasps. He *was* perfect. Despite—or perhaps because of—all his annoying ways, he really was perfect for her.

But she could never be with him. Not in the way she longed to be.

'Oh goodness, Shelley. What did I say? What's wrong?' Skye pushed out of her chair and leapt across the coffee table. Shelley had just enough time to put her mug of tea on the side table before Skye enveloped her in a hug. 'I'm so sorry I upset you. Tell me, what's wrong?'

How could she explain something that was so eternally painful? Something there was no shying away from, only enduring. The Pack Diaries, her aunt, the banshee—all had made it perfectly clear that all she would ever bring to Adam was death in exchange for her love. There was no way she was going to do that.

But how could she explain that to Skye? Her friend, who had once been a pessimist to match Shelley, was now the eternal optimist, always trying to find the bright side. Just like Bron. They'd think there was some way around hundreds of years of history and her aunt's prophecy. They'd make her hope. She didn't want to hope. Hope hurt. Especially given that even if the diaries were wrong about how Adam's powers worked, how they were affected by the Pact with the witches, even if her aunt was wrong, there was still the insanity so prevalent in her family. An insanity she had fought against for so many years, keeping it at bay through sheer stubborn will and a refusal to use her powers—the seat of her insanity. However, now that the banshee was inside her, she knew it was only a matter of time.

Every time the banshee hummed inside her, every time it raised its voice into a wail, it pulled her closer to the edge. That edge was like something jagged in her mind, snagging her thoughts with increasing rapidity, spinning them around. She grasped for control, and so far she had managed to keep herself from falling over that precipice like her aunt, but it was a frayed tightrope she balanced on. Very soon, it would snap and there was nothing she could do to stop it.

Even if Adam wasn't an empathic Trickster who would take the burden of that insanity from her until it killed him, she wouldn't burden him with the inevitability of what would happen to her. She loved him too much to ever do that to him.

She could never, ever, explain that to her friends who were in such perfect relationships that they thought everything could come right in the end. They simply wouldn't understand.

She swiped at the tears on her cheeks, sniffled, forced her lips to move. 'It's nothing. I'm just overtired, that's all.' She hiccoughed and rubbed her cheeks. 'I hate crying.'

'I know you do, Shells. Which is why I know this isn't nothing. Please tell me what's wrong. What did I say that upset you so much?'

The words trembled on Shelley's lips. Despite what she'd just told herself, she wanted to tell someone the burden in her heart. Wanted someone else to know that, despite how much love she felt for Adam, it could never be. Wanted someone else to carry the burden of why.

Her gaze raked over her friend and the thought died the death it deserved.

She took in the beautiful blue of Skye's eyes, swimming with worry, the deep circles under them, the paleness of her skin. Her friend was stressed enough already, what with helping the McClunes through the death of their Alpha and Cordy being in a coma. She was still trying to learn about her power and taking on the responsibilities of being mated to the Alpha of a strong pack. Not to mention trying to run her childcare business from afar and becoming a new mother to Tom, Jason and Adam's nephew. She'd also been sick with some form of recurring stomach complaint for the last month—most likely related to her already considerable stress and anxiety about everyone she loved.

Shelley couldn't add to that burden. She wouldn't.

She touched Skye's cheek. 'I really am just overtired and being silly. When you said Adam is the perfect man for me, I couldn't help thinking that it's typical that the perfect man for me is slowly dying and relying on me to help him to live and I can't seem to do even that.' Her voice broke, perfecting the lie, and she blinked rapidly. Well, it wasn't a complete lie. Simply a sleight of hand with a kernel of truth to divert her friend from the real, deeper truth.

'Oh, Shelley. I'm so sorry. It was thoughtless of me to put that burden on you as well. We all know you're doing your best. Nobody, Adam especially, would ask more from you than that.' Skye's arms tightened around her.

'I know,' she said, hugging back. 'But knowing it doesn't stop me from wishing I was better at all this. That I knew more.'

Skye sat back. 'You and me both. Although, I'm surprised to hear you say you want to learn more about your magic.'

'Only insofar as it will help bring Adam back. And help to fight off whatever Morrigan and Cain are going to do next.'

'Of course,' Skye said, a little smile playing at the corner of her lips.

'I mean it,' Shelley said, not liking that smile at all.

'I know you do.'

'Skye.'

'Shelley.'

They stared at each other for a long moment, but Shelley was the one to break the stare. She covered by grabbing her tea and sipping. 'Yuck.' She pulled a face. It was cold. She placed it back on the side table carefully, still not looking at Skye. 'So, you haven't told me if you've heard from Eloise, Iain and Patrick lately. Have they found anything?'

'Nice change of topic, Shelley. But we're not done with this one.'

'Yes, we are.' She squared her jaw, hands clenched in her lap. 'Please, Skye. I know what you all think, but I can't talk about this. Please don't make me.'

There was a long pause. 'Okay.' Skye's hands folded over hers, thumbs stroking, soothing. 'But I'm here if you want to tell me anything. You know that, don't you?'

Shelley's gaze snapped to Skye's. 'I know.'

'Good.' She took a deep breath then, moving a little shakily, she stood, swayed.

Shelley grabbed her friend. 'Skye? Are you okay?'

'I'm fine. Just stood too quickly. I'll be fine.'

'Perhaps you should sit down.' Shelley helped her sit on the lounge beside her and took her wrist to check her pulse.

Skye waved her away. 'Don't fuss. I get enough of that from Jason and Bron.' She folded her hands in her lap. 'Now, where were we? Ah, yes, you asked about Eloise.' Shelley nodded.

'So far, every lead they have leads them to another dead end. But Patrick is showing his worth and has always managed to track down another lead to follow.'

'I hope they find something. For Eloise if for nothing else. It must be horrible for her.'

'Yeah. But Iain says she's holding on to hope and isn't despondent.'

'Good. I'm glad she's got him. And Patrick.' Skye looked like she was about to say something but then swallowed hard and closed her eyes. A little frisson of worry skated up Shelley's spine. 'Are you okay?'

'Still a little dizzy.' She breathed in deep.

'You're dizzy again?' Jason said as he walked into the room, heading straight for his mate. She opened her eyes, smiled, and then her eyes rolled up into her head and she fell forward off the chair.

'Skye!'

Jason caught her before she hit the floor. 'Skye. Skye.' She didn't respond.

'Here, put her on the couch.'

Jason swept his mate up in his arms and placed her on the couch, hands grasping hers. Shelley checked her pulse and her breathing. 'Her pulse is a little fast, but she's breathing okay. I think she passed out.' She glared at him. 'Just how sick has she been?'

'She's been throwing up a little. Complaining of some tiredness. But that's it.' He met her gaze, his shadowed with fear. 'She wouldn't go and see a doctor. You know how she is.'

'I know.'

'What should we do?'

'Let's get her down to the hospital room. Bron's down there. She can check her out.'

'Good idea.' He picked Skye up, her head lolling worryingly against his shoulder, and ran out of the room too fast for Shelley to keep up. He was waiting in the SUV for her when she ran out onto the patio. She ran down the front steps. 'Put her in the back. I'll sit with her while you drive.'

A moment later she was sitting in the back, cradling Skye's head in her lap. Tension pushed at her—hers and Jason's—as he made his way carefully down the dirt track that led to the barn that sat over the entrance to the old mines. Shelley wanted to yell at him to hurry, but knew he was only taking care not to jostle Skye unnecessarily, especially given they didn't know what was wrong with her.

He pulled up outside the barn ten minutes later. Shelley ran to the lift to push the call button while Jason got Skye out of the car.

She'd just done so when Jason joined her, Skye cradled against his chest. Blue lightning zipped around Skye and over Jason's arms.

'Holy crap! Jason? Are you going to change? Give her to me.'

'No. It doesn't feel like that. I don't feel it building up inside me.'

'When did it start?' There had definitely been no lightning sparking on Skye in the car.

'Just now. As soon as you got out of the SUV.'

'Does it hurt?'

He rocked Skye in his arms, looking down at her, the love in his eyes almost painful to watch. 'No. She'd never hurt me. Not even when she's unconscious.'

'No. Of course.' Shelley turned from them as the lift doors opened. They hurried inside and she pushed the button that would take the lift down into the old mine tunnels.

The blue around Jason and Skye intensified. The lights flickered in the lift. The lift shuddered. 'No you fucking don't! You're not breaking down now!' She kicked at the door, her shout bouncing around in the narrow space. The lift shuddered again, and the lights flickered then exploded over their heads. Sparks flew down around them. Jason, even though he had Skye in his arms, bent so as to protect Shelley from the sparks as well.

'Are you okay?' he asked a moment later when the lift shuddered but kept going.

'I'm fine,' Shelley said. 'Just protect Skye.' She couldn't believe he'd done that. Nobody had ever tried to protect her like that before. Except for Adam. Her thoughts shied away from him immediately, her conversation with Skye too raw, too close, for her to want to even consider thinking about the feelings it had dredged up.

'It seems to be coming from her stomach.' He turned to her. 'Have you ever seen anything like this before?'

She shook her head. 'You're asking the wrong person.'

'I thought you might have come across something in the diaries.'

'No. Except ...' Her voice faltered as the words she'd read just after Christmas swam before her eyes. 'No. That's impossible.'

21

She stared at Skye's stomach, repeated, 'It's impossible.'

'What's impossible?'

She looked up at Jason, feeling a little sick. She didn't want to say anything, didn't want to be the person who gave hope only to have it sucked away when she was proved wrong. Which she had to be. Because this was impossible. Skye couldn't have children. Her womb and ovaries had been destroyed by some cruel surgery meant to save her from her magic, but that had just served to make things so much worse for her friend. 'Let's wait to see what Bron says, okay,' she hedged.

'Is it something bad? Please. Tell me. I'm going out of my mind here.'

'I ... it's just ...' What could she say? She didn't want to lie, didn't want to give false hope either. Her gaze flickered to Skye's stomach where the blue lightning moved, almost acting like a shield.

Jason followed her gaze. His eyes widened. 'Are you saying she's ...' He took in a deep breath. 'By the Moon! She's pregnant. I can smell the change in her scent. Her scent is mixed with the scent of another.' His gaze skittered up to hers. 'She's pregnant.'

Shelley nodded, even though it wasn't a question. 'I think, maybe she is.'

He stared down at Skye, eyes widening even further in wonder. 'I should have known. Everything was telling me she was pregnant, even my wolf knew, but I couldn't let myself even think it. Or bring it up. I knew how much it would hurt her. It's impossible. Supposed to be impossible.'

'I know.'

'Then how?' he whispered, joy and confusion vying for prominence.

Shelley didn't answer. She couldn't. She had no idea. Didn't even know why Skye's power was acting the way it was, covering her like that, but not going into Jason. The thing she'd read in the diaries never mentioned Were contact.

'A little boy or girl of our own,' Jason muttered. 'I can hear the flutter of their heart. Feel their presence already impacting the Pack-bond, mind linking with me. Our child is strong, my love. He or she is very strong. I don't know how I missed it up until now.' He leaned down and nuzzled his nose against her cheek. 'Your mate is a dunderhead.'

Shelley looked away. She couldn't stand to see his happiness. Not that she wasn't happy for them and the miracle of this pregnancy, but it hurt. And she hated that it did.

The lift jerked to a halt and the doors opened.

Bron stood in the hallway, eyes wide with worry.

Jason smiled at her. 'She's pregnant, Bron. She's pregnant.'

Bron's gaze slammed into Shelley, so that she almost stumbled back from it, the accusation in her eyes like a shove 'You know that isn't possible.'

'We know, Bron. But look at her. Check her out. I know it's impossible, but I think, I'm afraid, that it's true.'

Bron checked Skye's pulse, her temperature, then ran her hands over her friend, just a few centimetres above her skin, eyes intent as she watched their progress.

Skye's power flickered under her almost-touch. 'By the Moon. You're right.'

'Is that why her power is acting like this?'

'I don't know. I've never seen anything like it before.'

'Shelley's read something about this.'

Bron looked questioningly at her, but Shelley gestured to Skye. 'Shouldn't you get her to the hospital room and check her out? I could only do a basic physical—I have no idea if there's a deeper problem, either physical or magical.'

'Yes. Of course.' Bron hurried down the hall to the room at the end, Jason and Shelley following closely behind her.

'Where's River?' Shelley asked as Jason carried Skye over to the empty bed.

'Out for a run. I've called him. He's coming now.'

'Good.' Depending on what was wrong with Skye, Bron might need River's strength to pull on if she needed to do a Healing. Aside from that, River would want to be here for his sister.

Bron quickly examined Skye, hooking her up to the machine that read oxygen levels, blood pressure and heartbeat. Then she checked her eyes. 'It's not a coma. She simply appears to be asleep.' She turned to them. 'What happened?'

Jason quickly told her, with Shelley adding bits that she knew. Bron nodded throughout, arms crossed, a frown deepening on her forehead. She reached over after they'd finished and touched the power flickering over Skye. 'What do you know about this, Shelley? I imagine this is what you read something about?'

Shelley nodded. 'I think it's the baby. From what I've read, this sometimes happens with a powerful mother having a powerful child, especially if the mother hasn't been looking after herself—and we all know Skye has been pushing herself to exhaustion.'

'I should have stopped her.'

Bron touched Jason's arm, stroking. 'Nobody could stop her when she gets a bee in her bonnet.' Her attention returned to her patient. 'Do you think it's dangerous to her? Do the diaries say anything about that?'

Shelley went to answer, but there was a sound behind her, and then a soft, slightly husky voice said, 'It's not.'

They spun to face the familiar voice they hadn't heard for months.

'Cordy!' Bron gasped. 'You're awake.'

The McClune Head Witch pushed herself up in the bed, eyes shadowed by pain and grief, her face far too pale as she focused on Skye. 'Shelley was right. The baby is as powerful as its mother and it needs more than Skye has been giving it. Both physically and magically. This is the result.' She swung her legs over the edge of the bed, stood up, began to topple.

Shelley and Bron raced over and held her steady. 'You're awake. You're awake.'

Cordy didn't look at them, her gaze still pinned on Skye. 'I don't want to be awake. I was called.'

'You were?' Jason asked.

'By the babies. Your babies. They're worried about their mother. They sent out a call to the nearest midwife. I'm it.'

Shelley frowned. 'But I've had training as a midwife. Why didn't they call to me?'

'A magical midwife, Shelley. One with an essence in new life. That is not your gift. It is, however, mine. I had to wake up because I'm bound by my powers to help a child of power when it calls me.'

'They?' Jason's smile became goofily wide. 'There's more than one?'

Cordy smiled shakily at him. 'Yes. There are two.'

'Two what?' River asked, coming through the door, gaze immediately going to his sister. 'Is Skye okay?' He was by her side as he asked, touching her face, her arm, stroking. Shelley stayed where she was beside Cordy as Bron and Jason joined him. 'Please tell me she's okay.'

'She's pregnant.'

His gaze snapped to Bron, then widened as he saw Cordy. 'Cordy?'

She waved her hand to stave off his questions. 'This isn't about me. It's about your sister.'

'How do you know she's pregnant? Is that ...?'

Jason's smile widened at the look of dawning realisation on River's face. 'You can hear the heartbeat too.'

'Heartbeats,' Cordy corrected.

'But how? The surgery ...' River's mouth hung open. 'Heartbeats? She's having twins?'

Cordy nodded. 'Twins run in your family.'

'One witch and one Were like Skye and River?' Bron asked. Cordy shook her head, frowning. 'No. Both have power.'

'Two witches?' River asked.

Her frown deepened. 'Yes, except, I can also feel the Were in them too.' Her eyes widened as she looked up at Jason. 'They are both.'

Jason swallowed hard, hand gripping tight to Skye's. 'That can't be. Were can't hold the power of a witch. The lore is clear.'

'Not all the lore is written. Some is passed on from midwife to midwife because to write of it would be to create fear and from that fear, a schism could be created that would destroy the Were-Witch Pact. Believe me when I say, while it's rare, there have been cases of Were born with power.'

Jason turned to Shelley. 'Tricksters. That's what you said about the Tricksters, isn't it? That they had power that sat outside the magic that allowed Were to change.'

Shelley bit her lip. 'Yes. So what Cordy is saying is true. Adam is proof.' The words caught in her throat, the reality of what it all meant a kick in the ribs.

'Are you okay?' Cordy asked.

'I'm fine. It's you and Skye we're worried about right now.'

'Yes.' Cordy frowned down at her legs, which were trembling violently. 'How long have I been on that bed?'

'Almost two months.'

Cordy hissed in a breath, swayed.

Shelley held her up. 'It's okay. You'll be okay.'

Cordy's expression of disbelief tore into her. 'Okay? He's been gone for two months? I missed his funeral? How is that okay?'

'I didn't mean …'

Tears filled her eyes and her chin wobbled, but she shook her head. 'No. Don't talk about it,' she said, breathing hard. 'I don't want to think about it. I can't—' Her voice broke.

'It's okay to take a moment,' Bron said quietly, joining them again, her arm going around Cordy in a way that was more than just physically supportive. Shelley marvelled at the way her friend did that so naturally. 'It's okay to cry.'

Cordy shook her head furiously. 'No. It's not. If I cry, I'll never stop.' She stared at Skye. 'I have to keep myself together.' She made a little whimpering noise but then slapped her hand to her chest, clutching at the gown. 'I've got a job to do. I'm the only one who can do it. If I don't, Skye could die.'

'What?' Jason and River both barked.

'She won't die. She can't die,' Shelley said automatically, but inside her, the banshee shifted and stirred in a way that said it was a possibility.

'If I don't help the babies to control their power, she will.'

'What do you mean?' Jason frowned at the power cascading across Skye, centring around her stomach. 'Is that what's happening now?'

'No. That is happening to protect her. But as they grow, that protection will become more dangerous. The power of both of them combined with her own power could become too much.'

'I can channel it into the pack.'

'No. Not this power. You are not designed to channel this kind of power. It would burn through the bond and every synaptic link in your body and mind before you could use it to transform and then it would burn its way through every member of your pack until all of them were dead.' She glanced at Bron. 'It would probably spark a cascade in you and Shelley and Eloise as well, and with the pack all gone you would all die too.'

River clutched at Bron's hand. 'No.'

'This is one of the reasons Skye's grandmother did what she did.'

Jason's eyes filled with horror. 'Are you telling me I have to kill our babies to save Skye and the pack?'

'No.' Cordy looked as horrified as he did. 'Sorry, I'm not managing this well at all.'

'You're managing it fine,' Bron said, helping her forward.

Shelley moved with them, holding Cordy's other arm, giving her support, but suddenly, somehow, she felt like a third wheel. Their words swam around her and she only took half of it in, just enough to know that it was centuries since a witch had birthed a power-born Were and that Cordy knew what to do because she was a born midwife as her grandmother before her had been. She could help Skye. The babies had asked her. Nobody else. Not Jason. Not Bron. Not Shelley, despite her medical training and human midwifery skills.

The sensation of being on the outside increased. She tried to push it down, to ignore it, but it was difficult when she realised the only use she had here was as confirmation that if Cordy didn't do her job, Skye and her babies would die. Nothing else.

She should go. She was of no use here. She could only bring more worry.

She gestured with her head for River to come and help Cordy in her stead.

'What's going on?'

'Skye.' Jason was at her side in a moment, forcing her to stay supine.

Skye's eyes found Shelley's. 'What happened, Shells?' she asked huskily.

'You passed out. We brought you here for Bron to check over.' She gestured and Skye looked down at herself for the first time, noticing the lightning.

'Oh, my goodness. What's happening?'

'It's okay, Skye,' Cordy said as she reached Skye's side with Bron and Shelley's help.

'Cordy! You're awake?'

'Yes,' the other witch smiled down at her. 'I was woken by your babies.'

'My ... what?'

Shelley stood silently as Bron and Cordy explained that the impossible had happened—that she was pregnant, not with one baby, but with two.

'How? How did this happen?'

Cordy turned to Bron. 'I think, perhaps, that has something to do with the rather remarkable Healing Bron cast last year at Yule when she brought Eloise back from death and saved River from the Beast. I think, perhaps, that massive surge of Healing energy brought life to something that previously had no life in it at all.'

'Of course,' Shelley gasped. Why hadn't she realised something like this might have happened when she'd read about the creation of the warlock lightning and what it had originally been intended for? It was Healing energy. A massive amount, twisted and turned into something dark because of the weakness of the magic that had created it. But Bron wasn't weak. She was one of the strongest people Shelley had ever met, with a kindness and empathy that was rare to find in this world. A burst of that kind of energy from her would be enough to heal Skye's broken womb.

It wasn't a miracle. It was simply the nature of her friend and her beautiful gift. A gift that was the opposite of Shelley's.

No wonder she hadn't put two and two together. Her gift could never encompass something so life giving, so life affirming.

'Shelley?'

'What?' They were all looking at her. She shifted, forced her face into a smile. 'I'm so pleased for you and Jason, Skye.' She hugged her friend, hiding her face from Bron's watchful eyes. 'I'm so glad this happened. And so sorry I didn't realise what was going on with you earlier. If I had, you might not have got this bad.'

'How could you have known?' Skye pulled back to look in her face, but Shelley stood abruptly and looked away.

'I am a nurse for Christ's sake. I should have known the signs of pregnancy. They shouldn't have had to slap me up side of the face.'

'I didn't see it either,' Bron said. 'And I can read her aura. I should have seen that there were two other little auras sitting inside hers.'

'I think we've all been a bit blind—and with reason,' Skye said, taking both their hands. 'It was impossible.'

'Not impossible. Thanks to Bron,' Shelley said.

'Yes. Thanks to Bron.' Skye lifted Bron's hand and kissed it as Jason hugged the Healer to his side, pressing a kiss to her forehead.

Shelley nodded and smiled as their congratulations and talk wove around her, wanting to feel a part of their excitement, their joy, but struggling to feel anything but separated from it.

Cordy started telling them what they'd need to do to help the pregnancy along in a healthy way for mother and babies, none of which Shelley could help with. There was nothing she could do here. But there were things she could do back in Melbourne. They would all be better served if she took herself and her gift of death far away from those she loved the most. Skye had Jason and Bron and River. And Cordy, of course. She didn't really need Shelley hanging around bringing the mood down.

She frowned. Cordy was swaying on her feet. Nurse Shelley came to the fore, pushing "feeling sorry for herself Shelley" to the side with a massive shove.

'Okay, I think that's enough for the day. Cordy has only just woken from a long coma. She needs her rest as much as Skye.' She took Cordy's arm, letting the other woman lean on her again.

'Of course, you're right. You mustn't wear yourself out, Cordy, even for me and my twins.'

'You and your twins are giving me a purpose to move forward.' The smile she gave Skye was grateful, but endlessly sad.

Skye squeezed her hand. 'I know. And I'm glad for it on multiple levels. But now it's time for both of us to rest.'

'Yes. It is. But if you don't mind, I'd like a shower and something to eat first.'

Cordy leaned on Shelley and River as they took her down the hall to one of the other rooms where there was a bathroom and proper bed. Shelley helped her to shower while Bron sent River off to get

Cordy something to eat and headed off to fetch her fresh pyjamas. She was back just as Cordy finished her shower and then, despite Cordy's protests, they made her get into the bed—Cordy wanted to go back to the hospital room, but Bron insisted she have a good night's sleep in a proper bed for a change. 'I'll come and get you if there's any issues with Skye and the babies. I promise.'

'Can you go and check now?'

'Of course. I'll be right back.'

She left, leaving Shelley alone in the room with Cordy.

The other witch settled back on the pillows, her gaze on Shelley piercing. 'I know what you're thinking, Shelley, but you're wrong. It was you, too.'

'Me too what?' Shelley pretended she didn't know what the other woman meant.

Cordy's lips quirked into a patient smile. 'When you allowed your powers to be joined with Skye's to save her, you gave her and Bron everything they needed to get to this point.' She took Shelley's hand, squeezed. 'It's been more difficult on you than the others because your powers are so much more volatile. I know how hard this has been for you, how much it has hurt you. And it's going to hurt more. I can feel that.' She tipped her head on the side. 'You know I can.'

Yes, she did. She hadn't known that Cordy was a midwife born, but she had known that Cordy's powers included foresight.

Cordy's smile widened. 'In some ways, my powers are not so different from yours.'

'I don't believe that for a minute.'

'Believe what you will, but I know it to be true. Just as I know you think things will only get worse for you. That all there will ever be is pain.' Shelley didn't move, could barely breathe as the other woman kept speaking. 'But it will be all right in the end, you know. I can feel that too. For you. For Skye. For Bron. For Eloise. You are all going to be part of changing our world. I know it.'

'I don't know if that's a good thing or not,' Shelley managed.

'It's not just a good thing.' Cordy's eyes brightened, almost as with a fever, her face glowing. 'You and your friends are going to be what saves us all from the Darkness. The Nexus working alongside an Elemental, a Healer and a banshee-Medium, helped by the power of elemental energy from the unborn twin Witch-Weres and the Trickster who is spirit-bound.' She gasped. 'I can see it. Together you will unbind the Darkness from its heavenly plain and bring balance back to our world.'

The hairs on Shelley's arms stood up.

Then suddenly, Cordy's head jerked up and light glowed out of her face, eyes swirling gold as words gushed out of her; words that seemed torn from her and carried on a fae wind, spoken with a voice that was hers and yet echoed with ancient weight:

'Four with two and channelled through one
Will have the power to light the sun.
The power of all will have its way
To overcome the worst of Darkness' sway.
Together their Will will oversee
The coming of the new eternity
Three times three times three times three
So I say, so mote it be.'

The last word ended on a high gasp and Cordy fell forward into Shelley's arms.

Bron raced into the room, River behind her. 'What happened? I felt magic swell.'

Shelley looked down at Cordy and then back up at her friend. 'She spoke a prophecy.' She told them what the other witch had said.

'What does it mean?' River asked.

'It means I'm going to have to head back to Melbourne tonight. I've got more research to do.' If they were to do what Cordy had prophesied, then she needed to find more information and find it fast. And she needed to finally learn how to use her powers.

Leaving Cordy in Bron and River's capable care, Shelley headed for the lift.

Cordy said there was more pain to come and Shelley was horribly certain the other witch wasn't wrong.

22

'**I**'m done.' Adam collapsed on his back, staring up at the pure blue of the sky in this place that wasn't in any way natural or normal. It had no seasons. No wind. No rain. It wasn't warm or cold. He didn't feel hunger or thirst. And the smell of the place—it was all wrong. There were no bad smells, only lovely ones—it was doing his head in. Even his sweat—or whatever it was that covered his spirit body when he did the drills and exercises Morghanna insisted he do every day for hours and hours—smelled pretty.

He wanted to go home. He wanted to feel hungry. He wanted to sink his teeth into a burger and breathe in the scents of greasy meat and cheese and tomato and beetroot as the sauce and egg-yolk dripped down his chin and over his hands. He wanted to breathe in the soil and the fertiliser used in their farming, the sweet scent of the grapes growing on the vines, he wanted to nose a decent red and enjoy the crisp, thick, fruity taste of it on his tongue.

But what he wanted the most was to see Shelley again. To hear her voice. To smell that scent unique to her, the one that reminded him of the warmth and rich fullness of chocolate and shiraz. To feel the silk of her golden hair twined around his hands as he tasted her mouth and pressed his body against the soft curves of hers. He wanted her to tell him off, to argue with him, to challenge him in the way only she could. He wanted to hear her laugh—be responsible for making her laugh that husky exasperated chuckle that lifted the hairs on his body and made his cock stand to attention.

'You're thinking of Shelley again.'

'Of course I am. I miss her. I miss all of them.'

'Then that should make you work twice as hard to get back to them sooner.'

He opened his eyes and looked up at Morghanna as she stood over him, her lack of shadow irritating him. The light was so strange here, it came from everywhere at once so they didn't even have a damned shadow! 'Sorry I'm not a fast-enough learner for you, but you have kind of thrown me in the deep end here.'

She sat down beside him, legs crossed. 'You're learning faster than I expected, actually.' His brows rose at the unusual praise, but she forestalled any smartarse comment from him with a raised hand. 'It's just, we're running out of time.'

'And why is that? You've mentioned time before, but not what the deadline is.'

'Samhain. The Darkness will make his final move on Samhain.'

'Samhain?' He sat up, draping his wrists over bent knees. 'I've only been here for what? A week at most. Samhain's still more than four months away.'

She rose to her knees, brow furrowed—he'd discovered she hated having to look up at him. 'Samhain is only two and a half months away.'

'Two and a half months!' He surged to his feet. 'What the hell?'

'Time moves differently here from back on earth. One day here is more than a week there, sometimes less, sometimes more. It's not always consistent.'

'I've been gone for two months?' He scrubbed his hand over barely-there bristles, pacing. 'They must be frantic with worry. Is there some way we can give them an update on what's going on?'

'Not yet. It's not time.'

'But Shelley ... the pack. They need me.'

'They've got their own concerns to get on with.'

'So they're not missing me?'

'I didn't say that.' She patted the place he'd been sitting on the stuff that was too green and perfect to be called grass. 'Come. Sit down. There is something I need to tell you.'

He glared at her. 'I don't particularly feel like listening to anything you've got to say right now.' He raked his hands through his hair. 'Fuck. When were you going to tell me about the time thing?'

'It's not important, other than impacting on the amount we've got to get through and the time we have to do it in.'

'Not important?' He pushed to his feet, staring down at her. 'I don't think you know the meaning of the concept. How can this not be important? Take me back. Take me back now.'

'No. We have only covered the basics that will allow you to learn how to control your powers.'

'You know, I'm sick and tired of hearing about these fucking mythical powers of mine. Were don't have magical powers.'

'You do. All Tricksters do. It's a legacy from when your people were created, a way the Goddess had of working against the Darkness.'

'Why would she do that—give Tricksters powers and not anyone else? That doesn't make sense.'

'Tricksters aren't the only Were with powers. But that is another story for another time. The answer to your question is that my Goddess was following the trails of prophecy.'

He blinked. 'Prophecy? What the hell are you talking about?'

She patted the ground beside her again. 'If you sit down, I will tell you.'

He scowled at her. 'This isn't one of those bullshit times where you say you're going to tell me something and then talk in riddles so I can't understand a thing?' She'd done that plenty since he'd been here.

'No. No bullshit. Just a story about how this all began. It's essential you know this so you understand what's at stake and why it is so necessary for you to learn to control your power and your abilities.'

He flexed his fingers, still scowling at her, but when she did nothing but smile in that serene way that both calmed and annoyed the hell out of him, he folded himself onto the ground next to her. 'I'm listening. Tell me your tale.'

She looked down at her lap, picking at the soft material of her skirt. When she spoke, her voice was barely a whisper. 'What I tell you now is not spoken of, but I tell you because I think it will help you to understand the urgency of what we must do.'

'Okay,' he said, the word drawn out. For the start of a story, it was a pretty good one.

She nodded, picked at a thread that had come loose. 'There was a prophecy, spoken at the birth of my Goddess when she sprang fully formed from her mother's womb. "*The goddess of fertility and rebirth, the weaver of time and fate, known by many names but to herself as Arianrhod, will grow to betray the one she loves and he will become Darkness. Intent on seeking his revenge, he will work to take over the world her powers are most firmly tied to and subvert it to his will.*

"Arianrhod will battle the Darkness for millennia over the fate of this world, succeeding in keeping him at bay, until finally, a child is created, with the accidental help of light magic, by those with power and the blackest of hearts. Through this child, the Darkness may be born into this world on the night where the veil between worlds is weakest. If the Darkness becomes this child, he will call all creatures of death and destruction to him and rule over them to wreak havoc on all, mortal and immortal alike, and the Goddess Arianrhod will be no more."'

'Holy shit. That's unbelievable.'

Her violet gaze met his. 'The Goddess thought so too. She laughed in the face of this prophecy, vowing to never love any man. For eons, she was successful in turning from any other, devoting her love and her light to the world she was given dominion over. She wove a life for herself, bore children, orchestrated myths about her, all to belie this prophecy. But the prophecy proved stronger than her will. She fell in love with one who was a slave in her father's temple. Their love was forbidden, not because of the prophecy, which only my Goddess and her mother knew of, but because this servant was not a God. He was part mortal, born of a Goddess from another pantheon and a slave she had taken from a distant world. My Goddess and he met quite by chance and it was love at first sight for both of them. Even then, my Goddess thought nothing of the prophecy, because she could not think of any circumstance under which she would betray her beloved. She did not think of what her father or the other Gods would do when they found out.'

'What did they do?'

'As punishment, her father threatened to destroy the world that gave her power if she did not give up her love. Knowing she could not live without the power of the world that was hers, she turned from her love and did nothing when her father banished him from the temples of the Gods and set him on the path between the voids to wander in hunger and thirst for an eternity for his hubris. Unable to stand the thought of him in such pain, the Goddess pushed him off the path and into the seething darkness that had always been kept at bay by the light of the stars. She had meant for him to die, but instead, he survived.'

'Holy shit!'

'Precisely. Of course, when he crawled back onto the path, he was a changed being, no longer part mortal, but made of the dark stuff of the universe. He sought out the Goddess and her father, seeking revenge for all the pain they had brought to him. By the laws of her own people, they could not destroy him, as his essential being was a part of the tapestry that made up the universe, which made him, for all intents and purposes, like them: a God. The only thing they could do was tear him into smaller pieces and scatter those pieces among the stars, hoping they would never come together again. But all the time my Goddess despaired, because so far that prophecy had proved correct, and she was afraid that unless she found some way to stop it, the rest would be proved too.

'Given she was the Weaver of Fate, she was certain she could weave herself a new one. She created magic users to worship her, to share in her power, and by doing so, to increase her power tenfold. She then created creatures who had magic threaded into the fibre of their beings, enabling them to change shape. These beings were stronger than the humans, rarely sickened, and were fierce fighters. She had meant them for her guard. She imbued others with a different kind of power—still able to change shape, these were also designed as the first defence, for their skill was in gauging changes in the emotions and thoughts of their people. She then turned her attention to creating more mythical stories about herself for those who worshipped her in the different lands, calling her by different names, laying out for her many different stories about her origins. She delighted in all of them, for it was a mark of her cleverness in subverting the will of the prophecy.

'For a millennia, nothing happened and her world thrived. And then, one day, her Were empaths cried out in pain. She flew down to help, but it was too late. The Darkness had made its way to her world and had infiltrated the Were, using the power of change she had gifted them, subverting it, creating pain and misery out of what should have been joy. It did not stop there, reaching out to influence the humans and making them turn on the covens and the Were so they were forced into hiding. Unable to share their power with the world as they'd once done, the power she'd gifted them began to turn on her beloved witches and warlocks. Some turned to black magic to try to protect themselves, tipping the balance of power so that the ley lines of magic became further twisted and warped, making it impossible for her to ever return her world to the way it had once been.'

Adam's mouth was open, but he couldn't seem to close it as she told him all the hidden history of his people and their Goddess. It was almost more than his brain could take in.

'The Gods forbade her to use her powers as Weaver in such an open way again, binding her tighter to their laws. Unable to outwardly influence anything, my Goddess began to work in secret. She found those with an astonishing amount of good in their hearts, who were filled with love and hope for a better future and whispered to them an idea. And the Pact between the Were and the covens was born. It banished the Darkness from the Were and returned some control over the balance of their power to the covens. And for centuries all seemed well. The Darkness banished and the future saved.'

'But the Darkness was not banished.'

'No. Her machinations were not enough to stop the final part of the prophecy from coming to pass.'

'The child,' Adam whispered.

'Yes. The Darkness continued to work, twisting those like my sister to do its bidding, always aiming at gaining a final revenge against my Goddess and her kind.'

'It knew about the prophecy?'

'No. My Goddess and her mother managed to keep it secret. But they knew it would somehow find its way to this path, and when it did, it would be the end.'

'Why on earth do you think that myself and the others can possibly make any difference when the Goddess herself is unable to stop it?' Fear for all he loved trembled through him.

She regarded him for a long moment before saying softly, 'I know it seems like an impossibility, but it is not. There is a way. A way my Goddess told me of when I was brought to this place.'

'Which was?' Adam said, hope growing in his chest once again and dispelling the fear and despair that had taken him over as she told her story.

'The prophecy of the Goddess and the Darkness is not the only prophecy that was ever made. There are other prophecies that she has come to believe have bearing on her hope of success in defeating her ex-love. An ancient prophecy about a fight over one called the Nexus, a singular being who has the power to tie death, life, animal and human, and the four main elements of earth, fire, wind and water together and use it as a weapon to defeat a great power. There was another of the Healer who could turn the Beast from violence and bring life to barren wombs. Yet another spoke of the lost witch with the power of all the elements rising from denial and bringing life to the nearly dead. And finally, the one that made her believe there was an answer to her prayers to save herself and her world, the prophecy that spoke of the Trickster, spirit-bound, who would be mated to the banshee and could help her harness the power of the dead to save the living.'

'But those prophecies haven't all come true.'

'Oh, but they have. Skye became master of all the elements and saved her pack from the destruction I accidentally wrought. Eloise is the Nexus. Thankfully, she found your pack, mated with Iain and fought the Darkness from taking over her soul. She has chosen to be a weapon against the Darkness. Bronwyn rid her mate of the Darkness' influence, overcoming the Beast and in an incredible feat of Healing that saved not only him and Eloise, but all of your pack, she also enabled Skye and Morrigan to become pregnant.'

'Skye's pregnant?'

'Yes. Which is another bonus for us, as the power of the babies inside her womb will be added to the whole.'

'Babies? I'm going to be an uncle to twins?'

'Yes.'

'Fucking brilliant!'

She waved her hand at him, impatient. 'You focus on the wrong thing.'

'I hardly think Skye and Jason having a baby is the wrong thing. It's a fucking miracle.'

'No, it's not a miracle. It's prophecy. Skye's pregnancy also means Morrigan too can become pregnant.'

'Okay. But the last one isn't true. I'm not bound to the banshee.' She smiled at him, a knowing smile that made him shiver to his core and shake his head. 'I hope all this doesn't hinge on that, because if it does, we're all fucked.'

She waved her hand. 'We will focus on that when the time is right and when you are ready to do what must be done.'

'And what is that?'

'With your help, the power of the Nexus, along with the witch, the Were and spirit, can harness the magic of the world and use it to cast the Darkness into the void before it can fulfil the words of the prophecy.'

'The child. You said Morrigan could get pregnant too. And she is, isn't she?'

Morghanna nodded.

'Shit.' So, all the prophecies she had spoken of were true—including the one about him and Shelley. But he didn't have time to focus on the enormity of that because she said,

'We cannot allow what they want of that pregnancy to come to fruition.'

Adam swallowed hard, feeling every ounce of the weight of the responsibility she had just placed on his shoulder. 'You want us to kill the child?' Revulsion bubbled inside him. Even if it was a child with Darkness in its heart, he wasn't sure he could be a part of killing a baby.

'No. We simply need to stop the Darkness from being born into the babe.'

'He's not in the child already?'

'No. It is not possible. Not while it is growing in the womb. The only time it can move into the child is when the babe is about to be born. When the soul that is meant for it should settle into its flesh as it is brought into your world. That is the moment the Darkness must strike, killing the soul and taking its place in the flesh of the child. Once it has done this, because of the magical nature of the child and his own powers, it will be able to syphon all power from the ley lines of your world, destroying it and my Goddess and using the destructive force to cross the bridge between the worlds of the Gods and hold dominion over all.'

'Fucking hell. Why don't the Gods stop it then?'

'The Gods do not believe this can happen. They do not believe any being would be so stupid as to destroy another God or Goddess. The power unleashed in the universe by a destruction such as this could tear the fabric of everything apart and cause chaos that would take millennia to pass. But the Goddess believes the Darkness has come to be something that feeds only on destruction. It will only become stronger if it manages to do this and is no longer bound by the same rules as the rest of them. The others of her kind will not believe her, and she is forbidden to lift a finger herself to openly stop the Darkness from seeking its revenge. That is why she needs us all. We must play our parts to stop the Darkness from entering the world through the child in my sister's womb. Our only chance is to expel the Darkness into the void before the child is born, then the prophecy of its birth can play out without the Darkness having any influence over it. The child can live and grow a normal life—well, as normal a life as any child could have without its parents. Both Cain and Morrigan will be destroyed when the Darkness is expelled into the void.'

'And you are okay with that? With your sister dying like that?'

Her lips thinned and her chin wobbled, but she met his gaze, hers devoid of anything but determination. 'If that is what it takes to save this world and our peoples, then yes. I will be okay with that. So, are you ready to get back to work and stop worrying about how long you have been away from your home?'

He wanted to look away, suddenly feeling like a recalcitrant child being brought to task over a temper tantrum but forced himself to return her gaze. 'I still can't believe I can help, but if you're right, then yes. Bring it on and let's destroy this fucker.'

She smiled and held out her hand so he could help her to her feet. 'I thought you might say that. Now, we have tested your physical agility and stamina, let us see about your control over your power.'

ADAM CLOSED his eyes and concentrated on the emotions rushing through him.

'Yes,' Morghanna said somewhere to his left. 'Those emotions you have always felt and reacted to are not all your own.'

'I know that,' he said, opening one eye.

'Concentrate!' She clipped him across his shoulder.

He closed his eye. 'I can feel anger and frustration now.'

'You will feel more than anger and frustration if you do not concentrate and take this seriously.'

'I am taking it seriously.' He opened his eyes again.

'Good, because to understand and manipulate the emotions of others, you must first master your own.'

'I don't manipulate people.' She raised a single brow. 'Well, not like you make it sound. I do it to help people.'

'Yes. You have had great success in helping your pack.'

'So why do I need to do this if I'm already good at it?'

'Because you did it without thought. Without truly understanding what you did and how you did it. You are a creature of pure instinct, and while that will lead you so far, it will not lead you to the greater power that lies within. The power that will help the triumvirate and the Nexus rid this world of the canker of the Darkness.'

'And I can't do this from my body?'

She sighed her frustration with him. He didn't mean to harp on getting back to his pack, but that was where he was meant to be.

'No. It is important you are in this form so that you can help Shelley control and channel her powers with your powers. The connection is stronger for her this way.'

He sighed. It wasn't that he didn't believe her now when she spoke of his powers. He did. He knew with certainty that his Trickster nature made him an empath in the true sense of the word—one whose powers derived from the ancient heart of the universe where the different threads of magic first came into existence. With that power he'd been helping his packmates for years, especially through the years after his parents and brothers were murdered and the Curse really began to exact its toll. However, the bit he was struggling with was that to do his part, Shelley had to engage with her powers. 'I won't force her to use her powers.'

'You will not have to. She will choose to use them. To save her friends. To save the pack. To save you.'

'If I'm so strong, why do I need saving?'

'Everyone needs saving. Even you. Shelley is key in delivering you back to your body.'

He couldn't help smiling. 'So I do get back to my body?'

'That is one of the things we are aiming for.' She tutted and shook her finger at him. 'Enough procrastinating. Back to the task at hand.' She gestured for him to take up the meditation pose. 'Now, while you have been very successful in the past at reading the emotions of your pack and stabilising them, you have also often been overwhelmed by those emotions, causing you to behave in ways that were detrimental to you and others around you. This is what we seek to control. Like Shelley, who must learn to control the spirits around her so they don't overwhelm her, you must learn to control the influx of emotions that influence your own emotions.'

He groaned. 'Please don't bring that up again.' He was tired of being taken to task for refusing to come with her and leave Shelley. 'I was worried about Shelley.'

'Yes, but that was only part of it. You could feel her fear as if it were your own and you let it take you over. You cannot allow that to happen again. It would be too easy for the Darkness and its followers to influence you negatively and take you out of the equation.'

'Fuck.' His eyes snapped open. 'You're serious?'

'Yes. The Darkness is trying even now to infiltrate this part of you through your body. It wants you on its side—you would be an asset with your ability to read and manipulate the emotions of others.'

'I'd rather die.'

'And you will if you do not learn to control what you do. If you learn control, you will be of no use to the Darkness.'

'It will leave my body then?'

'Possibly. Or it will kill you.'

'Terrific. Great options I've got there.'

'Better that than no options at all.'

He swallowed hard. She was right. He had to do this. He knew the stakes now. 'Okay. I'm concentrating. Tell me what to do.'

Over the next few days, they practiced the drills for controlling his emotions until he was dripping with sweat and exhausted, and then she drilled him more, throwing an array of emotions at him— quite literally at him. She'd conjured what looked like balls of smoky glass out of thin air and lobbed them at him, each one breaking on contact and overwhelming him with emotions others had experienced in the past—terror, grief, happiness, anger, depressive sadness, passion and so on—and he had to create a syphoning barrier that allowed him to utilise his power to feel the emotion but not let it take him over, so he could then pull on the right positive force to channel back out into others. His head ached by the end of every day, but he felt far more serene inside than he'd ever felt before. A serenity that brought an endless sense of strength and surety.

Finally he got to a point where he managed to successfully create the syphoning barrier again and again despite whatever she threw at him. Exhausted and dripping with sweat, he managed to stand tall and smile at her with what he knew was his cocky smile. 'Is that all you've got?'

She conjured another ball. This one had a tinge of amethyst to it. 'I have saved the strongest for last.' She threw it at him.

The ball hit him right in the middle of his chest, the glass-like substance turning to insubstantial tendrils of smoke as the others had. He erected his syphoning barrier, but this time, as the tendrils sank into his skin, he was driven to his knees by such an intensity of emotion that the barrier simply flickered and went out.

The emotion covered him, shot through him, surrounded him.

Love. His love. For Shelley.

But not simply that. There was something more, something behind it, ugly and weak, and yet it threatened to overtake everything. It was fear: fear that she was his mate but would never accept him.

The knowledge felled him, driving him to the ground. He struggled to breathe through the overwhelming onslaught he'd been fighting against for so long, but that had secretly driven everything he'd done since he'd met her. Staring up at Morghanna, agonised, he said, 'You've made this into a weapon? My love for Shelley?'

'Not your love for her—your fear of it. Mastery over this is more important than mastery over all the other emotions combined.'

'I know I love Shelley. I always have. I don't deny it.'

'No. However, you will not let yourself admit that she is your mate because you fear the choice she will make will not match yours.'

'She doesn't love me.'

Morghanna smiled knowingly. 'Of course she does. However, she suffers from the same martyr complex as you. She will give up everything because of her love for you. She is as frightened as you, perhaps more.'

'She has good reason after what her ex and her family did to her.'

She shrugged. 'Perhaps. Perhaps not. However, it is essential you both face that fear and allow the bond already in place to strengthen, for if you do not, none of what we are doing here will make any difference and we will fail.'

'You're telling me this all hinges on Shelley and me mating?'

'Yes.'

'But ... I can't force a mating. Shelley has to accept it of her own volition. Coercion of any kind won't let the bond come into being.'

'That is true, which is why you both must stop fighting against what is meant to be and let the strength of it flow through you.'

'And how the fuck am I supposed to do that here?' He dragged himself to his feet, anger burning in his chest. 'You refuse to let me even try to speak to her, let alone start the mating with her.'

'The mating has already begun—as you would know if you opened yourself to it. And I am not stopping you from seeing her now.'

She waved her hand and the air shimmered and then suddenly, the shimmering became a mirror-like surface full of swirling black and ghostly clouds. The clouds began to clear and the blackness dissipated until an image wavered in the mirror.

'Shelley,' he whispered, taking a step forward.

She sat at the table in the living room of her house. The table was covered with diaries and grimoires. She held her head in her hands, her fingers threaded through her hair, almost as if she was about to tear out great chunks of it. She was too thin. What had she been doing to herself? And how had the others allowed it?

She lifted her head to glare at the ceiling, her violet eyes made even more intense by the pallor of her skin and the dark circles under them.

Beautiful. So beautiful. Although he'd have to kill someone for not making her look after herself. She made an aggravated noise in her throat and then, looking down, swore at the diary she had open.

He wanted to reach out and touch her. To take her pain and frustration away. To soothe her anger and set aside her despair. To hold her in his arms and watch as she slept. To bring her food that she turned her nose up at, but then later ate with a gusto that made warmth spark in his chest.

He wanted to make her laugh. To cry out in passion. He wanted to give her joy in every way he could. He wanted to be her mate in every sense of the word. She was so real, so much a part of him already, he knew what Morghanna had said was true.

However, there was the little issue of him being without a solid form. 'I can't mate with her while I'm not in my body. And according to you, I can't be in my body until this is over. So how is this supposed to work?'

She simply smiled at him and said, 'Touch the mirror, step through and I promise the way will become clear. All you need to do is trust in yourself and your love.'

It seemed like such a simple thing and yet ... 'One small step and all that,' he murmured and, reaching out, touched the rippling mirror-like surface.

Everything he was turned inside out.

23

'I want to know about the Trickster and warlock lightning,' Shelley told the diary in her hands.

The pages fluttered and opened on another entry about banshees.

Fuck. 'Okay. Then tell me about the Nexus.' The pages fluttered again and landed on an entry about a Medium learning how to communicate with multiple spirits at once. 'I don't want to know about that, you bloody book.' Her fingers curled beside the diary and she trembled with the effort not to pick it up and throw it across the room. Taking a deep, unsteady breath, then a steadier one, then another, she re-centred herself before asking, 'Tell me about births of magical beings.'

Again, the pages fluttered. This time they landed on a picture of a winged woman, mouth open on a scream, Death with his scythe in the distance. 'You're as fucking useless as the last one!' Shelley slammed the diary shut and shoved it across the table. It hit the tray that held the lunch she'd not touched and the whole lot went spilling onto the floor with a loud clang of metal and smash of broken glass and crockery. 'Oh, fuck. Just fuck.'

'Hey? What's the problem?'

She looked up to see Gareth in the doorway, another tray in his hands holding a steaming bowl and fresh jug of water. He looked down at the mess on the floor. 'If you didn't like your lunch, you didn't have to push it on the floor. I hope you're not planning on murdering your dinner in the same way.'

She looked down at the bowl of minestrone and the thick piece of freshly baked sourdough he placed before her and burst out laughing.

Gareth laughed with her.

'Oh, shit,' she wiped the laugh-tears from her eyes. 'I needed that.'

'So did I,' Gareth said, pulling out the seat beside her. His face fell into serious lines as he regarded her. 'We all miss Adam. He could always bring light to dark times. He brought me out of my depression after I was kidnapped and tortured by Morrigan.'

'Yeah. He always made me laugh despite myself. Just like you've done a few times.' She gave him a considering look. 'Maybe you have a little bit of Trickster in you.'

'As if that could help even if it were true.'

She raised her brow. 'It's possible.'

'No, it's not that. I'd be thrilled if it were true. It's nice to be able to make people laugh. Especially when they need it most. But Adam brought something so essential to our pack that I couldn't possibly replace even if I were a full Trickster. There was ... is something very special about him. I think most of us didn't realise it until he was gone.'

Her mouth trembled, but she sucked in a breath, determined not to cry. 'I know. I've learned so much about what a Trickster truly is to the pack.' And what that meant to her in particular. 'He is one of the strongest there's ever been. I think he saved all of you when the Curse enacted. He kept you sane and strong.'

Gareth sucked in a breath. 'What are we going to do without him?'

'You're not. I'm going to find some way to bring him back.' She stared at the soup so hard, it blurred in front of her eyes.

'Shelley?'

'Yes.'

'Why don't you eat your dinner and then take a break. Maybe get some sleep. I know you've barely slept lately.'

She stared at the diaries. 'I can't. I've got too much work to do.'

Gareth reached over and took her hands in his—she hadn't realised she'd begun to tear the serviette on the tray into shreds—and pulled her around to face him. 'Have you found anything useful in the last few hours?'

She glared at him. 'No. Obviously. I didn't throw my lunch across the room for fun.'

'And will you find anything being this tired?'

'Yes.' His brow rose slightly. She glared at him. 'Possibly.' That brow went up higher. 'Okay, no.' She glanced at the diary she'd pushed across the table. 'They're not being helpful.'

'I think maybe you're just not in the right frame of mind and they're letting you know that. You need to eat and then sleep. Those are the most important things right now.'

She narrowed her eyes at him. 'I think you do have some Trickster in you. You're as annoyingly perceptive as Adam.'

Gareth smiled. 'I take that as a compliment.'

'You would,' she grumbled. But she picked up her spoon and took a big mouthful of soup. She almost groaned as the flavours filled her mouth, and despite the fact that it was steaming hot, she spooned another mouthful up, and another. The bowl was empty before she knew it. She picked up the bread and before she knew it, it was gone too.

'Here.'

She took the glass of water Gareth held out to her, gulped it down. He refilled it and she gulped that down too. Then yawned.

'Now you need to go to bed.'

She was too tired to argue. He helped her to her feet and accompanied her down the hall to her bedroom. She was glad she'd brought the diaries to the house she shared with Bron and Skye a few weeks earlier. Aside from being more comfortable there, she didn't have to go far to get to bed. She yawned again, struggling to keep her eyes open. She wondered briefly if Gareth had put something in her soup or water to make her feel sleepy. It was just the kind of overprotective thing Adam would have done, and despite his words to the contrary, Gareth was more like Adam than any other Were she knew. But when she opened her mouth to ask him what he'd given her, she yawned again and stumbled.

She was suddenly in his arms, head against his shoulder. 'Don't.'

'You're falling asleep on your feet.' The rumble of his voice vibrated through his chest and into her.

'What you give me?'

'I didn't give you anything, Shelley. You're exhausted. Please don't tell anyone I let you get into this state. Jason will kill me. No, scrap that. He'll just have to scramble for my entrails after Skye and Bron are done with me.' He sucked in a breath. 'Fuck, if Adam was here, I'd be a bloody mess on the floor already.'

'He couldn't touch you. He's spirit-thingy.'

'Oh, believe me, he'd find a way. When it comes to you, he is unforgiving.'

Shelley huffed a tired laugh against his chest. 'Ridiculous.'

'Not ridiculous. It's the truth. He loves you.'

Her heart lurched in her chest. 'No. He doesn't.' Even after her conversation with Skye all those weeks ago and admitting the truth to herself, she couldn't admit it to anyone else.

'Of course he does.' Gareth smiled down at her. 'Everyone knows it.'

Her mind spun. Everyone knew it? Crappity-shit-fuck. Her mind was still spinning as he lowered her onto a soft surface—her bed. He tugged at her feet—taking her shoes off—and pulled the doona up around her, tucking her in like she was a little kid.

'Don't baby me,' she managed to say through the whirl.

Gareth looked around. 'I know you say he's not here anymore, but just in case he can see us from where he is, I don't want him to think I've done any more shit of a job than I've done.'

She pushed up onto her elbows. 'He doesn't love me.'

He pushed her back down. 'He does. But I'm not having this argument with you right now. You need to sleep.' He kissed her brow, as if she was the younger and he the older, then turned the light off and shut the door.

Black closed around her, but she didn't notice, her head too full of thoughts of Adam. Her thoughts were always full of him, even when she was supposed to concentrate on other things, but especially when she went to sleep. It was one of the reasons she hated going to sleep lately. Her dreams were agonising, because in them she couldn't deny that he loved her and she loved him, and yet in those dreams—nightmares—her aunt was always there to remind her of who she really was, the banshee always rose, and Adam, being Adam, always tried to save her from the insanity of it all. And because of that, he died.

Every.

Single.

Night.

Tears stung her eyes. Even the memory of loss she lived through in her dreams every night squeezed the breath from her. She couldn't live through it for real. She just couldn't. Hot tears ran down her cheeks, a flood she couldn't seem to stop. 'Shit. Shit.' She rolled onto her side into a foetal position, arms wrapped around her legs, rocking, sobbing.

But it didn't help, so after a while, chest aching, throat throbbing, she rolled onto her back. 'Why do you hate me?' she whispered to the universe that had never been her friend, only an enemy she was constantly fighting against. But there was no response, only an empty, gaping hole where Adam was supposed to be in her heart. The sobs took her again and she cried until, exhausted, she fell into a deep sleep.

Clouds moved around her in her dreams, shimmering grey and misty white, twirling around her, making her dizzy. She was falling, falling. She cried out.

Hands caught her.

'Shelley. Shelley, open your eyes. I'm here. I've got you.'

'Adam?' She opened her eyes slowly.

She was cradled in his arms. His face swam before her, then

cleared so that she could see his beloved lopsided grin. Her heart lurched in her chest.

'Are you real?'

'As real as I can be right now.'

She reached up and touched his cheek, her thumb running down to his mouth. 'Oh.' He felt so good.

Behind him, the sky was a brilliant kind of blue she'd never seen before and there was the scent of flowers all around. They weren't in the dam like in every other dream. Instead, they were on a big, canopied bed, like one she'd seen in an antique store and had wanted but couldn't afford, filmy drapes not completely obscuring the fact that they seemed to be in the middle of a forest. Tree shadows should have been flickering over them but weren't. There seemed to be no shadows.

She refocused on Adam. His face was perfectly lit, like the light came from all around.

'Where are we?'

'A special place.'

She began to smile. This dream, by some miracle, wasn't the horrible one that ended with his death. This was something completely different. She knew she should try to wake herself up—none of her dreams ended well—but something about it made her want to follow it to its end.

'Kitten? Are you okay?'

Her smile widened. 'I think maybe I'm more than okay.' She lifted her head until her lips met his and then nothing else mattered. The warmth of him, the joy of him, was everywhere and everything. Every fibre of her being came instantly awake and sang a harmony of passion and desire that crescendoed through her, building and building with an excitement she'd never experienced before she'd kissed him.

She moaned into his mouth, pressing closer, tongue tangling with his. He tasted so good. Cinnamon and chocolate and red wine had nothing on Adam's spicy, rich taste. She could get drunk on the taste of him alone.

Dizziness overwhelmed her and she gripped his muscled shoulders, breasts pressing tighter against his chest, clinging as if she feared he would fall away, or she would. And if she fell now, she'd fall forever and never recover.

But she didn't have to worry. Because every time she fell, he was there. He was always there. And even though this was only a dream, it felt more real than real life ever had. As if, feeling her need, he'd come to her in the only way he could.

Her fingers curled into his shoulders. His growl of satisfaction was captured in her mouth, vibrating through her chest. She smiled against his lips. She knew that growl. Had heard it in many forms. She raked her fingernails over his shoulders, down his back and back up to make him growl again.

Hands tightened around her, pulling her closer, the growl she'd provoked vibrating on her lips and down to her toes, followed by a laugh—her laugh, his.

She raked her hands up his neck and into his hair, the silky strands winding around her fingers. She gave a little tug.

'Michelline,' he growled into her mouth. She tugged again and he pulled away slightly, his amber eyes glowing with passion as he stared down at her. 'Behave, Kitten.'

'What if I don't want to?'

His mouth cocked into that half smile she so loved. 'Then I'll have to punish you.'

'Maybe I'll have to punish you.'

'Please do. I love a naughty kitty.'

Then his mouth was back on hers, his hands on her arse, pulling her closer, possessive. Owning her. She waited for her mind to rebel against the thought. But it didn't. Because her mind was finally giving her some peace in a happy dream and it didn't matter if she gave here what she could not give in reality.

And in this dream, he wasn't the only one who got to claim, to own.

She ran her hands down his back to his tight arse, and pulled him closer, shaping the hard length of him against her stomach.

Fuck! He was so big. She wanted to see it. Feel it, pulsing and hot and silky smooth in her hands. Before she'd even thought about it, her hands were at the button and zip of his jeans. She expected him to question her need, to stop her, slow her down, but he only groaned and moved to give her easier access.

Then her hand was inside his jeans, pushing down his boxers, and she had the hard, hot, silken length of him in her hand.

'Fuck. Kitten.'

She looked up at him, wondering if her eyes looked as wild with passion as his did. She stroked her hand along his cock, loving the way he shuddered and bucked against her. 'Beautiful,' she muttered.

He swallowed hard, his eyes heated embers drilling into her. 'Do you know what it does to me to see my cock wrapped in your hand?'

'About what it does to me,' she said, her voice nothing more than a passion-hazed husk. She watched as she moved her hand up and down his shaft, fingers delving into the crisp curls below, cupping his balls, squeezing.

'Christ! If you keep doing that, I'm going to come.'

'What about if I do this?' She knelt and before he could move, had his glorious penis in her mouth.

'Kitten!' His shout was like the Hallelujah Chorus in her ears as she twirled her tongue around his shaft, finding the ridges, dipping the tip into the sensitive hole, lapping the salty moisture beading there. He shuddered and said something unintelligible. Her fingers gripped around him tighter and she opened her mouth wider, angling to take him deeper.

Before she could sink lower onto him with her mouth, he grasped her shoulders, pulling her up. 'Not yet, Kitten. Not yet. When I come, I want to be buried deep inside you here.' His pushed his hand under her waistband, fingers spearing through her curls and into the wet heat of her.

'Adam,' she gasped as one long, hard finger pushed into her.

'Do you like that, Kitten?' he asked as he pumped the finger in and out of her, his thumb stroking through her folds.

She jerked and trembled, calling out something incoherent. And then his mouth was on hers again, taking her cry into his mouth, one hand working on bringing her to a screaming orgasm as the other one dipped under her top and up to grip her breast. 'Yes,' she gasped as one thumb rubbed over her aching nipple and the other over her throbbing clitoris. 'Adam, Christ! Adam. I'm going to come.'

'Not yet, Kitten. I want to taste you when you come.' He moved and tore her pants away, and then he was between her legs, his tongue pushing between the swollen petals of her sex and licking, lapping at her with sharp, quick strokes that drove her mad. Then with long slow ones that drove her insane.

She twisted and writhed, but his hands gripped her thighs, pushing her wider, exposing more of her to his wicked, amazing tongue. He found her clitoris again, twirled his tongue around it and, just when she thought her head might explode from the build inside, he sucked her into his mouth.

'Adam!' She arched off the bed, fingers clawing at the sheets, but his mouth stayed on her, his tongue working against her as he sucked harder. Waves crashed over her, through her, the world receding into a tiny pinprick before exploding into a hundred million stars.

'That's it, Kitten. By the Moon! Even here, in this form, you taste so good.'

The words came to her but made no sense through the crashing, twirling tornado of sensation that was her orgasm, an orgasm that didn't seem to want to let up, just kept her twirling in space as his mouth and tongue and fingers kept working magic on her body.

Finally, Adam pulled away and trembling, exhausted, Shelley fell back to the bed. 'By all that's holy. Adam.' She could barely breathe and every muscle inside her trembled and twitched with the glory of what he'd just done to her.

'I'm not finished with you yet, Kitten,' he growled as he crawled up her body, lips chasing along her skin, the crisp hairs of his chest tickling her stomach.

He was naked. She was naked. When had that happened?

It was a dream, she reminded herself. Anything could happen in dreams.

She dug her hands into his hair as he dipped his tongue in her belly button and suckled there for a moment, then jerked when he bit down lightly. He kissed and licked at the little hurt, before moving up her body, doing the same on each hip, the base of her ribs and finally, on each breast, taking long moments to lazily swirl his tongue over and around her aching, swollen nipples, before sucking them into his mouth.

She clutched his shoulders and moaned. She'd never before thought she'd like this kind of sexual play, but with Adam it was different. Necessary. She loved everything he did. Everything he made her feel.

Hell! He made her feel. She'd spent so long shut down, keeping herself apart from everything. But he wouldn't let her. He'd never stopped making her react, making her feel. And she responded to him every time, telling herself she hated him, that he was annoying. Annoying Adam. But all the time secretly longing for the next time she'd see him, the next time he'd antagonise her in some way, the next time he'd make her smile or laugh, the next time he'd make her feel.

She loved him for it.

She loved him.

'I love you, Adam.' The words burst out of her, but she didn't feel the shock of them, didn't want to call them back. Not here. Never here. She could be truthful with the dream version of him. Could be her true self with him in this place.

He stilled, gaze meeting hers, the blaze in his eyes even brighter. 'I love you too, Michelline. With everything in me, I love you.'

She wasn't sure who moved first, but their lips met and she wrapped her legs around him as he slid inside her—the place he was always meant to be. He filled her, making her whole in a way she'd never been whole before. It wasn't real, but it felt more real than anything ever had—as if she'd been living a dream and had finally woken up.

He slid out of her and back in and she moved her hips so that he filled her completely.

'Fuck, Kitten. You feel so good.'

'More,' she said, fingernails pressing into his shoulders. 'More.'

His movements were slow to begin, so slow she thought her brain would melt with the tension of it. She tried to change the pace, move her hips faster, but he ran one big hand down her side and gripped her hip, slipping his hand under her butt, tilting her hips up to take him deeper. And when he was deeper than she thought it was possible for him to go, he stopped, leaned back.

'Look at me, Kitten. I want you to look at me. I want there to be no misunderstanding here between us. We are doing this together.'

She opened her eyes, reached to touch his face. 'You are so alpha male. Even my brain can't change you in a dream to be anything other than what you are.'

He frowned a little. 'This isn't a dream, Kitten. This is real. You are here with me.'

'Of course I am,' she smiled up at him. That was exactly what a dream would say, would try to make her believe. But this was too beautiful, too perfect to be anything other than a dream. 'Now, are you going to keep talking or are you going to make me scream?'

That grin again. 'I think you'll scream louder if I stop right now.'

'You bet I will.' She pulled his head down and gave him a big, luscious, open-mouthed kiss. He moaned into her mouth and moved inside her in response. And once started, he didn't stop.

'Thank the Gods!' she panted as he moved harder, faster. She gripped him tighter with her legs, hanging on, wanting it to go on forever while the pressure built up inside her higher, tighter. She didn't want to let go. Not of this. Not ever. She wanted to carry this moment with her for the rest of her life. It had to be enough, more than enough, because she would never have this perfection in real life.

In the dream, though, she could have everything. She could have it all. And she was going to.

She rose up and bit down on his neck again, just like the Were did to their mates, almost orgasming when his hiss of pleasure vibrated against her skin, through her chest next to the tightening around her heart. She lapped at the mark her teeth had made before taking his mouth with hers again. He flipped them both over, eyes gleaming, hands on both her breasts and said, 'Ride me, Kitten.'

And she did, laughing, exalting in the feel of his large hands rubbing over her breasts, down her stomach. His thumb dipped into her curls and played with the sensitive nub at her core. She bucked against him, muscles tensing. 'Holy crap, Adam!'

He rose up, lips melding with hers, hips pumping harder and faster, holding her upright against him, her legs wound around him, his thumb riding her clit as she rode him. She clutched him, hands tense against tight muscle, fingernails digging in. He growled, the sound vibrating to her core.

She wasn't sure she could take much more—her panted breaths a sob in her throat, her skin sweat-slicked and sliding against him.

'Hold onto me, Kitten. Hold on.'

She held on tighter as he pumped into her once, twice, three more times, and then her release tumbled over her and she screamed. Adam cried out his release, let go of her mouth, and bit down on her pulse point, the pleasure-pain of it driving her orgasm higher until it flowed over her, a tidal wave, tumbling and tossing her up and up and up until she thought the fall would kill her.

It didn't. Something snapped tight inside her and she was pulled back to Adam.

He caught her and held her close, as she knew he would; as he'd always done.

She came to, trembling and breathless, still curled around him and upright—she had no idea how he was holding them both up. All her muscles had turned liquid.

He caressed the bite mark on her neck with his lips, tongue brushing over her skin making her shiver delightedly. He lifted his head, gaze clashing with hers. His eyes gleamed golden honey, that beloved smile on his lips. 'You are mine.'

'Yes,' she agreed, melting into him as he toppled backwards on the bed, taking her with him.

24

Shelley lay, sprawled on top of him; he was still hard inside her, larger than he should be given what they'd just done.

She frowned. Bron and Skye had told her about this quirk of the Were's sex life. It was part of mating. Why on earth would she include this in her dream?

Maybe, deep down, she didn't just want to share love with him, she wanted to be bonded to him in the most intimate way. With that thought came a wave of need, of want, that told her that was exactly what she wanted. She wanted to belong. Wanted a man who would love her and challenge her, who supported her and nurtured her and would always, always, be in her corner, no matter what.

Just like Adam. He already did all those things; had done so since she met him. He was her perfect man. Annoying Adam. The man she had been so afraid to get close to, the one who had refused to let her keep him at arm's length, the man who knew the heart of her and saw past her bluster and snappy bitchiness to the soft, hurt little girl at her core.

'What are you thinking?'

She made lazy circles around his nipple with her pointer finger. 'I was thinking that I wish I truly could mate with you.'

'You can. You are. All you've got to do is accept it and me.'

She smiled up at him, brushed the hair back from his forehead. 'Of course you'd say that. You're a dream.'

'I'm not a dream.'

'Of course you are. I would never have gone this far if you weren't.'

His frown deepened as he looked into her eyes. Outside the dream, she would have avoided such a look; a look that pierced her to her soul, a look that demanded to be let in, to know her. But in the dream, she could meet it. She could be bold and true to who she wished she could be.

She pressed her lips softly against his, her knuckles brushing up the side of his face, her fingers playing over the lines of his frown. 'What's wrong?' she whispered.

'You think this is a dream?'

'Of course it's a dream. What else would it be? Aside from the fact you went with Morghanna and I haven't seen you for months, you're some kind of spirit.' She twined her fingers in his and brought them to her lips. 'I know you can touch me, but you wouldn't feel this warm, this real if this wasn't a dream.'

'I wouldn't feel this real if it *was* a dream.' He tore his hand from hers and pushed back from her a little, although he was still joined with her. 'It feels this real, Kitten, because I brought you to the place Morghanna brought me, and here my form is what I want it to be.' He looked down at himself. 'And given you channelled your power into me, it has made me able to make this even more real.'

He was shimmering with the purple of her power. A tingling raced through her, over her, making her shiver. 'How?'

'I was watching from the astral. You were so sad. Your astral soul left your body once you were asleep. It cried out for me. Morghanna told me when I stepped into the astral I would know what to do and I did. I brought you here with me.'

'You separated my spirit from my body?'

'No. You were already in the astral—you were dreaming. You were falling, calling for me and I caught you and then we were here.'

'So, these aren't our real bodies?'

'Not the ones that are back on earth, but they are real. Can't you feel it?'

'Oh, Adam.' It shuddered out of her and she had to put a trembling hand to her mouth to stop more words from spilling out.

He touched her face. 'We've just begun the mating.'

'No. That's not possible. We're spirits.'

'The bond isn't simply made through our bodies, it encompasses our souls, our thoughts, our hearts, every fibre that makes us who we are, both physical and metaphysical. You are my mate. We began the bonding almost from the moment we met, but tonight, sharing this here, it's been strengthened.'

Something flashed in her eyes—shock, panic. 'No. No ...'

'What's the matter?'

She shifted under him. 'I need a moment. Can you give me a moment?' She began to push at him. 'I need a moment by myself. I need to think. I can't think like this, with you here, all around me.' She pushed harder, her hands slapping at him. 'I need you to go. I need ... I need—'

He caught her hands. 'Shh. Shh. It's okay, Kitten. It's going to be okay.'

'It's not going to be okay. I thought this a dream. I would never ... I can't ever ... We can't mate.'

'Of course we can. I know you were hurt in the past but—'

'Do you think that's what this is? Do you think I'd truly let something like that keep me from the man I love?'

'Then what is it?'

'I can't believe this. I can't believe after I've been so careful, it's happened.' Tears began to stream from her eyes. 'Oh, Adam. What have I done?'

She sounded as if she was going to die. Her tears were a knife slash to the gut.

He swore and let go of one of her hands to brush the tears from her cheeks. 'Don't cry, Shelley. Please don't cry. Being my mate can't be that bad?'

'It would be the best thing that ever happened to me, except ...' She reached up and touched his cheek, his lips. 'I do love you. I want more than anything to be able to mate with you. But I can't. I can't.' She began pushing at him again. 'Please, I need you to move away. I just need to think. I need to think.'

She struggled against him, but he couldn't move. Fuck. He wished he could give her what she needed at this moment—wished it with every part of him—but the mating had started and he was too large inside her to pull out. He could hurt her if he did. 'I can't right now. You know I can't.'

Fear flared in her eyes. 'I ... I can still refuse you.'

He winced at the slashing pain of her words. 'Yes. You can. But it will hurt both of us at this stage.'

'I don't want to hurt you.' Her lips trembled and more tears spilled from her eyes, wetting her hair splayed out on the pillow.

He swore again. It horrified him that his strong, sexy Kitten, was crying, was in pain, because of him. He cupped her head with both hands, swiping at the tears with his thumbs. 'Then accept me. Accept this mating.'

'I can't. I can't.'

'Can't or won't?'

'Can't. It will kill you.'

'What?' He froze, stared down at her. 'Mating with you couldn't kill me. It's the best thing that ever happened to me.'

She squeezed her eyes shut. 'No. It will destroy you. It's in the diaries. In what my aunt prophesied to me. If I mate with you, I will end up killing you.' Her hand trembled over her mouth.

'That's rubbish. You would never hurt me.'

'I wouldn't mean to. But it's all tied into your Trickster empathy, how that power works, and what the Pact did to it. I'm not the right mate for you. I'm not stable. And the moment the insanity begins to take me over, that will be the beginning of the end for you. You will give too much of yourself to save me, but the cost will be your life.'

'That doesn't make sense. That's not what the mating bond is about. It's about a sharing.'

'Not for you. Not for us.'

'I could choose not to do it. I could choose not to give too much of myself.'

'No you couldn't. Don't you understand? It's hardwired into the Were DNA to do everything they can to save their mates, even at the expense of their own lives. The Pact didn't just make that a possibility, but a certainty in cases like ours.' She laughed, the sound tinged with hysteria. 'It helped everyone else, but it screwed us. It screwed us.'

He stared down at her, speechless.

'Adam, please. Don't look at me like that.'

'I can't help it. What you're saying is insane.'

She laughed bitterly. 'That's because I am insane. And you can't do anything to stop it. You shouldn't be tied to it. And I won't let you be. I won't drag you down into the death and destruction that is my due.'

'Don't.' He gripped her face tightly in his hands, forcing her to look up at him. 'Don't you ever say that is your due. Your due has nothing to do with death and destruction. That's some stupid idiocy your family has made you believe and it's patently untrue.'

'No. No. Don't you see? It's got nothing to do with my family's beliefs. It has to do with everything I've learned about the banshee and the kind of Medium I am from the diaries. It's got to do with what I've heard spirits say to me all my life. It's got to do with what my own power has shown me, what it does to me when it takes hold.'

She bit her lip, and took his hands in hers, pulling them away from her face. 'I knocked you unconscious when I banshee wailed. I made your ears and nose bleed. I could have done a lot more damage, but the banshee in me wasn't fully formed.' She stared up at him, her expression grim, fearful. 'It's been getting stronger. It's showing me more all the time, whispering in my mind, willing me to let her take over, to take care of everything so I don't have to worry anymore. And at times, I am so tempted to let her, because it's all so hard. But I don't, because I do care about the pack and I love Skye and Bron and you. Heaven knows, I love you.'

His fingers tightened on hers. 'And I love you.'

She clung to his hand. 'I know. I think I've always known. And I've been so frightened of it. I couldn't figure out why, but I think it was because the banshee was warning me even before it came to the fore. I didn't want to encourage myself or you for fear of this moment coming to pass. I can't let it happen. Do you understand, Adam? It's not because I don't want it—God knows, I want it with everything in me. I want to belong. I want to be tied to you in every possible way. And yet, I can't let it go any further, because I won't be the death of you.'

Tears streamed down her face and she made no effort to stop them. 'I won't kill you. I just won't. And nothing you say or do will make me take that final step.'

Her voice broke and it killed him. 'Fuck, Kitten. Don't. Please, don't.' He gathered her in his arms, shifting their positions so she was on top, and held her as she sobbed into his neck, her tears like hot acid against his skin. 'I won't push you. We won't go any further. I won't ask you for the words. I didn't mean to hurt you like this. I never wanted this.'

She lifted her head, her face ravaged by grief, eyes swollen with tears, but she still looked so beautiful to him.

'I'm not sorry for making love to you tonight. I've wanted it for so long and I know it's selfish of me to be glad we finally shared what's between us, but I can't be sorry to have experienced this. I'll hold this feeling to me for the rest of my life.'

'As will I. There will never be another for me, Kitten. You are it.'

'I know.' Her lips trembled again, but she pressed them together and held the tears back by the sheer strength of her will; a will that both amazed and terrified him. 'I am so sorry that's true. I wish you could have the love you deserve.'

'I have got the love I deserve.' He brushed her hair back from her face in a caress that trembled with the strength of his feelings. 'I hold your love to my heart. Even if we can never fully express our love, it's still there and it's precious. You are more than I could ever have wished for. Beautiful, strong, determined, intelligent and fiercely loyal and loving. Loving you is a gift I can never be sorry for. Nobody else could hold a candle to it.'

She pressed a wet kiss to his lips. 'If this moment wasn't so painful, that would be the most romantic and wonderful thing anyone has ever said to me.'

He chuckled as he kissed her, little sipping kisses. 'That's me. Wonderful and romantic.'

She pulled back from him and cupped his face. 'You are, you know. Wonderful. I always knew it, even when I pushed you away and was so horribly snarky.'

'I loved your snark.'

Her lips curled. 'You always saw it as a challenge, didn't you?'

'Sure did. The best challenge ever.'

The humour faded from her eyes as her gaze met his. 'This isn't a challenge,' she whispered. 'You do understand that, don't you?'

'I believe you. But that doesn't mean I won't hope that something will change. That we'll find a way through.'

Her face twisted and the look in her eyes was such a mixture of sad and loving that it twisted his heart with hope and grief all at once. 'I wish that was true, but I can't let myself do the same. It hurts too much to hope.'

His fingers tangled in her golden hair. 'I know, Kitten. Let me hope for the both of us, okay?'

'I can't ask you to change your nature any more than you can ask me to change mine.'

'No.' He touched his forehead to hers. 'We're quite a pair, aren't we?'

'The worst ever.'

He kissed her nose and leaned back. 'The best ever.'

He waited for the laugh he knew his words would bring and when the sound burbled out of her, he bent and drank it from her lips. Then he pulled out of her as the first part of the mating bond subsided.

'You need to send me back.'

'All you have to do is wish it and your astral self will leave here and return to your body.'

She stared up at him for an agonising moment, her fingers trailing over his cheek. 'I'm sorry.'

Then she was gone.

He'd never felt such an aching sense of loss in his life, then that loss turned to fury.

'Morghanna! Where the fuck are you? What have you made me do?'

25

The bed and the sky and the forest dell disappeared. Greyness enfolded him, tinged this time by the deepest amethyst of Shelley's power still sparking on his skin.

The grey swirled and faded and he heard a gasp behind him. He swung around.

'Morghanna.' His growl resonated in the air and he took a step towards her. The surprise faded from her face and she backed away from him, hands held out.

'Now, Adam. Wait. You have it all wrong.'

'I don't think I have. You pushed me to go to her and you must have known she couldn't mate with me. That she believed it would mean my death. Is it true? Will she kill me?'

'Perhaps.' She blanched as his snarl ripped through the air between them. 'It is the nature of the Trickster to take into themselves the sadness and pain and uncertainty of those around them and turn it into something stronger, better, happier. This was amplified when the Pact was created, but unfortunately, that amplification meant they also could give too much of themselves to their mates, and if that mate was weak of mind, spirit or body, it became one-sided, rather than symbiotic. The Trickster most often died from the effect.'

'Shelley isn't weak.' He took a step towards her.

This time she held her ground. 'No. She is strong.' Her clear violet gaze met his. 'As are you. Especially after the work we've done.'

He narrowed his eyes. 'Are you telling me you think she won't go insane? Or that if she does, I'll be able to handle it?'

'It does not matter what I or anyone else thinks. What matters is what you believe. You are a Trickster. What you believe, what you desire, holds a lot of sway with those you love and look after.'

His anger hissed out of him as he stared at her. 'That makes no sense. If that was true, those other Tricksters would not have died trying to help their mates.'

'Those other Tricksters had not travelled between the veil. They were not the heart of the strongest pack there has been since Bridgette wielded the spell of the Pact and bound our people to yours. They did not have a coven made up of a triad of witches with the capability of becoming the triumvirate, with the Nexus feeding power into them. They had not fought their own battle for the sanity of themselves and their pack as you fought when my Curse began to pull your pack apart at the seams. And as I said before, they did not have your training.

'You are the strongest Trickster I have ever seen. The very fact that you would hurt Shelley by your death is the single thing that will keep you clinging to life. It is one of the reasons my Goddess is certain our plan will work. It is a virtual impossibility for you to be torn apart by Shelley's insanity if she was to slide down that slope, because it is not in your nature to give in.' She huffed out a laugh. 'You are quite simply the stubbornest Were I have ever seen.'

'You haven't met my brother.'

She laughed briefly and then grabbed his wrist, holding him still. 'Once this is over and you are back in your body, all you have to do is convince Shelley what she saw is not true for you, and you can become fully mated.'

'You make that sound so simple. You think I'm stubborn? Mix that with intractable and you've got Shelley.'

'She won't be intractable. Not about this.'

'How can you be so certain?'

She smiled serenely at him. 'Because there is no other option. When the time comes, it will all fall into place. You will see.' She let go of his wrist. 'But it is not simply our need for it to be so that makes me certain. My Goddess does not wish you or your pack and coven anything but the joy and happiness of a future free of the Darkness. She wants your pack to become strong, to help build the Were and covens back to what they were always meant to be—a strength to help shape the world for the better. To help humans understand how to live in harmony with each other and with nature. That all can thrive if only they work together.'

'Sounds like the words of an idealist. I'm not sure if that can ever happen in reality. Not with the world the way it is.'

'Without the Darkness there making the evil take shape and form, you will have a chance to make it true.'

'You said I had to be mated with Shelley to be able to do my part. We're not fully mated.'

'The bond is strong enough. You will make it work.'

He sighed. 'You hold a lot of hope in my ability to do what you wish me to do.' The weight of expectation pressed in on him, obscuring the joy of making love to Shelley, of the hope he had to mate with her, of his anger at that joy being manipulated and used even for the most righteous of reasons. 'This could all still go to shit. What if I'm not as strong as you think?'

'As I said, it does not matter what I believe. Only what you believe.' She smiled, a Mona Lisa smile that made his skin shiver with some unknown fear. 'Now, it is time you go back. Things build towards their climax. You must help prepare the Nexus so she is ready to bind all the powers of the living and dead together.'

'How am I supposed to do that? I'm not a warlock.'

'No, but you can give her this.' She waved her hand and a stone appeared in his palm. It was many-faced, like a well-cut diamond, but green, like Eloise's power. At its heart was the electric blue of Skye's power, the warm orange-gold of Bron's, the amethyst of Shelley's and a brilliant, dazzling red he'd never seen before. On the larger face, there was a design carved into it—a dot inside a triangle inside a square.

'What's this?'

'It is the Goddess Stone. It was created at her birth and is tied to her as she is tied to this earth. It has the powers of the elements, of healing, of the living and the dead. Shelley will be able to find the spell in her family's grimoire that will help weld this to the Nexus.'

'Why would that be in Shelley's family's grimoire?'

'A distant relative, a Medium with the power of foresight, wrote down what she saw so that Shelley would have that information when the time was right. The Goddess ensured she saw what needed to be done at this future point. The spell is essential. With the Goddess Stone welded to her flesh and soul, the Nexus will be able to stand at the centre of the triumvirate's power and channel it and the pack's heart to the ley lines of the earth and wield that power to expel the Darkness from the Earth for good.'

'How will she know how to wield the power and the ley lines? She's barely had time to do any training.'

'The stone will tell her once it is part of her. What is in her nature will do the rest.'

'I thought you said that this wouldn't happen until Samhain when the veils between worlds are blurred.'

'It *is* almost Samhain.'

'What?'

'I told you time here moves differently. Shelley was with you for over a week.'

'What?' he said again. 'The others must have been frantic about her.'

'They were worried, but Bron was able to sense she astral travelled, and assumed she was following a lead from one of the diaries. They were angry she did not inform them of her intentions. They gave her a rather amusing lecture when she woke up.'

'Did she tell them what had happened?'

'What do you think?'

No. She would never tell anyone about what they'd shared. 'How do you know all this?'

'The Goddess has been keeping an eye on things. She shares some of what she learns with me.' She glanced at the sky. 'Our discussion is over. Days have passed as we talked.'

'Shit. What do I have to do?' His fingers tightened around the stone. 'Surely getting this stone to Eloise and helping Shelley find the spell isn't everything?'

'Be a conduit for Shelley. You already know how to do that. Use your bond with her to funnel the powers she will have to pull from the veil into yourself for the Nexus to use. She will have to drop all her shields, but your new abilities will enable you to protect her from the full impact of the death she will feel while allowing her to channel it in the way that is needed without becoming over-whelmed.'

'Okay. But is it just me and the coven?'

'No. You and River and Jason and Iain, the mates of the triumvi-rate and the Nexus, are all bound together through your Packbond, but also through your mating with the most powerful coven there has ever been. You make up the four points that will protect them all as you give them power.'

He opened his fingers to stare at the stone. 'We're the square carved here.'

'Yes. And they are the triangle and the Nexus stands in the middle, taking power from you all.'

'Won't that amount of power kill her?'

'No. The stone will allow her to expel it into the earth to manipu-late the ley lines. Besides, the conduit can also run the other way. If the power does prove too much at the end, the mating bonds will allow you Were to take the power and expel it into all the Were packs.'

'But we're not bonded to other packs.'

'Ah, but you are. After what happened to me because of the weakness of the Alpha of the pack I was bonded to, intermarriage between the packs was encouraged to keep the bloodlines strong and to make certain all Were and coven members had choices.'

'I have never heard of this.'

'That's because the practice died out as trust between the packs became a natural state of affairs rather than something that had to be forced. The bonds of friendship the McVales have created with the McClunes and other packs was not something we ever saw in my day —but it is just as strong as the bonds of blood intermarriage created. Your pack has their friendships and those packs have ties of friendship and trust with other packs—it is a stone dropped into a pond. So you see, it is as I say. If needed, the power can flow to every Were on the planet and safeguard the covens. That is why it was so important that you solidified the bond with Shelley, so she would have a protector bonded to her like the others are bonded to their mates. Even without the mating complete, the bond is already enough. We can finally do what the Goddess has longed to do for a millennium. We can banish the Darkness and live our lives free.'

'You needed all of us?'

'Yes. The Goddess has spent thousands of years weaving this fate so it would come to pass. And finally, we are going to see it to fruition.' Her smile trembled. 'All I have sacrificed, all that my blood has sacrificed, will be worth it if we can manage this great feat. And I know we can, for we must. There is no other alternative. We cannot let the Darkness be born into the world. Your concerns about your mating with Shelley will not matter if it does, because it will bring forth all the evil in the world. The darkest parts that lie in all of our souls will come to the fore and not a single one of us will care about anyone but ourselves. You would happily destroy Shelley to use her power for the Darkness and she would do the same to you.'

'That could never happen.'

Her face blanched. 'I did not believe it either. Not until the Goddess showed me what would happen in the future if the Darkness truly made it into the world. As I will now show you.' She waved her hand and the air trembled in front of them, light sparking into a widening sphere, so bright that he had to shield his eyes.

The light in the sphere faded and an image wavered, then cleared.

It was the Packhouse in Red Hill, but not as he'd ever seen it. Half of it was burning, the other half gone, the orchards and fields beyond it destroyed. Fires burned across the hills.

Cries filled the air, echoing and distant, the evidence of battles still being waged in the distance. The sparks of witch and warlock lightning flared, followed by explosions and the pop of gunfire. Battle howls split the air. Were fighting Were.

'Fucking hell,' he breathed. 'This can't be.'

'It can. If the Darkness gets its way. This and worse will tear the world apart. Watch.'

The scene changed. The smoking wreck of a house—the house that Iain had designed as a front to cover the caves below—smouldered before Adam, its massive metal doors a twisted mess on the floor. In front of the doors was a pile of something …

Bile rushed to his throat. It was a pile of bodies!

Were bodies, some half changed, others fully changed, others in their human form, all dead and mangled. He recognised faces and fur colour. Members of their pack, the McClunes, friends and family. His stomach lurched as he saw a small hand at the edge curled around a dead puppy. 'Tom.' He reached towards his young nephew, but his hand only passed through the image, making it waver like water.

When it cleared, the image had changed.

Shelley stood atop of the pile of bodies, her golden hair black with dried blood, eyes vividly purple and swirling with dark madness. She wore some kind of black diaphanous robe that swirled wildly back from her body as she lifted her hand and pointed to something in front of her.

Wings rose from her shoulders, blacker than night, only visible because of the purple sparks of power chasing along their edges. She laughed, the sound tinged with insanity. 'I am banshee. I am Death. Woe to all those I see.'

Something moved in the night behind her. A Were leapt towards her. Blue lightning, edged with black, tore from the edge of the image, lighting up the Were in mid-leap. The lightning tore a hole through the centre of the Were's chest and lit up his face enough for Adam to see who it was.

'Jason!' he cried as his brother hit the ground, killed by his own mate who now walked into view. 'Skye. No.'

Her eyes were filled with the same edge of dark-tinged insanity that infested Shelley.

Behind her came Bron and Eloise. Each of them were lit up with their black-tinged power, each of them touched by madness.

'No, no, no, no, no.'

Shelley turned to face them. 'Thank you, my sister.'

'My pleasure, sister. The filth will infest us no more.'

'Speaking of which,' Bron turned and Eloise waved her hand forward. 'We caught these trying to save those who had fled through the caves.'

Figures were pushed, stumbling and bloodied, into his view. Iain. Gareth. Patrick.

Shelley waved her hand. 'Why do you bring them here? They should be dead.'

'I thought the Beast might have some fun with them.'

Shelley shrugged. 'I care little how they meet their death. Do what you will.'

Bron flicked her hand and a creature pounded into the scene. River. But it wasn't River. He had become the Beast again. The look he gave Bron was the one a slave gives their master—desperate dependence, not the love and devotion of a mate.

Bron smiled a cold smile. 'They are yours, Beast.'

The Beast leapt at his injured packmates, claws slashing. They tried to defend themselves, but Eloise waved her hand and her power shot out, holding them in place as the Beast tore them to shreds.

Skye, Bron and Eloise laughed.

'Enough. Enough,' Adam said, his voice breaking, but the scene continued.

Shelley turned from the murder of those she'd once cared for. Her wings flapped and it seemed she was about to take off when there was a cry from behind her and something shot out of the darkness of the caves. The projectile hit one of her wings. Blood sprayed. Shelley toppled backwards, disappearing behind the pile of bodies.

The vision shifted to show her as she rolled across the floor. Her wings snarled on the shards of twisted metal of the destroyed doors. She tried to rip them free, but every move tore shreds from them. Screaming in rage, she lay still, chest heaving, eyes wide with pain and madness.

A figure stalked out of the darkness towards her. Tall and dark-haired and full of hatred and rage. He came to stand over the banshee version of Shelley, a crossbow in his hands that sparked with magic. The banshee-Shelley's eyes lit up as she met his gaze. 'Finally, you have come for me, my love.'

Adam watched, horrified, as a raging and grief-fuelled version of himself snarled at her. 'I am not your love. I will never be your love.'

The banshee-Shelley smiled, a smile that almost looked like her own sad smile. 'Ah, but you are wrong. Our love will bind us together even in death.'

'That is the last word of death you will ever speak.'

'It is the only one that counts,' she said, just before he shot a magic-fuelled bolt through her heart. She jerked, the light in her eyes flaring. The Adam in the vision lifted his head and howled to the sky. Behind him, there was a howl of rage and blue, orange and green lightning tinged with black hit him at once, lighting him up. He cried out, a sound of pain-filled triumph, and then he fell forward on top of Shelley. Her arms moved to embrace him and she whispered in his ear, 'See. I told you I would be the death of you.'

The light left her eyes. Still and silent, she stared blankly up at the storming sky.

Adam tore his gaze away as the image wavered and faded. He bent double and vomited.

'I'm sorry I had to show you that. I wish I'd never seen it either. But it is necessary if you are to truly comprehend what we face.'

He lifted his head to see Morghanna, paler even than when she had appeared to him as a ghost in the living plane. 'It can't be true. Mate would never turn on mate.'

'They would when love is twisted into hate. At the moment, all of them have the power of the light in them, but their power can be corrupted by the dark given the right circumstances. Shelley in particular. Her power and the banshee skirt on the edges of the veil, neither light nor dark, subject to both, but influenced by her will and her will alone.'

'Her will is strong.'

'Yes, but not strong enough to survive the visions she will have to endure if the Darkness succeeds. Her fear of insanity will become a reality and when it does, the banshee will rise inside her as a dark force instead of a light one. It will take over and become the vessel of Death the Darkness wants her to be. Skye and Bron and Eloise will be drawn down into that evil with her, no matter how they might fight it, because their power is too intimately entwined with hers. Her insanity will become theirs. Her visions of death will be meted out by their hands, ensuring those visions become reality. The banshee sees the possibility of this even now, has been whispering its warning to Shelley all these months. It's why she believes that insanity is coming, although she doesn't comprehend it's tied into the success of what we do here.'

'We should tell her.'

'No! She can't know. You can't tell her. It would be too much of a burden for her to bear at this juncture. She already has so little faith in herself.'

'Fuck! Then if you don't want her to know, why are you telling me?'

'Because you must know. You must use all that you are to ensure our success, to save your pack, your coven, your mate.'

'Of course, I will.'

'I know.' She looked back at where the vision had been. 'What I showed you here is only the tip of the iceberg. The Darkness will corrupt everything if he is born into Morrigan and Cain's baby. The

Earth will become nothing but a battle ground between all supernatural beings and the humans. Nothing is sacred and nobody is safe.'

Adam straightened slowly. 'That can never come to pass.'

'You understand now what must be done and why.'

Hell, he did. He wished he didn't, but he did. Taking in a shuddering breath, he said, 'I will do whatever I have to do to ensure what you just showed me never comes to pass.'

'Good. Because despite what the Goddess wants for all of you, I think there is the strong possibility that we might have to sacrifice ourselves to ensure the future. Do you understand?'

Adam nodded. He understood. He was more than prepared to sacrifice himself to stop the Darkness. But there was one thing he wouldn't do: sacrifice Shelley.

She must survive. It was essential.

And for her to survive, to be happy, she must have her friends with her. And their mates. And the pack.

They would keep her safe and sane and happy, even if he wasn't there to ensure it.

And because he was the Trickster, he would make sure his wish came to pass. Morghanna had told him that was part of his birthright.

Now, he would use it.

<h1 style="text-align:center">26</h1>

Morrigan winced as the baby kicked her in the ribs. He was so strong and already grown so big. When Cain had said he would be born on Samhain, she'd thought it impossible—even for magical beings, gestation was still nine months. But as Cain had said over and over, this pregnancy wasn't a usual pregnancy, and she knew the baby would be born on Samhain like he insisted.

And when that happened, the Darkness would cast aside the baby's soul, killing everything he was meant to be. Her child would become a vessel of pure evil.

She could never let that happen.

Something had changed in her over the last few months as the baby grew inside her. It had been so subtle at first that she hadn't noticed. Then one day, when Cain was crowing about what would happen on Samhain, the evil he intended to wreak on the Were and their covens, she'd felt sick at the thought of causing that kind of death and pain. She'd clutched her bulging stomach with both hands, as if she could protect her baby from the avaricious gaze of the man she'd once thought to rule but who had somehow come to rule her, and she'd known he was wrong.

They were wrong.

She couldn't let this come to pass. Couldn't let him and Darkness use her baby like this. Her baby deserved to live, soul intact, and be whoever nature had meant him to be at that magical moment of creation.

She couldn't let the Darkness kill the possibilities within her son. She just couldn't. Not even if it meant gaining her revenge.

That revenge seemed so overblown now, an insane dream she'd woken from and was now trying to shake off.

She would never have gone so far without the influence of the Darkness. But the Darkness had left her and moved fully into Cain. It couldn't touch the baby in any way before his birth because he was too pure, created from the light of the Nexus power Cain had stolen from Eloise. Cain had thought it was their magic they'd used, but he was wrong. They practiced the blackest magic; life could not be created from magic seated in death and pain. But even if it hadn't been created by the Nexus' pure magic, the Darkness couldn't have stayed. It was everything opposite to creation, so its presence would have killed the baby growing in her womb. So the Darkness had left. And with it gone, she'd begun to see clearly for the first time in centuries and was horrified by what she had done.

'I'm so sorry,' she whispered to her baby, hand stroking over her stomach. 'I can't take it back, but I can change what I do in the future. I won't let them use you. I won't let them turn you into a horror like your father and me. You will have a better life; the kind of life Morghanna's progeny had despite my meddling. I promise.'

She had to get away from Cain. And she had to find some way to stop the Darkness from entering her baby at its birth. She didn't have long—Samhain was closing in fast.

What the hell was she going to do?

Her mind roiled as fear and uncertainty washed over her. She had no one to turn to and it was all her fault. She'd used her people and never shown them a thread of loyalty, treating them like dirt to be trod on if she so wished. They'd so easily turned to Cain when he had come into his power. The only one of them who might have helped her had run away and was now taken in by the Were and their powerful coven.

Her eyes widened.

Eloise!

She'd always derided her for having such a big heart; for being so forgiving. But now, it just might be her salvation.

The shifter-witch and her coven were powerful enough to help her. They were the only ones who could. Her fingers trembled over her mouth as she sucked in a breath. Could she go to them? Could she ask for help from the very people she'd been trying to destroy?

She had to. She had no choice. And neither did they—unless they wanted to risk the Darkness taking over the world.

Escape was going to be difficult though. Cain watched over her with covetous wariness. When he wasn't able to watch her, he had one of the coven doing so. Cain said they were guarding her and the child from harm, which was probably true given his paranoia. She was certain he still had no idea she'd changed. That she wanted to escape.

But his paranoia did complicate matters.

If only she could knock them all out at once, then she'd have a chance.

Knock them out. That was it. She would need to create some kind of sleeping potion and give it to all of them at once. It would be easy enough to lace the evening meal with whatever she managed to create.

It would have been easiest if she'd had some Valium or some other strong sleeping pills to use. But Cain never let her leave the property at all now, so there was no chance she could steal any. Herbal ingredients would have to do. They had valerian, kava elixir and chamomile in their medical stores. Mixed together with a simple spell, they should be strong enough to knock out a horse. Now all she needed to do was cook something with enough flavour to hide the bitterness of the herbs and with enough chilli to disguise the tingling heat the spell would create. She needed to cook more than the one meal like it though, otherwise Cain would become suspicious, especially as cooking wasn't something she did much of anymore. Strange. Once she had loved to cook.

The next morning she declared she was in a nesting mood and wanted to cook for the baby and the coven, taking over the duties Cain's adoptive parents had taken on years ago. Cain seemed happy for her to do so. His adoptive parents weren't quite so thrilled as they were sent out to do other duties around the farm less suited to their talents. She couldn't let herself care about that though.

Over the next week she cooked soups, casseroles and stews with increasing amounts of chilli and herbs. On the third night, Cain stared at her across the table as he breathed in the scent of the stew she'd prepared. 'Why so much chilli?'

Heart thumping in her chest so loud she was afraid he would hear it, she smiled and shrugged. 'The baby is craving the heat. It settles him. Don't you like it?'

Cain's gaze lowered to her stomach, and then he lifted a spoonful, placed it in his mouth and swallowed. 'It's not bad,' he said after a moment, spooning up another mouthful. 'Eat,' he said, gesturing to the others. 'If it's good enough for my child and me, it's good enough for all of you.'

The others began to eat, spoons clanking against bowls. There was no talk, just the sounds of nervous eating.

Sighing in relief, Morrigan ate her stew, certain now her plan would work.

A few days later, she asked Steven, the coven member watching over her that day as she cooked, to step outside and pick her some fresh thyme so she could make thyme bread to go with the casserole. He hesitated. She kept chopping. Begun to hum. He must have decided it was safe to leave her for the few moments it would take him to get the thyme from the kitchen garden, because he turned without another word and left. Almost sagging in relief, she took the opportunity to whisper her spell over the ingredients cooking in the pot, emptying the sachet of dried sleep-inducing herbs she'd prepared days earlier into the mix. Then she dumped in the freshly chopped chilli and meat. By the time Steven came back with the thyme, she was measuring out flour for the bread.

That night, Cain polished off his bowl, wiping up the dregs with the bread. 'You are quite the cook, Morrigan.'

'Would you like another?' She rose, trying to hide her shaking legs.

His gaze snapped to her empty place setting. 'You haven't eaten.'

'I had some earlier. I've been feeling so tired lately that by the time it's dinner for the rest of you, I've been too tired to eat.' She yawned widely. 'If you don't mind, I might go and lie down.'

'I'll help you.'

'Oh, but what about your meal? You seem so hungry. I can get myself to bed and you can have some more.'

'Peter can bring me a bowl in the bedroom.' He stood, coming around to take her arm.

She gritted her teeth, forcing herself to stop shaking, to not give in to the need to shudder and step back. 'Thank you.'

They barely made it to the bedroom before his hand fell slack from her arm and he turned to her, accusation in his eyes. 'What did you do?' he asked before his eyes rolled up and he slumped to the floor.

She held her breath, waiting to see if anyone came running. Waiting to see if he moved. The clock ticked loudly. She counted the seconds. One minute passed. Two. Three.

Cain hadn't moved. Nobody came in to check on the noise.

It had worked!

Leaving him where he lay, she grabbed her winter coat and headed to the door.

Cain made a noise behind her. She turned slowly to look, afraid to see him sitting up.

Oh Goddess! Had she not made the potion strong enough?

He was still slumped where he'd fallen, his mouth slack, breathing slow and steady.

Asleep. But for how long? She couldn't be certain. She had to get out of here now.

The bodies of the others were scattered through the house. She'd been worried one of them might not have eaten enough for the potion to work.

She raced into the kitchen, snatched up the keys for the old four-wheel drive and slipped out the back door.

The cold night air stung her cheeks as she left the house and headed to the barn that served as their garage. The night was cloudy and there was very little light outside to mark the garden surrounding the house from the fields that folded out around them on the valley floor. This had probably been the most picturesque place they'd lived in for years. It would have been a perfect place to raise a child. The thought almost made her sorry to be leaving it.

Almost.

She didn't bother turning on the light in the barn, using her magic to light her way. The red glow of it lit up in her hand. The vibrancy of it made her stop and stare in wonder. It had been so long since she'd seen that brilliant ruby colour. She hadn't realised how much she'd missed it. For so long, her magic had been affected by the Darkness, dulled and heavy and blackened. 'Welcome back, old friend,' she whispered, wiping at the tears tracking down her cheek.

She clambered into the four-wheel drive. Despite its age, it started up easily and she headed down the long drive and onto the highway, driving in the direction that would take her to the McClunes' Packland.

They'd come to this place because Eloise was here. They needed to be near her and her coven so that Cain and the Darkness could strike as the baby was born, taking them unawares, turning their powers to their own use. They were only a few kilometres away.

A quick drive and her baby would be safe from his father and the corruption eating at his soul.

CAIN CAME to with a roar of rage, knowing immediately what Morrigan had done. Power lashed out as he charged through the house, felling those of his coven still inside. Their bodies tumbled around him. He didn't care. They'd failed him in allowing Morrigan to escape.

He knew where she'd gone. There could only be one place. The Darkness agreed with him.

The Were.

Power arched out of his hands, setting fire to curtains, furniture, walls, bodies, as he stormed through the house and outside. He barely noticed the heat of the flames, his rage a hot pulsing thing inside him.

She'd betrayed him. Him! First Eloise and now Morrigan. How could things have gone so wrong?

'*Calm yourself,*' the Darkness whispered inside his mind as he stumbled down the front steps. '*You are of no use if you destroy yourself with your rage.*'

The Darkness was right. The power would eat him up if he didn't expel it.

Two figures—his adoptive parents—were running towards the garage, trying to escape him. He raised his hands and shot warlock lightning at them both, pouring the excess power burning in his chest into the arc of magic ripping through the air. The lightning hit them, lighting them up from the inside, holding them in shocked stillness. Their outlines were bright against the dark of the night, their mouths opened on silent screams.

There was a whump of sound as the power exploded outwards, throwing him back, away from the incinerating bodies of his so-called parents. He flew through the air before slamming into the hard, cold ground. Dirt and turf flew up around him as he skidded across the ground, finally coming to a stop in the middle of the home paddock.

A cow lowed in the distance, followed by the wicker of a horse. The sounds died quickly and all that was left was the sound of the cold wind whipping around him.

He stared up at the sky, full of millions of stars, and felt more alone than he'd ever felt in his entire life.

'Never alone. I will always be here with you, dear one.'

He smiled. That was true. For a moment, he'd let himself forget. He was never alone. He had the Darkness and he had himself. That was all he needed to get his son back. And get him back he would.

He pushed to his feet. He could focus now. Focus on what to do next.

Morrigan thought she had foiled his plans, but she was only playing into them. In running to the Were, she gave him exactly what he needed—closer proximity to the Were and their coven.

He would kill many more Were as he went to reclaim his son, and in doing so, the power of their deaths would ensure the success of the Darkness in entering his son.

He only had to wait until Samhain. It would be a difficult wait, but he would do it. They would all die. Including Morrigan, after she had given birth to his son. And together, he and his son, the Darkness incarnate, would rule over this world.

Nothing could stop them.

27

'Shelley! Thank Goddess you're here.' Bron raced up to her, grabbing her hands as she hopped out of the four-wheel drive Gareth had driven her up in.

She tried to smile at Bron, to allay the worry that was visible on her friend's face, but the effort made her feel even more tired. She'd barely slept since the night she had made love to Adam, afraid to fall asleep and have him pull her astral self to that place again where everything had felt so real. She was getting by on the bare minimum and it was taking its toll on her mind and her body. She knew the others were worried about it. Knew Bron and Skye had known she'd lied about what had happened with Adam. But she couldn't talk about it. The words were too raw to think, let alone say. She smiled when she had to, but it felt like moving putty into shape. She wouldn't smile properly until Adam was back. And even then, the pain of not being with him would probably dull the edges of any happiness she might feel.

She couldn't imagine truly smiling again.

'Cordy will be so relieved you're here.'

Bron's words brought her out of her dark thoughts with a snap. 'How bad is she?'

'She's doing her best, but she desperately wants to speak to Marcus. It's driving her insane feeling him there but unable to communicate with him.' Bron's grip on her hand tightened as she turned and started walking towards the barn. 'It's got to the point where she's refusing to leave the caves' hospital room.'

'Which means Skye won't leave it because of the babies; and Jason's worried about Skye being down there all the time. I get it.'

Another squeeze. 'I knew you would. I'm so sorry to ask you to come up and do this when you've got so much to do in Melbourne with the diaries and grimoires, but I can't help her with this like you can.'

'It's fine.'

'I know it's not really fine at all. I know it's difficult for you to be here with Adam's body.'

'It's fine. I'm happy to do this for Skye and Cordy. I'd be some kind of bitch to not be.' She tried to smile again.

Bron's expression was shadowed by sadness. 'Nobody would ever think you're a bitch.'

Shelley raised her brow. 'Really? Damn. I'll have to work on that.' Bron snorted out a laugh. Shelley's smile felt more natural as the wonderful burble of laughter washed over her. 'Thank the Goddess. I was getting worried you'd forgotten how to laugh or smile.'

Bron entered the keycode to open the barn door. 'River makes sure I laugh.'

'I'm glad you have that.'

Bron swung around as they stopped in front of the lift. 'I wish you had that too. You have been alone too much, Shelley, since Adam went with Morghanna.'

'I'm never alone,' Shelley answered. 'That's part of the problem.' Although it had been a little better ever since she'd done what the three ancient witches and all the diaries kept telling her to do— engage with her powers. She could no longer deny that it was essential she learn to lower her shields and deal with the impact of all the spirits on her if she was to help in the fight against the Darkness, so she'd been practicing dropping her shields and talking to those around her. At first she was barely able to stand a few seconds, but now she could manage more than ten minutes without feeling the slippery touch of madness on her mind. Being here now, helping Cordy, was just another step along the path towards learning to control her abilities, not just block them.

Bron's assessing gaze remained on her the entire way down in the lift, but her friend didn't say anything, and Shelley didn't feel like engaging either.

Soon, too soon, she was standing inside the hospital room, the door closing at her back. The reality of Adam's body—too still, too quiet—hit her as it always did when she was here, followed quickly by the sense of Cordy's desperation. The banshee hummed inside her, as it always did when she entered this room. Death was so close, its song a whisper in her chest bringing the discordant note of insanity with it. 'Shelley?'

Bron's hand on her shoulder, warm, comforting, making her want to cry. 'Are you okay?'

'I'm fine.' Christ. She was sick and tired of people asking her that. And looking at her like they did. Their worry was a heaviness that pushed at her, making her more aware of the slippery thing at the edges of her mind that threatened to take over.

No. She clenched her fingers at her side. Not here. Not now. She had things to do.

She took a step towards Adam's body—couldn't stop herself—and the spirits shrank away from the bed, giving her room. Since she'd been allowing them time with her, they'd stopped trying to touch her or call out to her all the time as they'd always done. She walked through them, unmolested, and came to stand beside Adam, fingers wrapping around the metal sides of the hospital bed. 'How is he?'

'Same as before.'

She nodded, staring at Adam's face, at the sharp definition of his nose, the angle of his cheekbones, the jut of his jaw, shaded with stubble that her fingers itched to touch. 'He looks thinner.'

'The IV can only give him so much,' Skye said from beside her.

She knew that.

'We'll just give you a moment with him.' She glanced up then at the note in River's voice.

He smiled his hope at her, but sadness lingered in his eyes. He knew. They all probably knew. It was ridiculous to think they wouldn't know what had happened between her and Adam. The pack always knew when a mating started. Even though they probably knew, she still couldn't talk about it.

Bron and River moved away quietly.

Adam's hair had grown. A long hank of black lay across his forehead. She brushed it away, fingers whispering over his brow. The cool silkiness of his hair slid over her skin. She'd dug her hands into his hair when they'd made love, the sensation of it tickling her skin as he'd kissed his way down her body.

The room blurred and she blinked rapidly.

There was a sound, like whimpering. She looked at his lips. They hadn't moved.

Hell. She longed to lean over and kiss him. Could she wake him like the prince woke Sleeping Beauty? True Love's kiss. That's what all the fairy tales always said would cure anything. Except she was more Maleficent than royalty. There was a heavy weight on her soul. She could feel it, even now, weighing her down, blighting her future.

The whimpering sounded again.

'I'm here. It's fine. I'm fine.' She stroked his arm, a light, brief touch. Anything more and she'd break apart. The whimpering changed in tone, worried with a plaintive edge. She stopped touching him and gripped the metal rail tighter. 'I'm sorry. I'm so sorry I can't be what you need.'

'Shelley?' Adam's voice in her ear, the soft, cold unreality of his touch. She looked up, couldn't stop herself.

'Adam?'

He smiled at her and she was lost.

She wanted to throw herself into his arms but was horribly aware of everyone staring at her—dead and living alike.

'Adam's here?' Multiple voices asked her at once.

Jason hurried to her side, glancing around. 'Where?'

Shelley pointed, unable to speak, unable to stop staring at the spirit form of the male she loved with everything in her. She didn't want to love him. Loving him hurt so, so much. But it seemed she couldn't stop.

There was one thing she could stop though. 'I'm not mating with him,' she said to the room.

Stunned silence met her announcement.

Then laughter split the silence. Adam's laughter. Despite everything, it still warmed her from the inside out. Her gaze raced over him as he laughed, his eyes alight with the joy of seeing her.

'Tell them how it is, Kitten. Don't hold back.'

Her lips twitched despite herself. 'Adam,' she said. 'You need to take this seriously.'

'Oh, believe me, Kitten, I take everything you say seriously.' He closed the distance between them, cupped her face, the feel of his hands on her far more welcome and familiar than they should have been. 'I know you believe you can't mate with me, and I won't push you on that. But you have to admit, the looks on everyone's faces were priceless.'

The image of all those shocked faces played in her mind's eye and she began to chuckle.

'See? It was funny.' He bent and kissed her, kissed the laughter from her lips. The kiss was soft, restrained, only lasted a breath. He pulled back, amber eyes gazing intently into hers. 'I missed you.'

'Adam.' She gripped his arms, fingers clenching. 'You don't feel quite real. I need you to feel real.'

Amethyst energy crackled up his arm. 'Shelley, no!' But it was too late. She'd already poured some of her magic into him. It cascaded through him, over his skin, and everywhere it touched, it left sparkling purple energy in its wake.

'Adam.' He spun around to find his brother staring at him, joy and relief on his face. 'I can see you.'

'Yeah,' he said, glowering down at Shelley. 'Shelley poured her magic into me again.'

'And that's bad?' River asked.

'Yes. We can't afford for her to use up her energy on me. Not now. Not when we're so close to being able to get rid of the Darkness for good. Our coven is going to need all its energies to pull this off. She shouldn't have wasted a skerrick of it on me.'

'Well, I for one am glad she did. It's insanely good to see you again.' Jason looked like he wanted to pull Adam into a back-slapping hug. Adam would have liked him to, but that wasn't the way this worked.

'Can she do the same for Marcus? Can I see him again?'

The pleasure in Shelley's eyes disappeared in a wave of sadness. 'Oh, Cordy. I wish—'

'Shelley. Please.' Not a breath could be heard as Cordy stumbled towards Shelley, her hands outstretched, pleading. 'Please, give him back to me. Let me see him.'

'I can't.' The tears in her eyes now weren't of laughter. 'I wish I could, but I can't.'

'You can make Adam be seen. Why can't you help me to see Marcus?'

'It's not the same thing. Adam is still alive. My power reacts to his life energy. Marcus is ... dead. Nothing can bring him back to you.'

'I want to see him. One more time. Please.'

'I can't. I wish I could. But I can't. I'll drop my shields now and then I'll be able to hear him clearly and you can speak to him through me.' She closed her eyes. 'There, done.' A few of the spirits lurched forward, but then stopped. None of them begged her for anything, though she had to still feel the press of their need. The circles under her eyes suddenly got darker, her lips tight as she said, 'I can only give you fifteen minutes max at the moment.'

'Fifteen minutes? Is that all?'

'I'm so sorry. I might be able to do more—'

'Shelley, no, you've already used up too much energy giving it to me.'

She shot Adam a look. 'I'll be fine. This is what I'm supposed to do. It's my fault I'm not better at this.'

'It's not your fault at all ...' he began but his voice died off as Cordy began to quietly sob.

'I need more time. More time.'

'This is torture,' Marcus said and then he rushed forward.

'Marcus, no!' Adam moved to stop him, but Marcus went right through him like he wasn't even there. He turned just in time to see Marcus jump into Shelley's body just like Adeline and Harrison had done the year before.

Shelley jerked, her eyes snapping wide. Her mouth opened on a pained gasp and then she slumped over.

River caught her before she hit the ground.

'What the hell just happened?' Jason asked.

'Marcus entered her body,' Adam snarled.

Shelley's eyes flickered open and she lifted her head, gaze finding Cordy. 'Baby,' she said, her voice deep, rough with the gravelly sound of Marcus' tone.

'Marcus?' Fingers shaking, Cordy touched Shelley's cheek.

'Yes.' Her arms wrapped around Cordy, gathering the smaller witch to her, hand cupping the back of her head in a way that was so intimate, Adam had trouble watching.

'Marcus.' Cordy's voice was a muffled sob, her shoulders shaking. Then she leaned back, hands cupping Shelley's face. Shelley looked down at Cordy, her eyes no longer violet blue, but the lighter, more electric blue of an Alpha. 'Oh Marcus, it is you.'

'Yes, baby. I'm here. I'm holding you. I'm sorry. I'm so sorry.'

Unable to hold back any longer, Adam grabbed Shelley's arm and jerked her around. Marcus glowered at him out of her eyes, her face. It was wrong. So wrong. 'You can't use her like this, you bastard.'

'I know. I'm sorry. I won't do it again. But just give me this one chance to say goodbye to Cordy. She needs it, man. My pack needs her and she needs this.'

'You didn't just do it for her. You did this for you.'

'Of course I did. This isn't normal. I know it isn't normal for a Were to hang around in the spirit like this. I know I should have gone with my body, but her grief, my pack's grief, it held me here.' He gripped Adam's shoulder, Shelley's touch allowing him to do so. 'Please, just let me have this. Let us have this.' He paused, tipped his head to the side. 'Shelley agrees.'

'You didn't give her a choice.'

'I know. But now I'm here, she wants me to do what I must before I leave her. I promise, I won't stay long.'

'Make sure you don't.' He had no idea if it would make any difference now, but he hoped that if Marcus got out within the next few minutes, Shelley wouldn't be completely drained.

Marcus nodded his thanks before turning back to cup Cordy's face. 'I wish I could kiss you, baby, but I don't think Adam or Shelley would approve.'

'Damn right,' Adam growled.

Cordy laughed, a hiccoughing sound. 'I can see you in her eyes, feel you in her touch. It's enough.'

'It better be.'

'Let's give them room.' Skye's touched Adam's arm, her power shivering over his skin.

He moved away with the others but didn't take his gaze off Shelley's body. If Marcus hurt her more than he already had, Adam swore, the dead Alpha would pay.

Shelley's fingers brushed down Cordy's cheek. 'I'm so sorry, my love.'

'What for?'

'For dying. For leaving you alone.'

'I've not been alone. I could feel you here. I knew you shouldn't be here, but I could feel you. It's helped.'

'Which was why I stayed.'

Cordy nodded, tears glimmering in her eyes. 'But you have to go, don't you?' she asked in a choked whisper.

He nodded. 'As soon as this is done. I can't stay. It's not our way.'

'I know. But promise me we'll find each other in the future.' Her fingers tightened on his shoulders. 'We have to find each other again.'

'Yes. I promise. I will wait for you, always and forever.' He pressed a kiss to her forehead. 'But for now, the pack needs you.' He glanced over at Skye. 'She needs you. And her babies. And I owe Pack McVale. You know why. I can no longer pay the debt myself, so you will have to do it for me. Help the McVale Coven. Guide my successor in our pack when they step forward. Help us be a force for good in the world again. I know you can do it. You were always the strongest of us.'

She blinked rapidly. 'It hurts so much—being without you.'

'I know. But you have me with you.' He touched her chest. 'Here.' And her forehead. 'Cherish the memories of us and do me proud, okay baby?'

'Okay.'

He kissed her forehead again and then let go of her. 'I'll be here until this has finished. I'll be standing by your side.' She nodded, lip wobbling. 'Please don't cry, baby. I hate it when you cry.'

She smiled through her tears. 'You always did.' She reached out, touched his face. 'I love you, Marcus.'

'I love you too, Cordy. Always have, always will.'

'Me too,' she whispered. He convulsed, eyes flaring wide. 'Marcus! Don't go.' But it was too late. He was gone and it was Shelley standing there again.

'Damn. I hate it when they do that,' she muttered and then collapsed forward. Cordy caught her, but almost dropped her—Shelley was much taller and heavier than she was.

Jason and River were at her side in an instant, but Adam got there first.

'Here. Let me.' He took her limp form from Cordy, thankful right in this moment that the power she'd given him earlier now allowed him to do this; his energy aligned with hers so that his body was real enough not only to touch her, but to hold, to carry. He really couldn't stand someone else holding her right now, especially in this weakened state. She wouldn't like it either.

'I'm sorry she's hurt.'

'So you should be,' he growled at Marcus. He carried Shelley towards the empty bed.

She moaned, lashes fluttering open, and then her gaze focused on him. 'Why are you carrying me?'

'You collapsed.'

'I did?'

'Yes. Marcus took over your body.' He placed her gently on the bed, not letting go of her hand.

'That explains why I feel like shit.'

'Bron?' he asked, but she was there already.

'She'll be fine.' Her eyes unfocused in that way that told him she was reading Shelley's aura. 'She's just been drained.'

'How much?'

Bron glanced at him, surprised by his tone. 'She'll be fine. She just needs to rest for a day or two.'

'Fuck.'

'It's fine,' Shelley said. 'I'm glad I could help Cordy.' She smiled wanly at the other witch.

'It's not fine. Not even close.'

'What's wrong, A?' Jason came up beside him.

'When's Samhain?'

'On the first of November, as it always is,' Skye said.

'I know the date. I mean, how many days away is it?' When they all looked at him as if he'd lost it, he swore and said, 'Time moves differently where I've been. I have no idea of the date.'

'It's the twenty-eighth of October.'

'Make that the twenty-ninth,' Jason said, looking down at his watch. 'It's just turned midnight.'

'Shit.' He focused on Bron. 'Will she be okay in two days? Is that enough time?'

'She will be if I do a Healing on her.'

'No!' The word exploded from his mouth, making Bron jump. River was suddenly there pushing in front of his mate, getting between her and Adam, a warning growl low in his throat. Adam held up his hands. 'Sorry, mate. I didn't mean to shout at Bron. But she can't use any of her powers for the next few days.' He glanced at Skye. 'Neither can you. You're all going to need everything you have on Samhain Eve.'

'I'll be fine,' Shelley said, her face paler than some of the ghosts hovering around. 'Two days is heaps of time.'

'No, it's not. Not when you have to find that spell and meld this stone with the Nexus.'

'What stone?' Skye asked.

'What are you talking about?'

He pulled the Goddess Stone out to show them, repeating what he'd learned from Morghanna. 'Shelley needs to use the spell in her family's grimoire to bind this to Eloise to—'

'Why Eloise?' Bron asked.

'Because she's the Nexus. If it's bonded to her, it will stop you all from exploding with the excess power you will be using through the ley lines.'

'Why would we do something insane like that?' Skye asked.

'To banish the Darkness for good.' Stunned silence met his words. 'I know it's hard to take it all in, and I'll explain it all in detail later, but what you need to understand right now is that every witch in Pack McVale's coven needs your full power on Samhain. So none of you can use any power until then, no matter how small.' He stared at Shelley. 'Shelley in particular needs to be fully juiced to make this work. Fuck.'

'I'll help,' Cordy said, voice small.

'This is a disaster.'

'I'll help,' Cordy said again, louder this time. 'I can help. I can give Shelley the juice she'll need to do what needs to be done.'

'But you're already giving the babies a lot of your energy to help balance theirs with mine,' Skye said.

'I have enough for both.'

'Are you sure?' Bron asked, taking Cordy's hand in hers. 'You're still very weak.'

Cordy's chin lifted, her eyes becoming steely. 'This is my fault. It's my problem to fix. Let me fix it.'

Bron looked at Adam. 'Are you sure this is necessary?'

'All I can tell you is what I've learned. You, Skye, Shelley and Eloise are essential to fighting the Darkness. You will need your full power for that. Apart from the spell that will need to be done to weld the Goddess Stone with Eloise, you can't use any of your powers until Samhain Eve when we all come together to expel that shit from our world.'

'Then there is no choice. I must do this.'

He gaze raked over Cordy—she seemed so frail, brittle with grief, yet there was a determined spark in her eye. Maybe this would work. He nodded. 'Cordy is right. Shelley needs her power. It's essential.'

Bron stared into his eyes before moving away from the bed. 'She's all yours,' she said with a gesture to Cordy.

'Right.' She placed her hands on either side of Shelley's head and stared into her eyes. 'Keep still,' she admonished Shelley when she went to flinch away from the intimate contact, obviously a too-close reminder of the moment just shared between Cordy and Marcus using her body.

Shelley nodded and then held Cordy's gaze, despite her obvious exhaustion. Adam could feel her need to close her eyes and sleep. 'Just stay with us, Shelley. It's important.'

'I'm not going anywhere.' Her gaze met his, full of the stubborn determination he loved. Even so, after five minutes, her gaze slid away and she closed her eyes.

Cordy let go of her. 'You really shouldn't be this drained. I know you've finally been studying your power, but you're still fighting it. We'll need to do something about that when this is all over.'

Shelley didn't say anything, but Adam noticed the white around her mouth and nostrils. 'Shelley might not want that.'

Cordy shot him a questioning glance, one he was unwilling to answer. He would never make Shelley do anything she didn't want to do after this. If she wanted to ignore her powers and leave them all, then he'd help her do it. He'd be unhappy and missing a part of himself for the rest of his life, but he'd still help her if that's what made her happy.

Her happiness was truly all that mattered to him.

Cordy's eyes widened, but then she shook her head and turned her attention back to Shelley. 'She might not have a choice.'

'I'm lying right here, you know.' Shelley glared at them both. 'I will decide what happens in the future. But the future is not right now. Right now, we've got other things to worry about.'

'You're right. The first is to re-energise your powers. So, close your eyes, stop fighting me and try to rest. This is going to take some time.' She took in a deep breath and blew it out slowly as she put one hand over Shelley's chest and the other over her belly. 'Think happy thoughts—it will help with the energy transfer. Do you have something to think of that fills you with joy?'

Shelley's gaze flickered to Adam then away. 'Yes.' She closed her eyes.

Adam blew out a breath and continued to watch until Jason called him over to the other side of the room. 'What is it?'

'You said that Eloise was needed for this?'

'Yes. She's essential. It's kind of what the Nexus was built for. I assume, given she's not here, that she, Iain and Patrick are still searching for her missing relative? Can you call them back in time?'

Jason's lips quirked up. 'I just did. They're already on their way back at Eloise's insistence. Iain said she couldn't explain it, but just had an overwhelming feeling like this was where she needed to be.'

'Maybe the Goddess called her?' Bron suggested.

'Or because she's the Nexus, she can feel what's coming,' River said. 'The Goddess did tell her she'd know the path she had to take once she'd chosen which way she was going to go.'

'That makes sense,' Skye said.

'And what of you?' Jason asked Adam. 'What part do you have in all of this? Why did Morghanna take you?'

Adam's mouth quirked into a derogatory smile. 'Don't you know, I'm the most important cog in the machinery?'

'Of course you are,' Skye said. 'Jason always said you were more important than any of us knew.'

Adam's smile faded as he turned to his brother. 'You have always believed in me.'

'Always.' Jason said, his gaze intent, serious. 'I always knew you were one of the most important members of the pack—and not just because you were my brother. I felt it here.' He touched his chest. 'You are special, Adam. I didn't need the Goddess or Morghanna to tell me that.'

Adam cleared his throat and shoved his hands into his pockets, fingers tightening around the stone. 'Thanks, J.'

'We all believe in you,' Bron said, River nodding behind her. 'But in this instant, can you be more specific? What is it precisely that you are supposed to do?'

He told them about what a Trickster was, his empathy, his power that stood outside the pack, the partial mating bond with Shelley.

'Fuck. That must be excruciating, A.'

River nodded at Jason's words. 'To have the bond there but for it to be out of reach.'

'Yes.' Both Were knew what that was like—they'd almost suffered the same fate as him. He was so glad neither of them had.

'It is what it is.' He blew out a breath, looked back at Shelley. 'Whatever else happens though, it had to be. I'm the one who can let Shelley do what she has to do so we have the power of not only the living, but the dead. And I can only be of true support, be a true channel, if she is bonded to me in a way deeper than friendship, deeper than pack. If we all live through the next few days, then both Shelley and I will have to find some way of living with it.' His lips cocked. 'And you never know, maybe there is a way I can make this all work out in the end.'

'If anyone can, it would be you,' Bron said. The others all nodded their agreement, their love and friendship warming him in a way he didn't realise he needed.

Jason clapped his hands together. 'But none of that tells us how to get you back. How do we heal your body and get you back into it?'

'It can't be done until the Darkness is expelled. There's a small piece of its evil in the wound. The only way to make my body heal and accept my astral spirit back into it again is to get rid of that Darkness. When we do the spell, it should be drawn out along with all the other pieces of Darkness in this world.'

'And you'll go back into your body?'

Adam nodded—keeping to himself the fact that the very thing Shelley was afraid of could come to pass while playing his part. He could give too much, could be separated from his body in a final way that meant even if they succeeded, he would never come back.

But they didn't need to know that.

'Right. So, what do we need to do, A? What were Morghanna's exact instructions?'

He told them everything he'd been told. 'So, we'll need some of the diaries and grimoires from Melbourne and we'll need a space readied outside where we can set up protection wards in full view of the moon when it rises on Samhain Eve. It needs to be fully prepped before then.'

'The McClune witches will help,' Jason said.

'Good. Skye, Bron, Eloise and Shelley will all need to save their energy from now until then. They have to be protected at all costs. If Cain or Morrigan get wind of this, they'll attack.'

'I'll call all the pack up here if necessary, quadruple the guard with the McClunes.'

'Good, but we'll need to call on others as well. We'll need to tap into every bond we possibly can both inside and outside our packs. Any connection, no matter how slight, will need to be used.'

'I'll help with that,' River said. 'I've been making contact with other packs since coming back. Jason thought it was a good idea.' He looked down. 'It's what Mum used to do for the pack, keep the connections alive.'

'That's great. The more involved worldwide, the better chance we have.'

'They'll all be scrambling to help when I tell them what's at stake. Nobody wants to return to what we were when the Darkness had control over us.'

'It will be worse than that. Far worse.'

'What do you mean?'

He shook his head. He couldn't share with them what Morghanna had shown him. Couldn't put those images and thoughts in their heads. His mouth tightened. 'Just believe me. If the Darkness wins, everything we know will be destroyed.'

'Then let's do everything we can to stop that from happening.'

The door behind them slammed open. A cold wind whipped through the room, the force of it knocking over a metal table of instruments and sending paperwork cascading around the room as if caught in a mini-tornado. It was so strong, those in the room were almost knocked off their feet.

'What the hell?' Jason snarled, grabbing hold of Skye.

Cordy cried out and threw herself over Shelley, a flare of yellow power shot with violet, pushed out, shielding her and Shelley.

The amethyst of Shelley's power sparked and jumped around Adam in response to what was coming through the door, as if pushing out in a protective shield. Unaffected by the fae wind as the others were, and sure that Shelley was protected, he turned to face the danger at the door.

A woman stood there, her dark red hair blowing wild in the wind she'd created to blow the door open, obscuring her face. But he didn't need to see her face to know who she was. He could feel her deep inside, the crawl of her presence skittering over his skin.

'Morrigan.'

She jerked at the sound of her name. Wild eyes, green tinged with black whorls, snapped wide as she saw him. 'Help me.' She took a staggering step into the room. 'You have to help me save him.' Her hands cupped convulsively around the bulge in her belly. 'Please. Help.'

28

Adam stood next to River at the base of the lift, waiting.

The doors opened. 'Adam?' Iain said, staring at him from inside the lift.

'I'm back,' he said, waving his hand, the purple power sparking. 'And do we have something shocking to share with you.'

'It's so good to see you,' Eloise began and then gasped. Her gaze snapped to the door at the end of the corridor. 'Morrigan. She's here.'

'What?' Iain moved in front of Eloise.

'You know Morrigan is here?' River asked her.

'I can feel her, the press of her power.'

'But that's not possible. We've got the cuff on her to suppress her magic,' River said.

She looked up at him, shrugged. 'I can still feel her. Although, something's changed. It's almost as if ...' She pushed past him and took off down the hallway.

Iain raced after her. 'Eloise, wait. She's probably here to hurt you.'

'No. She's not. She wants my help.' She stopped at the closed door, pushing the numbers on the panel. It didn't open. 'Come on, come on,' she said, trying again.

'We changed it,' River said, reaching past her. 'After she broke the door.'

'You can't go in there,' Iain said, stopping River from opening the door.

'I have to, Iain. Everything depends on it.' She pushed past Iain and River and opened the door.

'How the hell did she get in here?' Patrick asked Adam in a whisper as they followed the others inside.

'She apparently came in the same way Cain got out.'

'I thought these caves were secure.'

'They are. She used some kind of portal magic and stepped through the rock. At least, that's what she said.'

'Did she say anything else?'

'No. Only that she needed our help to save her baby and that she'd say no more until Eloise got here.'

Eloise had stopped a few paces into the room, Iain a tense sentry at her side. 'Morrigan,' she breathed.

Morrigan's beautiful face bloomed into a relieved smile. 'Good, you're here.'

'What do you want?' She took a step closer, ignoring Iain's growl. 'Why are you here?'

'I see you've changed.'

'So have you.' Eloise nodded at Morrigan's stomach. 'In more ways than one.'

Morrigan's green eyes widened. 'You can sense the change in me?'

'Yes. You're no longer malignant. The Darkness is gone.'

Tears welled in Morrigan's eyes. 'Oh Goddess. I thought I might have imagined it, that it might come back, but having your confirmation gives me hope.' She blinked rapidly, sniffling.

If Adam hadn't known who she was and what she'd done, he would have felt sorry for her.

'I'm sorry, Eloise. So sorry for everything I did to you, to your family.' She nodded around. 'To the Were. I wasn't myself. I was so filled with grief and anger. I know that's no excuse. It was my choice to invite the Darkness in. But I had no idea. No idea.' Her gaze, her horrible, burning gaze, fell on Skye and River. 'I almost destroyed everything and I didn't care. It made me not care.' Her gaze careened back to Eloise. 'I didn't listen to you and I should have. Blood *does* matter. You did the right thing. I know that now that I am freed of the Darkness' influence.'

'These are just words,' Iain said, lip turned into a snarl. There were mumbles of agreement from the rest of the Were in the room; even the spirits who were present nodded.

'You can't believe her,' Patrick said.

Eloise tipped her head, gaze firmly on Morrigan. 'Hear her out.'

Morrigan seemed to sag then. 'Thank you. I know I don't deserve it but thank you.' She took in a deep breath, eyes full of sorrow. 'I've been empty for so long, full of rage tinged with the coldness of revenge, but it was never enough to fill the hole torn in me the night my sister was taken from me. I hated everything.' Her fingers gripped convulsively around her stomach. 'Until my baby came along, and then everything changed.'

She glanced down at her stomach, love and joy clearly shining in her eyes. 'The Darkness couldn't stay in me when the baby took root. At first I didn't realise what was happening, but I began to feel love, true love, for my precious baby. And then I felt horror over all that I'd done. And alongside that horror was fear about what Cain and the Darkness planned.' She looked up then, the joy disappearing under a cloud of terror. 'They're going to kill the soul of my baby and use the flesh for the Darkness to fully come into this world.'

'Just like you did with my grandmother,' River snarled.

She blanched. 'Yes. In a way. But worse. So much worse.' Despite her obvious shame, her gaze went from one to the next of those facing her, meeting their hostile and disbelieving stares and persisted. 'You think I was bad? You have no idea what the Darkness will do when it's fully in this world. No power will be able to stop it. It will corrupt all, especially the purest, and turn them to its service.'

'And why would you care about that?' Jason asked. 'Haven't you done that very thing all these centuries?'

She shook her head slowly. 'What I did was nothing as compared to what it will do once it is whole once more and born into my baby. If it corrupts the innocent goodness growing inside me, nothing will be safe. Ever. You have to stop it.'

'What makes you believe we can do such a thing?'

She laughed. 'Because you have Eloise. And if you have the Nexus, you must have the Goddess Stone.'

Adam stiffened as the atmosphere in the room became even more electric with apprehension and mistrust. 'How do you know about that?'

'My sister and I once shared everything. Even when I broke from her because I thought her foolish to tie herself to the Pact, the connection remained. And despite having the Darkness in me, that connection didn't even break after her death, although it was dulled.'

'Morghanna would never have told you about her plans with the Goddess,' Adam said.

'She didn't have to. It took me a while to realise the flashes I kept having of her were not memory but something of what she saw wherever she'd been taken by the Goddess. It was a shadow of her knowledge, a whisper, but that whisper was enough for us to figure out the Nexus was important, as was the Goddess Stone, and why.' She twined her fingers around the material of her t-shirt as she gazed sorrowfully at Eloise. 'The Darkness desperately didn't want you and the stone to come together. It made me think I needed to go after you to help in my plan to destroy the Were. I was too full of rage and anger to see how it played me and its fear was what led me to suppress your power. For that, I am so sorry.'

'Only for that?' Iain snorted.

'No. Not only that. I've already said, I'm so sorry for it all. But it wouldn't matter how many times I said it, you still wouldn't believe me.'

'Why should we, after what you've done?' River asked. 'You've hunted us, tortured us, worked to enact the Curse on us and tried to kill us for hundreds of years. And now you expect us to believe that you are sorry for your actions? That you have only good intentions?'

'No. I don't expect you to believe that. But I do expect you to believe that I want to save my baby. After all, what matters more than saving the life of an innocent child?'

'How do we know it's innocent? How do we know the Darkness isn't in it already waiting to be born in our midst?' Iain asked.

'It has to be evil.' Patrick gestured sharply at her stomach before she could answer. 'You look like you're about to pop, which is impossible given we had Cain captured for the first four months of this year. You couldn't be more than six months along.'

'My baby was born of magic. That magic has led to a faster gestation.'

'That doesn't mean it's not evil.'

She shook her head vehemently. 'How could you still understand so little of the world you live in? Magic is neither good nor bad at its heart, as your witches could tell you. Each of their powers has a destructive bent as much as one that can be used for the good of others. It's a choice, nothing more.' She gestured at Eloise. 'You know that's true, more than any other here. The Goddess told you as much.'

Eloise gasped. 'How do you know that?'

Morrigan smiled sadly at her. 'I was not always what you see now. I was once beloved of the Goddess. She visited me many times to gift me with her wisdom. I recognised her touch on you when Cain described what was going on.'

Eloise flinched at mention of her twin. 'Why would the Goddess ever visit you?'

'Because I was her creature. She gave me multiple gifts, one of which was to bring more of our kind into the world safely.'

'You were a Midwife, like me?' Cordy asked, disbelief in her tone. 'How could you cause so much destruction and death when your gift was to give life?'

'As I said, every gift has both dark and light in it, and I had more gifts than most. It was a constant struggle to balance those gifts inside me, but I did it with the Goddess' help. But when I saw my sister taken by the Goddess' fire, I felt betrayed by not only the humans and the Were, but by the Goddess I had dedicated my life to. The Darkness joined with me and made me see how I could use my powers to enact my revenge. I took out the humans who had tortured and killed my sister first, but it wasn't enough. Others were truly to blame. My fury burned me up on the inside. I would have been swallowed whole by it except for the Darkness. It helped me to channel that power to use against those who had destroyed the person I loved most in the world. I had no idea what that decision would bring me to, and I didn't care.'

Her hands spread across her stomach, love and protection glowing in her eyes as she looked down at the evidence of the baby growing there. 'I didn't care until my baby's goodness and innocence began to make itself known to me and then I cared. Goddess only knows how I care—' Her voice broke and she looked up at Cordy, Eloise, Skye and Bron, her gaze finally lighting on Shelley who was pushing herself up on the bed. 'I ask for your help as I give you my help. Save my baby. Protect him as you would protect your own. And I will help you to expel the Darkness from this world.'

'How will you do that?' Shelley wobbled as she tried to sit up. Adam was at her side in an instant, helping.

Morrigan smiled at her. 'Now my powers are freed of the Darkness' influence, I can use them to stop my baby from coming forth on Samhain Eve.'

'How will that help?' Jason asked.

She didn't look at him, her gaze still on Shelley. 'I am a powerful Midwife.'

'You can't have used those powers for centuries,' Cordy said.

Morrigan nodded at her. 'You're right. But they are not so rusty that I can't use them to halt my labour for at least twenty-four hours, especially if I have another Midwife's help.'

'I ask again, why will that help?'

She sighed. 'Because the Darkness needs the power of Samhain to allow it to expel my baby's soul and enter his flesh as he is born into this world.' Her fingers splayed over her stomach again, stroking.

'Why does it have to wait until the baby is born?' Jason asked.

'While my child remains in my womb, he is part of the life force of the universe, his soul both of that force and in his body. At the moment of his birth, the soul will divorce its link with the universal lifeforce and will follow the link to the body to become seeded fully in the flesh. The Darkness will use the power of Samhain to cut the tie to the body and cast my baby's soul into the void, taking its place in the body so it can be born into this world.'

'Holy shit!'

'That shouldn't be possible. The soul-link to the body at birth was strong,' Cordy said.

'It is. Perhaps the strongest in a person's life. That's why the Darkness needs the power of Samhain, when the veils between worlds are their weakest, when the moon is at its zenith for this to work. Without it, he will not be able to twist Nature's work and come into this world through my child.'

'If you can just stop the birth from happening on Samhain, then why did you bother coming to us?' River asked.

'I am strong, but I may need help because the Darkness is also strong, particularly given it is linked to Cain right now.'

'Also there is the fact that the Darkness won't stop,' Adam added. 'We need to get rid of it once and for all.'

Morrigan nodded, her face rigid as she clutched her stomach. 'Yes. And just as the Darkness needs the power of Samhain to come into this world, you too need that power to expel it for good from this world.'

'We've got two days.'

'No. You don't. I know from the whispers I've heard recently that the spell to weld the Goddess stone to the Nexus takes time to prepare and the stone must be seated in the Nexus for a good twenty-four hours before it can become fully part of her.' She jerked her chin at Shelley. 'And by the looks of your Medium, she's in no state to be able to complete the spell in the next three days let alone the next twelve hours.'

'I'll manage,' Shelley said, pushing to her feet. Her knees buckled. She caught herself on the edge of the bed before anyone could help her.

Morrigan quirked her brow. 'Even if you did, you would have no energy left to be part of the triumvirate.'

'I'm giving her my power,' Cordy said.

'It won't be enough.' Morrigan looked down at the cuff on her wrist. 'But if you free me, I can do the spell to weld the stone to the Nexus, giving your Medium time to reenergise for the main event.'

Everyone was vehement in their response to her suggestion except the witches, who watched her carefully. Finally Morrigan lifted her hand up and said, 'Your argument is pointless. They know it's the only way.' She gestured at Eloise, Skye, Bron, Shelley and Cordy.

Eloise nodded slowly. 'It probably is. But why would you do this for us?'

Morrigan's hand dropped. 'I know you don't trust me, but I *have* changed—you said you can sense that's true. But even if I hadn't, I need you. I need this spell to work. To save myself and my baby.'

'Why can't someone else do the spell?' Eloise asked.

'It requires a certain kind of power to be able to handle the Goddess Stone and weld it to the Nexus. One of life or death. Your Medium and I are the only ones here who can manage it without burning ourselves out with our power.' She nodded at Shelley, who leaned against the bed to hold herself upright. 'Obviously, she can't do it. That leaves me.' She laughed briefly. 'This is obviously the universe's way of having a joke on all of us, because I am seriously your only hope of pulling this off.'

A long silence followed this statement.

'She's not lying,' Bron said. 'I can see it in her aura. Surely you can smell that she's telling the truth?' she asked of River and the other Were.

'We can't trust her.'

'No,' Skye said slowly. 'We can't.' Her gaze met Morrigan's. 'But Bron's right. She's not lying now. She needs us.' Her hand clenched over her stomach. 'She wants to protect her baby. That I understand.'

'Eloise? What do you think?' Shelley asked.

Eloise was looking curiously at Morrigan, as if seeing her clearly for the first time. 'If you lift so much as one hand to hurt me or any of those I love, I will pour all my power into you and burn you up from the inside.'

Morrigan's lips curled into a smile. 'I like this new you.'

'It's no thanks to you.' She let out a slow breath. 'Take the cuff off her.'

Iain spun her to face him. 'I don't want her to touch you, Little Bird.'

'Neither do I, but it has to be done. We need Shelley fully functional for the spell on Samhain. If she isn't, we will never be rid of the Darkness and it will never stop coming after us.'

'That is preferable to her hurting or killing you.'

'She won't do that. Not now.' She lifted her hand to his cheek. 'Do you trust me?'

'Always.'

Her face bloomed into a smile as she went up on her toes to brush her lips over his.

'As I trust you.' She looked around at the others. 'I trust that you all have my back.'

'If she makes one wrong move,' Jason said, 'She's dead.'

'You wouldn't hurt my baby,' Morrigan said, hand clutched over her belly.

'You have no idea what we'd do to save our mates. To save our pack,' Cordy said, her voice raw.

'You wouldn't hurt an innocent baby,' Morrigan said again, less certain this time.

'No. We wouldn't.' Jason took a menacing step towards her. 'But we would ensure that you never got the chance to know him or see him or even hear a single thing about him in the future if you do anything other than weld the Goddess Stone to Eloise.'

Morrigan's lips curled into something just short of a sneer. 'After doing this, I will only have enough power left to keep the baby from being born on Samhain. And believe me, protecting my baby far outweighs any thoughts of revenge I might still harbour about any of you. Nothing is more important than him. Nothing.'

Shelley grimaced.

'Are you okay, Kitten?' Adam asked when she gingerly sat back on the bed, one hand clutching her head.

'I don't have enough strength to create my shields and all the spirits are yelling at me.'

'What are they saying?'

Eyes full of tiredness and pain, she said, 'They say this is our only chance. We have to trust her.'

'Then that's what we'll do,' Adam said, gaze taking in everyone in the room.

Slowly, very slowly, they all nodded their agreement.

Morrigan held her hand out to Skye, eyes bright. 'Release me. We're running out of time and there is a lot to prepare for the ritual of binding.'

Skye stared at the outstretched hand. 'Tell us what must be done. I won't release you until all is ready.'

Morrigan dropped her hand. 'Very well.' She glanced at Cordy. 'Help the Medium regain her power. She's going to need it in two days.' She turned to the others. 'Firstly, you have to prepare an area outside in a clearing in direct line of sight with the moon.' She continued to give her instructions—the same as what Adam had already told them.

Adam didn't listen, his attention returning to Shelley. 'Lie down,' he whispered. 'Let Cordy give you her energy.'

'I should help.'

His hands firmed on her shoulders. 'You will help. But first you need to regain your energy.' He looked a question at Cordy.

She nodded. 'He's right. This is all we can do for now.'

Shelley looked up at him as she lay down. 'What are you going to do?'

'I'm going to help.'

As Cordy placed her hands over the energy points in Shelley's body, he took her hand, and slowly began to push the energy she'd given to him from his body and back into hers.

Shelley's eyes flared wide. 'What are you doing?'

'Giving you back what you should never have given.'

'But the others won't be able to see you.'

'They don't need to. Only you do.'

She stared up at him, eyes filled with the love she could not express. He wondered if she realised? Not that it mattered.

He smiled down at her, pouring his love into his expression as he poured the power she'd gifted him back into her. If this was all he could ever give her, it would have to be enough.

SHELLEY TRIED to let her mind relax as Cordy worked on her, but she couldn't. It was taking too long. Too much to do and she couldn't be a part of it lying here, unable to do anything but think.

Hours later, when Morrigan's magic prickled on the air as she did the spell to meld the Goddess Stone to Eloise, her frustration rose even higher. She should be out there, a part of whatever was going on, helping her friends, her packmates. Instead, she was stuck here being useless as the tension of the pack thrummed through her until she gritted her teeth so hard that her jaw hurt.

'You have to relax,' Cordy admonished.

'I'm trying.'

'I know you're worried, but the others will take care of Eloise. You must relax.'

'It's okay, Kitten,' Adam said, hand stroking through her hair. 'You'd feel it if something went wrong.' She nodded. He was right. Even though she'd fought it, she was connected to them. Would always be connected to them. Instead of making her more tense, somehow that knowledge helped her relax.

What seemed hours later, Cordy finally sat back. 'It's done.'

'Yes,' Shelley whispered. She sat up, tried her shields. They rose, layering one over the other until the general noise that surrounded her when her shields were down was gone.

Silence. It was blissful.

And not a little lonely.

She frowned.

The door opened and Jason entered, carrying someone in his arms.

'Eloise?' Shelley asked.

Bron shook her head as she came in behind Jason. 'No. Morrigan. She just finished the spell. It took a lot out of her.'

She watched as Bron fussed around Morrigan, checking on her without using her powers. 'Do you need me to help?' She was a nurse after all.

'No,' Cordy said, dropping to a chair, her face grey. 'You need to lie down and rest to give the power I just gave you time to energise and mesh with your own.'

'You should lie down too.'

Cordy flashed a weak smile. 'I think I will. Jason, can you help me up?' He pulled her into his arms and began to walk over to the bed that had been hers. 'No. I want to go back to the house. I want to sleep in my bed.'

'Okay.' He looked at River. 'Call me if anything happens.'

'I will.'

Then he was gone and there was quiet again.

Shelley closed her eyes, tried to sleep, but her mind was too full. Too full of everything she'd learned the last few months, too full of what she still must learn, too full of worry and doubt and fear.

The fear was like whispers inhabiting her thoughts.

Emotions swirled through her that didn't feel like hers and yet were an intrinsic part of her now—the banshee's. She was so afraid that if she gave in to those feelings and thoughts her slide into madness would be fast and merciless. The introduction of Cordy's power—so alien to her own—made the encroaching madness worse. It was like bugs under her skin, nipping and scratching. A vision of her aunt smashed into her mind— eyes wild, mouth a bitten mess, scratches all over her skin, chunks pulled out of her hair so you could see her scalp. Was this what had caused her to injure herself like that? The sensation of bugs under her skin? Would she end up the same way? It seemed the more she clawed to hold on to her sanity, the faster it slipped away.

What would happen if she just let go?

No! She had to keep tight control on herself or she might not be able to see through her part in what was to come. Marcus' possession had brought her that much closer to the fracture between holding her ground and sliding into the oblivion of madness. The more she used her powers, the faster it would happen. She probably only had the next few days of being sane. After that ...

She wished things could be different. But if wishes were fishes and all that.

'What are you smiling at, Kitten?'

She opened her eyes. Adam stood next to the bed, his brow furrowed. Could he feel what was going on inside her? Shit, she hoped not. 'Just thinking about what's to come.'

'And you're smiling at that?'

'It's either smile or cry.' She clutched his hand in hers. 'You taught me the value of a smile.'

He smiled down at her. That smile was such a comfort. That smile meant that if she could save her friends and their loved ones, save Adam and see him and them to a brighter future without the Darkness, then everything she had to do and become would be worth it because he would make certain of it.

He was her inspiration. Because of him, she had the strength not to go out by slow degrees, a whimpering, shrieking mess like her aunt. No, she would blaze for one instant like the brightest of suns and then she would be gone, nothing but a blank spot in a sky still full of bright stars. 'I'm going to be magnificent.'

'You already are.'

He pressed his lips against hers, the lightest of kisses, but one that still managed to touch deep into her soul.

'You know I will never find anyone like you, right? You are it for me.'

'As you are for me.'

'Then don't give up.'

'Adam.' Goddess, how could he always read her mind so easily?

'I'm not. I'm not giving up on the possibility that somehow, it will work out for us. We deserve that at least.'

'Oh, Adam,' she began. 'This is not a fairy tale where everyone gets what they deserve.'

His brow rose, lips twitching into a smile. 'No? Witches, Were people, shifters, meddling Gods and Goddesses and an ultimate evil we're fighting. If this isn't a fairy tale, I don't know what is.'

She couldn't help it—she laughed. A full-bodied, throaty laugh that made her wipe at her eyes and caught the attention of everyone in the room.

'What are you laughing at?' Bron said, bouncing over to her.

'Adam. He thinks this is a fairy-tale story we're in. Tell them, Adam.'

'Adam's still here?'

Bron looked around her blankly and Shelley realised that the hand holding hers was a mere whisper. 'What did you do?' she asked, snapping upright. 'Goddamn it, Adam! You gave me back too much power again.'

He smiled at her. 'I gave you back the power you gave me.'

'No, you gave me more.' She glared at him. 'You shouldn't have done it.' She was suddenly furious. She swung her legs down from the bed and stood—not even a wobble! Her fury increased. 'This is what I'm talking about!' She pushed against his too-insubstantial chest, her fingers sliding through the outline of him. 'You can't help yourself, can you! And you think there's a chance in the future that we could work things out between us when you would do this? You gave too much to me, you idiot! You always give too much of yourself.'

'What's the matter?'

'What's wrong?'

'Adam gave her her power back, maybe more,' Bron said in a harsh whisper.

Shelley turned to see the others all staring at her. She didn't care. Her fury was trembling through her, her power sparking along her skin. She swung back around to face him. 'Take it back. Take it back. I don't want it.'

He backed away from her. 'No. You need it more than I do.'

'No, I don't.' She blinked rapidly, her fury burning wetly in her eyes. 'I don't ever want you to do that, don't you understand? This is why we can't be together. This is what I fear more than I even fear going insane. I refuse to be the cause of you not being here anymore, Adam. I refuse. Do you hear me? I reject your empathy. I reject you giving me power. After Samhain and the spell we have to do, I reject everything you ever want to give me again.'

'Micheline, you can't do that.'

'If it will save you from your stupid self, I will,' she yelled, then ran from the room.

29

'It's time.' Adam's voice behind her made her jump.

Fuck.

Shelley stared out the window. Fury still roiled inside her. Fury and fear, making it hard to sit still, to eat, to talk to any of the others. But she had.

There'd been no choice.

They'd had so much planning to do since she'd run from Adam. The Were had been on high alert. Morrigan hadn't said anything, but they were certain Cain and his followers would be after her, trying to get her back. She'd been moved to the main house, the room she was in secured with wards cast by determined McClune witches and warlocks. She was resting and had managed to halt the onset of contractions with a little help from Cordy.

Even so, Shelley was worried. Even though both were strong Midwives, they were weak—Morrigan from the spell she'd done to bind the Goddess Stone to Eloise, and Cordy from the Healing she'd done on Shelley and the work she continued to do to keep Skye and her twins safe. At this rate, they'd run out of power and there was nobody apart from them strong enough in Midwifery to keep the contractions at bay until Samhain was well and truly over.

And if Cain managed to get a hold of her ...

Shelley shook her head. It didn't bear thinking of.

McClune witches and warlocks were feeding into them what power they could, but it wasn't an easy thing given there were no true Healers on Packlands right now except for Bron and Cordy, and neither of them could help.

They were walking a tightrope. Shelley just hoped it didn't snap before it was time.

Which, according to Adam, was now. On the one hand, she was glad of it, given the general tension and the impact of the power drain on the McClune coven, not to mention Morrigan and Cordy. But on the other hand, now the time was here, she was going to have to look at Adam, to use the fine tracery of bond she'd been tricked into allowing to be created, to use him. She hadn't wanted to think about it over the last few days, and it was easier to keep out of her mind if she didn't look at him, talk to him or acknowledge him in any way.

It had hurt so much to do so—but not as much as truly losing him would be. At least he was here. At least—

She bit her lip, trying desperately to stop herself from crying hot tears of anger and shame and loss.

'Come on, Kitten. You have to talk to me at some stage. We have to work together soon.'

'I know that.' Shit, how could he not know that? Idiot man.

'I don't understand why you're so angry with me.'

She turned to glare at him, the anger his words caused thankfully drying the tears that had threatened to flood her eyes only moments ago. 'You don't understand why I'm so furious with you?' She snorted. 'That's rich.'

'Well, you're blocking me.'

'Of course I am you idiot man. You've given me no choice. You've just done the very thing that proves what my aunt told me. Proves what the ancient witches wrote about Tricksters.'

'No it doesn't.'

'Of course it does.' She jabbed her finger towards him. 'You gave me more than my own power back. You gave me some of yours.'

'You were so weak and Cordy's power wasn't enough—yours is so much greater. I just did what I could to help you get stronger faster. I know how much it rankled you lying there unable to do anything.'

'But that's just stupid. I wasn't in any danger, but by doing what you did ... You could have died.' She blinked rapidly and looked away —damn tears!

'Things aren't that drastic.'

'Of course they are.' She shook her head. 'If you are too weak, if you give me or anyone else too much of your own life energy, you might never make it back to your body. Even if this insane plan works and we manage to banish the Darkness forever from this world, if you give too much of yourself, you might never come back to us.'

'And would that be so bad?' he asked, taking a step towards her.

Her gaze snapped to his. 'I can't believe you asked that. It would be world ending. For me. If you're not around, whatever sanity I might have grasped hold of after this would fly away. Especially if I was to blame. You can't do that to me. You can't. You can't.' His arms were around her before she realised either she or he had moved.

'I'm sorry, Kitten,' he murmured into her hair. 'I'm so sorry. I didn't think.'

She snorted out a laugh. 'Well you need to think.' She raised her head from his chest to stare into his eyes, those beautiful eyes that even in this form glowed with life and love and laughter. 'I need you to think.'

He cupped her face, ghostly fingers smoothing her hair back. 'I will. I'll think. I promise.'

Then his lips were on hers. And even though she could feel him, it wasn't enough. The cold insubstantiality of him would never be enough. She wanted him back in his body so she could feel the hard warmth of him pressed up against her, feel his lips warm and hungering against hers. But given this was all she had, she gave herself over to the mad joy of his kisses, of his love, just for this moment.

He pulled back first. 'You can't block me, Kitten. I can't stand it when you do that.'

'I'm sorry. But if you try to give me your life energy, it's the only way I have of stopping you.'

'We need to be connected for this to work.'

She sighed. 'I know. So please, don't do more than be a conduit between the dead Were and me. I don't want any more from you. I don't want your life. I won't accept it.' She touched his face. 'I'm only trying to protect you.'

'I know.'

Her hands fell to her side, the fury draining away. 'You're too special, Adam, to give up yourself. Too precious to this pack.' She swallowed hard, trying to stop her legs from shaking. 'To me. Please remember that and act accordingly.'

'I will. As long as you realise the same.'

'The pack doesn't need me.'

'I disagree. But I wasn't talking about the pack.'

'Oh.' She shifted, became aware that she was twining her fingers together and forced them back to her side. 'Please don't hope. I can't carry that too.'

'You don't have to.' He smiled at her as he touched her cheek. It was the briefest caress, but she felt it deep inside her where nobody but him had ever touched. 'My hope isn't a burden, Michelline. It's a gift.' His smile twisted. 'It's taken me too long to realise that. Too long to realise that my Trickster side is also a gift.'

'I know it's a gift, Adam. I've been trying to tell you that for months.'

'I didn't seem to be able to hear it then.'

'But you can now. What changed?'

'You. I saw myself through your eyes and I saw the strength in what I can do. The wonder of it. The sheer stubborn irascibility of it, never giving up. It's who I am. I have hope enough for all the pack, including you. So, don't ask me not to hope.'

She bit her lip, whispered, 'But I don't want you to be hurt by the inevitable.'

He shook his head. 'If you think it's inevitable, you must think I'm weak.'

Her anger flared once again. 'I don't think you're weak!'

'You seem to think that I'll fade away just because I give you a little of my own energy. You think I'm not strong enough to feed that energy into you when it counts. Into the pack.'

'That's because of what I've read. The histories. It has nothing to do with thinking you weak.'

His eyes flashed. 'I'm nothing like those Tricksters from the past. I've grown up with extra magic always there. It was new to them and they didn't know how to handle it. I didn't even know who I was or what I could do and I handled it better than any of them. It was me who kept the pack going when the Curse was enacted. If your histories are right, then I should have died giving too much of myself when there were so many who needed my energies. But I didn't. I got stronger.' He threw his head back and snapped out a laugh. 'I kept a whole pack from going insane and I didn't die. And since then I've learned so much more about what I can do from Morghanna. I've become even stronger. I think I can keep one mate from going insane without turning into insubstantial dust.'

'But I—'

'Don't you trust me?'

'With my life. It's *your* life I don't trust *myself* with.' The words spilled out of her before she had a chance to think about them. She wished she could suck them back in or find some way to make him forget she'd ever said them. But that was as useless as wishing that Adam would ever placidly do what she wanted.

'That's the problem, right there.'

'What?' She tried to act annoyed, as if she had a right to still be angry with him, but it didn't work, because everything she'd made herself believe was crumbling around her, making her footing very precarious on the tightrope she'd been standing on for so long. One strong breath and she was going to topple off and into the abyss.

'You know what. You don't trust yourself. That guff about the Tricksters and how they died by giving too much to their mates was never real.'

'Oh, it was real.'

'For them. But that's not me.' He jabbed himself in the chest. 'And it certainly isn't you. You're not anywhere close to going insane.'

'You have no idea what you're talking about.'

'Don't I?' He took a step closer. 'What am I, Shelley? What is it that I do that nobody else does quite the same way?'

'You're an Empath at heart. One that gives and receives.'

He pointed his finger at her. 'Yes. I receive. I can feel other's emotions. And I've got better and better at it, especially now that I know what it is I do. Even without my Trickster body, the human and the wolf hearts of me, I can feel everything.' He stepped even closer, crowding her back against the window. 'I can feel you. You love me. That's there. But you can't let it out because your fear is so huge, it's engulfing everything else. Engulfing your ability to be able to see what is right in front of you.'

'And what is that?' She thrust her chin up, meeting his glare, arms crossed, shoulders tense.

'You are not your aunt. You're not anyone else in your family. Hell, you're not like anyone else ever. You are a banshee-Medium. And you are so strong. Nobody has ever been stronger.'

'I'm not strong,' she said, stuttering over the words.

'But you are. And that's what you fear the most.' He cupped her face, gentle but firm.

She wanted to move away but couldn't, his touch fixing her to the spot.

'It's that fear that's scratching away at the edges of your mind. Not insanity. It's your family who made you think your power was something to fear, that it was the thing that would drive you insane. But they are wrong. You were made for greater things than they could ever dream. But only if you trust yourself and your powers.'

'You are so certain.'

'I am. With good reason.'

'But why?'

'Because ...' His eyes darkened and he took in a shuddering breath. 'I've seen the consequences of you letting your fear overcome everything you are, and believe me, it's not something any of us want.'

'What are you talking about?'

He shook his head. 'I'm not going into that now other than to say your banshee is not an enemy unless you make it one.' He dropped his hands, stepped back. 'When you realise the truth in that, I'll be there. Waiting. For you. My mate.'

He turned and walked away, disappearing before he'd even reached the door.

The cold of his touch burned into her skin long after he'd gone. Long after she'd closed her mouth and made her mind grind into action.

He was right. The problem wasn't him. He was strong. He would survive—he would thrive—mated to her. She knew it deep down. The mating bond would never have come into being if she had been so wrong for him.

It was her fear keeping her from him. Fear of her power. Fear of her strength. Fear of reaching for something so incredibly precious and having it snatched away before she could prepare herself for its loss. It was bad enough having the connection with Bron and Skye. Even with them, she'd always tried to keep herself a little apart, to protect herself from the eventual loss of them. She'd been convinced for years that they would leave her, as everyone always did. But they never had; never would.

And neither would Adam. She belonged with him.

She was so deep in love with him that the fear of losing him had made her push him away. Just like she was pushing away a part of herself that only wanted to be recognised, that only wanted to be accepted. She was the banshee-Medium. A woman with enough strength to fight back the Darkness and claim everything in life that she ever wanted. Including the Were who would wait for her always. Forever.

'Adam!' She ran after him, out of the room, into the hallway and almost collided with Bron. 'Shit!' She jumped sideways and slammed into the wall.

'Are you okay?' Bron asked as River helped steady her.

'Fine.' She rubbed at her shoulder. 'I just got a shock. I didn't expect you to be there.'

'Obviously. So, where's the fire?'

She stared at Bron. 'What?'

'Ah, I see. Lack of sense of humour. Things must be bad indeed.'

'What the hell are you talking about?'

Bron shared an amused look with River, lips twitching. 'Adam. You. The argument we all could hear from outside.'

'You heard us?'

'Well, truth be told, we could only hear you, but there's only one person you argue with like that, so it didn't take a rocket scientist to know what was going on.'

'Is that why you're here? Because you heard shouting?'

Bron chuckled. 'No. If anything, it was the silence afterwards that caused more worry. I said you were probably just having some really hot make-up sex.'

'And I pointed out that wasn't possible given he wasn't in his body.'

Bron poked her tongue out at River. 'Spoilsport.' She gestured her hand at Shelley. 'You know they did it a few months ago, even though he was in spirit form.'

'Yes, but that was obviously because of something the Goddess did to help create the mating link.'

Shelley gaped at them. 'You knew? How come you pretended like you didn't?'

'Because we were waiting for you to tell us.'

'I ... I ...'

'We know,' Bron said, saving her from her incoherence. 'We kind of figured you needed to talk to Adam first.' She peered into the room behind Shelley. 'Speaking of which, where is he?'

'I'm here.' Shelley spun around and saw him leaning against the wall, watching her. 'I never truly left.'

She closed her eyes as relief washed over her. There was so much she wanted to say. So much she needed to apologise for. Promises that should be made. She opened her mouth to say something to him, but all that came out was, 'He's here.'

'Hey! What's going on up here?' Skye appeared at the head of the steps, hand cupping her slightly rounded belly, Jason at her side. 'Morrigan says you have to come now.'

Shelley swore under her breath. Could she never get a break? Just five minutes to say what needed to be said to Adam? Was that too much to ask?

'Coming.' Bron hooked her arm through Shelley's and pulled her along. 'Whatever it is, it will wait,' she said softly. 'He will wait. If you have what I think you have, he will wait for you.'

'I know.' But that wasn't the problem. She glanced behind her. Adam followed, his gaze never leaving her. Hunger, longing, love, understanding, burned in his eyes. The heat of it followed her down the stairs and outside. She wanted to swing around, to ask him to forgive her, to promise him better in the future. But she would have to wait until after.

After.

She'd just have to make sure they all made it through tonight so there could be an after.

The silvery light of the moon bathed the land. She'd never noticed the power in the moon before, but she did now. It tingled over her skin, making her suck in her breath as her power responded.

Could the others feel that too?

A group of Were, witches and spirits stood inside the clearing they'd prepared with candles and wards earlier that day. The lines they'd drawn with ash and salt in the centre of the clearing glowed in the moonlight: a small circle inside a triangle, inside a triple circle— Morrigan's addition she said would add to the power in an essential way. All of it was inside a square. The representation of the Nexus standing inside the triumvirate, all encompassed with the circle of life and death, bound by the bonds of love and connection to their mates.

Each of them would stand at a point—Eloise in the middle, Skye, Bron and Shelley at the three points of the triangle, a ring of spirits, a ring of Were—both McVale and McClune—and a ring of the McClune Coven around them, then Jason, River, Iain and Adam at the four points of the square on the outside, binding all within, linked to all within, feeding everything back into the triumvirate, and from them into the Nexus.

They had chosen a clearing that transected with a ley line so that when the spell got going, Eloise would be able to pour all their power through the Goddess Stone, now embedded in her chest, into the ley line and use it to search out every last speck of the Darkness, tearing it from its moorings and expelling it from the earth.

Eloise stood just outside the square, Iain by her side. She was talking to Morrigan—or more correctly, Morrigan seemed to be doing all the talking while Eloise nodded. Iain's tension was obvious as he stood, arm around his mate, body angled so that he could move between Morrigan and Eloise in less than a breath.

'You okay, Eloise?' Bron said as they re-joined her.

Eloise looked up. Her eyes glittered with excitement and worry. 'Morrigan was just giving me some tips.'

'You don't need them,' Iain said.

She placed her hand on his arm. 'I need whatever help and advice I can get.'

Distrust and hatred snapped in his eyes, aimed at Morrigan. 'She's never done anything like this before.'

'No,' Eloise replied. 'But she's been wielding magic for longer than all our lives put together. She knows things we don't. And she wants this to work as much as we do.'

Skye took in a sharp breath, hand cupping the slight roundness of her stomach.

'You okay?' Jason asked.

Skye nodded. 'The babies just moved.'

He put his hand on her stomach. 'I feel them too.'

Joy beamed from her and she laughed. 'It feels so strange.'

'And wonderful,' Morrigan said. 'It's fortuitous you're pregnant.'

'Miraculous is more the word I'd use.' Skye smiled at Bron.

'Both our pregnancies are miraculous. But that's not what I

meant. The Darkness doesn't know about them, so he won't be expecting the extra juice you'll all get from them being a part of the spell.'

'I won't use my babies in this.'

'You don't have a choice. They're as much a part of this as any one of you.' She flinched, hand cupping her stomach, the other rubbing her back.

'Are you okay?'

Morrigan nodded, but didn't speak, her lips thin.

Cordy was at her side in a moment. 'How long have you been having contractions?'

Morrigan grimaced. 'For an hour or so. It's okay. I can hold on.' She glared at Cordy. 'The Darkness isn't going to get my baby.'

Cordy gripped her hand. 'No. It's not.'

Something seemed to pass between the two women and then Morrigan nodded once, sharply, and pulled her hand from Cordy's. 'Let's get this started. You need to be well into the spell before Cain and the Darkness get here.'

'They're not getting anywhere close,' Michael, one of the McClunes' lieutenants, said. 'Our soldiers will stop them.'

'No,' Morrigan said. 'They can't get in the way. Can't let him kill them. That will only give Cain and the Darkness more power to play with. They have to stay out of the way. Trust in the booby traps we've put in place.'

'They know their jobs,' Jason said.

'Is there any chance Cain will survive after the Darkness has left him?' Eloise asked.

Morrigan met her question unflinchingly. 'No. Unlike me, the Darkness won't leave him or the others it still inhabits, willingly. And in Cain, it has sunk its claws deeper than any other I know.' She reached out, touched Eloise's arm. 'The brother you once loved has been gone for a long time.'

'I know.' Eloise sucked in a deep breath, blinking hard and fast. 'I just hope it's quick.'

'You okay, baby?' Iain pulled Eloise into his arms and glared at Morrigan.

She hugged him hard for a moment and then stepped back. 'Yes. Let's get on with it.' The stone glowed through her shirt as if in agreement.

'All right.'

They were about to take their places when Morrigan gasped. 'Oh Goddess. He's coming. He's almost here. The booby traps you've set won't hold him back for long. We must hurry. You have to begin. Now!'

'Then let's begin,' Shelley said, nodding at her coven. They moved as one to take their places, the others surrounding them in the circles, their mates marking the encompassing square.

Once in position, Eloise placed her hands over the stone in her chest. Power glowed around her, shifting colours that represented all of them and the life they endeavoured to safeguard.

Then everyone looked to Shelley. She had to begin the ceremony.

Bron and Skye raised their arms, hands outstretched, linking fingertips, opening to each other. She linked her fingertips with theirs and with a quick glance to her left to ensure Adam was in place, ready to hold her steady and do his part, she took a deep breath and did what she'd never done so willingly before.

She dropped her shields and opened herself to all the dead.

30

S ilence.

It caught Shelley by surprise. She'd expected an immediate influx of noise, the cries of all the spirits pleading, needing, pushing at her. But there was nothing. She opened her eyes. They were all there, surrounding her, their mouths closed, their needs withheld.

Adeline and Harrison floated forward. 'You have opened yourself to us freely and we are here to help.'

Guilt sliced through her. They were so ready to help when she had always hated having to help any of them. All she could say was, 'Thank you.'

She opened herself further. Adeline and Harrison waved the spirits forward, one at a time. She tried not to stiffen, fear a living thing in her chest, a bitter taste in her throat. This was necessary. It was necessary. She would live through this. She would.

'I'm here, Kitten.' Adam's voice in her mind made her relax. She could feel him through their bond. It was a tentative thing, but it was enough for her to hear him, to feel him as if he stood behind her, holding her shoulders. Holding her steady.

The first spirit touched her, melting into her, melding itself to her power. She flinched.

'Are they hurting you?'

Bron's voice came from her left.

'No. It just feels … difficult.'

'We're here with you,' Skye said.

Shelley nodded. Their power built, surrounding her. Touching her like a caress of warm, summer-scented breeze. Their presence comforted, allowed her to hold back the flinch as the next spirit and the next melded with her, giving her the power of their deaths.

'It's not fast enough.'

She glanced at Morrigan, who stood in the circle of witches. She was weak and couldn't be part of the power transfer, but her knowledge was more than enough to make up for it. She was there to direct the others so the triumvirate could pull power from them freely. She would give advice to the triumvirate as they became part of the spell. Even so, Shelley resented her tone. 'I'm going as fast as I can.'

'Go faster. The others need to start building their powers before the moon rises higher. You must be ready to feed that power into the Nexus as one when the moon is at its zenith and the power of Samhain is upon us. They will be ready long before you if you don't go faster.'

Shelley breathed deeply. She looked at the spirits before her, at Adeline and Harrison. They were treating her with kid gloves because, even though she had opened to them willingly, she was still afraid. She was still keeping part of herself from them all because, despite everything she'd thought earlier, she was still afraid of letting go and what might happen if she did.

It was stupid. It was going to destroy everything. She had to let go and trust Adam and the others to guide her and keep her safe.

Trust. It was now or never.

'Come.' She gestured to the spirits before her. 'You have to come now. All of you.' She let go of the shields she'd been holding in place around her heart, her soul, and with eyes and breath and body she welcomed the unknown in.

The spirits hesitated. Then they rushed at her—hundreds of them—entering her in a way she'd never allowed any spirit to enter her before, not through her body, but through her soul, through the heart of her power.

They melded with her, one after another without surcease. Her chest froze. She struggled to breathe. Every muscle and tendon seized, her joints locking. The banshee began to hum inside her, responding to the power of all those deaths, the power that was usually held beyond the veil but was now open for Shelley to use. She swayed but didn't fall—the power of the others wrapped around her, holding her firm; particularly the bond with Adam. It was as if his hands held her, thumbs stroking across her shoulders.

'Are you okay?' A whisper in her ear.

She couldn't move, couldn't speak, but managed to send something through the bond, like a pulse of certainty.

The spirits kept coming.

When would they stop? When would it be enough? She was bloated with them, as if her skin was about to burst. She didn't think she could take any more, but she had to. It wasn't enough. She needed all of them, and then more. She had to take all the witches who had hung around through the ages, and then, through Adam and the Packbond, she had to take the spirit Were who had turned up too. They were there, unexpected, something she'd not known could happen, but they'd come. For her. For Adam. For the pack.

Adam and Jason's parents, their brothers and wives, Skye and River's mother and father, and so many others.

They kept coming. Slamming into her so fast she couldn't distinguish one from another.

'Almost there!' The yell reached her through the void of pain that was now her entire world. Her mind was slipping, fracturing, and yet she somehow managed to hold together even though she'd let everything go.

Her skin vibrated as the last spirits entered her; stretched so that it was raw, painful. A strange itching started up between her shoulder blades.

She glanced up at the moon. It was almost midnight. She could sense the power of her friends as they reached for their magics, building them towards their peak, pulling on the source of their power and that of the living Were through their mating bonds and the Packbond. Even Eloise was tapped into them, her power resonating through the crystal in her chest, vibrating so fast now it emitted a high-pitched tone that made the Were howl to the moon.

The spirit Were inside her joined them in their howl, their emotions so strong that she feared she'd be swept away on the tidal wave of them.

Suddenly, more Were spirits arrived, ancient ones filled with power because they were two souls, not one. They were so strong. She'd never had a true understanding of the symbiosis of the bond until now. The unerring oneness of it.

It was beautiful.

It was overwhelming.

She was too full. Too full. She couldn't do this by herself. She couldn't.

You don't have to.

She reached for Adam, for the link with him. 'Help me.'

'Always.'

He opened himself up and allowed her to use him as a receptacle for some of the power, the emotions, that flowed through her. He glowed with it, like an amethyst lit from within by moonlight.

'By the Moon, Kitten. That feels amazing.'

'Adam!' Gasps rose around her, but she couldn't stop to think about what it meant. Adam had given her the ability to take in any spirits that arrived. But not only that. She knew he held within him the ability to give it all back to her and more when she needed it. It was what she'd been so frightened and angry about earlier, and now it was the thing that might save them all.

If the power wasn't blistering through her, she might have laughed at the irony.

Except laughter was driven far away. The more she took into her, the louder the banshee hum became inside her. A song of horrific warning, getting louder. She had to stop it before it drove forth, pushing sanity and all she loved into the abyss.

'Now,' she cried out to the others, extending her hands towards Eloise. Skye and Bron did the same, their power built to almost intolerable levels.

Together, as if they'd rehearsed this over and over when they'd never done it before, they chanted:

'Receive our power, three for one
In service to the light, bright as the sun
Receive our love, four for four
In service to the light, open the door
Receive our present, future and past
In service to the light, ley lines vast
Receive our hope to set us free
In service to the light, so mote it be.'

There was a loud crackling in the air, and then power shot from each of their hands, hitting Eloise from all sides, arcing through her to where the Goddess Stone sat in her chest.

She jerked and cried out, her arms flinging wide, head snapping back. Power shot into the air and down into the earth, and for the first time Shelley could see the ley lines above and below as their power was fed into them and given back tenfold.

It was so beautiful. And yet, maybe it wouldn't be enough.

Because, the hum inside her had begun to turn into a scream.

'HURRY. They're trying to stop us.'

Cain pushed on. He didn't need the Darkness to tell him the obvious. Morrigan would have told the bastard Were and their sluts what he and the Darkness intended this night. They'd be foolishly trying to do something to stop them. Not that they could. Not without the Nexus and the Goddess Stone. Even if they'd managed to find the Goddess Stone—which he seriously doubted as it had been lost in the aether centuries ago—Eloise had no idea about her power or how to use it. They might be trying something, but it would fail. He would see to it as soon as he was close enough to tear apart their feeble magic.

The true hurry was that the moon was almost at its zenith and they needed to be near Morrigan when she gave birth.

Explosions went off around him—traps the animals had set to stop him.

They barely slowed him down as he used his shields to protect him. There were Were in the trees around him—he could sense them. Why didn't they rush out to fight him? Perhaps he should ferret them out, light them up with his magic, suck up the power of their deaths.

'No. Don't waste your time or energy. You must hurry. Use your power to make yourself go faster.'

He already was using as much power as he dared on his shield and his speed. More would make him vulnerable when he faced down the Were and Morrigan and forced the labour to begin. The bitch was halting her labour, her power an itch under his skin. Couldn't she see the damage she did? The more she held on, the more their baby would suffer when the Darkness destroyed the soul that was destined for the body and took its place. She was fighting against the inevitable. Was she so far gone that she didn't see that?

No matter. She would die. As soon as she'd given birth to the baby.

He glanced up at the moon.

Almost time. Power tingled through his skin. The power of Samhain. Of life and death and everything in between. Soon it would all be within his grasp. He laughed into the night.

Light shot into the sky, the brightness bringing tears to his eyes and forcing him to look away.

All around him, Were howled into the night. Then he saw them, brightly lit in the trees, held in some kind of stasis. Power ran from them—into the earth, into the sky, back towards the place he was heading, where the light was coming from. Lines of power glowed in the sky above him, in the earth at his feet. A terrible chill stabbed his skin, making his spine snap straight as he stared, as he began to comprehend what it was he saw.

'No! No!' He shoved power into a burst of speed. He had to kill those who would take his dreams, his destiny, from him.

He had to kill them now.

SHELLEY STARED AT ELOISE. Tears streamed down her face at the beauty of her. Coruscating colours of power lit her up, blue, green, gold and amethyst with the flicker of red at its heart.

Stunning.

The shifter-witch held the power inside her for longer than Shelley thought possible, and then, pulling on all that power, she tapped into the ley lines.

'Seek out the Darkness
Light the night
No place to hide
Expelled from earth's sight.'

The words exploded from her—a spell, but not. At the same time, more power burst from the crystal in her chest, lighting the landscape around her in a way the sun never could.

The pull on her powers was incredible, but she, along with Skye and Bron, continued to channel their powers into Eloise; the power of the living and dead; the power of Healing and Empathy; the power of Earth and Water and Fire; the variations on those powers from the other witches in the inner circle just beyond the triangle, and beyond them, the power of the packs, all steadied and strengthened by their four mates.

Three lines of power from the triumvirate, four to their mates, multiple lines of power from the witches, warlocks and Were who were in the square created by Jason, River, Iain and Adam. But more than that, lines of power came from the surrounds. Any Were in the vicinity were tapped for power too with a suddenness that made them stop in their tracks and light up with the magic of the change.

Except none of them shifted. They were, in that moment, both human and wolf, strong and timeless, born of the magic of the world they lived in, inexorably tied to it. They shared in the power from the centre of the clearing and gave back to it, not just because the Pact demanded it, but because they could. Because they wanted to. Because the sharing and togetherness made them stronger.

In her mind, that truth suddenly became clear. The wonder and beauty of it filled her with awe. She was part of that. It was melded into her skin, her soul, her heart, as surely as the Goddess Stone was melded to Eloise. It made her strong.

No. She was already strong. It simply added depth to what was already there. Gave it all meaning.

She belonged. For the first time ever, she truly belonged. What had she been fighting against all this time? It was magnificent. Truly magnificent.

Laughter filled her mind. Her laughter. Adam's. It was joy and life combined, filling her with both. For the first time in her life she was free of fear and full of love. His love. Hers. Skye's and Bron's and Eloise's. Their mates. The pack. Even the McClunes. They loved her. Cherished her. She was theirs as they were hers.

Family. She had family.

She was never going to let them go.

Her power brightened, strengthened, and something snapped in place inside her. The bond with Adam. It went from being a gossamer thread to something bright and unbreakable.

She'd been so empty without it. It filled her. Made her more.

Adam howled to the night as the mating bond strengthened. In the distance there was an answering echo—his wolf, coming to life in recognition of the thing it had always longed for, even though it still wasn't whole without Adam's soul intact. Shelley could feel it pulling at him—but he didn't go. Couldn't go. Not yet. Not while the canker was in his skin. But that evil was going. She could feel the power of it being burned out of his flesh as their spell lit up the world, driving the Darkness from its hiding places.

She couldn't wait to be truly wrapped in his arms again, his lips on hers, his hands on her flesh, him thick and hard and glorious inside her.

'I want that, too, Kitten. By the Moon, I love you.'

His voice echoed in her head and she couldn't help but return them. 'I love you, too.'

He laughed again, a burst of wild joy.

She wanted to roll in it, to cover herself with the bubbling happiness of the sound. But there was another sound, the banshee, screaming to life inside her, sucking all the joy and happiness from her in an instant.

Someone was going to die. They were going to die!

It wasn't simply Cain or the Darkness either. There was the possibility of others. Thousands of others. Millions.

No. No. She had to hold on to the scream. She couldn't let it out.

A scream—not the banshee, but another—echoed through the night. Sounds of fighting clashed through the night from within the trees behind where Adam stood. The sizzle of dark power skittered over her, flicking off the web of light that had grown over them as they wrought the spell.

Cain. He was here.

Fury flared through the bond from Adam. 'You won't kill anyone tonight, you bastard.'

'Adam, no!'

Bron and Skye shouted 'no' at the same time she did. But it was no use. He didn't listen. He had already turned to engage the evil warlock, to stop him from shooting his power at Shelley and the others. His snarl tore through the air, shuddering through her. There was another scream, frustration and rage, sizzling heat, a cry from Bron—'Adam, watch out!' A heated bolt of Bron's golden Healing power flew past Shelley, so close the sizzle of it played across her skin. Another cry in the night and then ...

He was gone.

'Adam!' she cried out, with mouth and mind. 'Adam!' He didn't answer. The bond was still intact, but he wasn't there.

The banshee scream was working up to her chest, rising, rising.

No, not Adam. Not Adam. It couldn't start with Adam. But she knew that it could. That it would.

And if he was dead, she wouldn't have the strength or will to stop what came after the banshee screamed its cry of death and destruction.

More screaming and yelling. More bursts of power that struck at their spell. She wanted to turn, to look, to try to find Adam, but she couldn't move, was fixed in spot now as the spell came to its peak, holding desperately to one thought: not Adam.

She fought not to release the banshee wail, to hold on to the fact that she could still feel the bond, even though Adam didn't respond. Even though Bron's eyes were wide with horror as she looked past Shelley, her golden power flaring all around her.

'Adam, no!' Tears spilled down the Healer's face as her gaze, filled with desperate sadness, met Shelley's.

'No. No.'

Bron shook her head and words spilled out of her, as if she couldn't withhold the truth. 'Cain shot warlock lightning at him. I tried to help. Tried to send out Healing power to where he stood, but there was a flare of light and then he was gone. I can't see him anymore.'

'No. No!' She had no idea what might happen if he were hit in spirit form by Cain's warlock lightning, but given he wasn't answering, it wasn't good. His body was still alive— which was why she could still feel the bond—but his spirit was no longer there. She called out to him again, desperate, with voice and mind, but he didn't answer. No. No. It couldn't be. But she was desperately afraid it was.

His spirit had been destroyed. And without a spirit, his body would soon die too.

No. No! Not Adam. They were supposed to be together. She'd only just decided. Had only just accepted the bond. It had snapped tight. She'd thought, for one insane moment, that she was going to be able to have everything she'd ever dreamed of.

Now that was gone. Taken away with no rhyme or reason. Before she'd even had a chance to tell Adam face to face. To actually hold him, body and soul, and cherish him in the way he always should have been cherished and be cherished by him in return.

Hell. She was in hell. And she wanted to die.

The wail—more a scream—tore from her mouth. A savage sound, it ripped through the crackle of power, echoing across the land, sending Were to their knees.

'Shelley—no!' Skye and Bron and Eloise cried out to her, but it was too late.

She'd been walking a tightrope for too many years, but after the banshee part of her had come to the fore earlier in the year, she'd been even closer to this, to the insanity of crossing the veil, of knowing and feeling things a human was never meant to know and feel. The insanity was a living thing inside her, tied into that part of her that came from the Gods.

And it knew, could feel, that Adam was gone. Cain had taken him from her. Her Adam. It wasn't his time. It should have been Cain. The Darkness. They should be the ones to die tonight. They would be the ones to die tonight.

And she was the one who would make it happen.

Death was her gift. She would take Cain and his master into oblivion with her in recompense for what they'd done.

The world turned darkly purple.

The itching that had been in her shoulder blades since the spell began suddenly became a tearing pain. She screamed and screamed again, not of pain—but of rage and grief and retribution.

Something tore from the skin on her back—wings. They snapped out, strong and glistening with blood and amethyst fire in the night. They flapped, bearing her upward, through the wards, through the powerful ley lines, until she could look down and see her enemy.

The astral spirit part of her still stood at the point of the triangle, mouth open, tears streaming from her eyes, her power billowing and enormous, a silver and amethyst thread flying into the air to the banshee part of her that had transformed her body and separated it from the witch and Medium parts of her soul.

Skye and Bron and Eloise stared at her as she hovered above

them, their faces full of horrified understanding of what she'd done —splintered her mind and soul to have her revenge.

Jason and River and Iain still held their places, trying to steady the gap of Adam's absence with sheer will. They shouted at the witches and Were in the circle around the triumvirate to hold their place, to help Skye, Bron and Eloise complete the spell. Which they could do so long as her astral self remained to hold onto her side of the spell. But it was a tenuous grip that could break at any moment if she didn't return the two parts of herself together. The others were trying to shore her up while desperately trying not to lose their hold on their own side of the spell. They were managing but wouldn't for much longer if Cain kept shooting his power at them.

He had to be stopped.

If she killed him, if she ensured the Darkness was destroyed, the millions of deaths building inside her would not come to pass. Even if she had to sacrifice herself, she would ensure that future would not unfold.

Where was he? There!

Cain stood at the edge of the clearing, protected by the trees, shooting bolts of magic at anyone close by while yelling something— a spell—at the place where Morrigan stood.

The ancient witch yelled words into the night in response, another spell, hands clutched over her distended stomach. But whatever she was trying to cant, it didn't work.

As banshee-Shelley watched, Morrigan was driven to her knees, her face screwed into an expression of terror and agony.

She was going into labour.

The power in the clearing buckled, almost broke, but Bron and Skye and Eloise and all the others poured more of themselves into it, holding it together.

Cordy ran to Morrigan's side, her Midwife powers flaring around her, trying to hold the labour at bay for a little while longer.

But Morrigan screamed and in that scream, banshee-Shelley heard the inevitable.

The baby was coming. It was going to be born.

And if she didn't do something now, Cain and the Darkness would have their way and all would be lost.

Her grief a sword, she opened her mouth on a scream and swooped down towards the bastard warlock and the Darkness that infected him.

She would make them pay for all they'd done; but mostly, she'd make them pay for taking her mate from her.

31

Screaming filled Adam's mind. And a searing burn that made him wonder if it was his scream he heard. Screaming seemed the appropriate response to what had happened, to the pain shooting through him, to the knowledge that he was dying.

That fucker, Cain, had hit him with warlock lightning again. And holy shit, had it hurt! His soul must now be completely severed from his body. He couldn't possibly survive a second time. Shit. Fuck!

Very soon, there would be no more pain. No more thought. Only this moment of endless regret at everything he was about to lose.

Shelley.

She'd accepted the mating bond. The moment had been a glory inside him; her acceptance strong and unique and utterly her. It shone with her love, with her trust and commitment to him, the pack, herself. He'd known she could do it, and she'd proved him right. He would howl his joy to the moon if only he wasn't in the process of dying.

The burning pain intensified. 'Holy mother fucker,' he said, teeth clenched around the words. Then there was a jerk and a popping sound and the intensity of the pain disappeared, only its echo remaining.

The screaming got louder. Okay ... not coming from him then. Holy shit it was loud. So loud, it hurt. He flinched. And there was howling. Who was howling?

And was that blood he smelled? Fresh blood. Warmth trickled from his nose, his ears. What the?

He opened his eyes.

He was lying on the bed in the hospital room in the caves that were part of McClune Packland. His hand twitched, banging against the metal safety barrier on the side of the bed.

Ow! He clasped it with his other hand, rubbing. He'd hit it so hard, he'd probably have a bruise.

He bolted upright, swayed as the room careened wildly around him, held onto the metal rails of the hospital bed. It took a moment, but the room finally righted itself.

He was back in his body. How?

He looked down at his bare chest.

The wound faded as he watched, the skin slightly pink where it had been, but normal. No hint of the taint left by the Darkness. Just a slight golden glow emanating from his skin.

Bron. Her Healing bolt had hit him at the same time as the warlock lightning, somehow managing to send him back to his body, to heal him and knit body and spirit before he was lost. He'd have to kiss her later. She was fucking brilliant.

His wolf howled in his mind, catching his attention. Welcoming him back. And warning him.

Warning him about what?

The screaming. He touched the sticky warmth coming from his nose, lifted his hands. Blood. He was bleeding despite the Healing. The only thing that could cause him to bleed from his nose and ears like this was ...

Shelley! The banshee was screaming. But it wasn't simply the warning scream of oncoming death he'd heard before. This was more. Different. It was almost like ...

No. A horrible aching tear sheered along the bond, scraping it to its core. 'Kitten, what have you done?'

He jumped out of the bed and almost fell to the floor. His limbs trembled with lack of use, the room spinning again. He tried to stand upright, to take a step, but fell to the floor.

Fuck, no. No. He couldn't do it. He was going to let her down.

'*I can do it*,' his wolf said, a fierce growl in his mind. Yes. Yes. All he needed to do was to go and open the door.

With his wolf howling in his mind, encouraging, pushing him along, he pulled himself across the floor, hauled himself up and yanked open the door. He fell through as it opened, the light of change taking him mid-fall.

He landed on all fours and then he was running, paws pounding along the concrete floor. He reared at the lift, hit the button, paced as he waited for the lift to arrive and the doors to open, then repeated the action to get to the surface.

He whimpered as the sensation of a knife paring away at the mating bond became sharper, colder. Shelley must think him dead. The banshee screamed for him. There was so much grief and anger and terrible, horrifying loneliness echoing down the bond to him from her. Such a horrible loneliness, it would drive a person insane. If he didn't get to her soon, didn't make her see she was stronger than this, that she didn't need to let it take her, not just because he was alive, but because she was fucking amazing ...

The horror of the vision Morghanna had shown him rose in his mind. Fucking hell. He couldn't let that come to pass.

He had to get to her. Now.

Why was the fucking bloody lift taking so goddamned long?

THE SCREAM HIT Cain like a tidal wave, smacking him to his knees, forcing him flat to the ground. She smiled, even though the Were he fought had been knocked down too, some smacked into unconsciousness by the force of the sound, others clutching at their ears. Even Jason and River and Iain went to their knees.

A frisson of worry splayed along her chest. Had she hurt them?

Should she feel bad about that? They were her friends, weren't they? The ones she was protecting?

But Adam! She must avenge Adam. So cruelly taken from her. Her mind swirled with the pain of it. And those other deaths. She had to stop them.

The banshee screeched again.

Blood scented the air. Worried cries reached out to her. Familiar voices. Skye. Bron. Eloise.

Cordy. Calling to their mates and pack. Calling to her. She couldn't listen to them. Couldn't. She was Death. It was her gift. She had to make Cain pay with his life. Adam would want her to do it, wouldn't he?

Would he?

The voice, calm in the nightmare roiling through her mind, cut through the horrible grief and confusion.

Adam wouldn't want her to do this. He wouldn't want to be avenged like this. He'd tell her she was stronger than this. That she shouldn't lose control. Didn't have to give in to the insanity of her gift. She'd begun to think that was true. Had allowed the mating bond to snap into place because of that belief. Was it true? Was it?

True?

The scream faltered in her throat. Was she truly Death? Was that her gift? Or was her gift understanding? Was it the strength to hold the bridge between life and death and allow communication? To allow closure. As she'd done for Cordy and Marcus. For Harrison with Skye. Adeline with Bron. Even the banshee, though powerful, wasn't destructive at heart.

She was a warning. A gift of time to try to alter an unnecessary future—like now.

She frowned. But if that were true, then why hadn't she sensed Adam's death?

Because the scream that had been building inside her hadn't been for him.

But if that were true, then why had he died?

Maybe it was because he was too close. Maybe she could only see oncoming death for others. If only she could have known. If only she could have been warned. She could have ... could have ... what?

Saved him? How? She would have had to break the spell to do that. Adam would never have wanted that. He would want her to get on with the spell, finish what they'd begun. He would have been happy to sacrifice himself for her, for the others. He was that good. That generous.

He was her love. He would hate this murderous creature she was about to become.

She might see death, but she didn't have to create it. Not even for him.

The banshee cried her despair of that truth, her wings slapping in the night, buffeting those below as she held herself aloft. The ley lines snapped and sparked, their power arcing up to touch her wings.

Oh Goddess. The power of the world tied into the power of the universe. The part inside her that was linked to the Goddess tied to her by blood, by DNA, awakened fully. It was amazing. The power that filled her! She could do anything. Anything. She could ensure life or she could bring death. It was her choice. She had to choose.

Cain moaned, pushed to his knees, grabbing her attention once more.

She shrieked at him. She wanted him dead.

No. Not dead. Just stopped.

She tipped her head to the side. Would that be enough? She *could* stop him with this power streaming through her. Hold him up long enough for the others and her astral soul to finish the spell and banish the Darkness forever.

Or she could strike him down.

He rose to his feet, lifting his hand to use his power.

She screeched at him, pushing her power towards him with a flap of her wings. He arched, arms wide, the power sparking over his body, through him, making him shudder and shake and then fall back to the ground.

What had she done? What choice had she made? She didn't know. Didn't—

He took in a shuddering breath.

Ah. *I didn't kill him.*

The screams of millions of deaths inside her dissolved as if they'd never been. She looked down at those below her—her friends, her pack. She'd protected them from Cain, without killing, but there was still danger. Her gaze flickered to the labouring Morrigan.

She must stop the Darkness from entering the baby and replacing its soul. That was her role in this now. The thing she could do that no other could.

Leaving Cain where he lay supine in the grass, she dived to hover over Morrigan. The ancient witch lay panting, her swollen stomach rippling with the force of her contractions.

'I can't stop it!' Cordy gasped.

'No.' Morrigan panted between the words. 'Cain hit me with a spell, undoing our work. The baby is coming. It's coming now.'

And so was the Darkness. The banshee could feel it. Feel the death it would bring if it got to its destination and did the unthinkable. She spun, wings furled protectively over the labouring Morrigan, and faced the enemy as it came at her through the sky.

Torn bits and pieces flying through the moonlit night, coalescing together into a massive, whirling whole.

Cain screamed, his chest rising, back arching so high it looked like he would break in half. The Darkness tore itself from him and he slumped back to the ground, face deathly pale, blood pouring from his eyes and ears and nose.

He would be dead in moments. Even though she knew now she couldn't have raised a hand to cause his death, she also wasn't sorry for it.

The banshee hissed, wings snapping again, reaching out to touch the ley lines, to fill her with more power. Behind her, another power sizzled, greater, rising, rising. Eloise. Skye. Bron. The astral-Shelley. Out of the corner of her eye, she saw their brilliance—all the colours of the rainbow—their power growing out from them like a faceted gem, pushing further and further out into the sky. They were almost there, but not quite. They needed longer to reach the full strength of the spell. And in the meantime, the Darkness was strengthening, more pieces joining what stood before her, taking the rough shape of a giant man.

It grinned at her, as if it found her amusing. 'You cannot stop me. You are but a mewling infant. Your wings are still wet. Let me take care of that for you.'

The Darkness shot something at her. Before she could think what to do, her wings snapped forward, buffeting the energy back towards the Darkness.

With a wave of its hand, it deflected the rebounding power, a snarl now clear on its almost-face. 'Beginner's luck.' It shot more darts of power at her. She raised the shields she'd become so adept at, using them as she'd used them against Cain all those months ago, and deflected every one of his darts.

Then she lifted hands and wings and shot her own power at this creature that hungered for their destruction. Amethyst-tinged lightning sizzled around the Darkness, lighting up its edges, pushing it back towards the trees. She blasted it again, pushing it back further. It seemed to become a little smaller.

She shot out another bolt.

The Darkness raised its hand and deflected her bolt. It shot into the trees and flared in the branches, setting the tree on fire.

It straightened. 'Impressive. You're not as weak as I thought.'

'I was never weak.' She wasn't. So foolish to have thought it for so long simply because her family had told her so. She would never fall prey to those thoughts again.

Morrigan's cries and panting became louder. Her contractions coming thick and fast.

The full power of Samhain would be on them soon and the baby with it. The Darkness knew. It could probably feel it better than she could.

'It's time,' it said, moving as if to breach the outer square of power —weakened now because she'd driven the Were to their knees with her screams. It gestured at the bodies lying around the clearing and beyond because of her, because of Cain. At the fires in the trees—one was her fire, the others must have been Cain's. 'This is exactly how I ordained it. Death and destruction ushering in my new reign over this little world. And all thanks to you and your stupid, pathetic Were.'

'They weren't so pathetic when you used them all those centuries ago. In fact, you spent all this time trying to get back to them.'

'They were easy to manipulate and more powerful than the humans, but still simply there to use until something better came along. I could never fully gain entry into this world through them. Not like I can through that magically created baby. Its very cells are fuelled with magic. Can't you feel it? Powerful. So powerful. Power that will allow me to stay without destroying it. It was made for me. Unlike your pathetic Were.'

'Liar. The Were were too strong for you to fully take over, so you turn to an innocent baby to help you live out your dreams of power. You're pathetic.'

The eyes in its almost-face blackened with hatred and fury. It let out a shout of rage and then came at her in a rush, exploding through the weakened outer lines of their working with no effort at all. Jason and River and Iain cried out as they were released from the working, but somehow she could still feel their strength, backing her, buoying her.

She lifted her wings, raised more shields.

The Darkness hit the edge of her shield and roared in fury. She laughed in his face, a strange sound in her banshee throat.

'You can't stop me from getting what I want. From getting what is mine.'

'The baby will never be yours. We will never be yours!' She held onto her shields as it battered at them, the things that were its hands clawing at her shields, tearing at them, sucking the power of them with its dark energy. It hurt, but she held on. She had to hold on. Her friends were almost done. She could feel it. Feel them.

She cried out as the two outer shields were destroyed, leaving only the two at the centre. She poured everything she was into them.

'You could have been my greatest soldier,' the Darkness roared as it ripped at her next shield, the feel of it like claws raking at already shredded skin.

'I'd rather die.'

'So be it.' It shattered her second last shield. Only one left.

Trembling, she reached for everything within her, the banshee, the Medium, the friend, the pack member, the lover, the mate, and pushed the strength of that into her one remaining shield. 'I won't let you in,' she cried, voice trembling with her effort. It had to be enough. It would be enough.

He kept battering at it. And for a brief moment, she thought she would win. But then, her shield wavered.

The Darkness cried out in triumph as it lifted its hands to pound one last time at her weakened shield. Oh Goddess, please let it hold for one moment longer.

'Hold on, Kitten. You are strong. I know you can do it.'

'Adam!' His voice was in her mind, the howl of his wolf loud in her ears.

He was alive.

She could feel the vibrancy of him close by, racing to her. He was returned to his body, pounding over the earth in wolf form. He was coming to her. Coming for her.

Her wings fluttered, shivering their anticipation, their dread. No. She didn't want him to see her like this. Not this thing that could choose to kill so easily.

'But you didn't. I've seen a future where that's all you were because you had no choice. You had a choice today and you chose to save, to protect but not to kill. You are magnificent. You are strong. Banshee, Medium, witch, lover, friend. You are all that and more. Use it to save yourself. To save us all.'

His words rang through her, his strength adding to her own through their bond. His strength, his life, his love, his never-ending trust that she was everything and more, it was all she needed. Standing tall, wings raised proudly to the sky, she filled her shield with the hopeful joy in her heart.

'Take my strength. Use it.'

She did. Without hesitation. All her old fears about him had melted away. They had always been about her, not him. She had mistrusted herself; had feared that in an effort to stave off the insanity she thought was inevitably hers, that she would use everything he was. That she would take and take and take until he was nothing.

But she'd been so wrong. She knew that now. So she took what he offered and poured all of that certainty—his, hers—all of her new knowledge of herself, into her shield, a final attempt to deny the evil that would destroy the kind of love they both deserved.

The Darkness came at her, the force and scope of it blotting out the light of the moon.

'Together,' Adam shouted in her mind.

Yes, together.

The Darkness hit her shield ... and was slammed back, tumbling over and over, crashing through trees which fell with cracking thumps at the force of it.

Yes! They'd done it. They'd repelled it.

Screaming its rage, the Darkness returned in a billowing flurry. It pounded on her shield, over and over, wrapped itself around the edges, twisting, tightening against it, trying to shatter it all at once.

She held strong. She *was* strong. Adam offered her more of his strength and she took it, because he was strong too and could take it if she could. 'I won't let you in. Not to this circle. Not to my world. Not ever.'

'You can't stop me forever with this pathetic shield. It will break and I will kill you.'

She tossed her head. 'It won't matter. Others will be there to stop you after I fall.'

'The Were? They're not strong enough. Your spirits? They run from me when I pass. Your witch friends? They don't have the power.'

'By ourselves, we don't. But together, we do.'

She looked back to see that her friends—the witches of the triumvirate and the Nexus—had turned to face her. The multicolour gem of their power was brilliant about them, almost blinding.

'Go to oblivion,' Eloise said. She lifted her hands, drew on the power of the triumvirate, the power of the Were, the power of the dead and the living, the power of the earth and the sun and the moon, and shot at their enemy with a blast of light.

Pure and bright, full of the colours of all their powers and all their bonds, it hit the Darkness. The strike lit it up, sizzled around it, through it.

The Darkness began to shake. Cracks began to form. A high, piercing keen shredded the night. The earth shook beneath them. It seemed like the Darkness would break apart at any moment, but somehow it held.

Their power wasn't enough. They weren't going to be enough.

'You won't have my baby, you fuck!' Morrigan had sat up, Cordy at her side, and despite the fact that both of them had almost depleted their power, they managed to pull on something deep inside, something primal, and added their power to the mix.

The Darkness began to shatter, bits of it flying into the sky. But as fast as it shattered, it pulled itself back together, its determination to hold on as great as their determination to rid the world of its evil.

'Help us,' Shelley cried to the moon with the banshee and Medium powers, Adam's pleading howl adding to the strength of it.

Morghanna appeared in front of them, glowing from within in a way Shelley had never seen before—she was filled with the Goddess' light. She smiled at them and then turned her attention to the Darkness. 'The Goddess sends a message to you—"it is over, my love".' She waved her hand.

A crack appeared in the night behind the Darkness, widening to show the greyish nothing of the void. The Darkness screamed as shattered bits of it were sucked back into the void before it could pull them back to itself.

'You are defeated,' Morghanna cried, her voice the voice of the Goddess. Her power was added to the others—the red and the silver of the moon.

There was a boom of noise, a thunder crack that made the earth and sky heave.

The Darkness tore apart and was sucked into the void.

Silence.

Broken when Eloise cried out. The gem in her chest pulsed, sending out a wave of light in every direction, and another and another until it seemed like there was nothing but light around them.

'Eloise!' Iain raced to her side, catching her as she fell, the gem in her chest now nothing more than a speck of light that flickered and then went out.

Eloise touched Iain's cheek, an exhausted smile quivering on her lips. 'I'm fine. It was just the power cleansing the world of the Darkness. Any small remnant of it out there will be destroyed by the—'

Her words were sucked away by the howling wind of the void as the tear in the fabric of space and time snapped to a close, trapping the Darkness in the nothing, forever.

'Is that it? Did we do it?' River asked as he pulled Bron into his arms.

'I think so.'

Adam was suddenly in front of the banshee. He rubbed his wolf head against her leg before the light of the change surrounded him. And then he stood before her, his naked, human self, a smile on his face. 'Well done, my love.'

Yes. She was his love. All of her. Human, Medium, witch, banshee. They all belonged. All were welcome and appreciated. There was no longer any war between them. Something inside her relaxed and the banshee retreated, enfolded in the body of one, whole, contented being for the first time in their life as astral spirit and flesh came together.

Shelley opened her eyes and saw the world in a way she'd never seen it before. It was no longer terrifying. The future splayed before her, filled with hope and love and friendship. And she wanted to race towards it.

Her gaze lighted on the naked man in front of her. She wanted to race towards it with him. 'Adam.' Suddenly she was in his arms, his lips on hers, his warmth finally wrapped around her. She'd never felt so alive.

'Neither have I,' he said, laughing against her lips.

She laughed back, no longer surprised he seemed to be able to read her mind as well as her emotions. She pulled back, hands on his face. 'I thought you had left me.'

'Never. I will never leave you. You will never be alone. We are together. Forever.'

He always understood, had always known, her true fear was not simply about losing her mind. 'I love you.'

'Ditto.'

'*Ghost?* You're quoting from *Ghost?*' She slapped him on the shoulder. 'I hate that movie.'

'I know,' he laughed and caught her mouth with his, his laughter spilling into her, and all she could feel was the joy of being mated to this male who would never let her be too serious for too long, who would never let her go, who would never let her feel alone.

'Morrigan!' Skye cried out, breaking into Shelley and Adam's reunion.

Shelley tore her lips from Adam, turned in his arms in time to see Cordy catching Morrigan as she fell back, lowering her to the ground. There was blood all over the grass, covering the pale flesh of the ancient witch's legs.

Shelley, Bron, Skye and Eloise dropped to her side. Morrigan clutched Skye's hand, and Shelley's, as Bron and Cordy went to work to birth the baby, to try to save her. But there was no magic to use. They were all spent.

Morrigan knew. Shelley could see it in her eyes. Could see as she looked behind Adam and saw her sister standing there. 'Morghanna.'

'I'm here to take you home with me.'

'My baby?'

'Will live. You give your life for his.'

'Good.' Tears streamed down her pallid face, but she pushed and laboured until with a cry, the baby was guided from her ruined womb and into the arms of Cordy.

Cordy gave him to Morrigan as she leaned against Jason. 'Beautiful.' She caressed the baby in her arms, fingers playing over his dark, bloody hair. 'Make good choices, little one. And remember how much I love you.' She looked at Eloise, held out trembling arms. Eloise took the baby, and Morrigan's arms dropped listless to her side. The light seemed to dim around her. 'I give him to you,' she whispered. 'He is your blood. You will love him as I can't.' Her gaze flickered to Skye and River. 'He's your blood, too. You will guard him, help look after him?'

They both nodded. Tears spilled down Skye's face. River looked more sombre than Shelley had ever seen him—which was saying something. 'Of course.'

Her gaze flickered to Shelley. 'He will be like you.' She swallowed hard, her lips trembling, breath hardly a whisper. 'Please help to make him as strong as you.' Her gaze found her baby again, cradled in Eloise's arms, her smile beatific. 'Love him. Take care of him. Teach him what I could never see until it was almost too late.'

Eloise shook her head, holding the baby out. 'I can't. You're going to live. You'll do it.'

'You know that I won't.' Her gaze went to Morghanna. 'It's time?'

Morghanna nodded, her mouth twisted. 'I am sorry you will never get to be a mother to your baby.'

'You never got to be a mother to yours.'

Morghanna's eyes clouded with pain. 'No. But he was loved well and lived a good life, thanks to Bridgette's mate, Malcolm and the McVale Pack and Coven he was bonded to. It is more than I could ask.'

'Then I ask the same for my son. I will love him from afar.'

Morghanna shook her head, gaze full of sorrow. 'You cannot watch him. I made a bargain so I could be here tonight and be a channel of the Goddess' power. Our souls have tarried here long enough. We must go on.'

Morrigan's lips trembled. Tears spilled from her eyes, dripping from her chin as she said, 'I understand.'

She gazed longingly at her son for a long, heart-wrenching moment, and then her gaze fluttered to Eloise. 'Make sure he knows how much I love him. My little Phoenix.'

A breath puffed out of her. Her head lolled to the side.

She was gone.

All the Were lifted their heads and howled to the moon. But it wasn't mournful sound. Instead, it was filled with hope of a better life ahead—for Morrigan and Morghanna, and for them all.

As they all stared at the baby in Eloise's arms, and as Adam's arms tightened around her, Shelley felt light and hopeful for the first time in her life.

Aside from Adam's love and the mating bond thrumming strong and secure inside her, it was the best feeling in the world.

32

They consecrated Morrigan's body at sunset after everyone had recovered enough to be able to give her the gift of the ceremony of light. She was laid in the centre of the McClunes' Dance; the ancient stones had been brought from their lands in Ireland when their family had first settled there almost a century earlier.

Morrigan's body—at least, it was the body she'd stolen from Skye and River's grandmother and done blood magic on to make it young again—was placed on the altar stone in the centre, where all bodies that were being farewelled were lain. McVale and McClune witches stood in a circle around it, their mates and packmates surrounding them, spilling out of the Dance and into the edges of the trees surrounding the sacred clearing.

All who could be there were there. Morrigan had been their enemy for centuries, but in the end, she had died to help save them all, and everyone wanted to pay respect to that.

Shelley waited, Adam behind her, his hand on her back, as all the witches lit the body with their power, then she tapped into her power and loosed it to join theirs. Brightest amethyst coalesced over the body, melding and sparking off the power of the other witches.

Shields down, Shelley tapped into the power of the spirits around her that they gifted willingly. The power flared, brighter than the sun, pure white light outlining the body. Morrigan's soul was lifted from the body, and for the first time, they saw her true face. She was quite a bit like her sister, although, not as small and her square chin carrying an air of stubbornness that strangely reminded her of Skye.

Morghanna appeared above her, holding out her hand. Morrigan reached up, fingers twining with her sister's.

The light became too bright to see them clearly after that. A sound, a single joyous note, rang through the air—the banshee loosing a song of fair-journey from Shelley's throat.

Then the light was gone, Morrigan and Morghanna along with it.

Shelley closed her mouth. All was silent.

'May she rest safe in the arms of the Goddess,' Cordy intoned. Everyone murmured the words together in response. After a moment of silence, they began to drift away.

There was a lot to do. Damage control in the wider community. Injured Were to see to. Thankfully, aside from Morrigan and Cain, nobody had died. They'd all, somehow, been protected by the triumvirate–Nexus spell. There was plenty of destruction though—trees had been felled and fires needed to be doused. Even the spirits seemed to have something to do. She'd expected them to rush her with their requests and questions now she'd dropped her shields, but some simply sent her smiles before disappearing, others just faded away.

She'd made things harder for herself by holding them at bay. It was a mistake she wouldn't make again. She would use her shields, but not to keep the spirits from contacting her. She would use them to protect those who needed protecting.

The Were spirits left. Even Marcus, who lingered to say one last goodbye through her to Cordy, departed with Jason and Adam's family. Cordy cried, but then she was called to help Skye with the babies—their power had been fluctuating wildly since the working the previous night. Her tears dried, even though the sorrow was in her eyes—Shelley had a feeling it always would be—and she busied herself checking on Skye.

Cordy soon decreed that Skye needed to rest and Eloise needed to get Phoenix back up to the house. They and their mates, along with Bron and River, came over to Shelley and Adam before heading back, giving her hugs and slapping Adam on the back. Bron and Skye didn't say anything to her, simply hugged her and kissed her cheek, showing their love and support in the way they knew she'd appreciate the most. They hurried away soon after, Cordy ushering Skye to the house while Jason left to check on the repairs and touch base with as many members of both packs as he could. No doubt he'd join his mate soon, the need to support and love too great to set aside for long.

She smiled. That need was inside her now.

She didn't have to ask where Bron and River were headed. Now that Bron had some of her power back, she would be using it to see to those who needed more than normal doctoring could offer. Shelley wasn't certain where she got the energy from. But her friend had always seemed to have more energy than ten people combined, so it shouldn't be a surprise she had bounced back so quickly. Especially given she had River.

Eloise took the baby from Patrick, who had held him during the ceremony. She buried her face in the baby's neck, but not before Shelley saw the tears sliding down her face. She'd held it together up until now, not showing the extent of her grief until nearly everyone was gone. Shelley understood why. For most of them, today was a celebration. For Eloise, it was that, but it was also a day of loss. Despite what Morrigan had done to her—hunting and killing her family, turning her brother into a psychopath, using her to gain her revenge—she had, for so long, been mentor and family. One of the only people, aside from Cain, who had ever shown any skerrick of interest or hint of love for Eloise before she came to them.

Her faux parents were dead too—their bodies having been found at a burned-down farm in the next valley. They'd never shown her much love, but she had to feel their loss regardless. Shelley wasn't so certain she'd be so generous about her own parents, but then, she wasn't as kind and good as Eloise.

And of course, there was her worry about what had happened to Cain. All of them were worried about that. After Morrigan had passed, and they'd started to take care of their dead and injured, Eloise had realised Cain's body wasn't among them.

'Maybe the Goddess took mercy on him and took him too,' Eloise had ventured, her voice full of sad hope. 'Like she took Gabbie's body after she died.'

Nobody had the heart to suggest otherwise.

Despite that hope, the shifter-witch's grief was a huge weight on her heart; one Shelley couldn't help but feel through the Packbond. It made her want to cry for her friend; or try to do something to cheer her up.

But of course, she needn't have worried. Iain put his arm around his mate, kissed her, brushing the tears from her face, then pulled her and little Phoenix close. The grief lifted from the Packbond and was replaced by the joy that only a mate could bring. Shelley knew that exact feeling now.

Tears of happiness in her eyes, she watched the new little family of three, with Patrick shadowing them, slip into the darkening night.

Adam pulled Shelley snuggly against him, lips on her brow, arms warming her against the nip of cold in the spring air. She held him tight, her face pressed against his chest, her lips on his throat. She couldn't get enough of touching him, of him touching her. Of breathing in the unique Adam scent of him. It was joy and warmth and desire as it threaded through her veins. It was all hers.

Excitement chased across her skin, need pulling at her muscles. They'd barely had a moment alone since they'd banished the Darkness. The witches had all been exhausted after the spell they'd cast and had been hustled back to the house to rest by the overprotective Were who were their mates. Shelley had slept for hours, held in the warmth, strength and love of Adam's arms. She knew the others had the same experiences with their mates—it was amazing what that bond gave to them all.

Those hours being held in his arms, asleep, were no longer enough. They'd had things to do when they'd finally got up to prepare for Morrigan's ceremony, and while Adam had mostly stayed by her side, touching her, holding her hand, kissing her briefly when he was able, it had only served to build the fire inside her to be touched, kissed, loved by him, sharing the act of bonding with their bodies as well as their souls.

An urgency that was mirrored through their bond from him.

'Come on,' he said, taking her hand.

They walked in silence away from the Dance, both moving with one accord until they came to the clearing where the battle with the Darkness had occurred. The lines of power still glowed on the ground—Cordy thought they might always be there. They warmed the air, filled it with a powerful buzz that skittered along her skin.

Shelley closed her eyes, breathed deep, taking in the wonder of it. The banshee hummed inside her in response, but she was no longer afraid of what might come when that hum rose to a cry once again. She saw it now for what it was—a way to help her protect those she loved. She was determined to learn how to read that side of herself better, to learn how to use her powers to help others. Thinking of that, she frowned.

'What is it?' Adam asked, slipping his arms around her, pulling her close.

'I know Iain is there for her, but I wish there was something I could do for Eloise right now.'

'You are. Your caring, love and friendship vibrates through the bond. She knows everyone's here for her. It's taking away a lot of the sting of grief. As is the fact that she's got Phoenix to look after.' Adam tipped his head to the side. 'Iain will call us if there's anything more we can do.'

'Is he okay with becoming an instant dad?'

'Are you kidding me? He's already full of fatherly pride, it's kind of sickening.'

'I think Jason's going to be worse.'

He rolled his eyes. 'You're not wrong there. I can see I'm going to have my uncle duties cut out for me to make certain the twins are capable of getting into all sorts of trouble. I can't have them becoming spoiled brats.'

'Unthinkable!' Shelley laughed, then sobered. 'Although, there are worse things than being smothered in love.'

Adam pressed his lips against her forehead, his hand stroking down her unbound hair. 'You will never be lonely again.'

The warmth and love in his eyes washed over her. 'I was never truly alone. I know that now. Bron and Skye made sure of that. Besides, my power is a friend, the banshee even more so. I need to get to know them both.'

'I'll be happy to help. I liked the banshee side of you. You are pretty kick arse by yourself, but with those wings ...' His hands stroked down her back where the banshee wings tingled under her skin, a part of her, content to stay put until needed. 'They were pretty bloody sexy.'

'Really?'

'Mm-hmm. I think I might end up with a few fantasies about those wings.'

She laughed. 'Does your wolf feel the same?'

'We are one and the same. You should understand that now given you've got another creature inside you too.'

She did understand—and it was as precious an understanding as her love for Adam and his love for her. She reached up and pulled his head down, taking his lips with hers in a hungering kiss he answered in full.

Panting, he pulled away, eyes glowing amber at her in the darkening night. 'Are you sure?'

She didn't need to ask what he meant. He was asking her if she wanted to fully complete the mating, here, now, or if she wanted to wait.

She had waited too long already. Besides, she could think of no better place to finalise the mating and bond herself to him forever than the place where she'd embraced who she was and could be and banished age-old fears along with the Darkness. 'Death might have occurred here, but so did life. There is no better place for us to share our love and desire and bonding to fulfil the eternal circle that is life.'

Adam gently removed her clothes as she removed his. They lay down on the grass between the point of the triangle and square where they had both fought the night before against the Darkness. Body sliding against body, lips explored, tasting, sucking, hands tracing patterns of fire along skin.

Power built inside her, covering both of them in an amethyst glow, but she was no longer afraid of it. She gloried in it, in sharing it with Adam as she shared her body and her soul. And he gloried in it with her.

Ready, she wrapped her legs around his waist and tipped her hips to meet his thrust as he finally joined with her. Their cries of passion and wonder rang in the night as he moved inside her, faster and faster. Shelley met every thrust, her hands flying over his skin as his were over her, her lips and tongue and teeth tangling with his until she wasn't certain they weren't one creature, melded together in a fever of passion, the tight coiling inside her mirrored in the tight coiling inside of him that she could feel so clearly through the bond.

'Mine forever,' Adam breathed into her mouth, his skin slick under her hands as he moved deeper within her in fast, glorious slides.

'Mine forever,' Shelley claimed, holding him tight.

Their lips met again, breaths mingling, hands moving to twine fingers over her head.

He pulled back to capture her gaze with his as they came together in a blaze of amethyst and rainbow fire that cascaded over their skin, through their muscles and held them for endless moments where nothing existed but themselves, their love, their bond, their trust, one in the other.

His eyes flashed to wolf amber and back again. Hers to banshee amethyst, then back to the violet-blue of her witch-Medium self.

Then they collapsed in each other's arms and held there, panting and sated—for now—while the mating took full hold.

A wolf howled in the night. Adam lifted his head and joined it.

She touched his throat, amazed at how familiar and at home she was with that sound.

He looked down at her then, eyes filled with such pride and love, it made Shelley feel more treasured than she'd ever felt before.

'The pack has accepted our mating.'

'As if they had a choice!' she laughed. 'You are a force of nature, my love.'

'Well matched by you.'

'Abso-fucking-lutely.' She kissed him, tongue tasting the intimate depths of his mouth.

Groaning, he pulled her with him as he rolled over onto his back so that he was lying on the ground. 'Promise to do that again when I have more energy to join in,' he said when she pulled away.

Her lips split into a grin she couldn't stop. 'I didn't think anything could ever wear you out, my love.'

'You, Kitten, are my special blend of kryptonite.'

'Kryptonite?'

'You are the only thing that can make me weak at the knees. Otherwise I'm always like Superman.'

'Tickets on yourself.'

'Abso-fucking-lutely.'

She kissed him again, and soon the heat between them rose once more as it always would.

They made love as full mates as the moon rose high in the sky, bathing them in a silver glow, lighting the fine web of coloured strands of power that spread out from them. That fine web bound them together just as it bound them to all the others they loved and to the wider packs and covens to whom they belonged, the whole made stronger by their love, their power, and their acceptance of who they were.

And now, with hope for a better future for everyone, they were finally able to exalt in the fact that they were not only one, but one part of a greater whole. Stronger. And getting stronger.

It was more than either had ever dared to hope for. But now they had it, they were never going to let it go.

I HOPE you enjoyed Shelley and Adam's story as much as I enjoyed writing it. This book brings to conclusion this arc of the Pack Bound Series. But don't worry, there's more of the packs and covens to come in the new prequel Series in the Pack Bound World: *Dawn of the Curse*.

Dive into the world of the ancient witches and packs as they come to terms with their new lives, bound together under Bridgette Colliere's Pact, and discover more of the secrets that bind the Pack Bound world together.

The first instalment of this prequel series is *Soul Bound* which follows Morghanna Cantrae and her mate Alistair Sinoir.

Read on for the first few chapters of *Soul Bound* ...

SOUL BOUND

DAWN OF THE CURSE BOOK 1

A PACK BOUND PREQUEL SERIES

LEISL LEIGHTON

THE PACT

The Pact was created, the Darkness was banished
Magical beings no longer vanish
In the fire and flame of power vast and killing
Now they share with the Were and are willing
To bless the future and worship the sun
Giving thanks for the freedom granted by the One
The first and true Goddess who looks after thee
Blessed be her glory and the power of three

Pack Witch Blessing to the Goddess
Anonymous

1

Scottish Highlands—1493

'Out ye get, Frenchie.'

Alistair Sinoir nodded at the farmer who'd rowed him across the loch then swung himself out of the boat. Water lapped over his boots, wetting his breeches. He cursed to himself as he turned to haul his pack out of the boat—he was in for an uncomfortable walk unless he soon found a patch of sun in which to dry off.

He glanced up at the sky and frowned at the grey clouds lowering above the mountains surrounding the loch. He didn't fancy his chances of finding any sun in this wild place. It was more likely he'd end up wetter than he already was if the heavy scent of rain in the air was anything to go by.

Not that he wasn't used to living rough. He'd put up with worse in the years after his parents were killed. Their deaths had forced him to do things he'd never thought to endure since fleeing their small cottage in southern France—all in an effort to keep his siblings safe, fed and dry. At least, that's what he told himself.

'It looks like a storm is coming o'er the loch yonder. I hope yer not plannin' to go into the hills thata way. The storms when they come at this time o' the year can be mighty fierce.'

Alistair looked to where the farmer pointed—the exact direction the never-ceasing compulsion pushed him towards. *Merde.* The urge was only an uncomfortable prickling across his chest though, so maybe he could find another way out of this valley and over the mountains. Surely the voice behind the force that made him travel from his home to this strange country would give him some leeway to—

The prickling became a blaze; agony spiked through his head, squeezing his chest. His wolf whimpered.

He refocused on the mountain the farmer had pointed to and the pain twinging his nerves began to fade—as it always did when he made the correct decision on which way to go. Right. So, he was going to get wet. And cold. 'Is there shelter in that direction?' he asked the farmer.

'There might be some caves up in yon hills behind the woods. But I wouldna be going there if I were ye.'

'*Pourquoi?* Why?'

'There be wolves in those hills.'

Alistair snorted. 'I am not afraid of wolves.' They were usually afraid of him. As were most humans—although, he'd managed to lessen that impression somewhat in the search for foster parents for his brother and sister, Frederique and Amandine. In fact, his younger siblings had been his teachers there. They smiled in a friendly unassuming way and struck up general chit-chat easily even though both of them were a bit shy. But it worked because people took to them. He'd mostly let them take the lead when entering new villages and meeting new people, because even though he practiced what he saw them do, he still wasn't as good at it as they were.

When he left them though, he'd had to use what he'd learned during that time. It was essential to appear more human on his travels to this land if he was to gain people's help and trust. He'd managed to get their help, but trust was another thing. Something inside them obviously told them he was still a predator; but he had found this was soon overwhelmed by the coin he placed in their hands. It was amazing how pieces of metal could make a human ignore their instincts.

But who was he to talk? Since coming to him six months ago, the voice and its compulsion had made him ignore every instinct he had. He'd wanted to stay with his siblings, to make certain they were safe and happy. But the voice impelled him to travel, leaving all he'd loved and worked for far behind.

The farmer eyed him up and down as he stood in the waves, the older man's gaze taking in the breadth and height of Alistair. Finally his mouth quirked and he nodded. 'Mayhap ye have the right to no' be afeared o' wild critters, but there be many more things to be afeard of in yon hills, as I tried to tell ye across the loch.'

'Like what?'

The old farmer leaned in closer, his voice a harsh whisper. 'The faeries dwell there. Beyond yon crag there be an old place: their sacred Dance. It no' be a place any man of sense would wander. Especially with such weather lowering o'er the crag.' He looked up at the darkening sky, his eyes twinkling with the horror of the tale he told. 'Tuatha de Dannon—the insane faeries o' the Wild Hunt—will be riding the storm clouds and could take ye for their Queen's slave. Young Euan McBane went into yon hills on an afternoon such as this 'un, and ne'er came back.'

Alistair hid his amusement at the old man's superstitions. In all his years roaming the woods of France and Europe he'd heard many tales of the faeries and their terrors; not once had he come across any sign of them. The only magical beings he'd ever come across were his father's coven and his mother's pack—both far more dangerous to wandering souls than imaginary faeries and their Wild Hunt. 'I think I will be safe from faeries. *Merci* for your concern.' He bowed his head slightly. 'But this is the way I must go.'

The old farmer glowered, obviously annoyed his warnings had

not been heeded, but then, after hocking up phlegm and spitting it over the side of the boat, said, 'Well, tha's yer business then, isna it? Ye've been warned and I've done my duty. Now, give me the rest o' the payment, laddie, then push me off, would ye? Ye ken I dinna want to get caught in the rain, and my Agatha has supper waiting for me.'

Alistair sighed and dug into the purse he kept inside his shirt, handing over the rest of the payment for the provisions they'd spared him, and for rowing him across the loch. It was the last of his coin. He would have walked around the body of water, should have, but the compulsion to move only in the direction the mysterious voice wished him to move wouldn't have it when he'd tried. The torture it inflicted on his nerves had almost driven him to his knees. It had forced him to turn towards the farmhouse to seek faster passage.

'Use your coin. It will be of little use to you where you are going,' the voice had whispered to him, its feminine tone soft yet unyielding; he knew from experience to disobey was to court pain; to question a futility he still struggled to accept. Acceptance of the inevitable apparently wasn't in his or his wolf's nature.

He still wanted to know why the voice and its compulsion had forced him to leave Frederique and Amandine before seeing them fully settled. It was a question it had never answered. He only had his guesses, and they were wild and fanciful: no matter how he wished the voice was leading him to the woman in his dreams, he knew it could not be so.

The girl, with her violet eyes, shining black hair and gentle voice, had grown into a woman in his dreams as he'd grown into a man. And while those dreams had become more ... sensual in the last six months, completely ousting the nightmares that had most often been his constant companion, they were nothing more than they'd ever been: an escape from the daily toll of a life on the run, the only protector of his younger siblings. A creation of a mind in desperate need of someone to lean on, someone to rely on, someone to keep him strong, even if it was only in his sleep that he could share his burdens on the nights the nightmares didn't take him over.

No, the compulsion to travel here was more likely to do with his magic, given the voice resonated with a power he felt in every fibre of his being; a vast power that revived him just enough to keep going when exhaustion overwhelmed him, and punished him whenever he challenged it.

It had come upon him suddenly—another reason it could not be his dream woman. He'd seen her all his life, whereas the voice had only come upon him just after Frederique and Amandine had been settled with the kind baker and his wife.

But whether it had something to do with his magic or not, one thing was certain: the closer he got to his unknown destination, the greater the compulsion to get there faster.

And as that compulsion grew, so had his wolf's need to be allowed free. Certainly, there were parts of the journey that would have been easier if he could have travelled in wolf form but giving it such freedom could not be allowed.

For years he'd only released his wolf when necessary, not trusting its violent urges beyond the need to bring down game to feed himself and his siblings or stave off attack by other wild animals; and occasionally roving bands of bandits. Even though the freedom that washed over him every time he let his wolf out was glorious, he couldn't trust it. He'd seen the damage others of his kind had done in years past—which paled in comparison to what it had done to those humans who had threatened the safety of his brother and sisters. He didn't want to be responsible for more of that violence and horror than he already had been.

'Laddie, yer eyes.'

The farmer skittered back in the boat, dropping one of the oars, his horror prickling stabs in Alistair's heart. *Merde*—his animal must be showing in his eyes. He was right not to trust his wolf when it had this effect on humans even when it only showed in his eyes. He shoved it down where it belonged, deep inside, then before he could give the farmer more reason to fear him, picked up the oar, handed it to the old man, then pushed the boat back into the loch, his strength sending it and the scared farmer well on their way.

'*Merci*,' he called out. The old man didn't respond, just rowed frantically, putting as much distance between them as possible.

Sadness washed over him but he didn't have time to give in to it. A little reminder stab of pain fired through his nerves, forcing him to turn and head ever on.

He waded out of the water and up the embankment. The shale and stones of the small beach crunched under his feet as he was pulled towards the darkest section of forest that skirted the highest mountain and its craggy peak. He hoped he could find a path over those crags because he didn't fancy mountain climbing in this weather.

Sighing, he made his way from the beach to the long grass and into the dark woods.

Not long after, rain swept down, hard and cold. Despite the fact it was summer, it chilled him to the bone within minutes.

His wolf growled to be let out—it could handle the wet and cold better than his human side would. But Alistair couldn't risk it. There was a familiar scent in the air here, one he could smell even through the drowning rain. It made him reluctant to let his wolf out, no matter how much it insisted. Werepeople had been through here at some stage in the last few weeks and he could not chance meeting them in wolf form if they were still around. Meetings with full-bloods never went well.

He trudged on, through the woods, the thickening canopy overhead slightly lessening the stinging impact of the rain.

There was no sign of any life in the woods around him; not even the small animals that called this place home were foolish enough to be out in this. His only company was the pounding of the rain and the sloshing thumps of his boots on the leaf-strewn ground. And his wolf. It wasn't letting up, pushing, pushing.

'No. I cannot let you free,' he said out loud. 'It is not safe.'

The wolf kept trying, claws spiking out of his fingertips, fur scratching under his skin. He stopped, needing to be still to get his wolf under control.

Agony spiked through his entire body, driving him to his knees.

His wolf whimpered and pulled back as Alistair tried to stand, hand against a tree; the rough bark scraped against his skin, cutting his palm.

But the pain was nothing to the bright torment that started to punish him for stopping. It flared in his mind, blinding him; squeezed his chest, making him gasp for breath.

Panting as if he'd run for miles, he cried out into the cold darkness around him. 'Please. Let me rest for a moment. I am losing control over my wolf.'

'Let it be free and you will feel no more pain.'

'No!' He lurched to his feet, stumbling forward. Freeing his wolf was not the answer to his problems—it would only make things worse.

Instead, he dug inside his mind, using his power in a way that sickened him. Pulling on threads of magic, he quickly wove an internal shield over and around his wolf before it could know what he was doing; an iridescent cage stronger than the strongest stone or metal. He could not keep it up forever, but it would at least allow him a little breather so he was not fighting his wolf and the voice's compulsion at the same time. If the violence of the urge was anything to go by, he was close to his destination and should be able to release the cage then. 'It's only for a little while,' he whispered to his wolf.

Understanding dawned in his wolf and it howled then began to fling itself against the shield; but due to the shield, its distress was a distant thing. Even so, it made his heart ache. If only ...

But no. There was no use wishing for a past that was long gone.

He stumbled on, shivering with cold as the rain whipped into his face. Thunder rumbled overhead, followed by a bright crack of lightning that zigzagged across the sky.

Damn. The lightning made it dangerous to be under these trees. He should find shelter, maybe those caves the farmer had spoken of. But the voice, merciless in its wish for him to keep going, wouldn't let him.

'Why can you not let me rest? Why am I doing this?' he cried out, his voice almost lost in the noise of the storm.

'*You know.*'

'You answered me,' surprise had him blurting out.

'*It seemed necessary.*'

'But why?'

'*Why what?*'

'Why now? Why not before?'

A pause, then, '*Your destination is your salvation. There you will find the reward you have long sought to relieve all your years of suffering.*'

Not an answer to his question, but it was an answer that forced him on. For the only reward he could think would ever be worth this was to know his siblings were safe, happy and accepted.

Would he ever know whether all his sacrifice had come to fruition? He could tell by the utter silence in his mind that if he asked, the voice wouldn't continue to answer.

Rather than play into its cruel games, he simply trudged on, trying not to think of the words that had brought fragile hope fluttering into his heart.

I HOPE you enjoyed that little snippet of *Soul Bound*. If you want to read the rest, you will find the buy links here:

If you don't want to miss out on news about books in this new prequel series, as well as special giveaways, sales, book signings and information on my other books, then sign up to my newsletter.

As an added bonus, when you join, you will get a FREE ebook copy of *Witch Bound*, a novella set 40 years before *Pack Bound*. Just turn the page to find out more:

LOVE A FREE BOOK?

YOUR FREE BOOK IS WAITING

One Fate, one mate, a bond too strong to deny ...

Paul Collins, duty-bound Pack Warlock and seer, must marry a strong witch for the good of Pack McVale. But his hidden feelings for his best-friend's sister, maternal wolf Ivy McVale, make this a more difficult pill to swallow every day. Especially when they begin to mate.

Then Paul has a vision: If they mate, Ivy will die. Desperate, Paul uses his powers to change destiny and make Ivy think she's always hated him. He can deal with any punishment the Fates make him pay for tampering with destiny, as long as Ivy lives.

After recovering from a bewildering month-long illness, Ivy notices her nemesis, Paul, is tormented by something. And strangely, she is

the only one who can feel it. Unable to endure such unhappiness—
even if he does call her Poison Ivy—she is determined to help him,
no matter the cost. Because Pack McVale cannot survive without him,
and curiously, neither can she ...

Simply sign up to my newsletter and I will email your free copy of
Witch Bound to you. You will also receive the latest on upcoming
books, sales, giveaways and relevant bookish news.

Get My Free Copy of Witch Bound Here:

But wait! There's more ...

If you're not into newsletters but think you might be into
subscriptions that give you serialised content, exclusive chapters to
new books, exclusive bonus content, signed print books and much
more, then turn the page to find out about **Leisl's Legends** ...

JOIN LEISL'S LEGENDS

Subscribe to (or follow) me (via the QR code) at my Leisl's Legends page on REAM—a new subscription app like Patreon except it's designed especially for readers and authors for an amazing reading experience—and you will get early access to *The Huntress and the Vampire King*, my hot enemies to lovers, witch-and-vampire-licious urban fantasy romance that readers over there are already in love with. It's the prequel novel to the first book in the Blood-Rites Series - *The Blood of the Seer*.

Be the first to find out where it all began with Anita and Hei's love story.

BECOME A LEGEND NOW!

https://reamstories.com/leislleightonauthor

You will also find serialised chapters of the next book in my popular **Gods Cursed Series** there and can comment on the story as I write it! Not to mention you will also get extra bonuses like exclusive NSFW Bonus Epilogues, Bonus Prologues and cut scenes and chapters from all of my books.

Be part of creating the stories you love AND get exclusive access to a whole range of goodies including other WIPs, bonus content, voting rights, signed books and more.

Read on to find out more about The Huntress and the Vampire King PLUS read the opening chapters …

The Huntress and the Vampire King

She hates the vampire who saved her; he holds the key to her fate …

Hunter-witch Anita Middleton wants revenge against the violent vampire cults that murdered her father and has worked hard to become one of the best vampire hunters there is. But on a difficult hunt she is caught in an ambush and is mortally wounded … only to be saved by a mysterious warrior. A warrior with brilliant blue eyes and long silver-blonde hair who fights with a grace and violence like nothing she's seen. It is only after she wakes in the heart of his palazzo that she realises her saviour is a vampire - and according to her brother and mentor, this vampire king is their ally.

Lord Hei rules over an empire of witches, humans and vampires who have been trying to keep the vicious vampire cults, the Wild and Dark Brethren, at bay for centuries. Then he saves Anita and knows with one look she is the prophecied Huntress who could be his downfall or his salvation - and she is also his fated mate. But she struggles to trust him as her hatred of vampires is deep-seated. And she *needs* to trust him because only he can offer the specialised training a Huntress needs so her power won't overwhelm her.

But with the Dark Brethren mysteriously amassing, he has little time to win her over. And Anita must go on a crash course to learn how to control her Huntress magic ... or go slowly and violently insane.

The Huntress and the Vampire King is the exciting action-packed prequel novel to *The Blood of the Seer*.

If you love your vampires hot with a bit of The Witcher thrown in and your heroines as kick-arse as Buffy and even more tortured, if you love fated mates, enemies to lovers, chosen ones and epically hot romance mixed with action and mystery, then *The Huntress and the Vampire King* is what you've been waiting for.

Sign up to Leisl's Legends and start reading exclusive early release chapters of it now!

BECOME A LEGEND NOW!
https://reamstories.com/leislleightonauthor

ALSO BY LEISL LEIGHTON

PACK BOUND SERIES

Pack Bound

Moon Bound

Shifter Bound

Wolf Bound

Witch Bound

(A Pack Bound Series Prequel Novella -

FREE ebook copy to Newsletter Subscribers)

BOX SET

Pack Bound Series Collection Books 1-4

DAWN OF THE CURSE

A PACK BOUND PREQUEL SERIES

Soul Bound

Alpha Bound

Hunter Bound

Fae Bound

(Coming in 2027)

GODS CURSED SERIES

A Love Cursed Christmas Wish

Love Cursed

Soul Cursed

Blood Cursed

Hearts Cursed

Fates Cursed

Witch Cursed

Dragon Cursed

(Coming 2026)

Blood-Rites Series

The Blood of the Seer

The Blood of the Sire

The Blood of the Son

(Coming 2027)

Blood-Rites Prequel and Bonus Material

The Huntress and the Vampire King

The Middleton Manifesto

(Available now via Leisl's Legends subscription)

Anthologies

A Perfectly Paranormal Valentine

A Perfectly Paranormal Halloween

A Perfectly Paranormal Easter

A Perfectly Paranormal Christmas

A Perfectly Paranormal Prophecy

(Coming in 2027)

As well as writing sexy, epic and romantic paranormal novels, I write mysterious and emotional romantic suspense novels too. Check out the following titles for amazing, suspenseful reads:

Storm Haven Series

Need You Tonight

The Devil Inside

CoalCliff Stud Series

Climbing Fear: Book 1

Blazing Fear: Book 2

Echo Springs Series

Dangerous Echoes: Book 1

Books 2-4 in this series, (written by Daniel deLorne, TJ Hamilton and Shannon Curtis) are also available now at all ebook retailers.

You can find all the buy links for Leisl's Books at her website:

ABOUT LEISL

Leisl Leighton is a tall red head with an overly large imagination. As a child, she identified strongly with Anne of Green Gables, and like Anne, is a voracious reader and born performer.

It came as no surprise when she went on to a career as a performer, script writer, script doctor, stage manager and musical director for cabaret and theatre restaurants.

After starting a family, Leisl stopped performing and began writing the stories plaguing her dreams. She now writes emotional stories mixed with mystery and a little bit of what goes bump in the night.

Her novels have won and placed in writing contests here and overseas. She is a passionate advocate for the romance genre, was President of Romance Writers of Australia from 2014-2017 and when she's not writing romantic stories of redemption, she is helping other authors reach their dreams with her Author Services. You can contact Leisl through her website via the QR Code above or here: https://www.leislleighton.com

And if you want to stay in touch and be the first to find out about new releases, appearances, special deals and exclusive content and give-

aways, sign up to her Newsletter and pick up your free copy of *Witch Bound* via the QR code.

Or sign up to *Leisl's Legends* via this QR code to get *Witch Cursed* plus serialised early access stories and bonus content including a bonus NSFW ending for Love Cursed.

You can also follow her on social media:

facebook.com/LeislLeightonAuthor

instagram.com/leisllleightonauthor

bookbub.com/authors/leisl-leighton

amazon.com/stores/Leisl-Leighton/author/B00DBYRGZY

ACKNOWLEDGMENTS

I am filled with a sense of sadness mixed with pride and gratitude at the release of Wolf Bound. The last novel in this arc of the Pack Bound Series, it was a labour of love, sweat, tears and grit to get to this point. I am sorry to never have the joy of playing with Skye and Jason, Bron and River, Eloise and Iain, and finally, Shelley and Adam again in the way I did in writing this series, but I am so grateful they came to me like they did and demanded I write their stories and explore the world I want to spend more time in. I am also very grateful that I am privileged enough to have the chance to do so.

A lot of that is because I am surrounded by people who support me in my dreams and goals and I will be forever grateful for that.

So huge thanks have to go to my Mum and Dad, Kerrie and Jim, who have always done so much for me during my life and have always supported me no matter if it was to perform on the stage or own a theatre restaurant or write novels. This wouldn't have happened without you. Big thanks also have to go to my Mum who did the final proof edit on the books for me.

Of course, my hubby, Mark, and my two beautiful boys, Jacob and Nathaniel, deserve so much thanks and love too. Mark helped so often with tech help and supporting me through the big step to give up work to pursue this full time. Jacob and Nathaniel had to deal with a mum who lived in different worlds when they were younger and then taking on extra duties in their teens with cooking and cleaning and washing so the house was kept in order so I wouldn't be tempted to procrastoclean/cook/wash etc.

And then there are my wonderful friends from my writing

groups. Their feedback and endless encouragement as I rode the often turbulent waves of this writing journey, gave me the strength to push on and taught me so much, well beyond how to write better. I am so lucky to have been on this journey with them. Laura, Chris, Marnie, Frana, Anita, Samantha and Helen, I couldn't have gotten here without you.

Big extra thanks to Laura and Chris as well for helping me to wrestle the old Pack Bound Series blurbs into something fresh and new and powerful—you are both amazing and talented and I'm so glad you're in my life. And huge thanks to Marnie and Anita who helped me come up with the idea of Permien Press in the first place and gave me the support and encouragement I needed to do this self-publishing thing finally. You are the best.

Massive extra thanks also have to go to Samantha Marshall for the amazing covers she did for me for the re-release of this series. I love them so much and feel finally that each story now gets to shine on its own. Your talent is boundless and your generosity equally so.

It fills me with sadness that two people who were not only essential to my writing journey but to me personally, cannot be here to see this. I know they would be so proud and would say that thanks aren't necessary, but they are. My bestie, Helen, encouraged me to write my first novel and was always there with her encouragement and a kick up the butt when I needed it before her death in 2018. And Liz, the first writing friend I ever had but who became so much more than simply that, was the first person who truly gave me feedback on my novels as a whole and helped me see what needed to be done to make them better. It is a tragedy that you left us at the beginning of 2020 and that the world never got to see your true talent and brilliance; I feel privileged to have read your work and been part of your life and your writing journey—a journey that ended far too soon.

Helen and Liz, you are both gone but are never forgotten and a part of you will always live on in my stories.

I would also just like to send out a big thank you to all my friends in Romance Writers of Australia—you are inspiration and mentor rolled into a big ball of supportive writerly love.

I also want to thank my agent, Alex Adsett, for believing in me and my work and always backing every decision I make. Your confidence in me helps me believe I can actually do this writing thing. Eternal thanks.

Finally, I dedicated this novel to my readers because without you and your passion for my work, I wouldn't be able to lose myself in these worlds and characters. Thank you for being a big part of my writing journey. I promise to continue to write books I love in the hopes that you will continue to love them too.

For now, keep well, stay safe and happy reading.

Leisl XX